PRIZE STORIES 1969:
The O. Henry Awards

Prize Stories 1969:

THE O. HENRY AWARDS

Edited and with an Introduction by
WILLIAM ABRAHAMS

Doubleday & Company, Inc.
GARDEN CITY, N.Y.   1969

Contents

Publisher's Note

THE present volume is the forty-ninth in the O. Henry Memorial Award series. The annual collection did not appear in 1952 and 1953, when the continuity of the series was interrupted by the death of Herschel Brickell, who had been the editor for ten years.

In 1918 the Society of Arts and Sciences met to vote upon a monument to the master of the short story, O. Henry. They decided that this memorial should be in the form of two prizes for the best short stories published by American authors in American magazines during the year 1919. From this beginning, the memorial developed into an annual anthology of outstanding short stories by American authors published, with the exception of the years mentioned above, by Doubleday & Company, Inc.

Blanche Colton Williams, one of the founders of the awards, was editor from 1919 to 1932; Harry Hansen from 1933 to 1940; Herschel Brickell from 1941 to 1951; Paul Engle from 1954 to 1959 with Hanson Martin co-editor in the years 1954 to 1956; Mary Stegner in 1960; Richard Poirier from 1961 to 1966, with assistance from and co-editorship with William Abrahams from 1964 to 1966. William Abrahams became editor of the series in 1967.

Doubleday has also published *First-Prize Stories From The O. Henry Memorial Awards 1919–1966.*

The stories chosen for this volume were published in the period from the summer of 1967 to the summer of 1968. A list of the magazines consulted appears at the back of the book. The choice of stories and the selection of prize winners are exclusively the responsibility of the editor. Biographical material is based on information provided by the contributors.

Introduction: Prize Stories 1969

OF THE thousand or so stories by American authors* published in periodicals during the past year, it could be safely predicted that the merits of perhaps two hundred of them would insure their being read with respect and attention. From these the winnowing would be made, and from the best of them (as many as thirty-five) the final choice for the collection. And so it proved. Similarly, at the other end of the spectrum, there would be another hundred, or even two hundred stories of no discernible merit whatever: one could only wonder at their publication. And this too was the case. Indeed, if one were to generalize from these polar extremes on the state of the American short story at the end of the 1960s, it would appear comparable to that of the little girl in the nursery rhyme—when good, very good, and when bad, execrable.

Would that it were as simple as this, a clear-cut line of demarcation between the good and the bad! But in fact there is a territory between, vast, flat, innocuous and unmemorable, and it is there that the majority of contemporary stories come into being, objects of manufacture with a built-in obsolescence of their own—in this respect how American they are!—for the expectation, at least on the part of the magazines that publish them, cannot be for more than a single inattentive reading. Literary non-events, they are pointed to by large numbers of intelligent readers—admittedly with no particular fondness for fiction—as a justification or explanation for their no longer reading short stories at all.

Such stories of the middle ground, however they may differ in content and style, have certain characteristics in common: they

---

* Here perhaps it should be emphasized that the O. Henry Awards are made for stories complete in themselves, and not for excerpts from larger works of fiction. In recent years magazine editors have abandoned the tradition of publishing a novel serially; instead, the preference is for a chapter or section from the novel which, however well it may seem to stand alone, gains noticeably from being restored to the text from which it was extracted.

are, in their various ways, competent, knowing, trivial. Competence—and most American stories nowadays achieve a high level of competence, as it were, automatically—at first a virtue, becomes a defect when, as in these stories, it serves as a substitute for thought and feeling. The words, phrases and sentences, the manipulations and programs that simulate thought and feeling are readily available to competent writers. So too are subjects, of all sorts and degrees of seriousness, which are dealt with in these middling stories with an invincible knowingness. Much as articles, adroitly skimming the surface of things and often reinforced by illustrations (cameras don't lie, do they?), have made instant experts of us all in fields about which, until the moment before, we knew nothing, so the contemporary story goes confidently about its work of telling us how we live, or more often, how *they* live —for the tendency is to pin specimens down. Much is made of truth to life—that catch phrase!—which turns out to be a generalized, newsworthy phenomenon as one might have seen it in *Life* the week before, rather than the private truth that originates in the story itself. Perhaps it is this that accounts for the deadening triviality of so many contemporary stories, however "significant" their chosen subjects. The gap between the "event," whether grandiose or tiny, and its realization as art is not bridged: merely to be competent or knowledgeable is not enough. Too often we are asked to settle for technical competence, a literate and sometimes complex arrangement of sentences, or else a lordly show of expertise, whether of scuba diving, *haute cuisine* or a pad in the East Village.

It may seem odd to lay stress upon these stories in the introduction to a collection from which they have been excluded. But their very numbers, their preponderance, give them importance. In the short run, they, not the exceptional stories, affect the cultural climate. These stories, it must be remembered, are not downright unmistakably bad. They are published in respectable magazines; respectable, often famous names are signed to them; their competence, unflawed by a truly individual quirkiness, makes them easily teachable. They are safe, each comfortable in its stereotype, involving no risks for either writer or reader—dispiriting demonstrations, so far as the short story is concerned, of nothing ventured, nothing gained.

Happily there is a minority of stories, at the positive end of the

spectrum, very different in kind, in intention and in achievement. Seventeen of them have been chosen for this collection;
still others might have been added to it—there has not been a
dearth of excellence. So that at the same time that one deplores
the prevailing mediocrity, it is not inconsistent to remark that it
has been a good year for the American short story, even—taking
into consideration stories such as Bernard Malamud's "Man in a
Drawer," Joyce Carol Oates's "Accomplished Desires," and John
Barth's "Lost in the Funhouse," to single out only three among
the seventeen—a vintage year. The merits of the chosen stories
will be apparent, I hope, to anyone who reads them with the
attention they deserve: accordingly I don't propose to conduct
a guided tour among them. But I would like to comment briefly
on the stories by Mr. Malamud and Mr. Barth, which between
them suggest in a most heartening way the range of possibilities
still available to writers who aren't willing to settle for stereotypes.

Indeed, Mr. Barth in his story "Lost in the Funhouse" ad-
dresses himself to the question directly, although "directly" may
not seem the appropriate word for a story notable for the com-
plexity of its construction. Yet almost from the first sentence he
is asking how shall the story be told, as he tells in a manner
that recalls a nest of Chinese boxes, the story of writing a story
that itself is the story we are reading. And how simple and
familiar the basic material is—a middle-class American family
spends a day at the beach, where the younger members of the
family frolic about in the funhouse. One of them, a schoolboy
on the verge of adolescence, is lost for a time among the crazy
mirrors and secret passages, and so is made aware of his apartness,
his difference: he is to become a writer, one day he will write
this very story as Mr. Barth has done, like Mr. Barth he will
scatter through it italicized advice on how the story is to be told
in a parody of a teacher or textbook of creative writing. But advice of that sort will no longer serve for material as familiar as
this, the stock heart-cry ("I am different") of countless novice
writers; nor will an act of fidelity to the experience itself (the
smell of popcorn, the glimpse of a tear-stained face in a distorting
mirror) prove sufficient to reanimate it for one further final version. We have no need to be made familiar with this material;
no, we must be made to rediscover its strangeness. Mr. Barth's
solution is to formalize, to artificialize, to estrange—not for a mo-

ment are we allowed to forget that this is a "story," something written and invented and arranged, not "life" lived. The three voices we hear antiphonally, of the boy in the funhouse and the man he will grow up to be and the man writing about them both, are not meant to bring about a "suspension of disbelief," but a disquieting uncertainty—we are to be dislodged from all the easy assumptions that go with lifelikeness. It might be thought that with so much cleverness—and at times, especially toward the beginning, Mr. Barth is perhaps a shade too clever, too Brechtian—"Lost in the Funhouse" could not go beyond the show of virtuosity it so conspicuously is. But what is marvelous about this adventurous story is its gradual metamorphosis from parody to poetry. For all Mr. Barth's determination to keep us at a distance, he engages us, he draws us in. Fascinated (or irritated) at first, in the end we believe in his story and are moved: something new, unexpected, and illuminating has been given us.

Mr. Barth makes a virtue of artfulness, Mr. Malamud of artlessness—or to be more accurate, of the art that conceals itself as artlessness: nothing is to come between the story and the reader. And where Mr. Barth will seek out what is strange in the familiar, Mr. Malamud will "naturalize" his foreign material, familiarize it. Which is only to say these are two very different stories. In "Man in a Drawer" Mr. Malamud is concerned with subject matter wholly new to the American short story—the encounter in the Soviet Union of a visiting American with a writer who had been effectively "silenced" by the regime, that is, whose writings can't be published and are consigned to a drawer. Until now this material has been the province of editorial writers, foreign correspondents, Kremlinologists, propagandists and politicians. Mr. Malamud is none of these things, but an artist and a man of good will. What he has written is not a tract for the times—though one fears it may be read as such, not least by those hard-reading, deep-thinking sincere politicians who grin at us from our TV sets and wouldn't know a work of art if it hit them over the head (would that it might!)—but a story that transcends the rhetoric and half-truths of politics, and says something truthful, painful and inescapable about the indignities and humiliations inflicted upon decent men in this century. The risks inherent in writing this story must have been immense—to raise one's voice patriotically as though running for office, to melodramatize, to editorialize, to fake—and Mr. Malamud has wonderfully avoided them. He has been helped immeasurably by his idiomatic style, plain in its language but complex in its rhythm so that it never descends to flatness, and by a reassuring absence of knowingness. (There are times, and this is one of them, when one prefers the limitations of the artist to the expertise of the publicist.) Harvitz, the narrator of the story, is a tourist in Russia, and this is very much a tourist's story—it accounts for a deliberate thinness of background. Harvitz will tell us only what he sees; all that is sharply drawn as the foreground. For the rest there is what he has read, enough to make him fearful (he is timid to begin with), to be convinced that he will never get out of the country; and all this indicated, mostly by the tone of his voice, rather than described. There is none of that density of texture that Mr. Barth's mock creative-writing textbook would insist upon. Curiously, its absence makes for credibility. Tactful blank spaces are more reassuring than high-colored cartoons. It also has the effect of thrusting Levitansky into full relief—nothing distracts us from seeing and believing in this writer, reduced to driving a taxi, with whom poor timid Harvitz, all anxiety and decency, inadvertently finds himself in relation. The encounters of these two men, from which the element of comedy is seldom missing, have a domestic, unpretentious flavor, a cadence of familiarity in what they say to each other, that adds to their credibility. Everything is most cunningly designed, the seeming casualness of the telling and the sequence of action alike, to bring about a suspension of disbelief. A story of this sort—whose theme is so obviously significant that it can diminish the tale that embodies it—must transcend the requirements of formal structure. Loosely constructed, it will have the impact of testimony, of an artless and unanswerable kind. We know that Levitansky must have his prototypes. But what is important here is that the man in the drawer, *that* Levitansky, exists—unforgettably—not as a noble stereotype extracted from a news item, but as a man and a writer palpably alive in this enkindling work of imagination.

—William Abrahams

PRIZE STORIES 1969:
The O. Henry Awards

Man in the Drawer

A soft shalom I thought I heard, but considering the Slavic cast of the driver's face, it seemed unlikely. He had been eyeing me in the rearview mirror since I had stepped into his taxi, and to tell the truth, I had momentary apprehensions. I'm forty-four and have recently lost weight but not, I admit, nervousness. It's my American clothes I thought at first, one is a recognizable stranger. Unless he was tailing me to begin with, but how could that be if it was a passing cab I had hailed myself?

He had picked me up in his noisy Volga of ancient vintage on the Lenin Hills, where I had been wandering all afternoon in and around Moscow University. Finally I had had enough of sight-seeing, and when I saw the cab, hallooed and waved both arms. The driver, cruising in a hurry, had stopped, you might say, on a kopek, as though I were someone he was dying to give a ride to; maybe somebody he had mistaken for a friend, whom, considering my recent experiences in Kiev, I wouldn't mind being mistaken for.

From the first minute our eyes were caught in a developing recognition although we were complete strangers. I knew nobody in Moscow except an Intourist girl or two. In the rectangular

"Man in the Drawer" – Bernard Malamud, *The Atlantic*, Copyright © 1968 by The Atlantic Monthly Company.

mirror his face seemed globular, the eyes small but canny—they probed, tugged, doubted, seemed to beg to know—give him a word and he'd be grateful, though why and for what cause he didn't say; then, as if the whole thing wearied him insufferably, he pretended no further interest.

Serves him right, I thought, but it wouldn't be a bad thing if he paid a little attention to the road once in a while or we'll never get where we're going, wherever that is. I realized I hadn't said because I wasn't sure myself—anywhere but back to the Metropole just yet. It was one of those days I couldn't stand my hotel room.

"Shalom!" he said finally out loud. It came forth like a declaration of faith.

"Shalom to you." So it was what I had heard, who would have thought so? We both relaxed, looking at opposite sides of the street.

The taxi driver sat in his shirt sleeves on a cool June day, not more than fifty-five Fahrenheit. He was a man in his thirties who looked as if what he ate didn't fully feed him—in afterthought a discontented type, his face on the worn side; not bad-looking even though the head seemed pressed a bit flat by somebody's heavy hand although protected by a mat of thick uncombed hair. His face, as I said, veered to Slavic: bony, broad cheekbones tapering to sensitive chin; but he sported a longish nose and distinctive larynx on a slender hairy neck, a mixed type, you might say. At any rate, the shalom had seemed to change his appearance, even of the probing eyes. He was dissatisfied for certain this fine June day—his lot, fate, himself, what? Also a sort of indigenous sadness hung on him, God knows from where, and he didn't mind if who he was was visible; not everyone could do that or wanted to. This one showed himself. Not too prosperous, I'd say, yet no underground man. He sat firm in his seat, all of him driving, perhaps a little frantically. I have an experienced eye for such details.

"Israeli?" he finally asked.

"Amerikansky." I know no Russian, just a few polite words.

He dug into his pocket for a thin pack of cigarettes and swung his hairy arm back, the Volga swerving to avoid a truck making a turn.

"Take care!"

I was thrown sideways, no apologies. Extracting a Bulgarian cigarette I wasn't eager to smoke—too strong—I handed him his pack. I was considering offering my prosperous American pack in return but didn't want to affront him.

"Feliks Levitansky," he said. "How do you do? I am the taxi driver." His accent was strong, verging to fruity but redeemed by fluency of tongue.

"Ah, you speak English? I sort of thought so."

"My profession is translator—English, French." He shrugged sideways.

"Howard Harvitz is my name. I'm here for a short vacation, about three weeks. My wife died not so long ago and I'm traveling partly to relieve my mind."

My voice caught, but then I went on to say that if I could manage to dig up some material for a magazine article or two, so much the better.

In sympathy Levitansky raised both hands from the wheel.

"Please watch out!"

"Horovitz?" he asked.

I spelled it for him. "Frankly, it was Harris after I entered college, but I changed it back recently. My father had it legally changed after I graduated from high school. He was a doctor, a practical sort."

"You don't look to me Jewish."

"Not particularly, I admit."

After a minute he asked, "For which reason?"

"For which reason what?"

"Why you changed back your name?"

"I had a crisis in my life."

"Existential? Economic?"

"To tell the truth I changed it back after my wife died."

"What is the significance?"

"The significance is that I am closer to my true self."

The driver popped a match with his thumbnail and lit his cigarette.

"I am marginal Jew," he said, "although my father—Avrahm Isaakovich Levitansky—was Jewish. Because my mother was gentile woman I was given choice, but she insisted me to register for internal passport with notation of Jewish nationality in respect for my father. I did this."

"You don't say?"

"My father died in my childhood. I was rised—raised?—to re-spect Jewish people and religion, but I went my own way. I am atheist. This is inevitable."

"You mean Soviet life?"

Levitansky did not reply, smoked, as I grew embarrassed at my question. I looked around to see if I knew where we were. In afterthought he asked, "To which destination?"

I said, still on the former subject, that I had been a reluctant Jew myself, one might say. "My mother and father were thor-oughly assimilated."

"By their choice?"

"Of course by their choice."

"Do you wish," he then asked, "to visit Central Synagogue on Arkhipova Street? Very interesting experience."

"Not just now," I said, "but take me to the Chekhov Museum on Sadovaya Kudrinskaya."

At that the driver, sighing, seemed to take heart.

Rose, I said to myself, you're really gone.

I blew my nose. After her death I had planned to visit the Soviet Union but couldn't get myself to move. I'm a slow man after a blow; though I confess I've never been one for making up his mind in a hurry, at least not on important things. Eight months later, when I was more or less packing, I felt that some of the relief I was looking for was, also, from the necessity of making an unexpected important personal decision. Out of loneliness I had begun to see my former wife, Lillian, in the spring, and before long, since she had remained unmarried and attractive, to my surprise—these things can slip from one sentence to another before you know what's going on—there was some hesi-tant talk of remarriage. In which case we could turn the Russian trip into a sort of honeymoon—I won't say second because we hadn't had much of a first. In the end, since our lives had been so frankly complicated—hard on each other—I found it impos-sible to make up my mind, though Lillian, I give her credit, seemed to be willing to take the chance. My feelings were so difficult to define to myself, I decided to decide nothing for sure. Lillian, who is a forthright type with a mind like a law-yer's, asked me if I was cooling off to the idea, and I told her that since the death of my wife I had been examining my life and needed more time to see where I stood. "Still?" she said, meaning the self-searching, and implying, I thought, forever. All I could answer was, "Still," and then, in anger, "forever." I warned myself afterward: stay out of any more complicated entanglements.

Anyway, that almost killed it. It wasn't a particularly happy evening, though it had its moments, you might say. I had once been deeply in love with Lillian. I figured then that a change of scene, maybe a month abroad, would be helpful. I had for a long time wanted to visit the U.S.S.R., and taking time to be alone, and, I hoped, at ease to think things through, might give the trip an additional value.

So I was surprised, when my visa was granted, though not too surprised, that my anticipation was by now blunted and I was experiencing uneasiness. I blamed it on a dread of traveling that sometimes hits me before long trips, that I have to make my peace with before I can move. Will I get there? Will I get lost? Maybe a war breaks out, and I'm surrounded by enemies on all sides. To be frank, though I've resisted the idea, I consider myself an anxious man, which, when I try to explain it to myself, means being this minute halfway into the next. I sit still in a hurry, worry uselessly about the future, and carry the burden of an overripe conscience.

I realized that what troubled me about going into Russia were those stories in the papers of some tourist or casual traveler in this or that Soviet city, who is suddenly grabbed by the secret police on charges of spying, "illegal economic activity," "hooliganism," or whatnot. This poor guy, like somebody from Sudbury, Mass., is held incommunicado until he confesses, and then is sentenced to a prison camp in the wilds of Siberia. After I got my visa I sometimes had fantasies of a stranger shoving a fat envelope of papers into my fist and then arresting me as I was reading them—of course for spying. What would I do in that case? I think I would pitch the envelope into the street, crying out, "Don't try that one on me, I can't even read Russian," and walk away with dignity, hoping that would freeze them in their tracks. A man in danger, if he's walking away from it, seems indifferent, innocent. At least to himself; but then in my mind I hear the sound of footsteps coming after me, and since my reveries tend to the rational, two KGB men grab me, shove both my arms against my back, and make the arrest. Not for littering the streets, as I hope might be the case, but for "attempting to dispose of certain incriminating documents," a fact it's difficult to deny.

I see Harvitz shouting, squirming, kicking his captors, till his mouth is shut by somebody's stinking palm, and he is dragged by superior force, not to mention a blackjack blow on the cranium, into the inevitable black Zis that I've read about and seen on movie screens.

The cold war is a frightening business, though I suppose for some more than others. I've sometimes wished spying had reached such a pitch of perfection that both the U.S.S.R. and the U.S.A. knew everything there is to know about the other, and having sensibly exchanged this information by trading computers that keep facts up to date, let each other alone thereafter. That ruins the spying business; there's that much more sanity in the world, and for a man like me, the thought of a trip to the Soviet Union is pure pleasure.

Right away, at the Kiev airport, I had a sort of fright, after flying in from Paris on a mid-June afternoon. A customs official confiscated from my suitcase five copies of *Visible Secrets*, a poetry anthology for high school students I had edited some years ago, which I had brought along to give away to Russians I met who might be interested in American poetry. I was asked to sign a document the official had slowly written out in Cyrillic except that *Visible Secrets* was printed in English, with "secrets" underlined. The uniformed customs officer, a heavyset man with a layer of limp hair on a small head and red stars on his shoulders, said that the paper I was required to sign stated I understood it was not permitted to bring five copies of a foreign book into the Soviet Union, but I would get my property back anyway at the Moscow airport when I left the country. I worried that I oughtn't to sign but was urged to by my lady Intourist guide, a bleached blonde with wobbly high heels, whose looks and good humor kept me more or less calm, though my clothes were frankly steaming. She said it was a matter of no great importance and advised me to write my signature because it was delaying our departure to the Dnipro Hotel.

At that point I asked what would happen if I willingly parted with the books, no longer claimed them as my property. The Intouristka inquired of the customs man, who answered calmly, earnestly, and at great length.

"He says," she said, "that the Soviet Union will not take away from a foreign visitor his legal property."

Since I had only four days in the city and time was going fast, faster than usual, I reluctantly signed the paper plus four carbons—one for each book?—and was given a copy, which I filed in my billfold.

Despite this incident—it had its comic side—my stay in Kiev, in spite of the loneliness I usually feel my first few days in a strange city, went quickly and interestingly. In the mornings I was driven around in a private car on guided tours of the hilly, broad-avenued, green-leaved city, whose colors reminded me of a subdued Rome. But in the afternoons I wandered around alone. I would start by taking a bus or streetcar, riding a few kilometers, then getting off to walk within a particular neighborhood. Once I walked into a peasants' market where collective farmers and country people in beards and boots out of a nineteenth-century Russian novel sold their produce to city people. I thought I must write about this to Rose; I meant, of course, Lillian. Another time, in a deserted street when I happened to think of the customs receipt in my billfold, I turned in my tracks to see if I was being followed. I wasn't, but enjoyed the adventure.

An experience I didn't appreciate so much was getting lost one late afternoon several kilometers above a boathouse on the Dnieper. I was walking along the riverbank enjoying the sight of the boats and island beaches, and before I knew it, was a good distance from the hotel and eager to get back because I was hungry. I didn't feel like retracing my route on foot—too much tourism in three days—so I thought of a taxi or maybe an autobus that might be going in the general direction I had come from. Nothing doing, though I searched on some of the inner avenues for half an hour. I tried approaching a few passersby whom I addressed in English, or pidgin-German, and occasionally trying "*pardonnez-moi*"; but the effect was apparently to embarrass them. One young woman ran from me a few steps before she began to walk again. I stepped into an oculist's shop to ask advice of a professional-looking older woman, wearing pince-nez, a hairnet, and white smock. When I spoke in English, after momentary amazement her face froze, and she turned her back on me. Hastily thumbing through my guidebook to the phonetic expressions in Russian, I asked, *"Gdye* hotel?" adding "Dnipro?" To that she answered, *"Nyet."* "Taxi?" I asked. *"Nyet,"* this time clapping a hand to her heaving bosom. I figured I'd better leave. Though frustrated, annoyed, I spoke to two men passing by, one of whom, the minute he heard my first word, walked on quickly, his eyes aimed straight ahead, the other indicating by gestures that he was deaf and dumb. On impulse I tried him in halting Yiddish that my grandfather had long ago taught me, and was then directed, in an undertone in the same language, to a nearby bus stop.

As I was unlocking the door to my room, thinking this was a story I would be telling friends all autumn, my phone was ringing. It was a woman's voice. I understood "Gospodin Garvitz" and one or two other words as she spoke at length in musical Russian. In fact, her voice was like a singer's. Though I couldn't get the gist of her remarks, I had this sudden vivid reverie, you might call it, of walking with a pretty Russian girl in a birch-wood or thereabouts, coming out on the other side in a field that sloped to the water, and then rowing her around on a small lake. It was a very peaceful business. That was the general picture; but when she was done talking, whatever I had to say I said in English, and she slowly hung up.

The next morning after breakfast, she, or someone who sounded like her—I recognized the contralto quality—called again.

"If you could understand English," I said, "or maybe a little German or French—even Yiddish, if you happen to know it— we'd get along fine. But not in Russian, I'm afraid. *Nyet Russki.* I'd be glad to meet you for lunch, or tea if you like; so if you get the drift of these remarks why don't you say *da?* Then dial the English interpreter on extension 37. She could tell me what's what, and we can meet at your convenience."

I had the impression she was listening with both ears but after a while the phone hung silent in my hand. I wondered where she had got my name, and whether someone was testing me to find out if I did or didn't speak Russian. I honestly did not.

Afterward I wrote a short airmail letter to Lillian, telling her I would be leaving for Moscow via Aeroflot, tomorrow at 4 P.M., and I intended to stay there for two weeks, with a break of maybe three or four days in Leningrad, at the Astoria Hotel. I wrote down the exact dates and later mailed the letter in a box some distance from the hotel, whatever good that did. I hoped Lillian would get it in time to reach me by return mail before I left the Soviet Union. To tell the truth, I felt uneasy all day.

But the next morning my mood had changed, and as I was standing at the railing in a park above the Dnieper, looking at the buildings going up across the river in what had once been steppeland, I had an expansive feeling. The vast construction I beheld —it was as though two or three scattered cities were rising out of the earth—astonished me. This sort of thing was going on all over Russia—halfway around the world—and when I considered what it meant in terms of sheer labor, capital goods, plain morale I was then and there convinced that the Soviet Union would never willingly provoke a war, nuclear or otherwise, with the United States. Neither would America, in its right mind, with the Soviet Union.

For the first time since I had come to Russia, I felt safe and secure and enjoyed there, at the breezy railing above the Dnieper, a rare few minutes of euphoria.

Why is it that the most interesting architecture is from Czarist times I asked myself, and if I'm not mistaken Levitansky quivered, no doubt a coincidence. Unless I had spoken to myself aloud which I sometimes do; I decided I hadn't. We were on our way to the museum, hitting a fast eighty kilometers, which translated to fifty miles an hour was not too bad because traffic was sparse.

"What do you think of my country, the Union of Soviet Socialist Republics?" the driver inquired, turning his head a half circle to see where I was.

"Please watch where we're going."

"Don't be nervous, I drive now for years."

"I don't care for needless risks."

Then I said I was impressed by much I had seen. It was obviously a great country.

Levitansky's face appeared in the mirror globularly smiling, his dark teeth eroded. The smile seemed to emerge from within the mouth. Now that he had revealed his half-Jewish background I had the impression he looked more Jewish than Slavic, and possibly more dissatisfied than I had thought.

"Also our system—Communism?"

I answered carefully, not wanting to give offense. "I'll be perfectly honest. I've seen some unusual things here—even inspiring —but my personal taste is for more individual freedom than people seem to have here. America has its serious faults but at least we're privileged to criticize, if you know what I mean. My father used to say, 'You can't beat the Bill of Rights.' It's an open society, which means freedom of choice, at least in theory."

"Communism is altogether better system," Levitansky replied calmly after a minute, "although is not in present stage totally realized. In present stage"—he gulped for air, swallowed, and did not finish the thought. Instead he said, "Our revolution was magnificent holy event. I love early Soviet history, excitement of Communist idealism, and victory over bourgeois and imperialist Russian masses. It was born a life of new possibilities for all in society. Pasternak called this 'splendid surgery.' Evgeny Zamyatin spoke thus: 'The revolution consumes the earth with the fire but then is born a new life.'"

I didn't argue, each to his own revolution.

"You told before," said Levitansky, glancing at me again in the mirror, "that you wish to write articles of your visit. Political or not political?"

"I don't write on politics although interested in it. What I have in my mind is something on the literary museums of Moscow for an American travel magazine. That's the sort of thing I do. I'm a free-lance writer." I laughed a little apologetically. It's strange how stresses shift when you're in another country.

Levitansky politely joined in the laugh, stopping in midcourse. "I wish to be certain, what is free-lance writer?"

"Well, an editor might propose an article, and I either accept the idea or I don't. Or I can write about something that happens to interest me and take my chances I can sell it. Sometimes I don't, and that's so much down the drain financially. What I like about it is I am my own boss. I also edit a bit. I've done anthologies of poetry and essays, both for high school kids."

"We have here free-lance. I am also a writer," Levitansky said solemnly.

"You don't say? You mean as a translator?"

"Translation is my profession, but I am also original writer."

"Then you do three things—write, translate, and drive this cab?"

"The taxi is not my true work."

"Are you translating anything now?"

The driver cleared his throat. "In present time I have no translation project."

"What sort of thing do you write?"

"I write stories."

"Is that so? What kind, if I might ask?"

"I will tell you what kind—little ones—short stories imagined from life."

"Have you published any?"

He seemed about to turn around to look me in the eye but reached instead into his shirt pocket. I offered my American pack. He shook out a cigarette and lit it, exhaling slowly.

"A few pieces but not recently. To tell the truth"—he sighed— "I write for the drawer. Like Isaac Babel, 'I am master of the genre of silence.'"

"I've heard the expression," I said, not knowing what else to say.

"The mice should read and criticize," Levitansky said bitterly. "This what they don't eat they make their drops—droppings?—on. This is perfect criticism."

"I'm sorry about that."

"We arrive now to Chekhov Museum."

I leaned forward to pay him and made the impulsive mistake of adding a one-ruble tip. He was immediately angered. "I am Soviet citizen." He forcibly returned the ruble.

"Call it a thoughtless error," I apologized. "No harm meant."

"Hiroshima! Nagasaki!" he taunted as the Volga took off in a cloud of smoke. "Aggressor against poor people of Vietnam!"

"None of that is any of my doing!" I called after him.

An hour and a half later, after I had signed the guest book and was leaving the museum, I saw someone standing, smoking, under a linden tree across the street. Nearby was a parked taxi. We stared at each other—I wasn't certain at first who it was but Levitansky nodded amiably to me, calling "Welcome! Welcome!" He waved an arm, smiling openmouthed. He had combed his

thick hair and was now wearing a loose dark suit coat over his
tieless white shirt, and yards of baggy pants. His socks, striped
red-white-and-blue, you could see under his sandals.

I am forgiven, I thought. "Welcome to you," I said, crossing
the street.

"How did you enjoy Chekhov Museum?"

"I did indeed. I've made a lot of notes. You know what they
have there? They have one of his black fedoras and also his
pince-nez that you see in pictures of him. Awfully moving."

Levitansky wiped one eye, to my surprise. He seemed not
the same man, at any rate somewhat modified. It's funny, you
find out a few personal facts about a stranger and he changes
as he speaks. The taxi driver is now a writer, even if part-time.
Anyway that's my dominant impression.

"Excuse me my former anger," Levitansky said. "Now is not for
me the best of times. 'It was the best of times, it was the worst of
times,'" he quoted, smiling sadly.

"So long as you pardon my unintentional blunder. Are you
perhaps free to drive me to the Metropole, or are you here by
coincidence?"

I looked around to see if anyone was coming out of the museum.

"If you wish to engage me I will drive you, but at first I will
show you something—how do you say?—of interest?"

He reached through the open front window of the taxi and
brought forth a flat package wrapped in brown paper tied with
string.

"Stories which I wrote."

"I don't read Russian," I said quickly.

"My wife has translated of them, four. She is not by her profession a translator, although her English is advanced and sensitive.
She has been for two years in England for Soviet Purchasing
Commission. We became acquainted in university. I prefer not
to translate my own stories because I do not translate so well
Russian into English although I translate beautifully the opposite.
Also I will not force myself—it is like self-imitation. Perhaps the
stories are a little awkward in English—also my wife admits this
—but at least you can read and form opinion."

He offered me the package as if it were a bouquet of spring
flowers. I thought to myself, can it be some sort of trick? Are they

checking up on me because I signed that damned document at the Kiev airport, five copies no less?

Levitansky seemed to read my mind. "It is purely stories."

He bit the string in two, and laying the package on the fender of the Volga, unpeeled the wrapping. There were four stories, clipped separately, typed on long sheets of thin blue paper. I took one Levitansky handed me and scanned the top page—it seemed a story—then I flipped through the other pages and handed the manuscript back. "I'm not much of a critic of stories."

"I don't seek a critic. I seek for reader of literary experience and taste. If you have redacted books of poems and also essays, you will be able to judge literary qualities of my stories. Please, I request that you will read them."

After a long minute I heard myself say, "Well I might at that." I didn't recognize the voice and could hardly understand why I was saying it. You might say I spoke apart from myself, with a reluctance that either he didn't recognize or didn't care to acknowledge.

"If you respect—if you approve my stories, perhaps you will be able to arrange for publication in Paris or either London?" His large larynx wobbled nervously.

I stared at the man. "I don't happen to be going to Paris, and I'll be in London only between planes to the U.S.A."

"In this event, perhaps you will show to your publisher, and he will publish my work in America?" Levitansky was now visibly miserable.

"In America?" I said, raising my voice in disbelief.

For the first time he gazed around cautiously before replying.

"If you will be so kind to show them to publisher of your books —is he reliable publisher?—perhaps he will also wish to put out volume of my stories? I will make contract whatever he will like. Money, if I could get, is not an ideal."

"What volume are you talking about?"

He said that from thirty stories he had written he had chosen eighteen, of which these four were a sample. "Unfortunately more are not now translated. My wife is biochemist assistant and works long hours in laboratory. I am sure your publisher will enjoy to read these. It will depend on your opinion."

Either the man has a fantastic imagination or he's out of his right mind, I thought. "I wouldn't want to get myself involved in smuggling a Russian manuscript out of Russia."

"I have informed you that my manuscript is only made-up stories."

"That may be, but it's still a chancy enterprise. I'd be taking chances I have no particular desire to take, to be frank."

"At least if you will read," he sighed.

I took the stories again and thumbed slowly through each. What I was looking for I couldn't say: maybe a booby trap? Should I or shouldn't I? I thought. Why should I?

He handed me the wrapping paper, and I rolled up the stories in it. The quicker I read them, the quicker I've read them. I got into the cab.

"As I said, I'm at the Metropole," I told him. "Come by tonight about nine o'clock, and I'll give you my opinion for what it's worth. But I'm afraid I'll have to limit it to that, Mr. Levitansky, without further obligation or expectations, or it's no deal. My room number is 538."

"Tonight?—so soon?" he said, scratching both palms. "You must read with care so you will realize the art."

"Tomorrow night, then. I'd rather not have them around in my room longer than that."

Levitansky agreed. Whistling softly through his eroded teeth, he drove me carefully to the Metropole.

That night, sipping vodka from a drinking glass, at first reluctantly I read Levitansky's stories. They were simply and strongly written—I can't say I was surprised, I sort of expected it—and not badly translated; in fact the translation read better than I had been led to think although there were of course gaffes here and there, odd constructions, ill-fitting words surrounded by question marks, taken, I suppose, from a thesaurus. And the stories, short tales dealing—somewhat to my surprise—mostly with Jews and you might say their problems, were good, really moving. The situation they revealed wasn't news to me: I'm a careful reader of the New York *Times*. But the stories weren't written to complain, nothing of the kind. What they had to say was achieved as form, no telling "the dancer from the dance." I finished reading, poured myself another glass of potato potion—I was beginning to feel high, with occasional thoughts of wondering why I was putting so much away—just relaxing, I guess. I then reread the stories with a sense of growing admiration for Levitansky. I had the feeling he was no ordinary man. At first I felt excited, then depressed, as if I had been let in on a secret I didn't want to know.

It's a hard life here for a fiction writer, I thought.

Afterward, having the stories around began to make me uneasy. In one of them a Russian writer starts to burn his stories in the kitchen sink. But nobody had burned these. I thought to myself, if I'm caught with them in my possession, considering what they indicate about conditions here, there's no question I'd be in trouble. I wish I had insisted that Levitansky come back for them tonight.

There was a solid rap on the door. I felt as though I had risen a good few inches out of my seat. It was, after a while, Levitansky.

"Out of the question," I said, thrusting the stories at him. "Absolutely out of the question!"

The next night we sat facing each other over cognac in the writer's small, book-crowded study. He was dignified, at first haughty, wounded, hardly masking his impatience. I wasn't myself exactly comfortable.

I had come out of courtesy and other considerations, I guess; principally a sense of dissatisfaction I couldn't exactly define, except it tied up in my mind with who I was and wanted to be, issues that disturb me, to say the least, because they sometimes compel me to get involved in ways I don't want to get involved, always a dangerous business.

Levitansky, the taxi driver rattling around in his Volga-Pegasus and amateur trying to palm off a half-ass manuscript, had faded in my mind, and I saw him simply as a serious Soviet writer with publishing problems. What can I do for him? I thought. Why should I?

"I didn't express what was on my mind last night," I apologized. "You sort of caught me by surprise I'm sorry to say."

Levitansky was scratching each hand with the fingers of the other. "How did you acquire my address?"

I reached into my pocket for a wad of folded brown wrapping paper. "It's right on this—Novo Ostapovskaya Street, 488, Flat 59. I took a cab."

"I had forgotten this."

Maybe, I thought.

Still, I had practically had to put my foot in the door to get in.
Levitansky's wife had answered my uncertain knock, her eyes uneasily worried, which I took to be the expression she lived with.
The eyes were astonished to behold a stranger, and outright hostile
once I had inquired in English for her husband. I felt, as in Kiev,
that my native tongue had become my enemy.

"Have you not the wrong apartment?"

"I hope not. Not if Mr. Levitansky lives here. I came to see
him about his—er—manuscript."

Her eyes darkened as her face blanched. Ten seconds later I
was in the flat, the door shut tightly behind me.

"Levitansky!" she summoned him. It had a reluctant quality:
come but don't come.

He appeared at once in apparently the same shirt, pants, tri-
colored socks. There was at first pretend-boredom in a tense, tired
face. He could not, however, conceal excitement, his lit eyes roving, returning, roving.

"Oh, ho," Levitansky said, whatever it meant.

My God, I thought, has he been expecting me?

"I came to talk to you for a few minutes, if you don't mind,"
I said. "I want to say what I really think of your stories that
you kindly let me read."

He curtly said something in Russian to his wife, and she snapped
an answer back. "I wish to introduce my wife, Irina Filipovna
Levitansky, biochemist. She is patient although not a saint."

She smiled tentatively, an attractive women about twenty-eight,
a little on the hefty side, in house slippers and plain dress. The
edge of her slip hung below her skirt.

There was a bit of British in her accent. "I am pleased to be
acquainted." If so one hardly noticed. She stepped into black
pumps and slipped a silver bracelet on her wrist, a lit cigarette
dangling from the corner of her mouth. Her legs and arms were
shapely, her brown hair cut short. I had the impression of tight
thin lips in a pale face.

"I will go to Kovalevsky, next door," she said.

"Not on my account, I hope? All I have to say—"

"Our neighbors in the next flat." Levitansky grimaced. "Also thin
walls." He knocked a knuckle on a hollow wall.

I chuckled politely.

"Please, not long," Irina said, "because I am afraid."

Surely not of me? Agent Howard Harvitz, CIA, a comical thought.

Their living room wasn't unattractive, but Levitansky signaled the study inside. He offered a slightly sweet cognac in whiskey tumblers, then sat facing me on the edge of his chair, his repressed energy all but visible. I had the momentary sensation his chair might begin to move, even fly off.

If he goes he goes alone.

"What I came to say," I told him, "is I like your stories and am sorry I didn't say so last night. I like the primary quality of the writing. The stories impress me as strong, if simply wrought, and I appreciate your feeling for people and at the same time the objectivity with which you render them. It's sort of Chekhovian in quality. For instance, that story about the old father coming to see the son who ducks out on him. I guess I can't comment on your style, having only read the stories in translation."

"Chekhovian," Levitansky admitted, smiling through his worn teeth, "is fine compliment. Mayakovsky, our poet, described him 'the strong and gay artist of the word.' I wish I was so gay in respect of enjoyment of art and life." He looked at the drawn shade in the room, though maybe no place in particular, then said, perhaps heartening himself, "In Russian is magnificent my style—precise, economy, including wit. The style is difficult to translate in English, which is less rich language."

"I've heard that said. In fairness I should add I have some reservations about the stories, yet who hasn't about any given piece of creative work?"

"I have myself reservations."

The admission made, I skipped the criticisms. I had been looking at a picture on his bookcase, and asked who it was. "It's a face I've seen before. The eyes are quite poetic, you might say."

"So is the voice. This is Boris Pasternak as young man. On the wall yonder is Mayakovsky that I mentioned to you. He was also remarkable poet, wild, joyous, neurasthenic, a lover of the revolution. He spoke, 'This is *my* Revolution.' To him was it 'a holy washerwoman who cleaned off all the filth from the earth.' Unfortunately he was later disillusioned and shot himself."

"I read that somewhere."

"He wrote: 'I wish to be understood by my country—but if no, I will fly through Russia like a slanting rainstorm.'"

"I bet it sounds magnificent in Russian. Have you by chance read *Doctor Zhivago?*"

"I have read," the writer sighed, and then began to recite in Russian, I guessed some lines from a poem.

"It is to Marina Tsvetayeva, Soviet poetess, friend of Pasternak." Levitansky fiddled with the pack of cigarettes on the table with the cognac. "The end of her life was unfortunate."

"I guess why I really came," I said, "is I wanted to express to you my sympathy and respect."

Levitansky popped a match with his thumbnail. His hand trembled, so he shook the flame out without lighting the cigarette.

Embarrassed for him, I pretended to be looking elsewhere. "It's a small room. Does your son sleep here?"

"Don't confuse my story which you read with life of author. My wife and I are married eight years but without children."

"Might I ask whether the other experience you describe in that same story—the interview with the editor—was that true?"

"Not true," the writer said impatiently. "I write from imagination. I am not interested to repeat contents of diaries or total memory."

"On that I go along with you."

"Also, which is not in story, I have submitted to Soviet journals sketches and tales many times but only few have been published, although not my best."

"Did you submit any of the Jewish stories?"

"Please, stories are stories, they have not nationality."

"I mean by that those about Jews."

"Some I have submitted, but they were not accepted."

Brave man, I thought. "After reading the four you gave me, I wondered how it was you write so well about Jews? You call yourself a marginal one—I believe that was your word—but you write with authority about them. Not that one can't, I suppose, but it's surprising when one does."

"Imagination makes authority. My work is work of imagination. When I write about Jews comes out stories, so I write about Jews. I write about subjects that make for me stories. Is not important that I am marginal Jew. What is important is observation, feeling, also the art. In the past I have observed my Jewish father. Also I

observe sometimes Jews in the synagogue. I sit there on the bench
for strangers. The gabbai watches me, and I watch him. But
whatever I write, whether is about Jews, Galicians, or Georgians,
must be a work of invention or it does not live."

"I'm not much of a synagogue-goer myself," I told him, "but I
like to drop in once in a while to be refreshed by the language
and images of a time and place where God was. That's funny
because I had no religious education to speak of."

"I am atheist."

"I understand, though, what you mean by imagination—for instance that praying shawl story. But am I right"—I lowered my
voice—"that I detect you might also be saying something about the
condition of the Jews—er—at the moment?"

"I do not make propaganda," Levitansky said sternly. "I am not
Israeli spokesman. I am Soviet artist."

"I didn't mean you weren't, but there's a strong current of
sympathy, and after all, ideas come from somewhere."

"My purpose belongs to me."

"One senses, if I might say, an attack on injustice."

"Whatever is the injustice, the product must be art."

"Well, I respect your philosophy."

"Please do not respect so much," the writer said irritably. "We
have in this country a quotation: 'It is impossible to make out of
apology a fur coat.' The idea is similar. I appreciate respect but
need now practical assistance."

Expecting words of the sort, I started to say something non-
committal.

"Listen at first to me," Levitansky said, smacking the table with
his palm. "I am in desperate condition—situation. I have written
for years, but little is published. In the past, one, two editors who
were my friends told me, private, that my stories are excellent,
but I violate socialist realism. This what you call objectivity, they
called it excessive naturalism and sentiment. It is hard to listen to
such nonsense. They advise me to walk but not with my legs.
They warned me; also they have made excuses for me to others.
Even they said I am crazy, although I explained to them I submit
my stories *because* Soviet Union is great country. A great country
does not fear what artist writes. A great country breathes in its
lungs work of writers, painters, musicians, and becomes more great,
more healthy. This is what I told to them, but they replied I am

not enough realist. This is the reason that I am not invited to be member of Writers Union." He smiled sourly. "They warned me to stop submitting to journals my work, so I have stopped."

"I'm sorry about that," I said. "I don't myself go for exiling the poets."

"I cannot continue longer anymore in this fashion," Levitansky said, laying his hand on his heart. "I must free from drawer my imagination. I feel I am myself locked in drawer with my poor stories. Now I must get out or I suffocate. It becomes for me each day more difficult to write. I need help. It is not easy to request a stranger for such important personal favor. My wife advised me not. She is angry, also frightened, but is impossible for me to go on in this way. I am convinced I am important Soviet writer. I must have my audience. I wish to have in someone's mind different than my own and my wife acknowledgment of my art. I wish them to know my work is related to Russian writers of the past, as well as modern. I am in tradition of Chekhov, Gorky, Isaac Babel. I know if book of my stories is published, it will make for me good reputation. This is reason why you must help me—it is necessary for my interior liberty."

His confession came in an agitated burst. I use the word advisedly because that's partly what upset me. I have never cared for confessions of this kind, which are a way of involving unwilling people in others' personal problems. Russians are past masters of this art—you can see in their novels.

"I appreciate the honor of your request," I said, "but all I am is a passing tourist. That's a pretty tenuous relationship between us."

"I do not ask tourist—I ask human being, man," Levitansky said passionately. "Also you are free-lance writer. You know who I am and what is on my heart. You sit in my house. Who else can I ask? I would better prefer to publish in Europe my stories, maybe with Mondadori or Einaudi in Italy, but if this is impossible to you I will publish in America. Someday will my work be read in my country, maybe after I am dead. This is terrible irony, but my generation lives on such ironies. Since I am not now ambitious to die, it will be great relief to me to know that at least in one language is alive my art. Osip Mandelstam wrote: 'I will be enclosed in some alien speech.' Better so than nothing."

"You say I know who you are but do you know who *I* am?" I asked him. "I'm a plain person, not very imaginative though I don't write a bad article. My whole life, for some reason, has been without much adventure, except I was divorced once and remarried happily to a woman whose death I am still mourning. Now I'm here more or less on a vacation, not to jeopardize myself by taking serious chances of an unknown kind. What's more—and this is the main thing I came to tell you—I wouldn't at all be surprised if I am already under suspicion and would do you more harm than good."

I told Levitansky about the airport incident in Kiev and the paper I had signed five copies of. "I signed a document I couldn't even read, which was a foolish thing to do."

"In Kiev this happened?"

"That's right."

Levitansky laughed dismally. "It would not happen to you if you entered through Moscow. In the Ukraine—what is your word? —they are rubes, country people."

"That might be—nevertheless, I signed the paper."

"Do you have copy?"

"Not with me. It's in my room in the hotel."

"I am certain this is receipt for your books which officials will return to you when you depart from Soviet Union."

"That's just what I'd be afraid of."

"Why afraid?" he asked. "Are you afraid to receive back umbrella which you have lost?"

"I'd be afraid one thing might lead to another—more questions, more searches. It would be foolhardy to have your manuscript in my suitcase, in Russian no less, that I can't read. Suppose they accuse me of being some kind of courier or spy?"

The thought raised me to my feet. I then realized the tension in the room was thick as steam, mostly mine.

Levitansky rose, embittered. "There is no question of spying. I do not think I have presented myself as traitor to my country."

"I didn't say anything of the sort. All I'm saying is I don't want to get into trouble with the Soviet authorities. Nobody can blame me for that. In other words, the enterprise is not for me."

"I have made inquirings," Levitansky said desperately. "You will have nothing to fear for a tourist who has been a few weeks in U.S.S.R. under guidance of Intourist and does not speak Russian. My wife said to me your baggage will not be further inspected. They sometimes do so to political people, also to bourgeois journal-

ists who have made bad impression. I would deliver to you manuscript in the last instance. It is typed on less than one hundred fifty
sheets thin paper and will make small package. If it should look to
you like trouble you can leave it in dustbin. My name will not be
anywhere and if they find it and track—trace to me the stories,
I will say I have thrown them out myself. They won't believe this
but what other can I say? It will make no difference anyway. If I
stop to write I may as well be dead. No harm will come to you."

"I'd rather not if you don't mind."

With what I guess was a curse in Russian, Levitansky reached
for the portrait on his bookcase and flung it against the wall.
Pasternak struck Mayakovsky, splattered him with glass, breaking
his own, and both pictures crashed to the floor.

"Free-lance writer," he shouted, "go to hell back to America!
Tell to Negroes about Bill of Rights! Tell them they are free
although you keep them slaves! Talk to sacrificed Vietnamese
people!"

Irina Filipovna entered the room on the run. "Feliks," she en-
treated, "Kovalevsky hears every word!"

"Please," she begged me, "please go away. Leave poor Levitansky alone. I beg you from my miserable heart."

I left in a hurry. The next day I left for Leningrad.

Three days later, not exactly at my best after a tense visit to
Leningrad, I was sitting loosely in a beat-up taxi with a cheerful
Intouristka, a half hour after my arrival at the Moscow airport.
We were driving to the Ukraine Hotel, where I was assigned
for my remaining few days in the Soviet Union. I would have
preferred the Metropole again because it's so conveniently located
and I was used to it; but on second thought, better someplace
where a certain party wouldn't know I lived. The Volga we were
riding in seemed somehow familiar, but if so it was safely in the
hands of a small stranger with a large wool cap, a man wearing
sunglasses who paid me no particular attention.

I had had a few pleasant minutes in Leningrad on my first day.
On a white summer's evening, shortly after I had unpacked in my
room at the Astoria, I discovered the Winter Palace and Hermi-
tage after a walk along the Nevsky Prospekt. Chancing on Palace
Square, vast and deserted, I felt an unexpected emotion, you might
say, in thinking of the revolutionary events that had occurred on

this spot. My God, I thought, why should I feel myself part of Russian history? It's a contagious business, what happens to men. On the Palace Bridge I gazed at the broad ice-blue Neva, in the distance the golden steeple of the cathedral built by Peter the Great, gleaming under masses of wind-driven clouds in patches of green sky. It's the Soviet Union but it's still Russia.

The next day I woke up anxious. In the street I was approached twice by strangers speaking English; I think my suede shoes attracted them. The first, gray-faced and badly dressed, wanted to sell me black market rubles. "*Nyet*," I said, tipping my straw hat and hurrying on. The second, a bearded boy of nineteen, with a left-sided tuft longer than that on the right, wearing a home-knitted green pullover, offered to buy jazz records, "youth clothes," and American cigarettes. "Sorry, nothing for sale." I escaped him too, except that he in his green sweater followed me for a mile along one of the canals. I broke into a run, then forced myself to stop. When I looked back he had disappeared. I slept badly at night—it stayed light too long past midnight; and in the morning inquired about the possibility of an immediate flight to Helsinki. I was informed I couldn't possibly get one for a week. Calming myself, I decided to return to Moscow a day before I had planned to, mostly to see what they had in the Dostoevsky Museum.

I had been thinking a good deal about Levitansky. How much of a writer was he really? I had read four of eighteen stories he wanted to publish. Suppose he had showed me the four best and the others were mediocre or thereabouts? Was it worth taking a chance for that? I thought, the best thing for my peace of mind is to forget the guy. Before checking out of the Astoria I received a chatty letter from Lillian, forwarded from Moscow, apparently not an answer to my recent letter to her, but one written earlier. Should I marry her? Who knows, I don't. The phone rang piercingly, and when I picked up the receiver, no one answered. In the plane to Moscow I had visions of a crash. There must be many in the Soviet Union nobody ever reads of.

In my room on the twelfth floor of the Ukraine I relaxed in a plastic "leather" armchair. There was also a single low bed, and a utilitarian pinewood desk, an apple-green phone plunked on it for instant use. I'll be home in a week, I thought. Now I'd better

shave and see if anything is left over downstairs in the way of a
concert or opera ticket for tonight. I'm in the mood for a little
music.

The electric plug in the bathroom didn't work, so I put away
my shaver and was lathering up when I jumped to a single
explosive knock on the door. I opened it cautiously, and there
stood Levitansky with a brown paper packet in his hand.

Is this son of a bitch out to compromise me?

"How did you happen to find out where I was only twenty
minutes after I got here, Mr. Levitansky?"

"How I found you?" the writer shrugged. He seemed deathly
tired, a bit popeyed, the face longer, leaner, resembling in a way
a hungry fox on his last unsteady legs but still canny. "My brother-
in-law was the chauffeur for you from the airport. He heard the
girl inquire your name. We have spoke of you. Dmitri—this is my
wife's brother—informed me you have registered at the Ukraine.
I inquired downstairs your room number, and it was granted to
me."

"However it was," I said firmly, "I want you to know I haven't
changed my mind. I don't want to get involved. I thought it all
through while I was in Leningrad, and that's my final decision."

"I may come in?"

"Please, but for obvious reasons I'd appreciate a short visit."

Levitansky sat, somewhat shriveled, skinny knees pressed together, in the armchair, his parcel awkwardly on his lap. If he
was happy to have found me, his face didn't show it.

I finished shaving, put on a fresh shirt, and sat down on the
bed. "Sorry I have nothing to offer in the way of an aperitif, but
I could call down for something."

Levitansky twiddled his fingers no. He was dressed without
change down to his red-white-and-blue socks. Did his wife wash
out the same pair every night, or were all his socks red-white-
and-blue?

"To speak frankly," I said, "I have to protest about this constant
tension you've whipped up in and around me. Nobody in his
right mind can expect a total stranger visiting the Soviet Union
to pull his personal chestnuts out of the fire. It's your own country
that's restricting you as a writer, not me or the United States of
America, and since you live here, what can you do but live with
it?"

"I love my country," Levitansky said with dignity.

"Who said you didn't? So do I love mine, though love for country, let's face it, is a mixed bag of marbles. Nationality isn't soul, as I'm sure you will agree. But what I'm also saying is there are things about a man's country he might not like that he has to make his peace with. I'm not saying it's easy but if you're up against a wall you can't climb or dig under or outflank in some way, at least stop banging your head against it, not to mention mine. Make your peace in some way. It's amazing, for instance, all that can be said in a fairy tale."

"I have written already my fairy tales," Levitansky said moodily. "Now is the time for truth without disguises. I will make my peace to this point where it interferes with work of my imagination —my interior liberty; and then I must stop to make my peace. My brother-in-law has also told to me, 'You must write acceptable stories, others can do it, so why can't you?' and I have answered him, 'They must be acceptable to *me. Ich kann nicht anders!*'"

"In that case, aren't you up against the impossible? If you permit me to say so, are those Jews in your stories, if they can't have their matzos and prayer books, any freer in their religious lives than you are as a writer? That's what you're really saying when you write about them. What I mean is, one has to face up to his society."

"I have faced up. Do you face up to yours?" he said, with a flash of scorn.

"Not as well as I might, I admit. My own problem is not that I can't express myself but that I don't. In my own mind Vietnam is a terrifying mistake, though I've never spoken out against it except to sign a petition or two. My first wife used to criticize me. She said I wrote the wrong things and was involved in everything but action. My second wife knew this but she made me think she didn't."

From the heat of my body I knew I was blushing.

Levitansky's large larynx moved up like a flag on a pole, then sank wordlessly.

My God, not another confession, I hoped.

He tried again, saying, "The Soviet Union preservates for us the great victories of our revolution. Because of this I have remained for years at peace with the State. Communism is still to me inspirational ideal, although this historical period is spoiled by leaders who have taken impoverished view of humanity. They have pissed on revolution."

"Stalin?"

"Him, but also others. Even so I have obeyed Party directives, and when I could not longer obey, I wrote for drawer. I said to myself, 'Levitansky, history changes every minute, and Communism also will change.' I believed if the State restricts two, three generations of artists, what is this against development of true socialist society—maybe best society of world history? So what does it mean if some of us are sacrificed to Party purpose? The aesthetic mode is not in necessity greater than politics—than needs of revolution. And what if are suppressed two generations of artists? Therefore will be so much less bad books, paintings, music. Then in fifty years more will be secure the State and all Soviet artists will say whatever they will. This is what I thought, but I do not longer think so in this manner. I do not believe more in *partiinost*, which is guided thought. I do not believe in bolshevization of literature. I do not think revolution is fulfilled in country of unpublished novelists, poets, playwriters, who hide in drawers whole libraries of literature that will never be printed, or if so, it will be printed after they stink in their graves. I think now the State will never be secure—never. It is not in the nature of politics to be finished with revolution. After revolution comes revolution. Evgeny Zamyatin told: 'There is no final revolution. Revolutions are infinite!' "

"I guess that's along my own line of thinking," I said, hoping for reasons of personal safety maybe to forestall Levitansky's ultimate confession—one he, with brooding intense eyes, was already relentlessly making—lest in the end it imprison me in his will and history.

"I have learned from my stories," the writer was saying, "as I wrote them, that imagination is enemy of the State. I have learned from my stories that I am not free man. This is my conclusion. I ask for your help not to harm my country, which still has magnificent possibilities, but to help me escape the worst errors. I do not wish to defame Soviet Union. My purpose in my work is to show its true heart. So have done our writers from Pushkin to Pasternak. If you believe in democratic humanism, you must help artist to be free. Is not true?"

I got up, I think to shake myself free of the question. "What exactly is my responsibility to you, Levitansky?"

"If I am drowning you must assist to save me. We are members of mankind."

"In unknown waters if I can't swim?"

"If not, throw to me a rope."

"I'm just a visitor here. Besides, I've told you already that I may be suspect, and for all I know you yourself might be a Soviet agent out to get me, or this room might be bugged, and then where will we be? Mr. Levitansky, I don't want to hear or argue anymore. I'll just plead personal inability and ask you to leave."

"Bugged?"

"Some sort of listening device planted in this room."

Levitansky turned slowly gray. He sat for a minute in motionless meditation, then rose wearily from the chair.

"I withdraw now request for your assistance. I accept your word that you are not capable. I do not wish to make criticism of you. All I wish to say, Gospodin Garvitz, is it requires more to change a man's character than to change his name."

Levitansky left the room, leaving in his wake some fumes of cognac. He had also passed gas.

"Come back!" I called, not too loudly, but if he heard through the door he didn't answer. Good riddance, I thought, not that I don't sympathize with him, which I do, but look what he's done to *my* interior liberty. Who has to come all the way to Russia to get caught up in this kind of mess? It's a helluva way to spend a vacation.

The writer had gone, but not his sneaky manuscript. It was lying on my bed.

"It's his baby, not mine." Seeing red, I knotted my tie and slipped on my coat, then via the English language number, called a cab. But I had forgotten his address. A half hour later I was still in the taxi, riding frantically back and forth along Novo Ostapovskaya Street until I spotted the house I thought it might be. It wasn't, it was another like it. I paid the driver and walked on till once again I thought I had the house. After going up the stairs and getting a whiff of the cooking smells, I was sure it was. When I knocked on Levitansky's door, the writer, looking older, more distant—as if he had been away on a trip and had just returned, or maybe simply interrupted at his work, his thoughts still in his words on the page on the table, his pen in hand—stared blankly at me.

"Levitansky, my heart breaks for you, I swear, but I can't take the chance. I believe in you but am not, at this time of my life, considering my condition and recent experiences, in much of a mood to embark on a dangerous adventure. Please accept deepest regrets."

I thrust the manuscript into his hand and rushed down the stairs. Hurrying out of the building, I was, to my horror, unable to avoid Irina Levitansky coming in. Her eyes lit in fright as she recognized me an instant before I hit her full force and sent her sprawling along the cement walk.

"Oh, my God, what have I done? I sincerely beg your pardon!" I helped the dazed, hurt woman to her feet, brushing off her soiled skirt, and futilely, her pink blouse, split and torn on her lacerated arm and shoulder. I stopped dead when I felt myself experiencing erotic sensations.

Irina Filipovna held a handkerchief to her bloody nostril and wept a little. We sat on a stone bench, a girl of ten and her brother watching us. Irina said something to them in Russian, and they moved off.

"I was frightened of you also as you are of us," she said. "I trust you now because Levitansky does. But I will not urge you to take the manuscript. The responsibility is for you to decide."

"It's not a responsibility I want," I said unhappily.

She said then as though talking to herself, "Maybe I will leave Levitansky. He is wretched so much it is no longer a marriage. He drinks; also he does not earn a living. My brother Dmitri allows him to drive the taxi two, three hours in the day, to my brother's disadvantage. Except for a ruble or two from this, I support him. Levitansky does not longer receive translation commissions. Also a neighbor in the house—I am sure Kovalevsky—has denounced him to the police for delinquency and parasitism. There will be a hearing. Levitansky says he will burn his manuscripts."

"Good God, I've just returned the package of them to him."

"He will not," she said. "But even if he burns he will write more. If they take him away in prison, he will write on toilet paper. When he comes out, he will write on newspaper margins. He sits now at his table. He is a magnificent writer. I cannot ask him not to write, but now I must decide if this is the condition I want for myself the rest of my life."

She sat in silence, an attractive woman with shapely legs and feet, in a soiled skirt and torn pink blouse. I left her sitting on the stone bench, her handkerchief squeezed white in her fist.

That night—July 2, I was leaving the Soviet Union on the fifth—I underwent great self-doubt. If I'm a coward, why has it taken me so long to find out? Where does anxiety end and cowardice begin? Feelings get mixed, sure enough, but not all cowards are necessarily anxious, and not all anxious men are cowards. Many "sensitive" (Rose's word), tense, even frightened human beings did in fear what had to be done, the fear in some cases giving energy when it came time to fight or jump off a rooftop into a river. There comes a time in a man's life when to get where he has to go—if there are no doors or windows—he walks through a wall.

On the other hand, suppose one is courageous in a foolish cause —you concentrate on courage and not enough on horse sense? To get to the nub of the problem on my mind, how do I finally decide it's a sensible and worthwhile thing to smuggle out Levitansky's manuscript, given my reasonable doubts about the ultimate worth of the operation? Granted, as I now grant, he's trustworthy, and his wife is that and more; still does it pay a man like me to run the risk?

If six thousand Soviet writers can't do very much to enlarge their freedom as artists, who am I to fight their battle?—H. Harvitz, knight of the free lance from Manhattan. How far do you go, granted you have taken to heart the creed that all men (including Communists) are created free and equal and justice is for all? How far do you go for art if you're for Yeats, Rouault, and Ludwig von Beethoven? Not to mention Gogol, Tolstoy, and Dostoevsky. So far as to get yourself internationally involved: the HH MS. Smuggling Service? Will the President and State Department, not to speak of the CIA, send up three loud cheers for my contribution to the cause of international social justice? And suppose it amounts to no more than a gaffe in the end?—what will I prove if I sneak out Levitansky's manuscript, and all it turns out to be is just another passable book of stories?

That's how I argued with myself on several occasions, but in the end I argued myself into solid indecision.

What it boils down to, I'd say, is he expects me to help him because I'm an American. That's quite a nerve.

Two nights later—odd not to have the Fourth of July on July fourth (I was even listening for firecrackers)—a quiet light-lemon summer's evening in Moscow, after two monotonously uneasy days, though I was still making museum notes, for relief I took myself off to the Bolshoi to hear *Tosca*. It was sung in Russian by a busty lady and handsome tenor, but the Italian plot was unchanged, and in the end, Scarpia, who had promised "death" by fake bullets, gave, in sneaky exchange, a fusillade of real lead; another artist bit the dust, and Floria Tosca learned the hard way that love wasn't what she had thought.

Next to me sat another full-breasted woman, this one a lovely Russian of maybe thirty in a white dress that fitted a well-formed body, her blond hair piled in a birdlike mass on her head. Lillian could sometimes look like that, though not Rose. This woman—alone, it turned out—spoke flawless English in a mezzo-soprano with a slight accent.

During the first intermission she asked in friendly fashion, managing to seem detached but interested: "Are you American? Or perhaps Swedish?"

"Not at all Swedish. American is right. How'd you happen to guess?"

"I noticed perhaps a certain self-satisfaction, if it does not bother you that I say so?" she remarked with a laugh.

"You got the wrong party," I said.

When she opened her purse a fragrance of springtime burst on the scene—fresh flowers, the warmth of her body rose to my nostrils. I was moved to memories of the hungers of my youth—desire, love, ambition.

In the intermission she said in a low voice, "May I ask a favor? Do you depart soon the Soviet Union?"

"In fact tomorrow."

"How fortunate for me. Would it offer too much difficulty to mail wherever you are going an airmail letter addressed to my husband, who is presently in Paris? Our airmail service takes two weeks to arrive in the West. I shall be grateful."

I glanced at the envelope, addressed half in French, half in Cyrillic, and said I wouldn't mind. But during the next act sweat

grew active on my body, and at the end of the opera, after Tosca's shriek of suicide, I handed the letter back to the not wholly
surprised lady, saying I was sorry. Nodding to her, I left the
theater. I had the feeling I had heard her voice before. I hurried
back to the hotel, determined not to leave my room for any reason
other than breakfast, then out and into the wide blue yonder.

I later fell asleep over a book and a bottle of sweet warm beer
a waiter had brought up, pretending to myself I was relaxed,
though I was as usual dealing beforehand with worried thoughts
of the departure and flight home; and when I awoke, three minutes on my wristwatch later, it seemed to me I had made the
acquaintance of a spate of nightmares. I was momentarily panicked by the idea that someone had planted a letter on me, and I
actually searched through the pockets of my two suits. *Nyet.*
Then I recalled that in one of my dreams a drawer in a table I was
sitting at had slowly come open, and Feliks Levitansky, a dwarf
who lived in it along with a few friendly mice, managed to scale
the wooden wall on a comb he used as a ladder, and to hop from
the drawer ledge to the top of the table, where he leered into my
face, shook his Lilliputian fist, and shouted in high-pitched but
(to me) understandable Russian: "Atombombnik! You murdered
innocent Japanese people! Amerikansky bastards!"
"That's unfair," I cried out. "I was no more than a kid in college
at the time. If it was up to me such things would never have
happened." I also remember crying, which was where the dream
had ended.
That's a sad dream, I thought.
Afterward this occurred to me: Suppose what happened to
Levitansky happens to me. Suppose America gets into a war with
China in some semi-reluctant way, and to make fast hash of it
(despite my loud protestations: mostly I wave my arms and shout
obscenities till my face turns green) we spatter them with a few
dozen H-bombs, boiling up a thick atomic soup of about two hundred million Orientals—blood, gristle, bone marrow, and lots of
floating Chinese eyeballs. We win the war because the Soviets
hadn't been able to make up their minds whom to shoot their
missiles at first. And suppose that after this slaughter, about ten
million Americans, in self-revulsion, head for the borders to flee
the country. To stop the loss of goods and capital, the refugees

are intercepted by the army and turned back. Harvitz hides in his
room with shades drawn, writing, in a fury of protest, a long epic
poem condemning the mass butchery by America. What nation,
Asiatic or other, is next? Nobody wants to publish the poem because it might start riots and another flight of refugees to Canada
and Mexico; then one day there's a knock on the door, and it isn't
the FBI but a bearded Levitansky, in better times a tourist, a
modern not medieval Communist. He offers to sneak the manuscript of the poem out for publication in the Soviet Union.

Why? Harvitz suspiciously asks.

Why not? To give the book its liberty.

I awoke after a restless night. I had been instructed by Intourist
to be in the lobby with my baggage two hours before flight time at
11 A.M. I was shaved and dressed by six, and at seven had breakfast—I was hungry—of yogurt, sausage and eggs, tea with lemon,
in the twelfth-floor buffet. I then went out to hunt for a taxi. They
were hard to come by at this hour, but I finally found one near
the American Embassy, not far from the hotel. Speaking my usual
mixture of primitive German and French, I persuaded the driver,
by slipping him an acceptable two rubles, to take me out to
Levitanskys' house and wait a few minutes till I came out. Going
hastily up the stairs, I knocked on his door, apologizing when he
opened it to the half-pajamaed, iron-faced writer, his head looking
slightly flatter, for awaking him this early in the day. Without peace
of mind or certainty of purpose, I asked him whether he still
wanted me to smuggle out his manuscript of stories. I got for my
trouble the door slammed in my face.

A half hour later I had everything packed and was locking the
suitcase. A knock on the door—half a rap you might call it. For the
suitcase, I thought. I was for a moment frightened by the sight of a
small man in a thick cap, wearing a long trench coat. He winked,
and with a sinking feeling, I winked back. I had recognized
Levitansky's brother-in-law, Dmitri, the taxi driver. He slid in,
unbuttoned his coat, and brought forth the familiar manuscript.
Holding a finger to his lips, he handed it to me before I could say
I wasn't interested.

"Levitansky changed his mind?"

"Not change mind. Was afraid your voice to be heard by Kovalevsky."

"I'm sorry, I should have thought of that."

"Levitansky say not write to him," the brother-in-law whispered. "When is published book please send to him copy of *Das Kapital.* He will understand what means this."

I reluctantly agreed.

The brother-in-law, a thin figure with sad Jewish eyes, winked again, shook hands with a steamy palm, and slipped out of the room.

I unlocked my suitcase and laid the manuscript on top of my things. Then I unpacked half the contents and slipped the manuscript into a folder containing my notes on literary museums and a few letters from Lillian. I then and there decided that if I got back to the States I would ask her to marry me. The phone was ringing as I left the room.

On my way to the airport in a taxi, alone—to my surprise no Intourist girl accompanied me—I felt, on and off, nauseated. If it's not the sausage and yogurt it must be ordinary fear, I thought. Still, if Levitansky has the courage to send these stories out, the least I can do is give him a help. When you think of it, it's little enough one does for freedom in the course of his life. At the airport, if I can dig up some bromo or its Russian equivalent I'll feel better.

The driver was observing me in the mirror, a stern man with the head of a scholar, impassively smoking.

"*Le jour fait beau,*" I said.

He pointed with an upraised finger to a sign in English at one side of the road to the airport.

"Long live peace in the whole world!"

Peace with freedom. I smiled at the thought of somebody, not Howard Harvitz, painting that in red on the Soviet sign.

We drove on, I foreseeing my exit from the Soviet Union. I had made discreet inquiries from time to time, and an Intouristka in Leningrad had told me I had first to show my papers at the passport control desk, turn in my rubles—a serious offense to walk off with any—and then check luggage; no inspection, she swore. And that was that. Unless, of course, the official at the passport desk found my name on a list and said I had to go to the customs office for a package. In that case (if nobody said so I wouldn't remind them) I would go get the books. I figured I wouldn't open the package, just tear off a bit of the wrapping, if they were wrapped, as if making sure they were the books I expected, and then sort of saunter away with the package under my arm. If they asked me to sign another five copies of a document in Russian, I would write at the bottom: "It is understood I can't read Russian," and sign my name to that.

I had heard that a KGB man was stationed at the ramp as one boarded the plane. He asked for your passport, checked the picture, threw you a stare, and if there was no serious lack of resemblance, tore out your expired visa, pocketed it, and let you embark.

In ten minutes you were aloft, seat belts fastened in three languages, watching the plane banking west. I thought maybe if I looked hard I might see in the distance Feliks Levitansky on his roof, waving his red-white-and-blue socks on a bamboo pole. Then the plane leveled off, and we were above the clouds flying westward. And that's what I would be doing for five or six hours unless the pilot received radio instructions to turn back; or maybe land in Czechoslovakia, or East Germany, where two big-hatted detectives boarded the plane. By an act of imagination and will I made it some other passenger they were arresting. I got the plane into the air again, and we flew on without incident until we touched down in London.

As the taxi approached the Moscow airport, fingering my ticket and gripping my suitcase handle, I wished for courage equal to Levitansky's when they discovered he was the author of the book of stories I had managed to sneak out and get published, and his trial and suffering began.

Levitansky's first story of the four in English was about an old father, a pensioner, who was not feeling well and wanted his son, with whom he had continuous strong disagreements, and whom he hadn't seen in eight months, to know. He decided to pay him a short visit. Since the son had moved from his flat to a larger one, and had not forwarded his address, the father went to call on him at his office. The son was an official of some sort with an office in a new state building. The father had never been there, although he knew where it was, because a neighbor on a walk with him once had pointed it out.

The pensioner sat in a chair in his son's large outer office, waiting for him to be free for a few minutes. "Yuri," he thought he would say, "all I want to tell you is that I'm not up to my usual self. My breath is short, and I have pains in my chest. In fact, I am not well. After all, we're father and son and you ought to know the state of my health, seeing it's not so good and your mother is dead."

The son's assistant secretary, a modern girl in a tight skirt, said he was attending an important administrative conference.

"A conference is a conference," the father said. He wouldn't want to interfere with it and didn't mind waiting, although he was still having twinges of pain.

The father waited patiently in the chair for several hours; and though he had a few times risen and urgently spoken to the assistant secretary, he was, by the end of the day, still unable to see his son. The girl, putting on her pink hat, advised the old man that the official had already left the building. He hadn't been able to see his father because he had unexpectedly been called away on an important state matter.

"Go home, and he will telephone you in the morning."

"I have no telephone," said the old pensioner impatiently. "He knows that."

The assistant secretary, the private secretary, an older woman from the inside office, and later the caretaker of the building all attempted to persuade the father to go home, but he wouldn't leave.

The private secretary said her husband was expecting her, and she could stay no longer. After a while the assistant secretary with the pink hat also left. The caretaker, a man with wet eyes and a ragged mustache, tried to persuade the old man to leave. "What sort of foolishness is it to wait all night in a pitch-dark building? You'll frighten yourself out of your wits, not to speak of other discomforts you'll suffer."

"No," said the father, "I will wait. When my son comes in tomorrow morning, I'll tell him something he hasn't learned yet. I'll tell him that what he does to me his children will do to him."

The caretaker departed. The old man was left alone waiting for his son to appear in the morning.

"I'll report him to the Party," he muttered.

* * *

The second story was about an old man; a widower of sixty-eight, who hoped to have matzos for Passover. Last year he had got his quota. They had been baked at the State bakery and sold in State stores; but this year the State bakeries were not permitted to bake them. The officials said the machines had broken down, but who believed them.

The old man went to the rabbi, an older man with a tormented beard, and asked him where he could get matzos. He was frightened that he mightn't have them this year.

"So am I," confessed the old rabbi. He said he had been told to tell his congregants to buy flour and bake them at home. The State stores would sell them the flour.

"What good is that for me?" asked the widower. He reminded the rabbi that he had no home to speak of, a single small room with a one-burner electric stove. His wife had died two years ago. His only living child, a married daughter, was with her husband in Birobijan. His other relatives, the few who were left after the German invasion—two female cousins his age—lived in Odessa; and he himself, even if he could find an oven, did not know how to bake matzos. And if he couldn't, what should he do?

The rabbi then promised he would try to get the widower a kilo or two of matzos, and the old man, rejoicing, blessed him.

He waited anxiously a month, but the rabbi never mentioned the matzos. Maybe he had forgotten. After all he was an old man with many worries, and the widower did not want to press him. However, Passover was coming on wings, so he must do something. A week before the Holy Days he hurried to the rabbi's flat and spoke to him there. "Rabbi," he begged, "you promised me a kilo or two of matzos. What has happened to them?"

"I know I promised," said the rabbi, "but I'm no longer sure to whom. It's easy to promise." He dabbed at his brow with a damp handkerchief. "I was warned one can be arrested on charges of profiteering in the production and sale of matzos. I was told it could happen even if I were to give them away for nothing. It's a new crime they've invented. Still, take them anyway. If they arrest me, I'm an old man, and how long can an old man live in Lubyanka? Not so long, thank God. Here, I'll give you a small pack, but you must tell no one where you got the matzos."

"May the Lord eternally bless you, rabbi. As for dying in prison, rather let it happen to our enemies."

The rabbi went to his closet and got out a small pack of matzos, already wrapped and tied with knotted twine. When the widower offered in a whisper to pay him, at least the cost of the flour, the rabbi wouldn't hear of it. "God provides," he said, "although at times with difficulty." He said there was hardly enough for all who wanted matzos, so one must take what he got and be thankful.

"I will eat less," said the old man. "I will count mouthfuls. I will save the last matzo to look at if there isn't enough to last me. God will understand."

Overjoyed to have even a few matzos, he rode home on the trolley car and there met another Jew, a man with a withered hand. They conversed in Yiddish in low tones. The stranger had glanced at the almost square package, then at the widower and had hoarsely whispered, "Matzos?" The widower, tears starting to his eyes, nodded. "With God's grace." "Where did you get them?" "God provides." "So if He provides, let Him provide me," the stranger brooded. "I'm not so lucky. I was hoping for a package from relatives in Cleveland, America. They wrote they would send me a large pack of the finest matzos, but when I inquire of the authorities they say no matzos have arrived. You know when they will get here?" he muttered. "After Passover by a month or two, and what good will they be then?"

The widower nodded sadly. The stranger wiped his eyes with his good hand, and after a short while left the trolley amid a number of people getting off. He had not bothered to say good-bye, and neither had the widower, not to remind him of his own good fortune. When the time came for the old man to leave the trolley he glanced down between his feet where he had placed the package of matzos but nothing was there. His feet were there. The old man felt harrowed, as though someone had ripped a nail down his spine. He searched frantically throughout the car, going a long way past his stop, querying every passenger, the woman conductor, the motorman, but no one had seen his matzos.

Then it occurred to him that the stranger with the withered hand had stolen them.

The widower in his misery asked himself, would a Jew have robbed another of his precious matzos? It didn't seem possible.

Still, who knows, he thought, what one will do to get matzos if he has none.

As for me I haven't even a matzo to look at now. If I could steal some, whether from Jew or Russian, I would steal them. He thought he would even steal them from the old rabbi.

The widower went home without his matzos and had none for Passover.

*   *   *

The third story, a folktale called "Tallith," concerned a youth of seventeen, beardless but for a few stray hairs on his chin, who had come from Kirov to the steps of the synagogue on Arkhipova Street in Moscow. He had brought with him a capacious prayer shawl, a white garment of luminous beauty which he offered for sale to a cluster of congregants on the synagogue steps, Jews of various sorts and sizes—curious, apprehensive, greedy at the sight of the shawl—for fifteen rubles. Most of them avoided the youth, particularly the older Jews, despite the fact that some of the more devout among them were worried about their prayer shawls, eroded on their shoulders after years of daily use, which they could not replace. "It's the informers among us who have put him up to this," they whispered among themselves, "so they will have someone to inform on."

Still, in spite of the warnings of their elders, several of the younger men examined the tallith and admired it. "Where did you get such a fine prayer shawl?" the youth was asked. "It was my father's who recently died," he said. "It was given to him by a rich Jew he had once befriended." "Then why don't you keep it for yourself, you're a Jew, aren't you?" "Yes," said the youth, not the least embarrassed, "but I am going to Kharborovsk as a Komsomol volunteer, and I need a few rubles to get married. Besides I'm a confirmed atheist."

One young man with fat unshaven cheeks, who admired the deeply white shawl, its white glowing in whiteness, with its long silk fringes, whispered to the youth that he might consider buying it for five rubles. But he was overheard by the gabbai, the lay leader of the congregation, who raised his cane and shouted at the whisperer, "Hooligan, if you buy that shawl, beware it doesn't become your shroud." The fat Jew with the unshaven cheeks retreated.

"Don't strike him," cried the frightened rabbi, who had come out of the synagogue and saw the gabbai with his upraised cane. He urged the congregants to begin prayers at once. To the youth he said, "Please go away from here, we are burdened with enough troubles as it is. It is forbidden for anyone to sell religious articles. Do you want us to be accused of criminal economic activity? Do you want the doors of the shul to be closed forever? Do us a mitzvah and go away."

The congregants went inside. The youth was left standing alone on the steps; but then the gabbai came out of the door, a man with a deformed spine and with a wad of cotton stuck in his leaking ear.

"Look here," he said. "I know you stole it. Still, after all is said and done a tallith is a tallith, and God asks no questions of His worshipers. I offer eight rubles for it, take it or leave it. Talk fast before the services end and the others come out."

"Make it ten and it's yours," said the youth.

The gabbai gazed at him shrewdly. "Eight is all I have, but wait here and I'll borrow two rubles from my brother-in-law."

The youth waited impatiently. Dusk was thickening. In a few minutes a black car drove up, stopped in front of the synagogue, and two policemen got out. The youth realized at once that the gabbai had informed on him. Not knowing what else to do he hastily draped the prayer shawl over his head and began loudly to pray. He prayed a passionate kaddish. The police hesitated to approach him while he was praying, and they stood at the bottom of the steps waiting for him to be done. The congregants then came out and could not believe their eyes or ears. No one imagined the youth could pray so fervently. What moved them was his tone, the wail and passion of a man truly praying. Perhaps his father had indeed recently died. All listened attentively, and many wished he would pray forever, for they knew that when he stopped he would be seized and thrown into prison.

It was grown dark. A moon hovers behind murky clouds over the synagogue steeple. The youth's voice is heard in prayer. The congregants are huddled in the dark street, listening. Both police agents are still there, although they cannot be seen. Neither can the youth. All that can be seen is the white shawl luminously praying.

* * *

The last of the four stories translated by Irina Filipovna was about a writer of mixed parentage, a Russian father and Jewish mother, who had secretly been writing stories for years. He had from a young age wanted to write but had at first not had the courage to—it seemed such a merciless undertaking—so he had gone into translation work instead; and then when he had, one day, started to write seriously and exultantly, after a while he found to his surprise that many of his stories, about half, were about Jews.

Well, for a half-Jew that's a reasonable proportion, he thought. The others were about Russians who sometimes resembled members of his father's family. "It's good to have such different sources for ideas," he said to his wife. "In this way I can cover a more varied range of experiences in life."

After several years of work he had submitted a selection of his stories to a trusted friend of university days, Viktor Zverkov, an editor of the Progress Publishing House; and the writer appeared one morning after receiving a hastily scribbled cryptic note from his friend, to discuss his work with him. Zverkov, a troubled man to begin with—he told everyone his wife did not respect him—jumped up from his chair and turned the key in the door, his ear pressed a minute at the crack. He then went quickly to his desk and withdrew the manuscript from a drawer he had first to unlock with a key he kept in his pocket. He was a heavyset man with a flushed complexion, stained eroded teeth, and a hoarse voice; and he handled the writer's manuscript as though it might leap up and wound him in the face.

"Please, Tolya," he whispered breathily, bringing his head close to the writer's. "You must take these dreadful stories away at once."

"What's the matter with you? Why are you shaking so?"

"Don't pretend to be so naïve. You know why I am disturbed. I am frankly amazed that you are even considering submitting such unorthodox material for publication. My opinion as an editor is that they are of doubtful literary merit—I do not say devoid of it, Tolya, I wish to be honest—but as stories they are a frightful affront to our society. I can't understand why you should take it on yourself to write about Jews. What do you really know about them? Your culture is not in the least Jewish, it's Soviet Russian. The whole business smacks of hypocrisy, and you may be accused of anti-Semitism."

He then got up to shut the window and peered into a closet before sitting down.

"Are you out of your mind, Viktor? My stories are in no sense anti-Semitic. One would have to read them standing on his head to make that sort of judgment."

"There can be only one logical interpretation," the editor argued. "According to my most lenient analysis, which is favorable to you as a person of let's call it decent intent, the stories fly in the face of socialist realism and reveal a dangerous inclination —perhaps even a stronger word should be used—to anti-Soviet sentiment. Maybe you're not entirely aware of this—I know how a story can take hold of a writer and pull him along by the nose. As an editor I have to be sensitive to such things. I know, Tolya, from our conversations that you are a sincere believer in our kind of socialism; I won't accuse you of being defamatory to the Soviet system, but others may. In fact I know they will. If one of the editors of *Oktyabr* was to read these stories, believe me, your career would explode in a mess. You seem not to have a normal awareness of what self-preservation is, and what's appallingly worse, you're not above entangling innocent bystanders in your fate. If these stories were mine, I assure you I would never have brought them to you. I urge you to destroy them at once, before they destroy you."

The editor drank thirstily from a glass of water on his desk.

"That's the last thing I would do," said the writer. "These stories, if not in tone or subject matter, are written in the spirit of our early Soviet writers—the free spirits of the years just after the Revolution."

"I think you know what happened to many of those 'free spirits.'"

The writer for a moment stared at him.

"Well, then, what of those stories that are not about the experiences of Jews? Some are simply pieces about homely aspects of Russian life; for instance, the one about the pensioner father and his invisible son. What I hoped is that you might recommend one or two such stories to *Novy Mir* or *Yunost*. They are innocuous sketches and well written."

"Not the one about the two prostitutes," said the editor. "That contains hidden social criticism and is too adversely naturalistic."

"A prostitute lives a social life."

"That may be, but I can't recommend it for publication. I must advise you, Tolya, if you expect to receive further commissions for translations from us, you should immediately get rid of this whole manuscript so as to avoid the possibility of serious consequences both to yourself and family, and for this publishing house that has employed you so faithfully and generously in the past."

"Since you didn't write the stories yourself, you needn't be afraid, Viktor Alexandrovich," the writer said coldly.

"I am not a coward, if that's why you're hinting, Anatoly Borisovich, but if a wild locomotive is running loose on the rails, I know which way to jump."

The writer hastily gathered up his manuscript, stuffed the papers into his leather case, and returned home by bus. His wife was still away at work. He took out the stories, and after quickly reading through one, began to burn it page by page, in the kitchen sink.

His nine-year-old son, returning from school, said, "Papa, what are you burning in the sink? That's no place for a fire."

"What am I burning?" said the writer. "My integrity." Then he said, "My heritage. My talent."

JOYCE CAROL OATES has now received six O. Henry Awards, including a First Prize in 1967. She has written two collections of short stories and three novels, the latest of which, *EXPENSIVE PEOPLE,* was published in 1968. *FALSE CONFESSIONS,* a book of her poems, will appear in the spring.

Accomplished Desires

THERE was a man she loved with a violent love, and she spent much of her time thinking about his wife.

No shame to it, she actually followed the wife. She followed her to Peabody's Market, which was a small, dark, crowded store, and she stood in silence on the pavement as the woman appeared again and got into her station wagon and drove off. The girl, Dorie, would stand as if paralyzed and even her long, fine blond hair seemed paralyzed with thought—her heart pounded as if it too were thinking, planning—and then she would turn abruptly as if executing one of the steps in her modern dance class and cross through Peabody's alley and out to the Elks' Club parking lot and so up toward the campus, where the station wagon was bound.

Hardly had the station wagon pulled into the driveway when Dorie, out of breath, appeared a few houses down and watched. How that woman got out of a car—you could see the flabby expanse of her upper leg, white flesh that should never be exposed—and then turned and leaned in, probably with a grunt, to get shopping bags out of the backseat. Two of her children ran out to meet her, without coats or jackets. They had nervous, darting bodies—Dorie felt sorry for them—and their mother rose, straightening, a stout woman in a colorless coat, either scolding them or teasing them, one bag in either muscular arm, and so the mother and children went into the house and Dorie stood with nothing to stare at except the battered station wagon, and the small, snowy wilderness that was the Arbers' front yard, and the house itself. It was a large, ugly, peeling Victorian home in a block of similar homes, most of which had been fixed up by the faculty members who rented them. Dorie, who had something of her own mother's shrewd eye for hopeless, cast-off things, believed that the house could be remodeled and made presentable—but as long as he remained married to *that woman* it would be slovenly and peeling and ugly.

She loved that woman's husband with a fierce love that was itself a little ugly. Always a rather stealthy girl, thought to be simply quiet, she had entered his life by no accident—had not appeared in his class by accident—but every step of her career, like every outfit she wore and every expression on her face, was planned and shrewd and desperate. Before her twenties she had not thought much about herself; now she thought about herself continuously. She was leggy, long-armed, slender, and had a startled look, but the look was stylized now, and attractive. Her face was denuded of makeup and across her soft skin a galaxy of freckles glowed with health. She looked like a girl about to bound onto the tennis courts—and she did play tennis, though awkwardly. She played tennis with *him*. But so confused with love was she that the game of tennis, the relentless slamming of the ball back and forth, had seemed to her a disguise for something else the way everything in poetry or literature was a disguise for something else—for love?—and surely he must know, or didn't he know? Didn't he guess? There were many other girls he played tennis with, so that was nothing special, and her mind worked and worked while she should have slept, planning with the desperation of youth that has never actually been young—planning how to get him, how to get him, for it seemed to her that she would never be able to overcome her desire for this man.

The wife was as formidable as the husband. She wrote narrow volumes of poetry Dorie could not understand and he, the famous husband, wrote novels and critical pieces. The wife was a big, energetic, high-colored woman; the husband, Mark Arber, was about her size though not so high-colored, his complexion was rather putty-colored, rather melancholy. Dorie thought about the two of them all the time, awake or asleep, and she could feel the terrible sensation of blood flowing through her body, a flowing of desire that was not just for the man but somehow for the woman as well, a desire for her accomplishments, her fame, her children, her ugly house, her ugly body, her very life. She had light, frank blue eyes and people whispered that she drank; Dorie never spoke of her.

The college was a girls' college, exclusive and expensive, and every girl who remained there for more than a year understood a peculiar, even freakish kinship with it—as if she had always been there and the other girls, so like herself with their sleepy unmade-up faces, the skis in winter and the bicycles in good weather, the excellent expensive professors and the excellent air—everything, everything had always been there, had existed for centuries. They were stylish and liberal in their cashmere sweaters with soiled necks; their fingers were stained with ballpoint ink; and like them Dorie understood that most of the world was wretched and would never come to this college, never, would be kept back from it by armies of helmeted men. She, Dorie Weinheimer, was not wretched but supremely fortunate, and she must be grateful always for her good luck, for there was no justification for her existence any more than there was any justification for the wretched lots of the world's poor. And there would flash to her mind's eye a confused picture of dark-faced starving mobs, or emaciated faces out of an old-fashioned Auschwitz photograph, or something—some dreary horror from The New York *Times'* one hundred neediest cases at Christmastime. She had, in the girls' soft, persistent manner, an idealism-turned-pragmatism under the influence of the college faculty, who had all been idealists at Harvard and Yale as undergraduates but who were now in their forties, and as impatient with normative values as they were with their students' occasional lockets-shaped-into-crosses; Mark Arber was the most disillusioned and the most eloquent of the Harvard men.

In class he sat at the head of the seminar table, leaning back in his leather-covered chair. He was a rather stout man. He had played football once in a past Dorie could not quite imagine, though she wanted to imagine it, and he had been in the war—one of the wars—she believed it had been World War II. He had an ugly, arrogant face and discolored teeth. He read poetry in a raspy, hissing, angry voice. "Like Marx I believe that poetry has had enough of love; the hell with it. Poetry should now cultivate the whip," he would say grimly, and Dorie would stare at him to see if he were serious. There were four senior girls in this class and they sometimes asked him questions, or made observations of their own, but there was no consistency in his reaction. Sometimes he seemed not to hear, sometimes he nodded enthusiastically and indifferently, sometimes he opened his eyes and looked at them, not distinguishing between them, and said: "A remark like that is quite characteristic." So she sat and stared at him and her heart seemed to turn to stone, wanting him, hating his wife and envying her violently, and the being that had been Dorie Weinheimer for twenty-one years changed gradually through the winter into another being, obsessed with jealousy. She did not know what she wanted most, this man or the victory over his wife.

She was always bringing poems to him in his office. She borrowed books from him and puzzled over every annotation of his. As he talked to her he picked at his fingernails, settled back in his chair, and he talked on in his rushed, veering, sloppy manner, as if Dorie did not exist or were a crowd, or a few intimate friends, it hardly mattered, as he raved about frauds in contemporary poetry, naming names, "that bastard with his sonnets," "that cow with her daughter-poems," and getting so angry that Dorie wanted to protest, No, no, why are you angry? Be gentle. Love me and be gentle.

When he failed to come to class six or seven times that winter the girls were all understanding. "Do you think he really is a genius?" they asked. His look of disintegrating, decomposing recklessness, his shiny suits and bizarre loafer shoes, his flights of language made him so different from their own fathers that it was probable he was a genius; these were girls who believed seriously in the existence of geniuses. They had been trained by their highly paid, verbose professors to be vaguely ashamed of themselves, to be silent about any I.Q. rated under 160, to be uncertain about their talents within the school and quite confident of them outside it—and Dorie, who had no talent and only adequate intelligence, was always silent about herself. Her talent perhaps lay in her faithfulness to an obsession, her cunning patience, her smile, her bared teeth which were a child's teeth and yet quite sharp. . . .

One day Dorie had been waiting in Dr. Arber's office for an hour, with some new poems for him. He was late but he strode into the office as if he had been hurrying all along, sitting heavily in the creaking swivel chair, panting; he looked a little mad. He was the author of many reviews in New York magazines and papers and in particular the author of three short, frightening novels, and now he had a burned-out, bleached-out look. Like any of the girls at this college, Dorie would have sat politely if one of her professors set fire to himself, and so she ignored his peculiar stare and began her rehearsed speech about—but what did it matter what it was about? The poems of Emily Dickinson or the terrible yearning of Shelley or her own terrible lust, what did it matter?

He let his hand fall onto hers by accident. She stared at the hand, which was like a piece of meat—and she stared at him and was quite still. She was pert and long-haired in the chair facing him, an anonymous student and a minor famous man, and every wrinkle of his sagging, impatient face was bared to her in the winter sunlight from the window—and every thread of blood in his eyes—and quite calmly and politely she said, "I guess I should tell you, Dr. Arber, that I'm in love with you. I've felt that way for some time."

"You what, you're what?" he said. He gripped her feeble hand as if clasping it in a handshake. "What did you say?" He spoke with an amazed, slightly irritated urgency, and so it began.

His wife wrote her poetry under an earlier name, Barbara Scott. Many years ago she had had a third name, a maiden name—Barbara Cameron—but it belonged to another era about which she never thought except under examination from her analyst. She had a place cleared in the dirty attic of her house and she liked to sit up there, away from the children, and look out the small octagon of a window, and think. People she saw from her attic window looked bizarre and helpless to her. She herself was a hefty, perspiring woman, and all her dresses—especially her expensive ones—were stained under the arms with great lemon-colored half-moons no dry cleaner could remove. Because she was so large a woman she was quick to see imperfections in others, as if she used a magnifying glass. Walking by her window on an ordinary morning were an aged, tottering woman, an enormous Negro woman—probably someone's cleaning lady—and a girl from the college on aluminum crutches, poor brave thing, and the white-blond child from up the street who was precocious and demonic. Her own children were precocious and only slightly troublesome. Now two of them were safe in school and the youngest, the three-year-old, was asleep somewhere.

Barbara Scott had won the Pulitzer Prize not long before with an intricate sonnet series that dealt with the "voices" of many people; her energetic, coy line was much imitated. This morning she began a poem which her agent was to sell, after Barbara's death, to *The New Yorker: What awful wrath/what terrible betrayal/and these aluminum crutches, rubber-tipped*. . . . She had such a natural talent that she let words take her anywhere. Her decade of psycho-analysis had trained her to hold nothing back; even when she had nothing to say the very authority of her technique carried her on. So she sat that morning at her big, nicked desk—over the years the children had marred it with sharp toys—and stared out the window and waited for more inspiration. She felt the most intense kind of sympathy when she saw someone deformed—she was anxious, in a way, to see deformed people because it released such charity in her. But apart from the girl on the crutches she saw nothing much. Hours passed and she realized that her husband had not come home; already school was out and her two boys were running across the lawn.

When she descended the two flights of stairs to the kitchen, she saw that the three-year-old, Geoffrey, had opened a white plastic bottle of ammonia and had spilled it on the floor and on himself; the stench was sickening. The two older boys bounded in the back door as if spurred on by the argument that ranged between them, and Barbara whirled upon them and began screaming. The ammonia had spilled onto her slacks. The boys ran into the front room and she remained in the kitchen, screaming. She sat down heavily on one of the kitchen chairs. After half an hour she came to herself and tried to analyze the situation. Did she hate these children, or did she hate herself? Did she hate Mark? Or was her hysteria a form of love, or was it both love and hate to-gether? She put the ammonia away and made herself a drink.

When she went into the front room she saw that the boys were playing with their mechanical inventors' toys and had forgotten about her. Good. They were self-reliant. Slight, cunning children, all of them dark like Mark and prematurely aged, as if by the burden of their prodigious intelligences, they were not always pre-dictable: they forgot things, lost things, lied about things, broke things, tripped over themselves and each other, mimicked class-mates, teachers, and their parents, and often broke down into pointless tears. And yet sometimes they did not break down into tears when Barbara punished them, as if to challenge her. She did not always know what she had given birth to: they were so remote, even in their struggles and assaults, they were so fictional, as if she had imagined them herself. It had been she who'd imagined them, not Mark. Their father had no time. He was always in a hurry, he had three aged typewriters in his study and paper in each one, an article or a review or even a novel in progress in each of the machines, and he had no time for the children except to nod grimly at them or tell them to be quiet. He had been so precocious himself, Mark Arber, that after his first, successful novel at the age of twenty-four he had had to whip from place to place, from typewriter to typewriter, in a frantic attempt to keep up with—he called it keeping up with his "other self," his "real self," evidently a kind of alter ego who was always typing and creating, unlike the real Mark Arber. The real Mark Arber was now forty-five and he had made the transition from "promising" to "established" without anything in between, like most middle-aged critics of prominence.

Strachey, the five-year-old, had built a small machine that was both a man and an automobile, operated by the motor that came with the set of toys. "This is a modern centaur," he said wisely, and Barbara filed that away, thinking perhaps it would do well in a poem for a popular, slick magazine. . . . She sat, unbidden, and watched her boys' intense work with the girders and screws and bolts, and sluggishly she thought of making supper, or calling Mark at school to see what had happened. . . . That morning he had left the house in a rage and when she went into his study, prim and frowning, she had discovered four or five crumpled papers in his wastebasket. It was all he had accomplished that week.

Mark had never won the Pulitzer Prize for anything. People who knew him spoke of his slump, familiarly and sadly; if they disliked Mark they praised Barbara, and if they disliked Barbara they praised Mark. They were "established," but it did not mean much; younger writers were being discovered all the time who had been born in the mid- or late Forties, strangely young, terrifyingly young, and people the Arbers' age were being crowded out, hustled toward the exits. . . . Being "established" should have pleased them, but instead it led them to long spiteful bouts of eating and drinking in the perpetual New England winter.

She made another drink and fell asleep in the chair. Sometime

later her children's fighting woke her and she said, "Shut up,"
and they obeyed at once. They were playing in the darkened living room, down at the other end by the big brick fireplace, which
was never used. Her head ached. She got to her feet and went out
to make another drink.

Around one o'clock Mark came in the back door. He stumbled
and put the light on. Barbara, in her plaid bathrobe, was sitting at
the kitchen table. She had a smooth, shiny, bovine face, heavy
with fatigue. Mark said, "What the hell are you doing here?"

She attempted a shrug of her shoulders. Mark stared at her.
"I'm getting you a housekeeper," he said. "You need more time for
yourself, for your work," he said, twisting his mouth at the word to
show what he thought of it. "You shouldn't neglect your poetry,
so we're getting in a housekeeper, not to do any heavy work, just
to sort of watch things—in other words—a kind of external con-
sciousness. You should be freed from ordinary considerations."

He was not drunk, but he had the appearance of having been
drunk, hours before, and now his words were muddled and dignified with the air of words spoken too early in the morning. He
wore a dirty tweed overcoat, the same coat he'd had when they
were married, and his necktie had been pulled off and stuffed
somewhere, and his puffy, red face looked mean. Barbara thought
of how reality was too violent for poetry, and how poetry, and
the language itself, shimmered helplessly before the confrontation
with living people and their demands. "The housekeeper is here.
She's outside," Mark said. "I'll go get her."

He returned with a college girl who looked like a hundred
other college girls. "This is Dorie, this is my wife Barbara, you've
met no doubt at some school event, here you are," Mark said. He
was carrying a suitcase which must have belonged to the girl.
"Dorie has requested room and board with a faculty family. The
Dean of Women arranged it. Dorie will baby-sit or something—we
can put her in the spare room. Let's take her up."

Barbara had not yet moved. The girl was pale and distraught;
she looked about sixteen. Her hair was disheveled. She stared at
Barbara and seemed about to speak.

"Let's take her up, you want to sit there all night?" Mark
snarled.

Barbara indicated with a motion of her hand that they should
go up without her. Mark, breathing heavily, stomped up the back

steps and the girl followed at once. There was no indication of her presence because her footsteps were far too light on the stairs, she said nothing, and only a slight change in the odor of the kitchen indicated something new—a scent of cologne, hair scrubbed clean, a scent of panic. Barbara sat listening to her heart thud heavily inside her and she recalled how, several years ago, Mark had left her and had turned up at a friend's apartment in Chicago—he'd been beaten up by someone on the street, an accidental event— and how he had blackened her eye once in an argument over the worth of Samuel Richardson, and how—there were many other bitter memories—and of course there had been other women, some secret and some known—and now this. . . .

So she sat thinking with a small smile of how she would have to dismiss this when she reported it to their friends: *Mark has had this terrible block for a year now, with his novel, and so . . .*

She sat for a while running through phrases and explanations, and when she climbed up the stairs to bed she was grimly surprised to see him in their bedroom, asleep, his mouth open and his breath raspy and exhausted. At the back of the house, in a small oddly shaped maid's room, slept the girl; in their big dormer room slept the three boys, or perhaps they only pretended to sleep; and only she, Barbara, stood in the dark and contemplated the bulk of her own body, wondering what to do and knowing that there was nothing she would do, no way for her to change the process of events any more than she could change the heavy fact of her body itself. There was no way to escape what the years had made her.

From that time on they lived together like a family. Or, it was as Mark put it: "Think of a baby sitter here permanently. Like the Lunt girl, staying on here permanently to help, only we won't need that one anymore." Barbara made breakfast for them all, and then Mark and Dorie drove off to school and returned late, between six and six-thirty, and in the evenings Mark worked hard at his typewriters, going to sit at one and then the next and then the next, and the girl Dorie helped Barbara with the dishes and odd chores and went up to her room, where she studied . . . or did something, she must have done something.

Of the long afternoons he and the girl were away Mark said nothing. He was evasive and jaunty; he looked younger. He explained carefully to Dorie that when he and Mrs. Arber were invited somewhere she must stay home and watch the children, that she was not included in these invitations; and the girl agreed eagerly. She did so want to help around the house! She had inherited from her background a dislike for confusion—so the mess of the Arber house upset her and she worked for hours picking things up, polishing tarnished objects Barbara herself had forgotten were silver, cleaning, arranging, fixing. As soon as the snow melted she was to be seen outside, raking shyly through the flower beds. How to explain her to the neighbors? Barbara said nothing.

"But I didn't think we lived in such a mess. I didn't think it was so bad," Barbara would say to Mark in a quiet, hurt voice, and he would pat her hand and say, "It isn't a mess, she just likes to fool around. *I* don't think it's a mess."

It was fascinating to live so close to a young person. Barbara had never been young in quite the way Dorie was young. At breakfast—they ate crowded around the table—everyone could peer into everyone else's face, there were no secrets, stale mouths and bad moods were inexcusable, all the wrinkles of age or distress that showed on Barbara could never be hidden, and not to be hidden was Mark's guilty enthusiasm, his habit of saying, "*We* should go to . . . ," "*We* are invited . . ." and the "we" meant either him and Barbara, or him and Dorie, but never all three; he had developed a new personality. But Dorie was fascinating. She awoke to the slow gray days of spring with a panting, wondrous expectation, her blond hair shining, her freckles clear as dabs of clever paint on her heartbreaking skin, her teeth very, very white and straight, her pert little lips innocent of lipstick and strangely sensual . . . yes, it was heartbreaking. She changed her clothes at least twice a day while Barbara wore the same outfit—baggy black slacks and a black sweater—for weeks straight. Dorie appeared downstairs in cashmere sweater sets that were the color of birds' eggs, or of birds' fragile legs, and white trim blouses that belonged on a genteel hockey field, and bulky pink sweaters big as jackets, and when she was dressed casually she wore stretch slacks that were neatly secured by stirrups around her long, narrow, white feet. Her eyes were frankly and emptily brown, as if giving themselves up to every observer. She was so anxious to help that it was oppressive; "No, I can manage, I've been making breakfast for eight years by myself," Barbara would say angrily, and Dorie, a chastised child, would glance around the table not only at Mark but at the children for sympathy. Mark had a blackboard set up in the kitchen so that he could test the children's progress in languages, and he barked out commands for them—French or Latin or Greek words—and they responded with nervous glee, clacking out letters on the board, showing off for the rapt, admiring girl who seemed not to know if they were right or wrong.

"Oh, how smart they are—how wonderful everything is," Dorie breathed.

Mark had to drive to Boston often because he needed his prescription for tranquilizers refilled constantly, and his doctor would not give him an automatic refill. But though Barbara had always looked forward to these quick trips, he rarely took her now. He went off with Dorie, now his "secretary," who took along a notebook decorated with the college's insignia to record his impressions in, and since he never gave his wife warning she could not get ready in time, and it was such an obvious trick, so crudely cruel, that Barbara stood in the kitchen and wept as they drove out. . . . She called up friends in New York, but never exactly told them what was going on. It was so ludicrous, it made her seem such a fool. Instead she chatted and barked with laughter; her conversations with these people were always so witty that nothing, nothing seemed very real until she hung up the receiver again; and then she became herself, in a drafty college-owned house in New England, locked in this particular body.

She stared out the attic window for hours, not thinking. She became a state of being, a creature. Downstairs the children fought, or played peacefully, or rifled through their father's study, which was forbidden, and after a certain amount of time something would nudge Barbara to her feet and she would descend slowly, laboriously, as if returning to the real world where any ugliness was possible. When she slapped the boys for being bad they stood in meek defiance and did not cry. "Mother, you're out of your mind," they said. "Mother, you're losing control of yourself."

"It's your father who's out of his mind!" she shouted.

She had the idea that everyone was talking about them, everyone. Anonymous worthless people who had never published a line gloated over her predicament; high-school baton twirlers were better off than Barbara Scott, who had no dignity. Dorie, riding with Mark Arber on the expressway to Boston, was at least young and stupid, anonymous though she was, and probably she too had a slim collection of poems which Mark would manage to get published . . . and who knew what would follow, who could tell? Dorie Weinheimer was like any one of five hundred or five thousand college girls and was no one, had no personality, and yet Mark Arber had somehow fallen in love with her so perhaps everyone would eventually fall in love with her? Barbara imagined with panic the parties she knew nothing about, to which Mark and his new girl went: Mark in his slovenly tweed suits, looking like his own father in the Thirties, and Dorie chic as a *Vogue* model in her weightless bones and vacuous face.

"Is Dorie going to stay here long?" the boys kept asking.

"Why, don't you like her?"

"She's nice. She smells nice. Is she going to stay long?"

"Go ask your father that," Barbara said angrily.

The girl was officially boarding with them; it was no lie. Every year certain faculty families took in a student or two, out of generosity or charity, or because they themselves needed the money, and the Arbers themselves had always looked down upon such hearty liberalism. But now they had Dorie, and in Peabody's Market Barbara had to rush up and down the aisles with her shopping cart, trying to avoid the wives of other professors who were sure to ask her about the new boarder; and she had to buy special things for the girl, spinach and beets and artichokes, while Barbara and Mark liked starches and sweets and fat, foods that clogged up the blood vessels and strained the heart and puffed out the stomach. While Barbara ate and drank hungrily Dorie sat chaste with her tiny forkfuls of food, and Barbara could eat three platefuls to Dorie's one; her appetite increased savagely just in the presence of the girl. (The girl was always asking politely, "Is it the boys who get the bathroom all dirty?" or "Could I take the vacuum cleaner down and have it fixed?" and these questions, polite as they were, made Barbara's appetite increase savagely.)

In April, after Dorie had been boarding with them three and a half months, Barbara was up at her desk when there was a rap on the plywood door. Unused to visitors, Barbara turned clumsily and looked at Mark over the top of her glasses. "Can I come in?" he said. "What are you working on?"

There was no paper in her typewriter. "Nothing," she said.

"You haven't shown me any poems lately. What's wrong?"

He sat on the window ledge and lit a cigarette. Barbara felt a spiteful satisfaction to see how old he looked—he hadn't her fine, fleshed-out skin, the smooth complexion of an overweight woman; he had instead the bunched, baggy complexion of an overweight man whose weight keeps shifting up and down. Good. Even his fingers shook as he lit the cigarette.

"This is the best place in the house," he said.

"Do you want me to give it up to Dorie?"

He stared at her. "Give it up—why? Of course not."

"I thought you might be testing my generosity."

He shook his head, puzzled. Barbara wondered if she hated this man, or if she felt a writer's interest in him. Perhaps he was insane. Or perhaps he had been drinking again; he had not gone out to his classes this morning and she'd heard him arguing with Dorie. "Barbara, how old are you?" he said.

"Forty-three. You know that."

He looked around at the boxes and other clutter as if coming to an important decision. "Well, we have a little problem here."

Barbara stared at her blunt fingernails and waited.

"She got herself pregnant. It seems on purpose."

"She what?"

"Well," Mark said uncomfortably, "she did it on purpose."

They remained silent. After a while, in a different voice he said, "She claims she loves children. She loves our children and wants some of her own. It's a valid point, I can't deny her her rights . . . but still. . . . I thought you should know about it in case you agree to help."

"What do you mean?"

"Well, I have something arranged in Boston," he said, not looking at her, "and Dorie has agreed to it . . . though reluctantly . . . and unfortunately, I don't think I can drive her, myself . . . you know I have to go to Chicago. . . ."

Barbara did not look at him.

"I'm on this panel at the University of Chicago, with John Ciardi. You know, it's been set up for a year, it's on the state of contemporary poetry—you know—I can't possibly withdraw from it now."

"And so?"

"If you could drive Dorie in—"

"If I could drive her in?"

I don't see what alternative we have," he said slowly.

"Would you like a divorce so you can marry her?"

"I have never mentioned that," he said.

"Well, would you?"

"I don't know."

"Look at me. Do you want to marry her?"

A nerve began to twitch in his eye. It was a familiar twitch—it had been with him for two decades. "No, I don't think so. I don't know—you know how I feel about disruption."

"Don't you have any courage?"

"Courage?"

"If you want to marry her, go ahead. I won't stop you."

"Do you want a divorce, yourself?"

"I'm asking you. It's up to you. Then Dorie can have her baby and fulfill herself," Barbara said with a deathly smile, "she can assert her rights as a woman twenty years younger than I. She can become the third Mrs. Arber and become automatically envied. Don't you have the courage for it?"

"I had thought," Mark said with dignity, "that you and I had an admirable marriage. It was different from the marriages of other people we know—part of it is that we don't work in the same area, yes, but the most important part lay in our understanding of each other. It has taken a tremendous generosity on your part, Barbara, over the last three months and I appreciate it," he said, nodding slowly, "I appreciate it and I can't help asking myself whether . . . whether I would have had the strength to do what you did, in your place. I mean, if you had brought in—"

"I know what you mean."

"It's been an extraordinary marriage. I don't want it to end on an impulse, anything reckless or emotional," he said vaguely. She thought that he did look a little mad, but quietly mad; his ears were very red. For the first time she began to feel pity for the girl who was, after all, nobody, who had no personality, and who was waiting in the ugly maid's room for her fate to be decided.

"All right, I'll drive her to Boston," Barbara said.

Mark had to leave the next morning for Chicago. He would be gone, he explained, about a week—there was not only the speaking appearance but other things as well. The three of them had a kind of farewell party the night before. Dorie sat with her frail hand on her flat, child's stomach and drank listlessly, while Barbara and Mark argued about the comparative merits of two English novelists —their literary arguments were always witty, superficial, rapid, and very enjoyable. At two o'clock Mark woke Dorie to say good-by and Barbara, thinking herself admirably discreet, went upstairs alone.

She drove Dorie to Boston the next day. Dorie was a mother's child, the kind of girl mothers admire—clean, bright, neat, passive —and it was a shame for her to be so frightened. Barbara said roughly, "I've known lots of women who've had abortions. They lived."

"Did you ever have one?"

"No," Barbara answered quickly but in a softer voice.

Dorie turned away as if in reproach.

"I've had children and that's harder, maybe. It's thought to be harder," Barbara said, as if offering the girl something.

"I would like children, maybe three of them," Dorie said.

"Three is a good number, yes."

"But I'd be afraid. . . . I wouldn't know what to do. . . . I don't know what to do now. . . ."

She was just a child herself, Barbara thought with a rush of sympathy; of all of them it was Dorie who was most trapped. The girl sat with a scarf around her careless hair, staring out the window. She wore a camel's hair coat like all the girls and her fingernails were colorless and uneven, as if she had been chewing them.

"Stop thinking about it. Sit still."

"Yes," the girl said listlessly.

They drove on. Something began to weigh at Barbara's heart, as if her flesh were aging moment by moment. She had never liked her body. Dorie's body was so much more prim and chaste and stylish, and her own body belonged to another age, a hearty nineteenth century where fat had been a kind of virtue. Barbara thought of her poetry, which was light and sometimes quite clever, the poetry of a girl, glimmering with half-seen visions and echoing with peculiar off-rhymes—and truly it ought to have been Dorie's poetry and not hers. She was not equal to her own writing. And, on the highway like this, speeding toward some tawdry destination, she had the sudden terrible conviction that language itself did not matter and that nothing mattered ultimately except the body, the human body and the bodies of other creatures and objects: what else existed?

Her own body was the only real fact about her. Dorie, huddled over in her corner, was another real fact and they were going to do something about it, defeat it. She thought of Mark already in Chicago, at a cocktail party, the words growing like weeds in his brain and his wit moving so rapidly through the brains of others that it was, itself, a kind of lie. It seemed strange to her that the two of them should move against Dorie, who suffered because she was totally real and helpless and gave up nothing of herself to words.

They arrived in Boston and began looking for the street. Barbara felt clumsy and guilty and did not dare to glance over at the girl. She muttered aloud as they drove for half an hour, without luck. Then she found the address. It was a small private hospital with a blank gray front. Barbara drove past it and circled the block and approached it again. "Come on, get hold of yourself," she said to Dorie's stiff profile, "this is no picnic for me either."

She stopped the car and she and Dorie stared out at the hospital, which looked deserted. The neighborhood itself seemed deserted. Finally Barbara said, with a heaviness she did not yet understand, "Let's find a place to stay tonight, first. Let's get that settled." She took the silent girl to a motel on a boulevard and told her to wait in the room, she'd be back shortly. Dorie stared in a drugged silence at Barbara, who could have been her mother—there flashed between them the kind of camaraderie possible only between mother and daughter—and then Barbara left the room. Dorie remained sitting in a very light chair of imitation wood and leather. She sat so that she was staring at the edge of the bureau; occasionally her eye was attracted by the framed picture over the bed, of a woman in a red evening gown and a man in a tuxedo observing a waterfall by moonlight. She sat like this for quite a while, in her coat. A nerve kept twitching in her thigh but it did not bother her; it was a most energetic, thumping twitch, as if her very flesh were doing a dance. But it did not bother her. She remained there for a while, waking to the morning light, and it took her several panicked moments to remember where she was and who had brought her here. She had the immediate thought that she must be safe—if it was morning she must be safe—and someone had taken care of her, and seen what was best for her and had carried it out.

And so she became the third Mrs. Arber, a month after the second one's death. Barbara had been found dead in an elegant motel across the city, the Paradise Inn, which Mark thought was a brave, cynical joke; he took Barbara's death with an alarming, rhetorical melodrama, an alcoholic melancholy Dorie did not like. Barbara's "infinite courage" made Dorie resentful. The second Mrs. Arber had taken a large dose of sleeping pills and had died easily, because of the strain her body had made upon her heart; so that was that. But somehow it wasn't—because Mark kept talking about it, speculating on it, wondering: "She did it for the baby, to preserve life. It's astonishing, it's exactly like something in a novel," he said. He spoke with a perpetual guilty astonishment.

She married him and became Mrs. Arber, which surprised everyone. It surprised even Mark. Dorie herself was not very surprised, because a daydreamer is prepared for most things and in a way she had planned even this, though she had not guessed how it would come about. Surely she had rehearsed the second Mrs. Arber's suicide and funeral already a year before, when she'd known nothing, could have guessed nothing, and it did not really surprise her. Events lost their jagged edges and became hard and opaque and routine, drawing her into them. She was still a daydreamer, though she was Mrs. Arber. She sat at the old desk up in the attic and leaned forward on her bony elbows to stare out the window, contemplating the hopeless front yard and the people who strolled by, some of them who—she thought—glanced toward the house with a kind of amused contempt, as if aware of her inside. She was almost always home.

The new baby was a girl, Carolyn. Dorie took care of her endlessly, and she took care of the boys; she hadn't been able to finish school. In the evening when all the children were at last asleep Mark would come out of his study and read to her in his rapid, impatient voice snatches of his new novel, or occasionally poems of his late wife's, and Dorie would stare at him and try to understand. She was transfixed with love for him and yet—and yet she was unable to locate this love in this particular man, unable to comprehend it. Mark was invited everywhere

that spring; he flew all the way out to California to take part in
a highly publicized symposium with George Steiner and James
Baldwin, and Dorie stayed home. Geoffrey was seeing a psychiatrist in Boston and she had to drive him in every other day,
and there was her own baby, and Mark's frequent visitors who
arrived often without notice and stayed a week—sleeping late,
staying up late, drinking, eating, arguing—it was exactly the kind
of life she had known would be hers, and yet she could not
adjust to it. Her baby was somehow mixed up in her mind
with the other wife, as if it had been that woman's and only
left to her, Dorie, for safekeeping. She was grateful that her
baby was a girl because wasn't there always a kind of pact or
understanding between women?

In June two men arrived at the house to spend a week, and
Dorie had to cook for them. They were long, lean, gray-haired
young men who were undefinable, sometimes very fussy, sometimes
reckless and hysterical with wit, always rather insulting in a light,
veiled manner Dorie could not catch. They were both vegetarians
and could not tolerate anyone eating meat in their presence. One
evening at a late dinner Dorie began to cry and had to leave
the room, and the two guests and Mark and even the children
were displeased with her. She went up to the attic and sat
mechanically at the desk. It did no good to read Barbara Scott's
poetry because she did not understand it. Her understanding had
dropped to tending the baby and the boys, fixing meals, cleaning
up, and shopping, and taking the station wagon to the garage
perpetually . . . and she had no time to go with the others to
the tennis courts, or to accompany Mark to New York . . . and
around her were human beings whose lives consisted of language,
the grace of language, and she could no longer understand them.
She felt strangely cheated, a part of her murdered, as if the
abortion had taken place that day after all and something had
been cut permanently out of her.

In a while Mark climbed the stairs to her. She heard him
coming, she heard his labored breathing. "Here you are," he said,
and slid his big beefy arms around her and breathed his liquory
love into her face, calling her his darling, his beauty. After all,
he did love her, it was real and his arms were real, and she
still loved him although she had lost the meaning of that word.
"Now will you come downstairs and apologize, please?" he said

gently. "You've disturbed them and it can't be left like this. You know how I hate disruption."

She began weeping again, helplessly, to think that she had disturbed anyone, that she was this girl sitting at a battered desk in someone's attic, and no one else, no other person who might confidently take upon herself the meaning of this man's words— she was herself and that was a fact, a final fact she'd never overcome.

JOHN BARTH has published many well-known novels, including *THE SOT-WEED FACTOR, GILES GOAT-BOY, THE FLOATING OPERA,* and *THE END OF THE ROAD.* The story appearing here is the lead story from a collection published last year entitled *LOST IN THE FUNHOUSE.* Mr. Barth is now a Professor of English at the State University of New York at Buffalo.

Lost in the Funhouse

FOR whom is the funhouse fun? Perhaps for lovers. For Ambrose it is *a place of fear and confusion.* He has come to the seashore with his family for the holiday, *the occasion of their visit is Independence Day, the most important secular holiday of the United States of America.* A single straight underline is the manuscript mark for italic type, *which in turn* is the printed equivalent to oral emphasis of words and phrases as well as the customary type for titles of complete works, not to mention. Italics are also employed, in fiction-stories especially, for "outside," intrusive, or artificial voices, such as radio announcements, the texts of telegrams and newspaper articles, *et cetera.* They should be used *sparingly.* If passages originally in roman type are italicized by someone repeating them, it's customary to acknowledge the fact. *Italics mine.*

Ambrose was "at that awkward age." His voice came out high-pitched as a child's if he let himself get carried away; to be on the safe side, therefore, he moved and spoke with *deliberate calm* and *adult gravity.* Talking soberly of unimportant or irrelevant matters and listening consciously to the sound of your own voice are useful habits for maintaining control in this difficult interval. *En route* to Ocean City he sat in the back seat of the family

car with his brother, Peter, age fifteen, and Magda G____, age
fourteen, a pretty girl an exquisite young lady, who lived not
far from them on B____ Street in the town of D____, Maryland.
Initials, blanks, or both were often substituted for proper names
in nineteenth-century fiction to enhance the illusion of reality. It
is as if the author felt it necessary to delete the names for reasons
of tact or legal liability. Interestingly, as with other aspects of
realism, it is an *illusion* that is being enhanced, by purely artificial
means. Is it likely, does it violate the principle of verisimilitude,
that a thirteen-year-old boy could make such a sophisticated observation? A girl of fourteen is *the psychological coeval* of a boy of
fifteen or sixteen; a thirteen-year-old boy, therefore, even one
precocious in some other respects, might be three years *her emotional junior.*

Thrice a year—on Memorial, Independence, and Labor Days—
the family visits Ocean City for the afternoon and evening. When
Ambrose and Peter's father was their age the excursion was made
by train, as mentioned in the novel *The 42nd Parallel* by John
Dos Passos. Many families from the same neighborhood used to
travel together, with dependent relatives and often with Negro
servants; schoolfuls of children swarmed through the railway cars;
everyone shared everyone else's Maryland fried chicken, Virginia
ham, deviled eggs, potato salad, beaten biscuits, iced tea. Nowadays (that is, in 19–, the year of our story) the journey is
made by automobile—more comfortably and quickly though without the extra fun though without the *camaraderie* of a general excursion. It's all part of the deterioration of American life, their
father declares; Uncle Karl supposes that when the boys take
their families to Ocean City for the holidays, they'll fly in Autogiros.
Their mother, sitting in the middle of the front seat like Magda
in the second, only with her arms on the seat-back behind the
men's shoulders, wouldn't want the good old days back again, the
steaming trains and stuffy long dresses; on the other hand, she
can do without Autogiros, too, if she has to become a grandmother to fly in them.

Description of physical appearance and mannerisms is one of
several standard methods of characterization used by writers of
fiction. It is also important to "keep the senses operating"; when
a detail from one of the five senses, say visual, is "crossed" with
a detail from another, say auditory, the reader's imagination is

oriented to the scene, perhaps unconsciously. This procedure may be compared to the way surveyors and navigators determine their positions by two or more compass-bearings, a process known as triangulation. The brown hair on Ambrose's mother's forearms gleamed in the sunlight. Though right-handed, she took her left arm from the seat-back to press the dashboard cigar-lighter for Uncle Karl. When the glass bead in its handle glowed red, the lighter was ready for use. The smell of Uncle Karl's cigar-smoke reminded one of. The fragrance of the ocean came strong to the picnic-ground where they always stopped for lunch, two miles inland from Ocean City. Having to pause for a full hour almost within sound of the breakers was difficult for Peter and Ambrose when they were younger; even at their present age it was not easy to keep their anticipation, *stimulated by the briny spume,* from turning into short temper. The Irish author James Joyce, in his unusual novel entitled *Ulysses,* now available in this country, uses the adjectives *snot-green* and *scrotum-tightening* to describe the sea. Visual, auditory, tactile, olfactory, gustatory. Peter and Ambrose's father, while steering their black 1936 LaSalle sedan with one hand, could with the other remove the first cigarette from a white pack of Lucky Strikes and, more remarkably, light it with a match forefingered from its book and thumbed against the flint-paper without being detached. The matchbook cover merely advertised U. S. War Bonds and Stamps. A fine metaphor, simile, or other figure of speech, in addition to its obvious "first-order" relevance to the thing it describes, will be seen upon reflection to have a second order of significance: it may be drawn from the *milieu* of the action, for example, or be particularly appropriate to the sensibility of the narrator, even hinting to the reader things of which the narrator is unaware; or it may cast further and subtler lights upon the thing it describes, sometimes ironically qualifying the more evident sense of the comparison.

To say that Ambrose and Peter's mother was *pretty* is to accomplish nothing; the reader may acknowledge the proposition, but his imagination is not engaged. Besides, Magda was also pretty, yet in an altogether different way. Although she lived on B____ Street, she had very good manners and did better than average in school. Her figure was very well developed for her age. Her right hand lay casually on the plush upholstery of the seat, very near Ambrose's left leg, on which his own hand rested.

The space between their legs, between her right and his left leg, was out of the line of sight of anyone sitting on the other side of Magda, as well as anyone glancing into the rearview mirror. Uncle Karl's face resembled Peter's—rather, vice versa. Both had dark hair and eyes, short husky statures, deep voices. Magda's left hand was probably in a similar position on her left side. The boy's father is difficult to describe; no particular feature of his appearance or manner stood out. He wore glasses and taught English in the T_____ County High School. Uncle Karl was a masonry contractor.

Although Peter must have known as well as Ambrose that the latter, because of his position in the car, would be the first to see the electrical towers of the power plant at V_____, the half-way point of their trip, he leaned forward and slightly toward the center of the car and pretended to be looking for them through the flat pinewoods and tuckahoe creeks along the highways. For as long as the boys could remember, "looking for the Towers" had been a feature of the first half of their excursions to Ocean City, "looking for the standpipe" of the second. Though the game was childish, their mother preserved the tradition of rewarding the first to see the Towers with a candybar or piece of fruit. She insisted now that Magda play the game; the prize, she said, was "something hard to get nowadays." Ambrose decided not to join in; he sat back in his seat. Magda, like Peter, leaned forward. Two sets of straps were discernible through the shoulders of her sun-dress; the inside right one, a brassiere-strap, was fastened or shortened with a small safety-pin. The right armpit of her dress, presumably the left as well, was damp with perspiration. The simple strategy for being first to espy the Towers, which Ambrose had understood by the age of four, was to sit on the right-hand side of the car. Whoever sat there, however, had also to put up with the worst of the sun, and so Ambrose, without mentioning the matter, chose sometimes the one and sometimes the other. Not impossibly, Peter had never caught on to the trick, or thought that his brother hadn't, simply because Ambrose on occasion preferred shade to a Baby Ruth or tangerine.

The shade-sun situation didn't apply to the front seat, owing to the windshield; if anything the driver got more sun, since the person on the passenger side not only was shaded below by the door and dashboard but might swing down his sun visor all the way too.

"Is that them?" Magda asked. Ambrose's mother teased the boys for letting Magda win, insinuating that "somebody [had] a girl-friend." Peter and Ambrose's father reached a long thin arm across their mother to butt his cigarette in the dashboard ashtray, under the lighter. The prize this time for seeing the Towers first was a banana. Their mother bestowed it after chiding their father for wasting a half-smoked cigarette when everything was so scarce. Magda, to take the prize, moved her hand from so near Ambrose's that he could have touched it as though accidentally. She offered to share the prize, things like that were so hard to find; but everyone insisted it was hers alone. Ambrose's mother sang an iambic trimeter couplet from a popular song, femininely rhymed:

> *What's good is in the Army;*
> *What's left will never harm me.*[1]

Uncle Karl tapped his cigar-ash out the ventilator window; some particles were sucked by the slip-stream back into the car through the rear window on the passenger side. Magda demonstrated her ability to hold a banana in one hand and peel it with her teeth. She still sat forward; Ambrose pushed his glasses back onto the bridge of his nose with his left hand, which he then negligently let fall to the seat-cushion immediately behind her. He even permitted the single hair, gold, on the second joint of his thumb to brush the fabric of her skirt. Should she have sat back at that instant, his hand would have been caught under her.

Plush upholstery prickles uncomfortably through gabardine slacks in the July sun. The function of the *beginning* of a story is to introduce the principal characters, establish their initial rela-tionships, set the scene for the main action, expose the background of the situation if necessary, plant motifs and foreshadowings where appropriate, and initiate the first complication or whatever of the "rising action." Actually, if one imagines a story called "The Fun-house," or "Lost in the Funhouse," the details of the drive to Ocean City don't seem especially relevant. The *beginning* should recount the events between Ambrose's first sight of the fun-

[1] *Copyright 1943 by M. Witmark & Sons. Used by permission.*

house early in the afternoon and his entering it with Magda
and Peter in the evening. The *middle* would narrate all relevant
events from the time he goes in to the time he loses his way;
middles have the double and contradictory function of delaying
the climax while at the same time preparing the reader for it
and fetching him to it. Then the *ending* would tell what Ambrose
does while he's lost, how he finally finds his way out, and what
everybody makes of the experience. So far there's been no real
dialogue, very little sensory detail, and nothing in the way of a
theme. And a long time has gone by already without anything
happening; it makes a person wonder. We haven't even reached
Ocean City yet: we will never get out of the funhouse.

The more closely an author identifies with the narrator, literally
or metaphorically, the less advisable it is as a rule to use the
first-person narrative viewpoint. Once five years previously the
three young people *aforementioned* played Niggers and Masters
in the backyard; when it was Ambrose's turn to be Master and
theirs to be Niggers, Peter had to go serve his evening papers;
Ambrose was afraid to punish Magda alone, but she led him to
the whitewashed Torture Chamber between the woodshed and
the privy in the Slaves Quarters; there she knelt sweating among
bamboo rakes and dusty mason jars, pleadingly embraced his
knees, and while bumblebees droned in the lattice as if on an
ordinary summer afternoon, purchased clemency at a surprising
price set by herself. Doubtless she remembered nothing of this
event; Ambrose on the other hand seemed unable to forget the
least detail of his life. He even recalled how, standing beside
himself with awed impersonality in the reeky heat, he'd stared
the while at an empty cigar-box in which Uncle Karl kept stone-
cutting chisels: beneath the words *El Producto,* a laureled, loose-
toga'd lady regarded the sea from a marble bench; beside her,
forgotten or not yet turned to, was a five-stringed lute. Her chin
reposed on the back of her right hand; her left depended negligently from the bench-arm. The lower half of scene and lady
was peeled away; the words EXAMINED BY _____ were inked
there into the wood. Nowadays cigar-boxes are made of pasteboard. Ambrose wondered what Magda would have done, Ambrose wondered what Magda would do when she sat back on
his hand as he resolved she should. Be angry. Make a teasing joke
of it. Give no sign at all. For a long time she leaned forward,

playing cow-poker with Peter against Uncle Karl and Mother and watching for the first sign of Ocean City. At nearly the same instant picnic-ground and Ocean-City-standpipe hove into view; an Amoco filling station on their side of the road cost Mother and Uncle Karl fifty cows and the game; Magda bounced back, clapping her right hand on Mother's right arm; Ambrose moved clear "in the nick of time."

At this rate our hero, at this rate our protagonist will remain in the funhouse forever. Narrative ordinarily consists of alternating dramatization and summarization. One symptom of nervous tension, paradoxically, is repeated and violent yawning; neither Peter nor Magda nor Uncle Karl nor Mother reacted in this manner. Although they were no longer small children, Peter and Ambrose were each given a dollar to spend on boardwalk amusements in addition to what money of their own they'd brought along. Magda too, though she protested she had ample spending money. The boys' mother made a little scene out of distributing the bills; she pretended that her sons and Magda were small children and cautioned them not to spend the sum too quickly or in one place. Magda promised with a merry laugh, and having both hands free, took the bill with her left. Peter laughed also and pledged in a falsetto to be a good boy. His imitation of a child was not clever. The boys' father was tall and thin, balding, fair-complexioned. Assertions of that sort are not effective; the reader may acknowledge the proposition, but. We should be much farther along than we are; something has gone wrong; not much of this preliminary rambling seems relevant. Yet everyone begins in the same place; how is it that most go along without difficulty but a few lose their way?

"Stay out from under the boardwalk," Uncle Karl growled from the side of his mouth. The boys' mother pushed his shoulder *in mock annoyance*. They were all standing before Fat May the Laughing Lady, who advertised the funhouse. Larger than life, Fat May mechanically shook, rocked on her heels, slapped her thighs while recorded laughter—uproarious, female—came amplified from a hidden loudspeaker. It chuckled, wheezed, wept; tried in vain to catch its breath; tittered, groaned, exploded raucous and anew. You couldn't hear it without laughing yourself, no matter how you felt. Father came back from talking to a Coast-Guardsman on duty and reported that the surf was spoiled with crude

oil from tankers recently torpedoed offshore. Lumps of it, difficult
to remove, made tarry tidelines on the beach and stuck on swim-
mers. Many bathed in the surf nevertheless and came out speckled;
others paid to use a municipal pool and only sunbathed on the
beach. We would do the latter. We would do the latter. We would
do the latter.

Under the boardwalk, cold sand littered with cigar-butts, treas-
ured with cigarette-stubs, Coco-Cola caps, cardboard lollipop-sticks,
matchbook-covers warning that A Slip of the Lip Can Sink a
Ship, grainy other things. What is the story's point? Ambrose is
ill. He perspires in the dark passages; candied apples-on-a-stick,
delicious-looking, disappointing to eat. Funhouses need men's and
ladies' rooms at intervals.

Magda's teeth. She *was* left-handed. Perspiration. They've gone
all the way, through, Magda and Peter, they've been waiting for
hours with Mother and Uncle Karl while Father searches for
his lost son; they draw french-fried potatoes from a paper cup
and shake their heads. They've named the children they'll one
day have and bring to Ocean City on holidays. Can spermatozoa
properly be thought of as male animalcules when there are no
female spermatozoa? They grope through hot dark windings, past
Love's Tunnel's fearsome obstacles. Some perhaps lose their way.

Peter suggested then and there that they do the funhouse; he
had been through it before, so had Magda, Ambrose hadn't and
suggested, his voice cracking on account of Fat May's laughter,
that they swim first. All were chuckling, couldn't help it; Ambrose's
father, Ambrose and Peter's father came up grinning like a lunatic
with two boxes of syrup-coated popcorn, one for Mother, one for
Magda; the men were to help themselves. Ambrose walked on
Magda's right; being by nature left-handed, she carried the box
in her left hand. Up front the situation was reversed.

"What are you limping for?" Magda inquired of Ambrose. He
supposed in a husky tone that his foot had gone to sleep in
the car. Her teeth flashed. "Pins and needles?" It was the honey-
suckle on the lattice of the former privy that drew the bees.
Imagine being stung there. How long is this going to take?

The adults decided to forgo the pool, but Uncle Karl insisted they
change into swimsuits and do the beach. "He wants to watch the
pretty girls," Peter teased, and ducked behind Magda from Uncle

Karl's pretended wrath. "You've got all the pretty girls you need right here," Magda declared, and Mother said: "Now that's the gospel truth." Magda scolded Peter, who reached over her shoulder to sneak some popcorn. "Your brother and father aren't getting any." Uncle Karl wondered if they were going to have fireworks that night, what with the shortages. It wasn't the shortages, Mr. M____ replied; Ocean City had fireworks from pre-war. But it was too risky on account of the enemy submarines, some people thought.

"Don't seem like Fourth of July without fireworks," said Uncle Karl. The inverted tag in dialogue-writing is still considered permissible with proper names or epithets, but sounds old-fashioned with personal pronouns. "We'll have 'em again soon enough," predicted the boys' father. Their mother declared she could do without fireworks: they reminded her too much of the real thing. Their father said all the more reason to shoot off a few now and again. Uncle Karl asked *rhetorically* who needed reminding, just look at people's hair and skin.

"The oil, yes," said Mrs. M____.

Ambrose had a pain in his stomach and so didn't swim but enjoyed watching the others. He and his father burned red easily. Magda's figure was exceedingly well developed for her age. She too declined to swim, and got mad, and became angry when Peter attempted to drag her into the pool. She always swam, he insisted; what did she mean not swim? Why did a person come to Ocean City?

"Maybe I want to lay here with Ambrose," Magda teased.

Nobody likes a pedant.

"Aha," said Mother. Peter grabbed Magda by one ankle and ordered Ambrose to grab the other. She squealed and rolled over on the beach blanket. Ambrose pretended to help hold her back. Her tan was darker than even Mother's and Peter's. "Help out, Uncle Karl!" Peter cried. Uncle Karl went to seize the other ankle. Inside the top of her swimsuit, however, you could see the line where the sunburn ended and, when she hunched her shoulders and squealed again, one nipple's auburn edge. Mother made them behave themselves. "*You* should certainly know," she said to Uncle Karl. Archly. "that when a lady says she doesn't feel like swimming, a gentleman doesn't ask questions." Uncle Karl said excuse *him;* Mother winked at Magda; Ambrose blushed; stupid Peter kept saying "Phooey on *feel like!*" and tugging at Magda's ankle;

then even he got the point, and cannon-balled with a holler into
the pool.

"I swear," Magda said, in mock *in feigned* exasperation.

The diving would make a suitable literary symbol. To go off
the high board you had to wait in a line along the poolside and up
the ladder. Fellows tickled girls and goosed one another and
shouted to the ones at the top to hurry up, or razzed them for
bellyfloppers. Once on the springboard some took a great while
posing or clowning or deciding on a dive or getting up their nerve;
others ran right off. Especially among the younger fellows the idea
was to strike the funniest pose or do the craziest stunt as you fell,
a thing that got harder to do as you kept on and kept on. But
whether you hollered *Geronimo!* or *Sig heil!*, held your nose or
"rode a bicycle," pretended to be shot or did a perfect jackknife
or changed your mind halfway down and ended up with nothing,
it was over in two seconds, after all that wait. Spring, pose, splash.
Spring, neat-o, splash. Spring, aw shit, splash.

The grown-ups had gone on; Ambrose wanted to converse with
Magda; she was remarkably well developed for her age; it was
said that that came from rubbing with a Turkish towel, and there
were other theories. Ambrose could think of nothing to say except
how good a diver Peter was, who was showing off for her benefit.
You could pretty well tell by looking at their bathing-suits and
arm-muscles how far along the different fellows were. Ambrose was
glad he hadn't gone in swimming, the cold water shrank you up so.
Magda pretended not to be interested in the diving; she probably
weighed as much as he did. If you knew your way around in the
funhouse like your own bedroom you could wait until a girl came
along and then slip away without ever getting caught, even if her
boyfriend was right with her. She'd think *he* did it! It would be
better to be the boyfriend, and act outraged, and tear the funhouse
apart. Not act; *be.*

"He's a master diver," Ambrose said. In feigned admiration.
"You really have to slave away at it to get that good." What would
it matter anyhow if he asked her right out whether she remembered,
even teased her with it as Peter would have?

There's no point in going farther; this isn't getting anybody
anywhere; they haven't even come to the funhouse yet. Ambrose
is off the track, in some new or old part of the place that's not

supposed to be used; he strayed into it by some one-in-a-million chance, like the time the roller-coaster-car left the tracks in the nineteen-teens against all the laws of physics and sailed over the boardwalk in the dark. And they can't locate him because they don't know where to look. Even the designer and operator has forgotten this other part, that winds around on itself like a whelk-shell. That winds around the right part like the snakes on Mercury's caduceus. Some people, perhaps, don't "hit their stride" until their twenties, when the growing-up business is over and women appreciate other things besides wisecracks and teasing and strutting. Peter didn't have one-tenth the imagination *he* had, not one-tenth. Peter did this naming-their-children thing as a joke, making up names like Aloysius and Murgatroyd, but Ambrose knew *exactly* how it would feel to be married and have children of your own, and be a loving husband and father, and go comfortably to work in the mornings and to bed with your wife at night, and wake up with her there. With a breeze coming through the sash and birds and mockingbirds singing in the chinese-cigar trees. His eyes watered, there aren't enough ways to say that. He would be quite famous in his line of work. Whether Magda was his wife or not, one evening when he was wise-lined and gray at the temples, he'd smile gravely, at a fashionable dinner-party, and remind her of his youthful passion. The time they went with his family to Ocean City; the *erotic fantasies* he used to have about her. How long ago it seemed, and childish! Yet tender, too, *n'est-ce pas?* Would she have imagined that the world-renowned whatever remembered how many strings were on the lute on the bench beside the girl on the label of the cigar-box he'd stared at in the toolshed at age eight while she, age nine. Even then he had felt *wise beyond his years;* he'd stroked her hair and said in his deepest voice and correctest English, as to a dear child: "I shall never forget this moment."

But though he had breathed heavily, groaned as if ecstatic, what he'd really felt throughout was an odd detachment, as though someone else were Master. Strive as he might to be transported, he heard his mind take notes upon the scene: *This is what they call* passion. *I am experiencing it.* Many of the digger-machines were out of order in the penny arcades and could not be repaired or replaced for the duration. Moreover, the prizes, made now in USA, were less interesting than formerly, pasteboard items for the most part, and some of the machines wouldn't work on white pennies. The gypsy-fortuneteller machine might have provided a foreshadowing of the climax of this story if Ambrose had operated it. It was even dilapidateder than most: the silver coating was worn off the brown metal handles, the glass windows around the dummy were cracked and taped, her kerchiefs and silks long faded. If a man lived by himself he could take a department-store mannequin with flexible joints and modify her in certain ways. *However:* by the time he was that old he'd have a real woman. There was a machine that stamped your name around a white-metal coin with a star in the middle: A_____. His son would be the Third, and when the lad reached thirteen or so he would put a strong arm around his shoulder and tell him calmly: "It is perfectly normal. We have all been through it. It will not last forever." Nobody knew how to be what they were right. He'd smoke a pipe, teach his son how to fish and softcrab, assure him he needn't worry about himself. Magda would certainly give, Magda would certainly yield a great deal of milk, although guilty of occasional solecisms. It don't taste so bad. Suppose the lights came on now!

The day wore on. You think you're yourself, but there are other persons in you. Ambrose gets an erection when Ambrose doesn't want one, *and obversely.* Ambrose watches them disagreeing; Ambrose watches him watch. In the funhouse mirror-room you can't see yourself go on forever, because no matter how you stand your head gets in the way. Even if you had a glass periscope, the image of your eye would cover up the thing you really wanted to see. The police will come; there'll be a story in the papers. That must be where it happened. Unless he can find a surprise exit, an unofficial backdoor or escape-hatch opening on an alley, say, and then stroll up to the family in front of the funhouse and ask where everybody's been; *he's* been out of the place for ages. That's just where it happened, in that last lighted room: Peter and Magda found the right exit; he found one that you weren't supposed to find and strayed off into the works somewhere. In a perfect funhouse you'd be able to go only one way, like the divers off the high board; getting lost would be impossible; the doors and halls would work like minnow-traps or the valves in veins.

On account of German U-boats Ocean City was "browned out": streetlights were shaded on the seaward side; shopwindows and boardwalk amusement-places were kept dim, not to silhouette tankers and Liberty-ships for torpedoing. In a short-story about Ocean City, Maryland, during World War II the author could make use of the image of sailors on leave in the penny arcades and shooting-galleries, sighting through the cross hairs of toy machine-guns at swastika'd subs, while out in the black Atlantic a U-boat skipper squints through his periscope at real ships outlined by the glow of penny arcades. After dinner the family strolled back to the amusement end of the boardwalk. The boys' father had burnt red as always and was masked with Noxzema, a minstrel in reverse. The grown-ups stood at the end of the boardwalk where the Hurricane of '33 had cut an inlet from the ocean to Assawoman Bay.

"Prounced with a long *o*," Uncle Karl reminded Magda with a wink. His shirt-sleeves were rolled up; Mother punched his brown biceps with the arrowed heart on it and said his mind was naughty. Fat May's laugh came suddenly from the funhouse, as if she'd just got the joke; the family laughed too at the coincidence. Ambrose went under the boardwalk to search for out-of-town matchbook-covers with the aid of his pocket flashlight; he looked out from the edge of the North American continent and wondered how far their laughter carried over the water. Spies in rubber rafts; survivors in lifeboats. If the joke had been beyond his understanding, he could have said: *"The laughter was over his head."* And let the reader see the serious wordplay on second reading.

He turned the flashlight on and then off at once even before the woman whooped. He sprang away, heart athud, dropping the light. The man had snarled: "Cut da friggin' light!" Perspiration drenched and chilled him by the time he scrambled up to the family. "See anything?" his father asked. His voice wouldn't come; he shrugged and violently brushed sand from his pantslegs.

"Let's ride the old flying-horses!" Magda cried. I'll never be an author. It's been forever already, everybody's gone home, Ocean City's deserted, the ghost-crabs are tickling across the beach and down the littered cold streets. And the empty halls of clapboard hotels and abandoned funhouses. A tidal wave; an enemy air raid; a monster-crab swelling like an island from the sea. *The Inhabitants fled in terror.* Magda clung to his trouserleg; he alone knew the maze's secret. "He gave his life that we might live," said Uncle Karl with a scowl of pain, as he. The woman's legs had been twined behind the man's neck; he'd spread her fat cheeks with tattooed hands and pumped like a whippet. *An astonishing coincidence.* He yearned to tell Peter. He wanted to throw up for excitement. They hadn't even chased him. He wished he were dead.

One possible ending would be to have Ambrose come across another lost person in the dark. They'd match their wits together against the funhouse, struggle like Ulysses past obstacle after obstacle, help and encourage each other. Or a girl. By the time they found the exit they'd be closest friends, sweethearts if it were a girl; they'd know each other's inmost souls, be bound together *by the cement of shared adventure;* then they'd emerge into the light, and it would turn out that his friend was a Negro. A blind girl. President Roosevelt's son. Ambrose's former arch-enemy.

Shortly after the mirror-room he'd groped along a musty corridor, his heart already misgiving him at the absence of phosphorescent arrows and other signs. He'd found a crack of light—not a door, it turned out, but a seam between the plyboard wall-panels—and squinting up to it, espied a small old man nodding upon a stool beneath a bare speckled bulb. A crude panel of toggle- and knife-switches hung beside the open fuse-box near his head; elsewhere in the little room were wooden levers and ropes belayed to boat-cleats. At the time, Ambrose wasn't lost enough to rap or call; later he couldn't find that crack. Now it seemed to him that he'd possibly dozed off for a few minutes somewhere along the way; certainly he was exhausted from the afternoon's sunshine and the evening's problems; he couldn't be sure he hadn't dreamed part or all of the sight. Had an old black wall fan droned like bumble-bees and shimmied two flypaper streamers? Had the funhouse operator—gentle, somewhat sad and tired-appearing—murmured in his sleep? Is there really such a person as Ambrose, or is he a figment of the author's imagination? Was it Assawoman Bay or Sinepuxent? Are there other errors of fact in this fiction? Was there another sound besides the little slap slap of thigh on ham, like water sucking at the chineboards of a skiff?

When you're lost, the smartest thing to do is stay put till you're found, hollering if necessary. But to holler guarantees humiliation as well as rescue; keeping silent permits some saving of face—you can act surprised at the fuss when your rescuers find you and swear you weren't lost, if they do. What's more you might find your own way yet, *however belatedly.*

"Don't tell me your foot's still asleep!" Magda exclaimed as the three young people walked from the inlet to the area set aside for ferris-wheels, carrousels, and other carnival rides, they having decided in favor of the vast and ancient merry-go-round instead of the funhouse. What a sentence, everything was wrong from the outset. People don't know what to make of him, he doesn't know what to make of himself, he's only thirteen, *athletically and socially inept*, not astonishingly bright, but there are antennae; he has . . . some sort of receivers in his head; things speak to him, he understands more than he should, the world winks at him through its objects, grabs grinning at his coat. Everybody else is in on some secret he doesn't know; they've forgotten to tell him. Through simple *procrastination* his mother put off his baptism until this year. Everyone else had it done as a baby; he'd assumed the same of himself, as had his mother so she claimed, until it was time for him to join Grace Methodist-Protestant and the oversight came out. He was mortified, but pitched sleepless through his private catechizing, intimidated by the ancient mysteries, a thirteen-year-old would never say that, resolved to experience conversion like St. Augustine. When the water touched his brow and Adam's sin left him, he contrived by a strain like defecation to bring tears into his eyes—but felt nothing. There was some simple, radical difference about him; he hoped it was genius, feared it was madness, devoted himself to amiability and inconspicuousness. Alone on the seawall near his house he was seized by the terrifying transports he'd thought to find in summershed, in Communion-cup. The grass was alive! The town, the river, himself, were not imaginary; time roared in his ears like wind; the world was *going on!* This part ought to be dramatized. The Irish author James Joyce once wrote. Ambrose M_____ is going to scream.

There is no *texture of rendered sensory detail*, for one thing. The faded distorting mirrors beside Fat May; the impossibility of choosing a mount when one had but a single ride on the great carrousel; the *vertigo attendant on his recognition* that Ocean City was worn out, the place of fathers and grandfathers, straw-boatered men and parasoled ladies survived by their amusements. Money spent, the three paused at Peter's insistence beside Fat May to watch the girls get their skirts blown up. The object was to tease Magda, who said: "I swear, Peter M____, you've got a one-track mind! Amby and me aren't *interested* in such things." In the tumbling-barrel, too, just inside the Devil's-mouth entrance to the funhouse, the girls were upended, and their boyfriends and others could see up their dresses if they cared to. Which was the whole point, Ambrose realized. Of the entire funhouse! If you looked around, you noticed that almost all the people on the boardwalk were paired off into couples except the small children; in a way, that was the whole point of Ocean City! If you had X-ray eyes and could see everything going on at that instant under the boardwalk and in all the hotel-rooms and cars and alleyways, you'd realize that all that normally *showed*, like restaurants and dance-halls and clothing and test-your-strength machines, was merely preparation and intermission. Fat May screamed.

Because he watched the goings-on from the corner of his eye, it was Ambrose who spied the half-dollar on the boardwalk near the tumbling-barrel. Losers weepers. The first time he'd heard some people moving through a corridor not far away, just after he'd lost sight of the crack of light, he'd decided not to call to them, for fear they'd guess he was scared and poke fun; it sounded like roughnecks; he'd hoped they'd come by and he could follow in the dark without their knowing. Another time he'd heard just one person, unless he imagined it, bumping along as if on the other side of the plywood; perhaps Peter coming back for him, or Father, or Magda lost too. Or the owner and operator of the funhouse. He'd called out once, as though merrily: "Anybody know where the heck we are?" But the query was too stiff, his voice cracked, when the sounds stopped he was terrified: maybe it was a queer who waited for fellows to get lost, or a longhaired filthy monster that lived in some cranny of the funhouse. He stood rigid for hours it seemed like, scarcely respiring. His future was shockingly clear, in outline. He tried holding his breath to the point of unconsciousness. There ought to be a button you could push to end your life absolutely without pain; disappear in a flick, like turning out a light. He would push it instantly! He despised Uncle Karl. But he despised his father too, for not being what he was supposed to be. Perhaps his father hated *his* father, and so on, and his son would hate him, and so on. Instantly!

Naturally he didn't have nerve enough to ask Magda to go through the funhouse with him. With incredible nerve and to everyone's surprise he invited Magda, quietly and politely, to go through the funhouse with him. "I warn you, I've never been through it before," he added, *laughing easily;* "but I reckon we can manage somehow. The important thing to remember, after all, is that it's meant to be a *fun*house; that is, a place of amusement. If people really got lost or injured or too badly frightened in it, the owner'd go out of business. There'd even be lawsuits. No character in a work of fiction can make a speech this long without interruption or acknowledgment from the other characters."

Mother teased Uncle Karl: "Three's a crowd, I always heard." But actually Ambrose was relieved that Peter now had a quarter too. Nothing was what it looked like. Every instant, under the surface of the Atlantic Ocean, millions of living animals devoured one another. Pilots were falling in flames over Europe; women were being forcibly raped in the South Pacific. His father should have taken him aside and said: "There is a simple secret to getting through the funhouse, as simple as being first to see the Towers. Here it is. Peter does not know it; neither does your Uncle Karl. You and I are different. Not surprisingly, you've often wished you weren't. Don't think I haven't noticed how unhappy your childhood has been! But you'll understand, when I tell you, why it had to be kept secret until now. And you won't regret not being like your brother and your uncle. *On the contrary.*" If you knew all the stories behind all the people on the boardwalk you'd see that *nothing* was what it looked like. Husbands and wives often hated each other; parents didn't necessarily love their children; et cetera. A child took things for granted because he had nothing to compare his life to, and everybody acted as if things were as they should be. Therefore each saw himself as the hero of the story, when the truth might turn out to be that he's the villain, or the coward. And there wasn't one thing you could do about it!

Hunchbacks, fat ladies, fools—that no one chose what they were was unbearable. In the movies he'd meet a beautiful young girl in the funhouse; they'd have hairsbreadth escapes from real dangers; he'd do and say the right things; she also; in the end they'd be lovers; their dialogue-lines would match up; he'd be perfectly at ease; she'd not only like him well enough, she'd think he was *marvelous;* she'd lie awake thinking about *him,* instead of vice versa—the way *his* face looked in different lights and how he stood and exactly what he'd said—and yet that would be only one small episode in his wonderful life, among many many others. Not a *turning-point* at all. What had happened in the toolshed was nothing. He hated, he loathed his parents! One reason for not writing a lost-in-the-funhouse story is that either everybody's felt what Ambrose feels, in which case it goes without saying, or else no normal person feels such things, in which case Ambrose is a freak. "Is anything more tiresome, in fiction, than the problems of sensitive adolescents?" And it's all too long and rambling, as if the author. For all a person knows the first time through, the end could be just around any corner; perhaps, *not impossibly* it's been within reach any number of times. On the other hand he may be scarcely past the start, with everything yet to get through, an intolerable idea.

Fill in: His father's raised eyebrows when he announced his decision to do the funhouse with Magda. Ambrose understands now, but didn't then, that his father was wondering whether he knew what the funhouse was *for*—especially since he didn't object, as he should have, when Peter decided to come along too. The ticket-woman, witchlike, mortifying him when inadvertently he gave her his name-coin instead of the half-dollar, then unkindly calling Magda's attention to the birthmark on his temple: "Watch out for him, girlie, he's a marked man!" She wasn't even cruel, he understood, only vulgar and insensitive. Somewhere in the world there was a young woman with such splendid understanding that she'd see him entire, like a poem or story, and find his words so valuable after all that when he confessed his apprehensions she would explain why they were in fact the very things that made him precious to her . . . and to Western Civilization! There was no such girl, the simple truth being. Violent yawns as they approached the mouth. Whispered advice from an old-timer on a bench near the barrel: "Go crabwise and ye'll get an eyeful without upsetting!" Composure vanished at the first pitch: Peter hollered joyously, Magda tumbled, shrieked, clutched her skirt, Ambrose scrambled crabwise, tightlipped with terror, was soon out, watched his dropped name-coin slide among the couples. Shamefaced he saw that to get through expeditiously was not the point;

Peter feigned assistance in order to trip Magda up, shouted "I see Christmas!" when her legs went flying. The old man, his latest betrayer, cacked approval. A dim hall then of blackthread cobwebs and recorded gibber: he took Magda's elbow to steady her against revolving discs set in the slanted floor to throw your feet out from under, and explained to her in a calm deep voice his theory that each phase of the funhouse was triggered either automatically, by a series of photoelectric devices, or else manually by operators stationed at peepholes. But he lost his voice thrice as the discs unbalanced him; Magda was anyhow squealing; but at one point she clutched him about the waist to keep from falling, and her right cheek pressed for a moment against his belt-buckle. Heroically he drew her up, it was his chance to clutch her close as if for support and say: "I love you." He even put an arm lightly about the small of her back before a sailor-and-girl pitched into them from behind, sorely treading his left big toe and knocking Magda asprawl with them. The sailor's girl was a string-haired hussy with a loud laugh and light-blue drawers; Ambrose realized that he wouldn't have said "I love you" anyhow, and was smitten with self-contempt. How much better it would be to be that common sailor! A wiry little Seaman 3rd, the fellow squeezed a girl to each side and stumbled hilarious into the mirror-room, closer to Magda in thirty seconds than Ambrose had got in thirteen years. She giggled at something the fellow said to Peter; she drew her hair from her eyes with a movement so womanly it struck Ambrose's heart; Peter's smacking her backside then seemed particularly coarse. But Magda made a pleased indignant face and cried, "All right for *you*, mister!" and pursued Peter into the maze without a backward glance. The sailor followed after, leisurelily, drawing his girl against his hip; Ambrose understood not only that they were all so relieved to be rid of his burdensome company that they didn't even notice his absence, but that he himself shared their relief. Stepping from the treacherous passage at last into the mirror-maze, he saw once again, more clearly than ever, how readily he deceived himself into supposing he was a person. He even foresaw, wincing at his dreadful self-knowledge, that he would repeat the deception, at ever-rarer intervals, all his wretched life, so fearful were the alternatives. Fame, madness, suicide; perhaps all three. It's not believable that so young a boy could articulate that reflection, and in fiction the merely true must always yield to the plausible. Yet Ambrose M_____ understood, as few adults do, that the famous loneliness of the great was no popular myth but a general truth—and moreover, that it was as much cause as effect.

All the preceding except the last few sentences is exposition that should've been done earlier or interspersed with the present action instead of lumped together. No reader would put up with so much with such *prolixity*. It's interesting that Ambrose's father, though presumably an intelligent man (as indicated by his role as high-school teacher), neither encouraged nor discouraged his children at all in any way—as if he either didn't care about them or cared all right but didn't know how to act. If this fact should contribute to one of his children's becoming a celebrated but wretchedly unhappy scientist, was it a good thing or not? He too might someday face that question; it would be useful to know whether it had tortured his father for years, for example, or never once crossed his mind.

In the mirror-maze two important things happened. First, our hero found a name-coin someone else had lost or discarded: *AMBROSE*, suggestive of the famous lightship and of his father's favorite dessert, which his mother prepared on special occasions out of coconut, oranges, grapes, and what else. Second, as he wondered at the endless replication of his image in the mirrors— second, as he *lost himself in the reflection* that the necessity for an observer makes perfect observation impossible, better make him eighteen at least, yet that would render other things unlikely, he heard Peter and Magda chuckling somewhere in the maze. "Here!" "No, here!" they shouted to each other; Peter said, "Where's Amby?" Magda murmured. "Amb?" Peter called. In a pleased, friendly voice. He didn't reply. The truth was, his brother was a *happy-go-lucky youngster* who'd've been better off with a regular brother of his own, but who seldom complained of his lot and was generally cordial. Ambrose's throat ached; there aren't enough different ways to say that. He stood quietly while the two young people giggled and thumped through the glittering maze, hurrah'd their discovery of its exit, cried out in joyful alarm at what next beset them. Then he set his mouth and followed after, as he supposed, took a wrong turn, strayed into the pass *wherein he lingers yet*.

The action of conventional dramatic narrative may be represented by a diagram called Freitag's Triangle

$$\underset{A}{}\diagup\overset{B}{}\diagdown\underset{C}{}$$

or more accurately by a variant of that diagram

$$A \overset{B}{\underline{\quad}}\diagup\overset{C}{}\diagdown D$$

in which *AB* represents the exposition *B* the introduction of conflict, *BC* the "rising action," complication, or development of the conflict, *C* the climax or turn of the action, *CD* the *dénouement* or resolution of the conflict.

While there is no reason to regard this pattern as an absolute necessity, like many other conventions it became conventional because great numbers of people over great numbers of years learned by trial and error that it was effective; one ought not to forsake it, therefore, unless one wishes to forsake as well the effect of drama or has clear cause to feel that deliberate violation of the "normal" pattern can better can better effect that effect. This can't go on much longer; it can go on forever. He died telling stories to himself in the dark; years later, when that vast unsuspected area of the funhouse came to light, the first expedition found his skeleton in one of its labyrinthine corridors and mistook it for part of the entertainment. He died of starvation telling himself stories in the dark; but unbeknownst unbeknownst to him, an assistant operator of the funhouse, happening to overhear him, crouched just behind the plyboard partition and wrote down his every word. The operator's daughter, an exquisite young woman with a figure unusually well developed for her age, crouched just behind the partition and transcribed his every word. Though she had never laid eyes on him, she recognized that here was one of Western Culture's truly great imaginations, the eloquence of whose suffering would be an inspiration to unnumbered. And her heart was torn between her love for the misfortunate young man (yes, she loved him, though she had never laid though she knew him only—but how well!— through his words, and the deep, calm voice in which he spoke them) between her love et cetera and her woman's intuition that only in suffering and isolation could he give voice et cetera. Lone dark dying. Quietly she kissed the rough plyboard, and a tear fell upon the page. Where she had written in shorthand *Where she*

had written in shorthand Where she had written in shorthand
Where she et cetera. A long time ago we should have passed the
apex of Freitag's Triangle and made brief work of the *dénouement;* the plot doesn't rise by meaningful steps but winds upon
itself, digresses, retreats, hesitates, sighs, collapses, expires. The
climax of the story must be its protagonist's discovery of a way to
get through the funhouse. But he has found none, may have ceased
to search.

What relevance does the war have to the story? Should there
be fireworks outside or not?

Ambrose wandered, languished, dozed. Now and then he fell
into his habit of rehearsing to himself the unadventurous story of
his life, narrated from the third-person point of view, from his
earliest memory parenthesis of maple-leaves stirring in the summer breath of tidewater Maryland end of parenthesis to the present
moment. Its principal events, on this telling, would appear to have
been *A, B, C,* and *D.*

He imagined himself years hence, successful, married, at ease
in the world, the trials of his adolescence far behind him. He has
come to the seashore with his family for the holiday: how Ocean
City has changed! But at one seldom at one ill-frequented end
of the boardwalk a few derelict amusements survive from times
gone by: the great carrousel from the turn of the century, with its
monstrous griffins and mechanical concert-band; the roller-coaster
rumored since 1916 to have been condemned; the mechanical
shooting-gallery in which only the image of our enemies changed.
His own son laughs with Fat May and wants to know what a funhouse is; Ambrose hugs the sturdy lad close and smiles around his
pipestem at his wife.

The family's going home. Mother sits between Father and Uncle
Karl, who teases him good-naturedly who chuckles over the fact
that the comrade with whom he'd fought his way shoulder to
shoulder through the funhouse had turned out to be a colored boy
—to their mutual discomfort, as they'd opened their souls. But
such are the walls of custom, which even. Whose arm is where?
How must it feel. He dreams of a funhouse vaster by far than any
yet constructed; but by then they may be out of fashion, like
steamboats and excursion-trains. Already quaint and seedy: the
draperied ladies on the frieze of the carrousel are his father's

father's mooncheeked dreams; if he thinks of it more he will vomit his apple-on-a-stick.

He wonders: will he become a regular person? Something has gone wrong; his vaccination didn't take; at the Boy-Scout initiation campfire he only pretended to be deeply moved, as he pretends to this hour that it is not so bad after all in the funhouse, and that he has a little limp. How long will it last? He envisions a truly astonishing funhouse, incredibly complex yet utterly controlled from a great central switchboard like the console of a pipe-organ. Nobody had enough imagination. He could design such a place himself, wiring and all, and he's only thirteen years old. He would be its operator: panel-lights would show what was up in every cranny of its cunning of its multifarious vastness; a switch-flick would ease this fellow's way, complicate that's, to balance things out; if anyone seemed lost or frightened, all the operator had to do was.

He wishes he had never entered the funhouse. No: he wishes he had never been born. But he was. Then he wishes he were dead. But he's not. Therefore he will construct funhouses for others and be their secret operator—though he would rather be among the lovers for whom funhouses are designed.

NANCY HUDDLESTON PACKER was born in Washington, D.C. in 1925, but grew up in Birmingham, Alabama. Her stories have appeared in the *Kenyon Review*, the *Southwest Review*, the *Yale Review*, *The Reporter*, *Harper's*, and elsewhere. She teaches fiction writing at Stanford University, where she lives with her husband, a professor of law, and their two children.

Early Morning, Lonely Ride

FRANCES BENEDICT's husband, Emery, was a lawyer. Successful. Frances herself might yet become anything, having tried nothing. She was only thirty-three. She had three children and live-in help at home. Sleeping. She was nothing among strangers at a rich man's party. She said to Emery,

"Notice how new money smells like a cross between wet copper and Cashmere Bouquet?"

"Please don't," said Emery.

"Cash, cashmere, coppers, copper, and a can of room freshener I think they call it wafting in from the downstairs drains. Rich people always trying to undo the natural odors of the universe. New rich. What about dying? Buried with a can of aerosol spray and a couple of lavender sachets?" She thought she was going just great, about to zoom off holding Emery by the collar.

"Grow up," said Emery, making his choice against her. "Please just grow up!"

"Right here?" she asked sweetly. "On his gorgeous handwoven rug? Think of the aroma for God's sake, Emery."

Gazing beyond her with the look of a guest who expects momentarily to catch the party's beat, Emery professed to ignore her, having other fish to fry or why had they come in the first place. To cope with her, she believed, required his full attention. Hell with

it. She sat on a pumpkin velvet window seat and vowed to view
the dark Bay all evening. Maybe the rich didn't like smells but
they sure bought the sights. If anyone noticed. Occasionally she
nodded amiably about her. Grins hung from her teeth like old
moss. People seeing her saw only Revlon and Maidenform. She was
just one of the girls, boys: chic, shrewd, and stupid. Look out.
Their hostess, whose barbiturated face flamed up from a purple
dress that weighed in at close to five hundred dollars, claimed
Emery, rescued a man from his wife. From time to time, the host,
porpoise of body but ferret of eye, came to sit beside Frances and
to press thighs with her. Frances shortly ran out of amusing things
to say and was a wallflower. With contemptuous lack of embarrassment she warded off other wallflowers seeking solace. She was not
a woman's woman. With a bold blue mirthless eye she forewarned
idle men she might have ridden straight through the evening. She
was not a man's woman.

It was Emery's crowd, not hers. It was a tired coupling of business and pleasure. She did not count. She was, if anything at all,
only a helpmeet the color of the background. Forgetting her,
Emery enjoyed himself. At that thought, many grievances sur-
faced. The children slept like tops; like tops they were spinning
on their own. Strings dangled from her hands, cut loose by time
and condition. Nothing short of the rapt attention of everyone
would satisfy her and, sadly, she knew it. She grew restive. This
was the world she lived in, a world she never made, the best of all
possible worlds, but hers, alas, was not the hand that rocked it.

"O brave new world," she said aloud.

"Darling?" asked Emery, standing at the empty fireplace with
their host's brother-in-law, for all the world as if conducting the
world's affairs.

"That has such people in it," she finished.

Emery laughed gaily, apprehensively, and moved away. The
brother-in-law, who smelled of oil and litigation and pine needles,
cast her an appraising and impersonal look. The sort of man, she
decided, who grandly bestowed upon a grateful wife a white
Lincoln Continental (What's wrong with that? Emery might ask.
If you don't know . . . Did *she* give *him* a Cadillac?) Frances
preferred Emery, gentle, rational, accepting. Mutual. Slyly she
coughed for his attention and signaled for them to go home. He

hesitated but then set his face to stay. All right all right go fly a kite.

A waiter moved among them like a matador, a towel over his arm, a tray of drinks poised for the kill. He was Filipino, colors of golden hills and black patent leather. The host called him Robert. Soon, Frances called him Bob. An hour passed and she called him Bobby. He said, Yes Mrs. Benedict, and she thrilled at the sound from strange luscious lips. Later, having crossed the hearth to the other window seat, she caught his eye. One enchanted evening. His white teeth gleamed for her. She played with the thought of lust. She saw them naked and exhausted upon hot sand but found that she had nothing further to say to him. To fill the void, she curried, combed, painted, filed, smoothed, roughed in order that she would want to talk to him. Why? Reality, as usual, impinged and she saw him sliding down the corridors of forever, happily passing drinks to friends of the rich. Let him climb some other snow-capped mountain. Poor Frances, she thought.

Two in the morning came none to soon and Emery, she thought, was none too sober. He did not so much approach as accost her. He took her elbow. She heard his trumpets blaring and the martial beat of his drums. He had not forgotten her, but he preferred himself. She was not defenseless but she was demanding. She reclaimed her elbow. At the front door he swooped down on a half-finished and deserted drink and after proffering it to her downed it with a flourish. His gesture was at once a reprimand, a warning, and a defiance. He apparently felt deeply guilty at having deserted her, but nonetheless he proclaimed that he was his own man by right, be quiet.

By reason and a long-standing agreement, she should have driven home. By happenstance she did not, for their host marched them down the stairs to the car. Before such a client as that, dear Emery lacked the courage to let her drive. She might have insisted, made a small scene, but she did not, out of pity and fortitude and a desire to justify all her grievances.

Gesturing grandly, drunkenly, Emery slid behind the wheel of the car and unerringly slipped the key in the ignition. Smiling grimly, Frances announced to herself that she was going to die on the Bloody Bayshore because their host wished, under cover of darkness, to pat her bottom one more time. She contemplated giving the old fool a punch in his belly and her resentment reached a climax. Is this the age we live in? No one counted her, protected her, nor was she free and equal. She wished ill on everyone.

As Emery bucked away from the curb, she looked back and saw their host sprawled face down in the entrance to his house. Now that, she said, will do for a starter.

"There's a stop sign," she said.

"I'm not blind," said Emery.

"Oh?" said Frances. She withdrew into her most maddening silence.

"Great party," said Emery, making amends. He glanced at her quickly as if to judge her mood. What right had he to smile who had no right not to smile? What gift was this? He drove, did he not?

"Absolutely tiptop, one in a million," she said. "Shall I drive?" She extended her hand as if literally to take the wheel.

He heard, saw, ignored. "They're first-rate people, really first-rate. Know what I mean?" It was his way of making friends, but he had no grievance.

"Well now let me see," she said. "You mean salt of the earth, don't you? May I drive now?"

Emery appeared to ruminate. "It's going to be a very fruitful relationship."

"He said you were the greatest lawyer since . . . John Jay. I'd like to drive, Emery."

He laughed. "That guy never heard of John Jay. I'm doing all right, ain't I? Driving?" His voice was reasonable, not thick, just very careful and reasonable. He bore no grudge. He was, in fact, managing the car well enough. He had smoothed out the clutch and he traveled at moderate speed. All the same, she wanted to drive.

"In the early years of their marriage," she intoned as if reading from a document, "they agreed together, both parties complying without dissenting voice, that so-called role-playing was less important than life-saving, that error would be on the side of over-safety, that should one or the other imbibe too deeply, that one automatically relinquished his or her rights to the wheel of the car, the body of the baby, the tray of Orrefors, or the handle of the hot pan. It was a bargain struck in good faith and high reason. It has no doubt saved them many a goblet."

"Agreed," he said, turning up the ramp to the Bayshore. "So?"

She had been acutely alert to him for years and she saw the components of his resistance, the pride, the threat, the daring, the fear. Nevertheless, it infuriated her.

"Tomorrow morning you'll give me that cute little crooked little smile of yours and you'll say Boy was I crocked last night, I didn't know whether I could drive home or not. If we live until tomorrow."

"Goddammit," said Emery, speeding up, "you know I'm not drunk but you just keep pounding away as if your life depended on it, just so you can win the round, just so you can show me."

"Merging traffic," she said.

"I see the merging traffic." His face became, for him, brutal and flushed. Suddenly he braked and swerved to avoid a sideswiping Thunderbird. His face quieted. "Got your seat belt fastened?" he asked in rueful apology.

She quoted a headline. "Lawyer and Wife Killed on Bayshore."

He thought he had her, he looked delicious. "*Prominent* Lawyer and *Beautiful* Wife Only Injured." When he heard himself, his smile soured. "Not injured either, dammit. Why do you act this way? What do you want?"

"I'd be mad as hell if I got killed coming home from a party as nasty as that one," she said.

At first he laughed at the absurdity of what she had said. And then he surrendered to her anger and its demands for combat. He drew back his lips and said, "You just can't stand it, can you? How many years and you just can't stand it when people are more interested in me than they are in you. You just got to cut me down someway."

Her skin felt like plaster of Paris and her teeth ached, but her voice was gay. "It's a man's world, you know. Poor Emery. Poor dear old Emery, with his hag of a nag of a bag of a wife. I mean, what the hell, if you want to drive while intoxicated, what difference does it make that I'll get killed too?"

Sour and silent, he drove the car. Stubbornly they built up the battlements of silence. The Bayshore swept down the countryside to the flat country and the bay and darkness. The hills to the right held pockets of light. A jet swooped upward from the runway at the airport. The moon vanished. Occasionally cars sped toward them on the other side of the parkway. Rarely, a car passed them heading south. Their own car began to lug. Emery gripped the wheel. He shifted down a gear. The car began to thud and bump. He switched off the ignition. Understanding struck them both but Frances rushed to speak it.

"It's a flat."

"I know it's a flat," he said, turning off to the shoulder of the road. "I am not a fool."

He applied the brakes and the car stopped. His face was sober and ashamed. She relented at the sight and wished to touch his face, give comfort, offer love and forgiveness. She devised a smile but not soon enough.

"You are so superior," he said. "You never had a flat in your whole life. You'd have seen the nail, whatever it was."

Rebuffed, she said warningly, "Perhaps."

"From you, that's a concession."

She knew that all he wished was one kind word, to be asked to share in the comedy or rue that lay beneath their quarrels. He was a bookish man, not a fighter. He hated to quarrel, as he inevitably, too late, proclaimed. She saw clearly, not for the first time, how she drove him to it, with her vanities and irritations, her untapped powers and her vast need for consolation. She saw, too, that he had not this time consoled her but had instead himself concocted a grievance. She refused then in all conscience to help him. Was it ever different?

"You may recall," she said, "that I asked to drive. Perhaps, just perhaps but nevertheless perhaps, we might have avoided this flat."

"Oh for Christ's sake stop it."

"But you had to show everyone how big and tough . . ."

"Can you stop it? Can you please stop it?"

"If I wanted to," she said.

"Can you forego just this one time the intense pleasure you get from hammering on me?"

"He said, hammering on her."

Her stomach cramped and her jaws ached, but she smiled to prepare herself for further battle. He was what he was, but so was she. She did not know what laws governed them. But loving each other (for all they knew or cared), they rubbed mild abrasions into deep rawness. Moments of contempt and anger had always come and gone, had often wracked and strained them to breaking, and always been inconclusively put away and forgotten. She was no fool, she of course wished for peace. But she said, "Can you change a tire?"

"That's helpful, that's real helpful," he said. "Leave it to you to make a man feel manly and confident."

He got out of the car, took off his coat and folded it neatly, placed it on the seat, rolled up his sleeves, loosened his necktie, and idly walked up and down beside the flat tire. Finally he got his keychain and opened the trunk. Staring ahead at oncoming lights, Frances listened to his work. She thought that she wished him success, but she was not sure. He removed the jack from the trunk and placed it under the back axle. Frances felt the car rise. She thought of going to stand with him but gave it up. They would only antagonize each other. She would create his mistakes. Once he had accomplished his task, he would be so happy that they would be friends again. He would be irresistible. If he succeeded.

She heard him bump the spare out of the trunk. He popped the hubcap off the flat tire. She heard his startled cry of pain. She opened the door and peered back at him. He held the heel of his thumb to his mouth. Blood darkened his arm and shirt front.

"Damn thing slipped," he said.

She took the handkerchief from his hip pocket and wrapped it around the wound. A car coming in their direction slowed. She raised her hand in greeting but lowered it in fear. Who were they and why? Emery turned, still holding his hand to his mouth. He looked at Frances, gleaming and relieved, as the car stopped behind them. Frances thought that she might herself have changed the tire. She feared strangers at such an hour.

Three young men got out of the car. They wore sports coats and white shirts and loosened neckties. They smelled of men's cologne and stale whiskey. They stopped before Emery and bowed low. Their manners were comic, impersonal, and threatening.

"Sir," said the shortest of the three, a boy of twenty or so with a crew cut and glasses. The largest one came to stand before Frances. "Madame," he said with a low bow.

The third boy said, "You talk entirely too much, bear," and all three commenced to laugh. Frances backed away. The big one did look like a bear, with his short arms and heavy torso and triangular head. A bear.

"I'm awfully glad to see you boys," said Emery. "I seem to have hurt myself." He presented his wounded hand for their inspection.

The shortest one grasped it and shook it vigorously. Emery cried in pain.

"Leave off, Larry," said the third boy, apparently the leader. He was sharp-featured, yet soft and sensual. The other two, the bear and the one called Larry, watched and waited for his reactions. The three were, it seemed to Frances, a closed group, performers and audience at once. She and Emery were only props for them. Or toys. "Okay, doc," said the leader.

The bear approached Emery and extended his hand. He said, "I make no pretense at being adept at the healing arts but may I look at your wound?"

Emery held out his hand and the boy took it. He held the wound close to his eyes, pulled the handkerchief away and carefully pressed open the still bleeding gash in the heel of Emery's hand. Emery jerked away.

"What the hell, are you crazy?" he said.

"I wanted to see what was inside," the bear said.

"He's a sadist," said the leader.

"I was a teen-age sadist," said the bear. All three boys whooped with laughter.

"You boys run along," said Emery. "Find your fun someplace else."

Frances wondered where the highway patrol was. The vaunted highway patrol. Cars were fewer and fewer now.

The smallest of the boys, Larry, pushed his glasses up higher on his nose and after a glance at the leader walked to peer under the car. He put his hand on the bumper and gently, slowly began to rock the car.

"Stop that!" said Emery. With his hand at his mouth, he started toward Larry. The bear touched Emery's arm.

"He isn't hurting you, is he, mister?" The bear shot a glance at the leader. "Ever heard the story of the Good Samaritans? I mean, anybody else stop to help you? He's just trying to help, mister, in his own little way. Don't kill the instinct for brotherhood, mister, not in our Larry."

Emery paused. "He's going to rock the car off the jack."

"Larry ain't mean, mister," said the bear. "Ain't a mean bone in that kid's body."

"By accident, maybe," said Emery. He didn't look at anyone, nor did he move. Frances knew that he was uncertain and nervous, that he was unsure of how to handle the boys. He wouldn't want to act on impulse or do anything dangerous. And he did want the boys' help. He hesitated, staring at the roadway and sucking the wound on his hand.

"Larry ain't accidental, either, mister," said the bear. "Ain't an accidental bone in that kid's body. Is there, Larry?"

Larry turned toward Emery. He was not smiling, but his expression was trancelike. He began to shake his head, slowly, rhythmically, as if dancing. On that signal the other two boys also began to shake their heads, to wear trancelike expressions, and to move toward Emery. They moved in quite close, shaking their heads, but silent. Emery looked at the highway, up and down the highway. Frances said to herself that the boys were obviously kidding, that they would fold if Emery just showed a little authority, confidence. They were just kids. Clean kids, at that. Out on a lark. Showing off for each other. Not dangerous, not if someone laughed at them and said Fix the flat or go away. Emery said nothing. He did not feel comfortable or strong, perhaps it was his aching thumb, or the quarrel. Seconds ticked off. A car whipped past them.

"You want this tire fixed or not?" asked the bear.

"I seem to have hurt this hand rather badly," said Emery. He appealed to them with a smile.

"We ain't asking for a health report," said Larry. "You're taking too much time talking. You want the tire fixed or not?"

Frances said, "Yes," and Emery said, "Yes, if you would be so kind." His voice sounded choked and she knew he was angry to ask directly for help, from them. He had taken too much from them. She shrugged off the accusing look he gave her. If she hadn't said Yes, would he have said No? She didn't think so.

"We'd be delighted to be so kind," said Larry.

The bear walked to Emery and laughed when Emery backed off. "I won't hurt you, mister, not a mean bone in my body either. I don't want your wife to hear this." Emery looked suspicious but allowed himself to be involved. The bear cupped his hand around Emery's ear as if to whisper and he brought his mouth close. In a loud shouting voice he said, "You real scared, ain't you, mister?"

Emery jerked loose and Frances thought he was going to hit the boy. He stopped himself but his face clenched. "Now look here," he said, "you boys are having fun, but I don't find it at all funny. What are you up to, what do you want?" He looked from one to the other, demanding an answer, a rational explanation.

"Easy easy easy," said the leader in a soft sibilant voice. He held his hands up and shook them, as if to forestall Emery. He seemed deeply embarrassed. Emery went on.

"I say, if you are going to help, then help. If you are going to change the tire, then change it. But if you are going to rob, then rob. If you are going to hurt, then hurt. If you are going to . . ."

The bear interrupted. "Rape?" he said.

"Shut up," said the leader. He gestured for Emery to go on, that he for one found Emery's words interesting and he was intent on listening.

"I'm sick of it," said Emery. "I've had as much of your clowning as I am going to. Either . . ."

"Inside," said the leader, gesturing toward the car door.

Emery did not answer. He stared as if he did not believe his ears. Larry took a step toward him. Spacing his words as if for a particularly stupid and stubborn person, he said, "Get—in—side. We will—fix—the flat. Get it?" He turned to the other two boys and then looked back at Emery. Very quickly he said, "The lady stays outside."

"Oh no," said Emery. He went to Frances and put his arm protectively about her shoulders. "Oh no," he repeated with finality. Larry went to the back of the car and began to rock it on the jack, back and forth, back and forth, with increasing tempo. He smiled sweetly, as if deeply engaged in the music of the rocking car. The bear began to move his hips and snap his fingers.

Emery pulled Frances farther away and then he turned back in fury to the boys. Frances put a restraining hand on his arm. His hands were locked in fists at his sides. She tightened her grip. She had thought the boys meant no great harm; but if Emery challenged them, would they be able to resist? What chance had a paunchy forty against three young bulls who were twenty and raging? Emery tugged at his arm but she held fast. Let them have their fun.

"Don't be a fool," she said. She pressed her body against his and forced him to move backward. They walked away from the car. She held his elbow and applied a gentling rhythmic pressure. She said, "They're just showing off. If you try to take them on, well . . ." She slipped her hand into his and they walked off hand in hand. Emery seemed blind and agonized.

"Christ!" he said. He stopped, forcing her to stop too.

She said, "They could easily rock the car off the jack. What could you do? You can't win. They could rock the car off the jack."

"Let them," said Emery. "I don't have to take their insolence."

She put her arms around him and leaned her head against his chest. His head strained over her shoulder, asserting himself at the boys. Silently the boys watched and waited for Emery's next move, to play out their game against him and to defeat him. They despised him and Emery knew it and Frances knew it. But she thought it was useless for him to try to remedy their opinion of him.

"I'm in it, too," she said. "You can't just decide by yourself to start a fight."

"Start a fight Christ!" said Emery. He put his hands on her shoulders to shove her aside, but she locked her arms around his back.

"Get in the car," she said. "Please. For my sake. You aren't a child, proving something. What would be gained?"

"I don't know, something, I don't know." His breath was staccato, like obstructed sobs. Abruptly the strain left him and he grew slack, surrendered. She knew he was ready, needing now only a bit more persuasion. She wondered briefly, had it all been a charade? his willingness to fight? She did not dwell on the thought nor did she commit herself to it, but it was there. Automatically she marshaled the opposing force: his tension, his anger, his self-respect, and, of course, her own unfortunate instinct to comprehend the seamiest motive of everyone. She said,

"For my sake. Think what might happen to me. Those stupid toughs. Bully-boys. Bulls. Animals. Do it for my sake. Get in the car."

She urged him toward the door, her arms still locked behind him, as if they were dancing. He stared over her shoulder at the silent boys, from time to time made as if to challenge them. At the door of the car, she released her hold on him. Hesitancy gripped him and then he folded into the back seat.

The bear and Larry began to change the tire. Frances leaned against the front fender and drew her light jacket tighter. She felt quite chilled, and as she looked at the sky it seemed to recede and she seemed to shrink. She was on a vast empty darkened desert. She was delicate and exposed in a senseless universe and she was mortal and alone. All else was diversion, and useless.

She became aware of a presence near her and she was at once her intact self again. The third boy, the leader, had come to stand beside her, leaning, as she did, against the fender.

"You're a tough one, ain't you, a real tough one," he said. Polishing his teeth with his tongue, he nodded his head and looked at her under lowered lids. "I like tough women. Not cheap: tough. Know something? You ought to pick on somebody your own size, not a little guy like that one." He motioned with his head toward the car. "I bet not once, not once, you been with a guy as tough as you are."

How absurd, Frances cried to herself, how awful, she cried, and momentarily her body seemed to open wide and to close and she felt a chill on her neck and a tremble. As if by signal the boy pushed off from the car and came to stand face to face with her. He put his hands on his hips, thumbs hooked into his belt. He rocked back and forth, back and forth, from the balls of his feet to his heels, swinging closer and closer to Frances. He was grotesque, and lewd, a caricature, obscene, threatening, appealing. And she was herself and tough.

"You filthy little animal!" she said. "Don't dare touch me! You fix the tire and then leave us alone, all of you."

The boy laughed hollowly. "Tough," he said, "see what I mean?" He moved away and as he walked past the other boys he said, "Fix the tire like the lady said and then git." He shook a cigarette from a pack and went on to his own car. The other boys bent back to work. Frances felt the back end of the car go down and she heard the trunk slam. They were finished. With the leader at the wheel and without speaking or acknowledging Frances and Emery, the boys got in their car. Whatever they had wanted, they either had or would never have. Grinding, spitting stones, blowing smoke and the stench of burning rubber, the car sped away.

"They're gone," said Frances.

Emery's muffled voice came to her. "I hope you're satisfied. I hope one time in your life you're satisfied."

She did not answer. She knew what he meant, or thought she did, but she did not know what the truth was. After a moment she got behind the wheel and started the car. Slowly she gained the roadway and set out for home. Once home, she would consider Emery. She would help him. She would restore him with a final drink, with ice and coldness. She would persuade him, and herself, that really nothing important to either of them had been at stake. She would help him to discover the comedy of it all and to laugh. Slowly, between them, they would begin to build a little anecdote to relate to friends and to reduce the episode to dust. And in the darkness they would soothe each other's frail raw nakedness to a forgiving sleep. When they got home. But for now, as Emery wept silently in the back seat, she drove the car and she was exhilarated.

LEO LITWAK was born in Detroit and lives in San Francisco. He teaches at San Francisco State College. Mr. Litwak's stories have appeared in numerous periodicals and anthologies; his novel, *TO THE HANGING GARDENS*, was published in 1964; and his latest, *IN O'BRIEN'S HOUSE*, will be published in 1969.

In Shock

THE war against Germany took a bad turn; several divisions along the Belgian border were overrun; replacements were needed. So finally my time had come. What a relief to be drafted. I was ready for war. They took me from a college campus where I had been allowed to practice liberal arts and sent me to a camp in South Carolina.

I had no talent in the medical line but they made me an aid man. I wore red cross brassards pinned at each shoulder. My steel helmet was marked with red crosses on a white field. I bore two kits suspended from a shoulder harness, anchored by a pistol belt. My kits held gauze bandages, ammonia capsules, small compresses, belly compresses, bandage scissors, merthiolate, sulfa packets, sodium amytol tablets, a hypodermic needle for blisters, tags for the wounded and morphine syrettes for shock.

Each day after morning calisthenics, we sat baking in a rubble field, dusted by South Carolina clay while noncoms lectured us on the aid man business. I was told all that might happen—from blisters to amputations—and the proper responses. For blisters draw the fluid, clean with merthiolate, cushion with gauze. For amputations, apply a tourniquet, cover the stump, inject morphine to prevent shock. Get the patient in shock position and keep him warm. I learned the venereal diseases from clap to lymphogranuloma inguinale. Bare literacy was an achievement for most. I alone volunteered the right answers. But no one was fooled. The least literate of them could draw blood, give injections, apply splints.

I had no talent for it. I couldn't even do a proper job bandaging a compliant buddy simulating a broken clavicle. Instead of a neat mummy, hand strapped to the chest, the upper swathed in two-inch gauze, there was a tangle of loose folds, undone by the first movement.

Sergeant Carrol, unstringing my mannequin then rewrapping with flourishes of gauze, asked me, "How the hell did you ever get into this outfit?"

Dewey Carrol was a sack of beef with mechanic's hands, little eyes in a pumpkin face, his belt notched beneath a swollen paunch. He knew the whole repertory of bandaging. He could wrap any part of a man. He had deft fingers and a fumbling mouth. For lymphogranuloma inguinale he had to say "blue balls."

I was bigger than most. I had good shoulders and could do fifty push-ups. I ran the obstacle course on my own time in order to be ready for the day when I'd meet the dead and dying. But I showed small promise as a medic. My hands wouldn't serve me. We practiced giving each other injections, angling the needle for the different shots—subcutaneous, intramuscular, intravenous. I didn't flinch when my novice buddy punctured my arm. When I jabbed in return I pierced a vein and stained his forearm with a bruise.

Dewey Carrol said, "With hands like that you got a tough job eating breakfast. Too bad you can't work with your tongue. Then you'd be champ." I laughed with him, agreeing to appear as a clown.

Dewey wasn't alone in taking that line. The other GI's spotted me as an eager-beaver college boy, trying to get ahead with big talk in lieu of physical grace. They were as suspicious of me as if I were queer. Yet I could take as much punishment as the best of them. I never fell out on a march. I made good time around the obstacle course. I could bear to look at anything. I was even ready to look at dead men. I knew that I could make myself very still and cold, and so long as I didn't stir nothing would offend me. If they didn't ask my help I'd be fine. I could always trust my mouth to distract others from my blunders.

Joe Witty didn't have to rely on his mouth. He was the other college boy in the outfit, a premed student from the University of Michigan. He was a tall, wiry, Irish boy, long-faced, with a hard chin. He had no intention of allowing anyone to treat him as a clown. He volunteered no answers. He respected the laconic tradition of our American knighthood. He only offered his judgment when it was asked. And then he was authoritative. He was helped by a fine baritone voice whose tone was more convincing than any good argument. When he took over drill we marched for him. He was aimed for Officer Candidate School after basic training. He was a gentleman private who condescended to noncoms. Dewey Carrol scraped low for Witty, recognizing future brass and preparing the ground for handouts. Witty meant to rise and he kept the men in line. He didn't want screwups in any outfit he was in. Anyone who lagged in preparing for inspection got reamed by Witty. He looked like a fighter. He had clever hands. I admired Witty even though he steered shy of me. He was disgusted, I suppose, by my fumbling. Perhaps he didn't want anyone to confuse us. He wanted it made clear that he was a different sort of collegian.

I wasn't liked. That I knew. I didn't know how much until one day, after a speed march, we lined up naked in the latrine, waiting a turn at the shower room. Nine miles in two hours, up a dirt road, one hundred degrees of a naked sun, every man lobster red, first striding in cadence, then jogging, beginning to gasp early in the game, wobbling under the burden of full packs, trailed by an ambulance that inched up on stragglers and accumulated the fallen. I pushed for my shower, grumbling like the rest, but pleased to have outsuffered the whole lot. We called to those already in the shower to hurry it up. Joe Witty, about to enter the shower room, heard only my voice and it triggered his revulsion.

"Step in here and I'll kick the shit out of you."

I followed him into the shower room. It was steamy. We slid along duckboards. Witty shoved me against the wall and hauled back. Then he dropped his fist.

"Why get in trouble over you?"

He said *you* as though I were vermin. When he hauled back to slug me my arms were numb at my sides. I stayed in the shower room after he left. None of the boys looked at me. When I came out Witty was drying himself with a khaki towel.

"Let's go behind the barracks, Witty."

"I'm not getting in trouble over you." He again said *you* in that contemptuous tone.

"You pushed me."

He left the latrine. "He won't fight," I said, but no one was interested in my side of the argument.

I was so numb that if we'd have gone beyond the barracks I could only have pawed him.

I went to his bed. He was in khaki shorts, putting on khaki socks. He was lean with ropy muscles.

"You pushed me."

"So what?"

"Fight me, Witty."

"Anytime. In the gym. With gloves."

If I'd answered a challenge that way, they'd have put me down as yellow. But in the case of Witty it was just a knight refusing to credit a knave. They were pleased by my humiliation, no mistaking that. It was evident in blank looks when I hunted for support.

I had a friend, Jason Diedrich, a clerk in Headquarters Company. We met in the music room of the post USO. He introduced me to his crew, three Harvard boys, also with Headquarters. They maintained a bookish world in their off-hours. I read *Nightwood* to share their vocabulary. It was a book of loonies. A wise man crawled in woman's clothing. Keening ladies embraced. A queer book, a queer crowd, but I wasn't put off by that queerness. With everything about to crack under that Carolina sun, the book only seemed a foreshadowing.

I went to Jason for relief. "My impulses aren't good," I told him. "Why didn't I swing? I couldn't move. I stood there as if I couldn't be insulted. By the time it gets through to me it's too late. I'm numb."

"Get out of it, Arthur," Jason advised me. He spoke with precision. He deliberated before he spoke. His voice was high-pitched. He wore spectacles, a raw, lumpy face perched on a long throat. I was impressed by his calm. I never found him short of advice. He looked brand-new, only half-made, hair just beginning to sprout on his chin and upper lip. Yet he claimed an ancient tradition. He had a monkish faith in the liberal arts. His model was a Frère Lupus Servatus who preserved Ovid despite a shortage of parchment for more pious work. This monk faked allegiance to boors in order to save what he loved. And Jason, too, wanted to save what he loved. He lapsed into protective shock during the working day, appearing servile and unimportant. After hours he attended to the

French symbolist poets. He read Baudelaire, Rimbaud, Valéry, Mallarmé.

Jason invited me to join their otherwordly retreat at head-quarters. He had pull. I, too, could become a clerk. They had a cozy thing going. They had each other during the day. They had their own bedroom in the HQ barracks. To Jason, the war was a holding operation, an intermission between his junior and senior years at Harvard.

I'd invested too much in the war to settle for anything less than combat. I'd so often fantasied my ordeal that to stop now, before anything was proved, would have left me dreamy.

I kept my eye on Witty. He, too, flaunted being a college boy but somehow he didn't antagonize. He led the current events dis-cussion in our Information and Education classes. He rallied us against the traitor, John L. Lewis. Those goldbrick miners were striking for a larger share of the pie while we were stuck in the army getting sixty-five a month. Those slackers were making hay with the girls. That was how Witty, the college boy, saw current events. He lived in Grosse Pointe, Michigan, a fancy place. His father was a big-shot Detroit surgeon. Witty had never worked a day in his life. About women he was very collegiate, copping feels at USO dances. And yet he lectured these red-necks and slum kids about what a rotten deal it was to be deprived the earnings of sweaty labor and other men's wives. He took the words right out of Dewey Carrol's mouth. Dewey Carrol accepted the word of the nobleman. He didn't give any credit to frauds, though, and he clearly spotted me as a fraud.

"You sure do talk, don't you, boy?"

That shrewd peasant. He understood that my gabbiness dis-guised a lack of grace.

I saw Witty at a USO dance go straight for a hostess who was officer material. He took charge, a confident dancer. He made her dip with him. He swung her out and back. He ended by forcing her arms behind, locking her hands, so that her breasts were shoved against him. He was polished in everything he tried, in contrast to me who couldn't hit a man, shoot a man, bandage or inoculate a man. I was afraid to touch. I knew that I could endure being hit. I didn't want to make the first move though.

Dewey Carrol went to Charleston once a month. "To get my gun off," he explained. That was the medicine Dewey prescribed

for growing boys. He took Witty with him one weekend. On their
return Witty informed the barracks that anyone who couldn't get
laid in Charleston didn't have man's equipment. The procedure
was to go to a hotel where the bellhops pimped.

So I went to Charleston on a weekend pass. I visited the Citadel.
I went to the Battery and looked out on Fort Sumter. I walked
through streets garlanded with filigree ironwork. I took a room in a
hotel and asked the bellhop for a woman.

"Ten bucks," he said.

"That's too much." He was my age, a shrimp who lacked a chin
and was obviously shrewd enough to avoid the draft. He studied
me as if he could read my competence. I didn't want to allow him
any advantage.

He asked how much I was willing to pay. I told him five dollars.

"I'll see what I can do."

I lay down to kill time and it was more than time that was
killed. I could feel the freeze coming over me, the loss of feeling in
my skin, in my limbs, numb in the head, all my senses ducking
down to my belly and cowering there. I lay in my shorts and saw
myself shrivel up. I felt nothing when I touched. I stayed awake all
night but no one came. Next morning I left for camp.

The insult was unavenged and that made me fair game for anyone in the bullying line. There was a chunky ambulance driver
named Kish. Going over the obstacle course we climbed a wall and
he gave me the hip. Then crawling through a concrete tube he
butted me with his Neanderthal head.

"What gives?" I asked.

"Move, creep."

There was a tug of war. Kish was on the opposite team. Our
anchor man fell and the other boys gave way and we slipped
toward the ditch. Then I dug in. I held against their whole team. I
held against Kish and three others. They couldn't haul me over.
When the rest of my team recovered we pulled Kish and his boys
into the ditch.

That night after lights were out I went to Kish's bed and sat
down. I said, "Take hold."

"What do you mean?"

"Get any grip you want."

He grabbed me from behind. I braced and heaved and threw

him over my head and sprawled on him and wrapped my arm around his throat and squeezed until he surrendered.

"You're as strong as any man in this outfit," he said. "You don't have to take crap from Witty."

We were told that when a man's in shock, his face is grey, he's in a cold sweat, his pulse is fluttery, his lips purple. The blood leaves the brain and collects in the solar plexus and elsewhere. Blood vessels collapse. The brain brooks no starving and will perish from the insult. Lift the legs, lower the head. Give plasma to raise the pressure in the veins.

I took the challenge on Witty's terms and we faced each other in a corner of the gym, wearing sixteen-ounce gloves, naked save for GI shorts. I shivered. The blood was in my belly. There was cold sweat on my face despite the heat. The gym was a great shed with naked steel beams, sun dazzling through clerestories. We were beneath an elevated running track. In an opposite corner were mats for wrestlers and tumblers. Several basketball games occupied the center of the gym. Balls pounded, shoes thudded, players called for balls. I heard basket rims vibrate from missed shots.

We circled each other, alone in our corner.

I launched my arms. He jabbed. Wild swings. We circled, clinched, pounded backs. I held tight and gasped. Just before the whistle which summoned us to retreat he hit me hard in the eye with the lacings of his glove and for the first time I felt something and swung with purpose, rapping him on the shoulder, then winding around his neck. It ended in a clinch.

"Okay," Witty said, "it's time."

We didn't shake hands. We walked to the locker room without speaking, both of us breathless.

After the shower I looked in the mirror and saw that he had blacked my eye.

"It's not enough," I told him.

"Anytime you want more," he said.

"Now."

"It's time for retreat."

My eye got worse and by the time we stood retreat I was marked for everyone to see.

"It's not enough," I told Jason. "I didn't lose. He didn't hurt me. I gave as good as I got. But I'm marked."

Jason told me to stop being foolish. "He's not worthy of you,

Arthur. Don't play his game. It's unnecessary to expose yourself."
Why did I resist, he wondered, joining my own at Headquarters?

But I didn't want to become queer. I wanted revenge for my eye.
Kish who had learned the strength of my arms and so was a friend
offered more congenial advice. "Don't go to a gym. Just clobber
the stuck-up bastard."

Dewey Carrol stuck me on extra KP and when I complained he
said, "We're changing the duty assignments. We're starting at the
end of the alphabet." Then why not Witty? They were going to
send Witty to a surgical technician's school for a few weeks. Basic
training was a waste of time for so talented a kid.

When I got back from KP, I saw Witty entertaining a crowd
around his bed. I pushed through.

"What a shame you're leaving, Witty. I hate to see you go. I'll
miss you."

"To hell with you," he said, putting the usual stress of contempt
on the *you*.

"You're leaving with clear eyes. I wanted a chance to fix that."

Witty jumped up. "Here's your chance now. Do something."

"In back of the barracks."

He led the way out, swaggering for the benefit of the crowd that
followed us. They were his partisans. "Finish the job this time,
Joe." "Wipe the snot off his face." "Get the other eye, Joe." "Don't
forget to shut his mouth for good."

I was bowled over by their ill wishes.

We were stopped at the door by Carrol. He told us to take our
trouble to the gym or off the post. He would personally like to see
me smeared but being a noncom he had to forgo that pleasure.

Witty was steamed up by their encouragement. "Alright," he said.
"Tomorrow. In town. After retreat, you clown. See this?" He held
his fist close to my face. "I'm going to shove it down your throat."

"It suits me." I was numb again. They were as offended by me
as though they'd stumbled across the root of evil.

Kish said to me afterwards, "You sure don't have friends in this
outfit." He excepted himself. He was also a foulup, a clumsy, ill-
educated loser, an obvious sucker for any malevolent noncom. He
was relieved to have another like himself. He saw my defects
clearly enough.

"You always knock," he told me.

"I'm not the only one to bitch."

But Kish told me that when I bitched the tone was wrong. "You got a way of getting under a guy's skin."

"Like the other night in the PX you're telling me about gas engines. It turns out you don't even know how to drive."

"That's just high school physics."

"And speaking up for niggers."

"Why should we listen to Witty? He's no authority."

"He's no nigger-lover either." Kish had my interests at heart and ticked off my faults and I was convinced. When I thought of meeting Witty the following night I experienced that familiar retreat of my blood to the sanctuary in my belly.

I hunted for Jason to tell him to get me into Headquarters. The Headquarters gang was in the music room, playing the *Liebestod*. They weren't bigots and saved all traditions irrespective of race, creed and nationality. They saved the Kraut, Wagner. They were also interested in African art.

Jason was delighted with my decision. He dreamed of the day when we'd have enough power to unmask ourselves and flail the peasants. I was surprised at his venom. The idea of Dewey Carrol particularly excited Jason. That frail boy was a precocious hater. His voice became shrill, his body stiff when he thought of the beasts who ranked above us. They should be groveling at our feet. He was only twenty years old but knew already how to manipulate authority by pretending to be obsequious. He despised officers and gentlemen. He favored the black heroes of literature such as Iago. He called Lear a gassy old man and praised the bastard Edmund.

Jason's father was a butcher by trade, a taciturn, abstracted man who came alive in bursts of violence. He once accused Jason's sister of being a whore and pursued her with a cleaver. She jumped from the second floor window and shattered her ankles. That butcher didn't trifle with Jason though. Jason was delicate but ferocious. A Harvard scholarship rescued him from his family.

He dreamed of a day when our kind would be able to force a redress of grievances. As for now, he was willing to settle for invisibility. We had a vantage point in the music room from which we could see each other. That was enough.

"Get me in, Jason," I told him. "I don't want any war."

The next day, while I was out on rifle range duty, Jason got the transfer underway. The rifle range was a lazy job for a medic. I took off my kits and lay under a tree while the men fired at targets. When they got up from the firing line they staggered. The heat and noise were stunning. On the right was Battle Village, surrounded by mine fields and barbed wire. Men wiggled beneath the barbed wire. Machine guns fired overhead. Dynamite blasts simulated artillery. Afterwards the GI's charged the mocked-up village, firing at false fronts. Dummies in windows represented snipers. Immobilized vintage tanks gave bazooka teams a target.

With these cozy sounds of battle as background, I sent my dreams ahead to scout the terrain of war. I dreamed of what would happen if someone should cry, "Aid man!" I'd hook up my pistol belt, run toward the wounded man, dodging shellfire, my hands on my kits to keep them from flapping. That action was imaginable. I could face shellfire. When I reached the wounded man, I'd look. And then what? What if it was a chest wound, the cavity penetrated, the lungs collapsed? Plug up the hole. With what? What if the bandages didn't fit? What if an artery were severed? Walk away and let him die. I didn't have the knack of finding pulses or pressure points. My hands lost their feeling. Use a tourniquet. A tourniquet tied too long meant gangrene. Any move of mine risked another man's life. I was unfit for that responsibility. Let them send for Witty or Dewey Carrol. They'd plug up the hole. They'd stop the bleeding. They had sure hands. After retreat those sure hands of Joe Witty's would clobber me. Then I'd withdraw to the music room and listen to Wagner and hold out till the end of the war as a clerk. Everyone would be better off.

Someone shrieked. "Aid Man!" Then again, "AID MAN!" I was almost asleep and dreamy and had imagined just this call, just this screechy, desperate wail and I didn't jump up, but turned on an elbow and looked toward Battle Village. The dynamite blasts had stopped. The machine gun had stopped. I saw a GI running across the fields, tumbling in shell holes, running with wild arms. He waved to me. "AID MAN!" Raging, as though I'd done something terrible. I shivered. I stood numb as he ran up to me. He shouted in my face, "AID MAN!" He grabbed my shoulders, his mouth agape, heaving air, his eyes big, his pupils dilated, his face grey, a trim platoon Sergeant from C Company with a fox face, one of the permanent cadre who had been to Ranger school and, it was said, could jog fifteen miles without showing the strain.

"A man got his leg blowed off. Let's go."

I woke the ambulance driver. We drove across the field toward Battle Village.

A squad leader had tripped into a hole just as a dynamite charge exploded. The Sergeant said, "His leg's off."

"Off?"

"His foot's in the shoe."

The ambulance launched off ruts, slammed down on the field, the carriage groaning. The ambulance driver, saucer-eyed behind his spectacles, his teeth clicking, hit every furrow and we bounced high. My kits slammed my thighs. Men were clustered at the side of a shell hole. We almost drove into them.

A lieutenant crouched over the screaming man who was covered with a blanket. They stepped aside for me. I saw a shoe some distance away. I pulled back the blanket and looked. He reared and bucked. Gone at the calf. The skin pulled back up the leg, showing the shreds of flesh. A hot, shitty smell. The skin above was peppered. A tourniquet was tied above the knee. I untied the tourniquet and blood spurted on the blanket. I could see raw flesh, gristle, the artery gulping, the veins pinched shut. I retied the tourniquet. No spurt of blood now. A slow welling. The scissors came out and I cut away the pant leg. The syrette came out. I thrust the plunger into the hollow needle and broke the seal. I jammed the needle into his thigh and squeezed it out like toothpaste. I bent down and got a good smell of the stump. He was under my hand. I could feel the muscles jumping. My hand was slimy where I'd touched the blanket.

We lifted him on a stretcher into the ambulance.

The ambulance driver went fast, hitting everything. I tried to figure out how to cover the stump. When I raised the leg to get the bandage-roll underneath he screamed. I yelled at the driver to slow down.

I took out a belly compress and placed it over the stump and looped the strings around the upper calf.

He screeched, "My balls!"

I cut away the pants and looked at his balls. Darts of powder peppered the sac and the surrounding flesh.

I told him, "You're alright."

They were waiting for us at the post hospital with a stretcher on wheels. Four orderlies carried him from the ambulance. A white smocked doctor lifted the belly compress as they wheeled him toward emergency.

"I gave him morphine," I called after them. "An eighth of a grain." They were already inside when I remembered that I had forgotten to fill out the tag. Describe the wound, its treatment, give your name, rank, serial number and medical organization.

The ambulance driver said, "You did great."

We returned to the rifle range but the day was finished.

They had heard back at battalion. The lieutenant who tied the tourniquet had called to praise me.

Our CO, a southern doctor, slapped my back. "Nice going, boy."

Kish wanted to know what happened to the foot.

It was all so dreamy. I'd made him scream in the ambulance. The belly compress hadn't been neatly tied: I looped the free strings over his leg and fumbled with the knot. A lousy job. And yet they were awed by my audacity. I had looked at the stump and wasn't altered by the sight.

"I'm ready," I told Joe Witty after retreat.

He invited me to the PX for a beer. "I understand you did a great job out there." He was boyish and charming. "I hear the leg was off. Entirely off. That takes a lot of guts, Artie. Nice going, buddy." He tapped my arm with his fist.

"We were going to fight."

"Listen," he said, his Irish face ruddy with sincerity, "I owe you an apology." His hand reached for mine and before I could prevent it, my hand engaged his.

I had a bloody field jacket. That was good enough credentials for Joe Witty. I was a bona fide medic, a soldier. What had been put down as big talk was now reevaluated. I was to be accepted on different terms.

Witty even became collegiate with me, spoke of campus life, wanted to sing an old Ann Arbor tune. This hard-chinned Irish boy was crammed to the brim with nostalgia. "Remember the old P-Bell on Saturday nights, Artie?" He talked as if we owned a common experience.

What a disappointment this moment I'd dreamed of in the PX. The dream of a villain had owned my fantasies. My desperate condition was remedied by something so trivial as a good word and a slap on the back. We drank beer in the PX and Witty advertised me as a credit to the battalion. He was no more adequate as a friend than as a villain. I had allowed him to black my eye. I had been numb in his presence. And now it was clear that he was only a fool.

"You got to pay for my eye," I told him. I interrupted him at his mellowest. "It's after retreat. I'm ready."

He reached for my hand again. "Listen, old buddy, I'm really and truly sorry about that. It was an accident."

"But there it is, Witty. An eye for an eye."

He told me that it had been accident. A lucky punch. "It was more of a backhand than a punch. I didn't even hit you right."

I pushed Witty against the counter of the PX. The men circled us. Someone yelled, "Break it up."

"Hey now," Witty said, "what gives?" But he didn't raise his hands to protect himself. I hauled back my fist but couldn't hit.

"And who wants to get in trouble over *you?*" I asked.

He came after me, caught my arm. "I know you're sore," he said. "You have every right to be. How can I convince you that I *really* am sorry? *Really.*" And in front of the men we shook hands again.

He was a coward and a fool. Like myself.

I had squeezed a bloody stump and vanquished Joe Witty. What achievement was that? Still, I didn't need to withdraw to the music room. I had earned the right to follow my dreams into combat and there confront the dying and wait for my own death to swoop down on me, hoping that in the penultimate moment I'd come out of shock and scream bloody murder.

I can't begin to tell you what a disappointment it was.

LEONARD MICHAELS lives in Berkeley and teaches at the University of California. This is his second O. Henry award story. He has twice won the *Massachusetts Review* Quill Award for Fiction, an award for fiction from the National Foundation on the Arts and Humanities, and presently holds an appointment at the Creative Arts Institute of the University of California. His stories have appeared also in *The Paris Review, Transatlantic Review,* and *New American Review,* and a collection of his stories entitled *GOING PLACES* is being published in 1969. Mr. Michaels is married and has one child.

Manikin

AT THE university she met a Turk who studied physics and spoke foreigner's English which in every turn expressed the unnatural desire to seize idiom and force it to speak exclusively for himself. He worked nights as a writer, summers on construction gangs, and shot pool and played bridge with fraternity boys in order to make small change, and did whatever else he could to protect and supplement his university scholarship, living a mile from campus in a room without sink or closet or decent heating and stealing most of the food he ate, and when the University Hotel was robbed it was the Turk who had done it, an act of such speed the night porter couldn't say when it happened or who rushed in from the street to bludgeon him so murderously he took it in a personal way. On weekends the Turk tutored mediocrities in mathematics and French. . . .

He picked her up at her dormitory, took her to a movie, and later, in his borrowed Chevrolet, drove her into the countryside and with heavy, crocodilean sentences, mutters and shrugs, communicated his agony amid the alien corn. She attended with quick, encouraging, little nods and stared as if each word crept visibly before her face, and she felt power gathering sensuously in their difficult motion as he leaned toward her and with lips still laboring words, made indelible sense, raping her, forcing her to variations of what she never heard of though she was a great reader of avant-garde novels and philosophical commentaries on the modern pre-dicament. . . .

In the cracking, desiccated leather of the Chevrolet she was susceptible to a distinction between life and sensibility and dropped, like Leda by the swan, squirming, arching, so as not to be touched again, inadvertently, as he poked behind the cushions for the ignition key. She discovered it pulling up her pants and, because it required intelligent speech inconsistent with her moan-ing, could not bring it to his attention; nor would she squat, winding about in her privates, though she hated seeing him waste time bunched up twisting wires under the dashboard.

Despite her wild compulsion to talk, and despite the frightened, ravenous curiosity of her dormitory clique whom she awakened by sobbing over their beds, Melanie was not able to say clearly what finished happening half an hour ago. She remembered the Turk suddenly abandoned English and raved at her in furious Turkish, and told them about that and about the obscene tattoo flashing on his chest when she ripped his shirt open, and that he stopped the car on a country road and there was a tall hedge, maples, syca-mores, and a railroad track nearby, and a train was passing, passing, and passing, and beyond it, her moans, and later an animal trotting quickly on the gravel, and then, with no discontinuity, the motor starting its cough and retch and a cigarette waving at her mouth already lighted as if the worst were over and someone had started thinking of her in another way.

The lights of the university town appeared and she smoked the cigarette as the car went down among them through the empty streets, through the residential area of the ethical, economic com-munity and twisted into the main street passing store after store. She saw an armless, naked manikin and felt like that, or like a thalidomide baby, all torso and short circuited, and then they were into the streets around campus which were narrow and shaky with trees, and neither of them said a word as he shifted gears, speeding and slowing and working the car through a passage irregular and yet steady, and enclosed within a greater passage as tangible as the internal arcs of their skulls. At the dormitory he stopped the car. She got out running.

Quigley, Berkowitz and Sax could tell that Melanie Green had been assaulted with insane and exotic cruelty: there were finger-prints on her cheeks the color of tea stains and her stockings hung about her ankles like Hamlet's when he exposed himself to Ophelia and called her a whore. So they sucked cigarettes and urged her to phone the Dean of Women, the police and the immigration authorities, as if disseminating the story among representatives of order would qualify it toward annihilation or render it accessible to a punitive response consistent with national foreign policy. Though none of them saw positive value in Melanie's experience it was true, nevertheless, in no future conversation would she complain about being nineteen and not yet discovered by the right man, as it happened, to rape with. Given her face and legs, *that* had always seemed sick and irritating crap, and in the pits of their minds where there were neither words nor ideas, but only raging morality, they took the Turk as poetic justice, fatal male, and measure for measure. Especially since he lived now in those pits vis-à-vis Melanie's father, a bearded rabbi with tear bags. "What if your father knew?" asked Quigley, making a gesture of anxious speculation, slender hands turned out flat, palms up, like a Balinese dancer. Melanie felt annoyed, but at least Quigley was there, sticking out her hands, and could be relied on always to be sym-bolic of whatever she imagined the situation required.

She didn't tell the rabbi, the Dean of Women, police, or im-migration authorities, and didn't tell Harry Stone, her fiancé, with whom she had never had all-the-way sexual intercourse because he feared it might destroy the rhythm of his graduate work in Classics. But once, during Christmas vacation, she flew east to visit him and while standing on a stairway in Cambridge, after dinner and cognac, he let her masturbate him and then lay in bed beside her, brood-ing, saying very little except, "I feel like Seymour," and she answer-ing, "I'm sorry." Quigley, Berkowitz and Sax called him "Harry the fairy," but never in the presence of Melanie who read them his letters, brilliantly exquisite and full of ruthless wit directed at everything, and the girls screamed and could hardly wait till he got his degree and laid her. "It'll be made of porcelain," said Sax, and Melanie couldn't refute the proposition (though the girls always told her everything they did with their boyfriends and she owed them the masturbation story) because they were too hot for physiology and wouldn't listen to the whole story, wouldn't hear its tone or any of its music. They were critical, sophisticated girls and didn't dig mood, didn't savor things. They were too fast, too eager to get the point.

She didn't tell the rabbi or any other authority about the rape, and wouldn't dream of telling Harry Stone because he tended to become irrationally jealous and, like homosexual Othello, would assume she had gone out with armies of men aside from the Turk, which wasn't true. The Turk had been a casual decision, the only one of its kind, determined by boredom with classes and dateless weekends, and partly by a long distance phone call to Harry Stone in the middle of the night when she needed his voice and he expressed irritation at having been disturbed while translating a difficult passage of Thucydides for a footnote in his dissertation. Furthermore the Turk was interesting-looking, black eyes, a perfect white bite of teeth between a biggish nose and a cleft chin, and because he was pathetic in his tortuous English going out with him seemed merely an act of charity indifferently performed, and it was confirmed as such when he arrived in the old Chevrolet and suggested a cowboy movie. He held the door open for her, which she could never expect Harry to do, and he tried to talk to her. To her, she felt—though it was clear that his effort to talk depended very much on her effort to listen.

She went to parties on the two weekends following the rape and sat in darkened rooms while a hasheesh pipe went around. She said things too deep for syntax and giggled hysterically, and in the intimate delirium of faces and darkness asked how one might get in touch with an abortionist if, per chance, one needed one. She didn't talk about the rape but remembered the Turk had held her chin and she felt guilty but resistless and saw that his eyes didn't focus and that, more than anything, lingered in her nerves, like birds screaming and inconsummate. She asked her clique about the signs of pregnancy, then asked herself if she were peeing more than usual. It seemed to spear down very hot and hard and longer than before, but she ascribed it to sphincters loosened upon the violent dissolution of the veil between vaginal post and lintel. When she asked the girls about an abortionist they laughed maniacally at the idea that any of them might know such a person, but, one at a time, appeared in her room to whisper names and telephone numbers and tell her about the different techniques and the anaesthetic she might expect if the man were considerate or brave enough to give her one. "They're afraid of the cops," said Sax, a tough number from Chicago who had been knocked up twice in her freshman year. "They want you out of the office as soon as possible."

Harry surprised her by coming to town during his intercession break and she was so glad to see him she trembled. She introduced him to her house mother and her clique and he ate dinner with her in the dormitory the first night. The next day he went to classes with her and that evening they ate in the best restaurant in town, which wasn't nearly as good as some Harry knew of in the east but it was pretty good, and then they walked in the midwestern twilight, watching swallows, listening to night hawks whistle, and she felt an accumulation of sympathy in the minutes and the hours which became an urge, a possibility, and then a strong need to tell him, but she chatted mainly about her clique and said, "Quigley has funny nipples and Berkowitz would have a wonderful figure except for her thighs which have no character. I love Sax's figure. It's like a skinny boy's." Harry made an indifferent face and shrugged in his tweeds, but quick frowns twitched after the facts and she went on, encouraged thus, going on, to go on and on. In his hotel room they had necking and writhing, then lay together breathless, tight, indeterminate, until he began talking about his dissertation. "A revolution in scholarship. The vitiation of many traditional assumptions. They say I write uncommonly well." She told him about the rape. He sat up with words about the impossibility of confidence, the betrayal of expectations, the end of things. He was amazed, he said, the world didn't break and the sky fall down. As far as he was concerned the ceremony of innocence was drowned. While he packed she rubbed her knees and stared at him. He noticed her staring and said, "I don't like you."

Wanda Chung was always in flight around corners, down hallways, up stairs and into bathrooms, and never spoke to people unless obliged to do so and then with fleeting, terrified smiles and her eyes somewhere else. She appeared at no teas or dances, received no calls and no boys at the reception desk, and Melanie and her clique gradually came to think of her as the most interesting girl in the dormitory. One afternoon after classes they decided to go to her room and introduce themselves. She wasn't in so they entered the room and while waiting for her casually examined her closet which was packed with dresses and coats carrying the labels of good stores in San Francisco. Under her bed there were boxes of new blouses and sweaters, and they discovered her desk drawers were crammed with candy and empty candy wrappers. They left her room, never returned, and never again made any effort to introduce themselves to her, but Wanda, who for months had harbored a secret yearning to meet Melanie, decided, the day after Harry Stone left town, to go to Melanie's room and present herself: "I am Wanda Chung. I live downstairs. I found this fountain pen. Could it be yours?" She bought a fountain pen and went to Melanie's room and an instant after she knocked at the door she forgot her little speech and her desire to meet Melanie. The door gave way at the vague touch of her knuckles and started opening as if Wanda herself had taken the knob and turned it with the intention of getting into the room and stealing something, which is how she saw it, standing there as the door unbelievably, remorselessly, opened, sucking all motion and feeling out of her limbs and making her more and more thief in the possible eyes of anyone coming along. And then, into her dumb rigidity, swayed naked feet like bell clappers. She saw Melanie Green hanging by the neck, her pelvis twitching. Wanda dashed to the stairs, down to her room, and locked herself inside. She ate candy until she puked in her lap and fell asleep. . . .

When the Turk read about the suicide he said in a slow, sick voice, "She loved me." He got drunk and stumbled through the streets looking for a fight, but bumping strangers and firing clams of spit at their feet wasn't sufficiently provocative, given his debauched and fiercely miserable appearance, to get himself punched or cursed or even shoved a little. He ended the night in a scrubby field tearing at an oak tree with his fingernails, rolling in its roots, hammering grass, cursing the sources of things until, in a shy, gentle way, Melanie drifted up out of the dew. He refused to acknowledge her presence but then couldn't tolerate being looked at in silence and yelled at her in furious Turkish. She came closer. He seized her in his arms and they rolled together in the grass until he found himself screaming through his teeth because, however much of himself he lavished on her, she was dead.

ANNE TYLER was born in Minnesota in 1941, but spent most of her life in North Carolina. Her two novels, *IF MORNING EVER COMES* and *THE TIN CAN TREE*, were published in 1964 and 1965, and her short stories have appeared widely. She now lives in Baltimore, Maryland with her husband and two small daughters.

The Common Courtesies

ALL during May, Miss Lorna sat on her front porch eating Sunshine biscuits. She kept the package in her lap, and while her fingers fumbled among the cellophane, she stared straight ahead, unblinking, watching the cars that slid past the house. Her face was the kind that had melted with age. It ran in downward lines toward her triple chin, and the sheer weight of her body seemed to drag at the corners of her mouth and at her eyes, which were small brown points behind tunnels of webbed skin. Although she didn't leave the porch, she wore crepe-soled walking shoes every day and heavy-duty stockings with crooked seams. On her head was a visored cap made of nylon net. One of her neighbors said she looked like Andy Devine in a golfing costume.

The Sunshine biscuits were brought out to her by Ida Donner, the cleaning woman. Several times a day Miss Lorna would call, "I-*duh?*" and there would come Ida, loping flat-footed across the porch and waving a pack of biscuits as if she had been waiting all this time just behind the screen. "Miss Lorna," she would say, "you ought not to be *staying* out here in this sun. Haven't I told you to go on inside?" Ida was colored, but her heart was in the right place. With her, Miss Lorna knew where she stood. "No, Ida, I thank you," she would tell her. "I know you mean well, but I am having to keep a watch over my health." Then Ida would shake her head and go back inside, and Miss Lorna would return to her own thoughts.

Miss Lorna's chair was made of wicker, splintered and darkened with age. It was the only chair she would sit in. Last year her husband, Mr. Billy, had given her a reclining Strato-Lounger for her birthday, but she had never used it—not even on the night he gave it to her, with the circle of guests crowding in around her and the birthday cake blazing a halo just beneath her chin. "Why, thank you, Mr. Billy," she had said. "That's mighty thoughtful of you." But she had remained in the wicker chair, with its gracefully curving arms grown ragged at the ends from her fidgety fingernails and its fan-shaped back towering high above her. Hawaiian-style, she called it. Beneath her weight the legs had spraddled outward, wider and wider, year by year, lowering her gradually to the ground. Miss Lorna didn't care. She took the chair with her wherever she went—to the porch, to the dinner table, to the bedroom where she sat undressing in the dark. She took it to Carolina Beach every July and to all her acquaintances and relations when she went to call. Mr. Billy would load it in the back of the car for her. "Miss Lorna, I just don't *see*," he told her every time. And then he went and bought her that reclining Strato-Lounger. "That's mighty thoughtful of you," she had said, "but I believe I'll just sit here, thank you." After that she blew the candles out, and her daughter handed her the silver-plated cake knife.

That May, which she spent sitting on the porch from breakfast to bedtime with the Sunshine biscuits in her lap, the seat of her chair began to give way. It made a splintering sound whenever she shifted her weight. "That's the chair making that noise," she told Ida. "Ida, you're the only one I can turn to, and that's the truth of it. What will I do? If I tell Mr. Billy my chair is breaking, he'll throw it in the trash. What will I do?"

"Miss Lorna, *you* know he wouldn't do that," Ida said. But the next afternoon she brought a circular piece of plywood out to the porch, along with a remnant of cotton cloth. "Inside I'm putting padding, stuff from an old quilt I had around," she said. "See there?" And she showed Miss Lorna how it would work—the padding tacked to the plywood, the cotton sewn over the whole thing, to reinforce the seat as efficiently as anything a professional repairman could do. While Miss Lorna rustled her fingers through cellophane, Ida sat in the porch swing and sewed, humming beneath her breath. Her voice was thin and aimless, as slippery as the whine of a mosquito. Miss Lorna felt soothed just hearing it.

"Ida, this is the kindest thing anyone has ever done for me," she said. "I mean that sincerely, now." As the sound of her own voice hit her she felt a huge tight ache beginning in her chest, but whether it was something happening to her health or merely the start of tears she couldn't be sure. Ida hummed on, unaware, while Miss Lorna stared out at the boxwood and tried to focus her thoughts.

It was a Monday, the twenty-first of May. For three weeks she had been sitting here with the neighbors all around her asking why, first to her and then, in whispers, to each other, and Mr. Billy begging her just please to step inside and away from that hot sun. "I am having to watch over my heart, Mr. Billy," she always said, and Mr. Billy said, "What good would sunstroke do to a heart?" He was a small man, much smaller than Miss Lorna. He had a round pink face creased with smile lines and his suits hung wrong on him, although heaven knew he could buy out every tailor in town. When he stood there on the porch inviting her inside, the bald top of his head began to shine; drops would run down to his eyebrows when he mentioned the sun, as if the word alone were enough to overheat him. What did he know about hearts? Miss Lorna was the one with nerves, and nerves made you prone to heart disease as any doctor would tell you. "Dear Lord, will you just go on *in?*" she would say. "You're perspiring all over my porch." Then Mr. Billy would sigh (although with all those smile lines, he couldn't even seem to do *that* very seriously) and leave her to herself again. After he had gone she would have to breathe very slowly for several minutes, taking care that her heart didn't just bounce up and spin around inside her.

The jolt to her heart had happened on the thirtieth of April, but ever since the ninth of October it had been under a considerable strain. On the ninth of October her daughter Melissa had marched up these very same steps, wearing a coat that was much too light for the season and no hat at all, and she had said, "We're expecting a baby at the end of April, Mama," and then just stood there smiling uncertainly with her hands in her pockets. Miss Lorna couldn't tell to this day how she had lived through that. Oh, Melissa herself had been shock enough—born in Miss Lorna's middle age, just when she had finally gotten it through Mr. Billy's head that she didn't hold with childbearing, arriving at midnight after an ordeal that Miss Lorna had been trying for

thirty years to forget. It was a miracle that she had even survived.
Then there was Melissa's health, always so delicate. She coughed
nights. She got asthma. She had every childhood disease twice,
even the ones you can only have once, and each summer she had
to be isolated from her playmates in case the polio epidemics came
around. (If there was a germ within ten miles, Melissa would find
it.) And she grew up so shy and strange, although Miss Lorna
herself was as sociable as they come, that it looked for years as if
she would be an old maid. When she finally did get married (to
a nice enough boy, though no one anybody *knew*—an insurance
salesman), Miss Lorna said, "Now, Melissa, there's something I
have to say to you. What with your delicate health and all, I do
hope you'll be *careful*." Should she have put it more plainly? There
was Melissa, standing with her hands in her pockets and smiling so
gently, talking about doctors and rooming-in. "Dear Lord, give me
strength," Miss Lorna had said, and she had felt her way to the
wicker chair and sat down heavily.

That had been seven months of sheer strain, something a heart
like hers should never have been asked to bear. Toward the end
she stopped seeing Melissa altogether. Melissa wore skirts with
elastic panels in the front and walked all over town as if she hadn't
a care in the world, but when she came visiting her parents, Miss
Lorna shut herself in her room. "How could she do this to me?"
she asked Ida. "The whole town knows it must have been sheer
carelessness. I told them all at the wedding her health was much
too delicate." Ida only clucked her tongue. Melissa stopped coming
around, but she still went to see Mr. Billy at his office. He admitted
it, right out. What did he care about health? He was plain silly
over children. When he had found out that Miss Lorna was expecting Melissa he had handed out cigars right then, six months
ahead of time, not even noticing how Miss Lorna vomited all
morning and cried all afternoon. "Go ahead, then," she had told
him. "Pass them out now, for in six months you'll be too busy buying
funeral wreaths." Mr. Billy didn't care.

Melissa's baby came on the thirtieth of April. It was a boy. It
must have nearly killed her, but Miss Lorna never heard the details because she didn't want to be told. Instead she took her
chair to the porch and started sitting there, and she told Ida that
from now on the entire house would be in Ida's hands. "I plan to
stay here a month," she told her. "I have to watch over my heart,

Ida. The slightest thing I do, it leaps up and flips over inside of me." Mr. Billy, of course, went to see the baby constantly. At first he kept it secret but later he grew bold and tried to tell her all about what he had seen. "His *hair*—" he began one day.

"I don't believe I care to hear just now," Miss Lorna said.

But today, with Ida's humming forming a soft, thin veil behind her thoughts, Miss Lorna heard again the way his sentence had begun. "His *hair*—" He had started so importantly, but what color could a baby's hair be but blond or dark? Not red, surely. "Ida?" she said.

Ida stopped humming.

"Never mind," said Miss Lorna.

But as if she could read minds, Ida said, "Miss Melissa's baby is being christened today."

"I don't care to hear," said Miss Lorna.

"Mr. Billy took the afternoon off to attend. Wouldn't it be fine if they all stopped by here after the ceremony?"

Miss Lorna didn't answer, since Ida already knew what the answer would be. She picked at one arm of the chair and waited for Ida to start humming again, but instead Ida said, "They're naming him William the second. For Mr. Billy."

"William. Ha," said Miss Lorna.

"Mr. Billy suggested they come by to see you. He said, 'Melissa, just apologize and tell her you're sorry. Then show her the baby, because who could turn a baby down?' He said that on the telephone, he says that all the time. Miss Melissa always says no, being proud, but who can tell about today? It's the christening day."

"What's she got to be proud *of*, I'd like to know," said Miss Lorna.

"What's she got to be sorry for?"

Miss Lorna looked up, but Ida already knew she had overstepped. She was biting her lip, sewing rapidly around the circle of flowered cotton. Miss Lorna sighed.

"Families are not what they used to be," she said. "I can tell you that."

She thought of the baby named William, after Mr. Billy. It was a no-account name. She favored Randolph, or Daniel. Not that anyone had asked her. When Mr. Billy had first come calling, carrying flowers and perspiring, even then, and she had known that he would probably turn out to be her husband, she had told

her father, "*Billy?* What kind of a name is *Billy* for a man?" Her
father hadn't seen the importance. "He's a fine boy," he had said,
"and he'll rise in the world." Oh, she should have told him it takes
more than money to raise a man. For all of their married life she
had called him "Mr. Billy," hoping to give him at least that much
stature, but no one else had ever followed her example. Neighbors
and colleagues and even employees, all but the servants in the
house and the shoeshine boy, called him "Billy" behind his back
and to his face. When she spoke to him about it he only laughed.
"You can laugh all you want," she told him, "but if there's one
thing I know it's this: the little things are the ones that count in
the end. The little graces, the common courtesies. My father was
Mr. Benjamin until the day he died, and not a person in the
county would have referred to him any differently."

"Your father was a fine old gentleman," said Mr. Billy, "but my
name is Billy. Anyone who wants can call me that."

"My father," Miss Lorna told Ida, "would spin in his grave to see
me here."

"How's that, Miss Lorna?"

"Sitting on this porch so sickly, having to watch my health. Why,
when he died I didn't eat for weeks, but if I'd known then what
I know now! First Melissa being born, he would have died of
worry for me. And now this. Oh, it sounds terrible when I say it
but I thank the Lord he's safely buried."

"Didn't he want no grandchildren?" Ida asked.

But Miss Lorna had drifted back inside her mind again. She
groped for another biscuit and frowned, watching the boxwood
through a ripple of heat waves. Her father had thought the sun
rose and set in her. He had admired everything about her—her
figure, which he had referred to as "baby fat" till she was past
twenty-five, her piano playing, and above all her singing. Why, he
had said time and time again that when he died he hoped all the
angels in heaven sang as sweet as she did. "Did I ever tell you
about my voice lessons?" she asked Ida. "Ida, if I told you how
much my father spent on my voice lessons you'd never in this
world believe me."

"Thousands, you said," Ida told her.

"Thousands. I don't know *how* many thousands. He had plans
for me to go on the concert stage in Europe, but I never got that
far. Oh, here, though—I sang at every benefit in the county for

just years and years. This was before I was married. They hung my maiden name on a banner across the stage—"Miss Lorna Love" from wing to wing, and the people came for miles. I sang the old-style songs. Sometimes the more elderly people in the audience just broke down and wept, and when I was through they kept begging for Miss Lorna to give them one more." '

"Yes, ma'am," said Ida.

"That was how they put it in the music world. 'Give them one more, Miss Lorna,' the manager would say, 'I guess you better just give them one more.' And I would go out on the stage again and see my father, spang in the middle of the very first row with a huge bouquet in his lap and his eyes just as *bright*—"

"Yes, ma'am," said Ida.

The porch swing creaked, sending a grating clean through Miss Lorna's nerves. Now Ida was humming again, but the sound was all but lost among the confusion of her thoughts. Where was Mr. Billy? At the christening; she had forgotten. Christening a baby. Time all ran together nowadays. She had to pull herself up short and concentrate before she could remember which baby it was, of what generation, and whose father was attending the christening. The porch she was sitting on could have been her father's veranda, or even Mr. Billy's porch but at another time. The last time she had sat here so long was that business last summer, with her husband's secretary. She had caught them red-handed—answered the telephone one day to hear only breathing and then a click at the other end. "That was your secretary's breathing," she told Mr. Billy. "I know that for a fact, and I know that there is something going on or she wouldn't have breathed that way and hung up when she heard my voice." "Secretary my foot," said Mr. Billy. "How would you know a thing like that? My secretary is a third my age and engaged to boot, and you've never even seen her, much less heard her breathing."

"Don't ask me how, I just know," she said. Then she had dragged her chair out to the porch, refusing all help, and sat there for twenty-nine days—all there was left of the month of August. That was nearly a year ago but it was hard to tell time today, with the porch swing making that same creaking sound and the box-wood still giving off that hot, musky smell. "Ida," she said before she thought, "why did he do it? How could I have married a man with such a coarse streak running through him?"

"Ma'am?" said Ida.

Tears were sliding down Miss Lorna's face. She remembered now, too late, that this had been back in August and that Mr. Billy had already apologized, after Melissa had come and reasoned with him for her, six separate times. Now it was something else; now it was Mr. Billy urging *Melissa* to apologize. She forgot what for. She leaned her head against Ida, who had risen to bend over the wicker chair. "There now, Miss Lorna," Ida said. She smelled of laundry starch and freshly ironed cotton. "Now *don't* take on, you hear?"

"I don't know why it is, Ida," Miss Lorna said, "but you're the only one I can turn to any more and that's a fact. Now, isn't that silly?"

She cried harder, with half of her face pressed against Ida's stomach and her eyes still fixed upon the front yard. A Sunshine biscuit crumbled away in her hand. Down in the street a long black car drew up and out stepped Mr. Billy, rumpled as ever, perspiring all over his white starched shirt. If he saw Miss Lorna, he didn't give a sign. He bent and spoke to someone else in the car, and after a while the back door opened and a woman got out. It was Melissa. She was carrying a baby in a blue receiving blanket, although any fool would know a baby could get heat exhaustion wrapped that way in May. "Yonder's Miss Melissa," Ida said. Ida's stomach was still pressed against Miss Lorna's face. "I see her," said Miss Lorna. "Do you want me to suffocate?" She pulled away from Ida and straightened the shoulders of her dress. "Fetch me more biscuits," she said.

Melissa was mounting the steps with her father beside her. Her figure was just ruined. Her one good feature, and now she had let it slide. When she raised her face, Miss Lorna saw that her eyes were puffy and dull, the way they were when she had a sullen fit. But at least she spoke—something she wouldn't have done during any ordinary fit. "Hello, Mama," she said.

"Well," Miss Lorna said.

Down in the street, one more person was climbing out of the car. It was Melissa's husband Joel, with a thermal crib blanket tossed over his shoulder. It looked as if they were bound and determined to smother that baby in the middle of summer. Of the three, Joel was the only one who smiled—flashing it at her, salesmanlike, as he climbed the first set of steps. "Hello there, Mother

Johnson!" he called. Miss Lorna only glanced at him and then
turned her attention back to Melissa.

"Melissa must have something to say to me," she said.

"Yes, Mama," said Melissa.

"Well, I'm waiting."

Melissa stopped on the last step and hugged the baby to her
shoulder. "I apologize for the concern I caused you," she said.

"Concern? My *heart* nearly gave way."

"Well, I'm sorry," said Melissa.

Then Mr. Billy suddenly came alive, springing up on the porch
to fetch an aluminum chair and calling, "Ida? You there? We'll
want iced tea all around." He shouted as if Ida were stone deaf,
though she must be waiting just on the other side of the door
and listening to every word. "Well, Miss Lorna, here's your grand-
son," he said. "William the second, bright as a button and you
can tell it already. Want to hold him?"

"Not just now, I don't believe," said Miss Lorna. "Melissa, if
you're planning to stay you'd best sit down. Won't you take some
of that baby's wraps off?" She watched while Melissa unfolded
the receiving blanket and lifted out the baby—only a tiny,
screwed-up pink thing, nothing to him yet. To look at him you
would never guess the pain he had caused. Momentarily, she
forgot again who he was and who he belonged to; she frowned
at Melissa's husband, who stood just behind Melissa like a father
in an old family album. Hard as she searched his face, she couldn't
think what he had to do with her. "Have you been here long?"
she asked him. Then, seeing the others' blank looks, she came to
herself. "Ida has been working on a cushion for me," she said.
"That girl just won't sit still, always finding little favors she can
do me. We were talking about my voice."

Joel cleared his throat. "Oh, yes. Your singing," he said.

"My singing. Yes." She was back on familiar ground now. She
raised her head and spoke slowly and clearly, going over the words
she knew so well that they came ready-made to her mind, set in
a pattern, stripped of the "he said's" and "she said's" that other
people would have used. "A year before I married, a professional
singer heard me," she said. She accepted, without looking at it, the
packet of biscuits that Ida handed her. "He came up to me after
my performance. I had sung three encores that night. 'Miss Love,
may I compliment you upon your delivery?' 'Why, I thank you,

sir.' 'Not at all, Miss Love, not at all. The pleasure was entirely mine.'"

In the patch of sunlight on Melissa's lap the baby slept, making tiny snoring sounds with every indrawn breath. Old Billy Johnson and Joel creaked side by side in the rusty porch swing. "'And may I remark,'" said Miss Lorna, "'that it was a very great pleasure indeed?'" She smiled at something a long way off while the three of them watched her—a large, ugly woman sinking through the seat of a wicker armchair, chewing Sunshine biscuits and looking like Andy Devine in a golfing costume.

EVELYN SHEFNER was born in Chicago, attended the University of Chicago, and lives in New York City. Her short stories have appeared in the *Southern Review, The Paris Review*, the *Hudson Review*, the *North American Review*, and the *Denver Quarterly*. She has just completed work on a short novel.

The Invitations

ADA WINTERGREEN had been living in the Grove Street apartment six years before the Jenners entered her life. One warm Saturday in November the tortoise-shell cat owned by the old lady across the street was gone from the windowsill overlooking the fire-escape, as were the tangle of begonias, the withered pots of ivy, the boxes of geranium that never bloomed. Instead, a young woman was leaning halfway out, rubbing a rope of red-gold hair with a towel.

At the apparition Ada was stunned. She had not seen the old lady so very often, but she had grown accustomed to her. Their front windows looked directly into one another's across this narrow street. The old lady had been an ideal neighbor, living with her cat and the sooty jungle on the windowsill, lowering her shades each evening when she sat down to eat, extinguishing the lights behind them promptly at nine. Occasionally Ada met her coming down the block, pulling an overloaded shopping cart. She wore a cape and sweeping-brimmed hat that all but hid the eyes, and funny flat shoes with a strap across the instep, like a child's. There seemed to be something wrong with her feet.

These encounters had made up her contact with the unknown neighbor, ostensibly gone out of her life now for good. Had the lonely woman fallen ill one night across from where Ada sat playing Gershwin on the phonograph behind closed blinds? At what point had they come to take her away, together with the cat, the mementos, the flowerpots—the lost clutter and debris of a lifetime? Deep in unfamiliar questions, she failed to realize that for minutes she had been staring directly across at the new neighbor, who went on without concern fluffing up her hair with a towel.

With a blush and thin smile of apology, Ada started to move away. At this, as if an unspoken colloquy between them had come to an end, the young woman gave her hair a last fillip and leaned back into her own apartment—not before signaling Ada a lengthy indiscreet, altogether an over-friendly smile. Unanswered, the smile hung in the air above the row of tenements and mouldering brownstones like a fume, insistent, cloying.

Ada wondered if she had suffered a shock over her old friend's disappearance! Above the uproar and clamor of a shabby corner of the city, it was startling enough to see a Rhine Maiden leaning out the window, calmly sunning her locks. Then the sun's rays struck a swarm of highlights from the young woman's mane as she leaned backward from the sill. Almost blinded, Ada had read into the other's face an appeal, an invitation out of proportion to the fact of two neighbors' meeting for the first time over so many empty feet of space.

She flattened the Venetian blinds, and began getting ready for the evening, pulling a black sweater over her head, stepping into low-heeled pumps, combing back her hair, short, thickly striped already with gray. She was expecting a visit later from a young man who had been coming to see her with clocklike punctuality a couple of times a week for the past half-year. They had not proved to be highly charged evenings, and by now Ada got ready for them with the same detached efficiency as if she were setting out on a coke date with one of the less-sought-after boys from Sumach High, one of those pebble-faced youths, below her in height, who had fallen her way as if by a fixed competition.

Compounding the troubles that her height had let her in for, Ada all too soon had to begin making allowances for her prematurely graying hair and a tendency toward a rigidness of temperament, an insistence on seemliness and order, that nothing— not the move to New York and settling into a ratty little apartment in Greenwich Village, the night courses in ceramics and membership in an experimental film society—had apparently any power to exorcise. On the other hand, at the medium-sized oil company where she worked as chief of the file room, she was considered a genius at cleaning up messes. Rather than crushing her, chaos—up to a point—roused her fighting spirit. Disorder left to flourish for years, however, like the unkempt growth on her former neighbor's windowsill, she considered beyond her dispensation. "What you need around here is a demolition squad, not a filing system!" she spoke up on one dramatic occasion, reaching for her hat. She regulated the rows of lettered boxes, and the girls who bent over them, with an unfaltering hand. Behind her back, she knew well enough, her severe young face and graying hair had earned her the nickname "Grandma Wintergreen."

Well, name-calling hardly mattered; she could shut that out at night. But the privacy of her home did. As she thought it over, walking out for a quick supper before her friend Roy should turn up, the young woman's displaying her hair at the window like Godiva was an intrusion into her personal line of vision. She glanced at the window, expecting some new, disturbing revelation, but was reassured by slats shutting out the view in regular, metallic procession.

"What's going on there across the street?" Roy turned from the window with a grin, inviting her to join him in gaping at a public spectacle.

"Then what could it be?" At his side, Ada peered through the crack in her Venetian blind enlarged by his pointing finger. In a white-painted room, fully open to the public eye, floodlighted by two immense ceiling fixtures—bare of furniture except for a low couch and some mats on the floor—a man and woman were performing a nervous, whiplash dance.

Although her bountiful hair had been skinned back into a knot on top the head, she was recognizably the young woman of the fire-escape that afternoon. Her partner was tall, wheatish fair, bullety close-cropped. His jeans clung intimately, with swagger, to the hips. The arm and shoulder muscles were defined with some brutality under the lightly tanned skin. Either the long paint-brush he held straight out from the shoulder or something in the way he stood brought up visions of a billboard poster announcing a circus: had it been leopards spitting defiance the man in the braided trousers had been cracking into line, or merely little dancing dogs?

As they watched, the red-haired woman stopped in her circling around the man, leaned close, one hand on his bare chest, and arched her neck back in an eloquent movement of pleading or distress. Perhaps the move annoyed him, or he was furious because of some word said. The man dropped the paintbrush and let go with two energetic, hard-handed slaps. They were executed with such refined timing the woman's face bobbed from one side to the other in anticipation of the second blow. As it was delivered, she sank to the floor and buried her face in a full skirt. Without another look the man walked out of the room, leaving the woman framed, alone, like a well-lit museum exhibit.

As Ada turned away she was aware that her own face was burning, her breathing not easy. Ignoring what they had witnessed, she heard herself ask, "Well, what should we do this evening? There's a new Peter Sellers movie around. If we hurry I guess we can make the last show."

When they came up the street a few hours after, Ada in spite of all good resolves, found herself staring directly ahead at the neighbors' windows. Their blinds were still raised to the heavens, but the overhead spotlights had apparently been replaced by a collection of small lamps and candles. People were moving around up there in a diffused glow. Loud conversation and laughter poured out, competing with the thump of drums. Head high, laughing, the woman with the flaming headpiece moved among her guests.

That night Ada said goodby to her friend at the door instead of letting him come upstairs to sit a certain time, one arm around her shoulder, while with the other he went through a routine which both of them, when they finally sat up, red-faced, fussing at their clothes, pretended had not taken place. This night she sent him away before her firm hands pushed him off. Watching him vanish down the street, four-square, familiar, plain—a large part of herself—Ada had a suspicion of putting out on a voyage that might lead farther than that first daylong excursion down from Sumach, New Hampshire, where a recent visit back home had demonstrated that New York City had no monopoly on ceramics classes—nor for that matter offered much reason for continuing a life except the decision, for reasons by now nearly forgotten, that it be lived out here.

During the honeymoon phase with the Jenners—with all going out on their part and nothing going out on hers—Ada made the discovery that there were more people to talk to in this world than she had previously been willing to credit. Arriving on the job early of a morning, she would find a circle of fellow-workers hanging around the coat closet or waiting expectantly in the vicinity of her desk. Pink-faced and smiling faintly, Ada would sit down to describe the latest knock-out quarrel over the way (the quarrels nearly always ended with blows thrown by one side or the other); the man's bare-chested struggles nightly at the easel, where he spent a good deal of time staring out into the dark; the meals taken cross-legged off little tables, with esoteric hand motions which one of the office girls figured out must mean they were using chopsticks; the alarming exercises, which no one could figure out, performed before or after dinner, on straw mats. And the parties. For the sake of these she began to spend whole evenings alone in the dark, face flushed against the tilted blind.

Unwilling to be separated from the diversion, she offered absent-minded regret when Roy rang up one evening, in the middle of a party, to announce that he was being sent on a selling swing down South. The tone of his voice implied he was unlikely to call again when he returned. She set the telephone down and hurried back to where she had been kneeling against the window on a bedroom pillow. Her legs felt stiff, and her knees were starting to ache in spite of cushioning. During the interruption the men and women in the apartment had split up into groups or teams and were starting to act out some childish charade. But as Ada strained to guess what title or message was being mimed, amid shrieks of laughter, by their bearish or awkwardly self-conscious gestures, a woman deliberately unbuttoned her blouse and slid a hand under one breast, offering it to public view. During the static minutes before she rearranged her clothing it swung, outsize and pendulous, like a great, quivering eye.

All during the late fall and winter the new neighbors continued to lead their morbidly attractive and excessively public existence. Theirs was, in fact, the life Ada had secretly visualized taking place behind closed blinds in every apartment on the street except her own—and the old lady's. The familiarity allowed an easy-going feeling of ownership. During her lunch-hour sessions and occasional unexciting evenings on the town with the other girls in her office, Ada began to pick and sort over what she chose to let them hear, sparing some incidents, adding others at will.

Had she wished, for instance, to tell about the woman unbuttoning her dress, she would have added that there had been a scream, following which all the lights had gone out. Not what really had followed, which was that a man and a woman led the disrobing one, who seemed to be crying, off into a corner and sat talking with her; the game broke up, and soon afterwards the hostess came in with coffee cups on a tray. More and more, she was tending to alter or to hold back details.

When they were up there alone now, the young woman often came to the window and stood a considerable time monotonously brushing the waterfall of hair over one shoulder. These manifestations, less intimate than many that she could take in without disturbance, invariably made Ada drop her finger from the tiny space raised in the blind and turn away in a kind of fear. Other times the man, in turn, seemed to be attempting communication when he came to the window and looked beyond his reflection on the glass. The spotlights overhead made caves of his nostrils and eye sockets, shaded the heavy pectoral muscles, nearly obliterating what was beneath, so that the dark trousers seemed a flattened, tapered extension of the naked torso. But within the high band of light the man's face swam out fixed, rebellious, grim. There was always a strong shiver when the stare searched and stopped at her window; worse, when after a heavy silent interchange he turned back to his work. Watching the man stab what must be a long incision down the canvas, or cover an area with cheerful methodical haste, Ada was frightened to think he had been able to see through to a likeness until now kept hidden from view. Reluctantly, she came to accept that a new vision of herself was being shaped and witnessed in the dark.

Beyond these encounters it was a disappointment to run into the couple out of doors, and she did her best to avoid having to pass them out walking, caught up in the same routines as everyone else. Outside, both lost their distinctiveness and took on a look that was indefinably shabby and unwholesome. Ada was forced to admit, for example, that the woman's complexion was not good, that there was a shrewish expression on her face, although the torch of her hair did make her visible in the daylight for blocks away. Wearing a work jacket and torn sneakers with rainbow spatters of paint, the man lost the aura Ada had invested on his half nude body. They seemed to have hardly a word to lose between them, as they carried the laundry or pushed the shopping-cart down the block; they appeared hampered or embarrassed by each other's presence. For some reason it annoyed Ada that they were so badly matched. He was far too tall for his companion, or she too short for him. The disparity was awkward, close to comic.

So she tried to turn a corner when she was able to recognize them in time bearing down in her direction. Or she ran back into the house with the start of someone who has left behind something extremely important when, by one of those coincidences which happened all too often, they walked out of their respective houses simultaneously. Even so, there were occasions when she could not help finding them in her path.

Both Jenners, on the other hand, seemed able to retrieve something from these accidental meetings. By now their expressive "Hi!" had broadened to a handsome "Hello, neighbor!" whenever they got near enough to deliver it. And by now prepared, Ada was able to deliver a weak smile, tentatively displayed, which left the corners of her mouth tingling. Beyond this she did not care to go—she had gone far enough already—and she would look down at the bag of groceries or the cleaner's package in her arms, admitting shyness to be inappropriate in a girl her size. Other times, especially after she had begun to claim the benefit of their private lives, she was hard on herself for this public withdrawal. Seeing the man or woman advance from the far end of the block (worse when they appeared one at a time), Ada would flinch, waiting for the reproaches, the corrupt smiles, the references that could never be taken back. On these occasions she would make a stringent effort to be polite. "My yes, isn't it!" she would respond energetically to their "Lovely day!" or "Brrr, nasty!" depending on weather conditions.

Finding the pair of them practically on her doorstep one Saturday afternoon as she was returning from Macy's with a pair of binoculars in a paper bag, Ada was staggered into cordiality. She tightened her hold on the bag, wondering if the contents could be guessed by the shape. This time she was first to comment on the weather—"Hello there; hasn't it been a lovely day?"

Now they were the ones to be cautious and uncertain. "Yes," the man agreed slowly, looking to his wife for confirmation. "It shore has been great."

Again Ada wondered at the impression of seaminess they managed to give off. Slouched against her doorpost, rubbing the dun-colored bristles on his cheek, the man suggested something both anonymous and ever-present. He might have stepped out of a book in which the pages were yet to be written or been slapped together out of unbaked, imperfectly mixed compound. Not exactly riffraff, they were yet people of no quality. At this hour the low-lying sun clamorously contended with the woman's chignon. The fabric of her skin was marred by bumps and pale freckles, and her eyes had a mean slant. But she beamed at Ada a luminous, intimate smile.

"I'm Bob Jenner," the man said suddenly, shooting out a hand. "And this is Hildy, my wife."

"How do you . . ."

"You must be Wintergreen," the woman broke in breathlessly.

"As a matter of fact"—he grinned—"you caught us in the act of looking at your doorbell. Kurtz and Mellon we know already, and you can't be Seligmann . . ."

"I'm Ada Wintergreen," she admitted in a dry voice, shifting the package in her arm.

"That's what we thought. I mean, it seemed to fit. . . ."

"She means," her husband interpreted, "you seemed a Grade-A-Eastern product. Not like the rest of us mongrel pups running around the neighborhood. I'm from Tennessee, myself, and my wife is from the state of Washington . . ."

"Oregon."

"Have it your way, baby, Oregon. We live in that beat-up brown-stone across the street." He supplied this information with no trace of irony. "Are you acquainted with Bob Kurtz or Jerry Mellon by any chance?"

As she silently shook her head he said, "You don't know many people around here, do you?"

"I do have a few . . ."

"We've been having some parties lately." He reached inside his jacket and began to scratch. "Since you're right over the way, I hope they haven't been bothering you?" ("You do seem to get to bed early," his wife expanded.)

"Why no," Ada replied miserably. "I'm not much troubled by noise."

"Well, if it bothers you any time, you can come right over. You know the old saying, if you can't beat it, join it."

"Thank you for thinking of me." That seemed to settle matters, and she took out her keys.

"We plan a little get-together this evening." He pulled his hand away from his chest and looked at the nails. "Think you can make it?"

"I certainly would," she told them, "if I weren't already taken."

"As a matter of fact"—again, no implication that he might not be dispatching fresh news—"we generally have open house on Sunday afternoons, too. Why don't you drop around tomorrow instead, 'bout five?"

She spun the keys in her open palm. "I'm afraid this weekend is going to be awfully busy for me."

"Any old time then. You don't have to call, remember. Just ring the bell."

He snapped a rigid salute as they crossed the street; but his wife's smile, lingering, followed Ada upstairs, settling into her hair, nostrils, the folds of her clothing. She made an impatient movement of brushing herself off before opening the door. As soon as she was inside, she put the Macy bag down where she would see it and remember to take it back with her on Monday. The binoculars had cost thirty-seven dollars, charged to her account, and it had been difficult selecting a pair that so well accommodated her degree of farsightedness.

That evening Ada joined six other women from her office for dinner at a heavily-advertised Italian restaurant in the theatrical district. The restaurant was crowded with people stoking away an oversized meal before curtain time. Because of the inconvenient number, their group was given a round table near the kitchen; Ada felt the breeze of passage whenever the waiters swung by with laden trays. She suspected their waiter of being subtly insulting because the party was all women. The portions served up were so gross that she was hardly able to make inroads on the main course—two girls later fell asleep at the theater. When it was over, she excused herself from going off for a final drink with the others, who had grown giggly and boisterous, and got into a taxi. It had been an extremely dull and remarkably expensive evening.

From halfway down the block she could tell while still in the cab that the Jenners' social get-together was well under way. She hurried up her stairs and then made certain the blinds were securely shut over her front windows and the curtains fully drawn before she ventured to turn on one small light. Without a glance at the noise out there, which was increasing, she went to bed and managed to sleep.

Around noon the next day, however, she began to wonder how to fill in the long afternoon. A few Sundays lately she had taken the bus ride up to the Metropolitan Museum to look over the Chinese porcelains. Today, the thought of the blue and yellow pots brooding in the quiet in their impervious glazes gave her a hemmed-in sensation. Just to get out of the house she went up to the Museum of Modern Art. Then when her feet hurt she went downstairs to the auditorium to watch an early Ginger Rogers-Fred Astaire musical. She had supper out, so it was after nine when she got home.

Before uncatching the street door, she shot one tentative look up toward the Jenners', recoiling when a heavy shape swung away from the glass. She was hardly up the stairs and out of her coat when the phone rang.

"Hello, Miss Wintergreen. Bob Jenner speaking. How are you? Good. Good. We have a few friends here, and wondered if you might still be in the mood for a little get-together tonight."

"I'm sorry; it isn't possible." She hoped the wobble in her voice was too minimal to be detected. "I've just got in—I have to go to work tomorrow—it's rather late."

"Shore, just as you like." Over the phone he seemed more Southern, ruminative, relaxed. "—What say, doll? One moment there. My wife says what about next Sunday?"

"It's still too early to make plans." Ada tightened one hand around the cradle of the phone and tried to think of something cheerful and far away.

"Quiet, men. Wha-a-t? She says how about setting a date for a drink before dinner early next week then, Monday, Tuesday? All right," he gave in. "You'll owe us the visit. We'll be in touch. One second there." He came back to the telephone the last time to say, "My wife sends regards."

About midnight, after traffic and passing footsteps died down, Ada began to be disturbed by repeated resonating thumps traveling

over from a familiar direction. Fighting the impulse a respectable
time, she finally got up, fastened her robe, pulled aside the curtains
and poked the slats of the blinds very slightly apart. Bob Jenner
was sitting crosslegged on the floor of his living room, half-stripped
as usual, tapping a pair of bongo drums. His head and shoulders
swayed, his eyes seemed closed. Hair fluffed out around her body
like drapery, his wife crouched at his feet. There were three
others, sitting on chairs: the older woman who had created the
sensation at that memorable party and two very young men. One,
a permanent fixture at the Jenners, had provided his own memorable evening, once, when presumably too drunk to get up or to
care he had vomited, like a baby, down the front of his clothes.

Windows nearby creaked, shouts closed in. "Cut that noise!
Quiet, or we'll call the police!" Bob Jenner started, tossed the
drums aside, and crossed to look out. Before Ada could step back,
he was staring directly into her observation-post. He raised a hand
loosely and smiled. One eye screwed down its hinge in a monstrous
wink.

The following Wednesday Roy telephoned to say he was back
in town. Ada was astonished by the warmth of her own greeting.
He may have been surprised, too, because it took a while for him
to get around to asking when they might get together. Usually
he could be relied on to settle essentials before branching out to
details—Florida beaches, New Orleans drinking-places, the Wil-
liamsburg cousins who had shown him such a fine time. Before
hanging up he did ask, "By the way, are you free Saturday?"
and tossed off, "Let's make it for dinner then, there's a lot to talk
about—anything new on your side?"

Thursday night Ada went out after work and bought a new hat
at rather an expensive store and a pair of shoes with heels. Balanc-
ing the bulky packages, she let herself into the house—sending
skyward one of those furtive glances that were becoming an habitual tic. If the Jenners were home, they were being unusually
secretive about it. The dark frames of their unreflecting windows
looked deserted. Most likely, for a change, they had taken themselves out.

She made a couple of ham sandwiches, shampooed and set her
hair, and went to bed with her head trussed up with loops of
plastic and wire. Past two in the morning, after she had fallen

heavily asleep, the sounds began to filter in, commanding wakefulness. Shrill piped battle clamor, yowls of pent and ambushed
rage.

Ada sat up and stuck her fingers into her ears, hoping to blot
out the noises. Instead, piercing and imperative, they vibrated past
her fingertips; this time double murder might indeed be in the
offing. Civic duty demanding at least a witness, she went to the
window, raised it, and this time making no attempt to camouflage,
leaned out.

Over across the way nothing so exceptional was happening after
all, no more than she had watched from hiding a dozen times at
least. No weapons were on show, neither side seemed to be getting
the explicit worst. The woman was only more dishevelled than
usual: the neck of her deep-cut sweater had slipped down past
the cleft, the hair was tossed forward, swathing her eyes. Trembling
and nearly sightless, she seemed ready to hurl herself on the
grinning giant who stood with one huge palm raised to meet the
charge. On similar occasions, Ada had seen her duck past his
defenses and draw blood with teeth or fingernails before he succeeded in pinning her arms or knocking her down. But quite
suddenly, before Ada could escape or catch her breath, the game
slid over into something else. It was as if a signal both had been
waiting for had been raised finally from outside of them. Whoever
provoked the first move, the other sprang ready to answer. The
combatants met and closed together like the halves of a mollusk
shell. In a turmoil of arms and legs they fell, and rolled on the
floor. As an afterthought, and none too soon, the man lifted himself from the mat and turned off the light. In his armpit the hair
lay thick, lion-colored.

"Doing?"

Ada toyed with the crabmeat cocktail bedded on ice in a silver-
metal bowl. On the table, in a bucket, sat a bottle of champagne,
as yet unopened. Roy watched critically as the waiter wrapped a
towel around the bottle and loosened the cork with a satisfactory
but not overly explosive pop. Wine gushed into their boat-shaped
glasses. She clinked "Cheers, Skol," lowered her eyes, and started
to eat.

"Doing? You know, the usual."

"Believe me, it's great being back in civilization." Roy buttered a cloverleaf roll. "The hours I spent, trying to hammer home one simple point. Even so, it was never simple enough. That backwoods mentality—you can keep it. I like to be around where things are happening." He had put on a little weight, and had a good suntan.

"I thought you liked New Orleans."

"Naturally. Sure. New Orleans is a different story."

"So you expect to be sent out again soon?" she asked.

"Not, I hope, until next summer. If I can help it, not then." Roy wiped his mouth, and reached a hand toward her fingers, curled around the wineglass. "Say, if I'm not being inquisitive, what happened the last time I called? You sounded—I wondered if I'd reached you at the wrong time or something. I don't want to meddle in your personal life, but is there a special reason you couldn't talk?"

Ada tried to blush; it came with no effort. "I've been meaning to explain. I'd just got to the door, you see, when the phone rang, and there were people parked illegally, waiting for me downstairs. I'm sorry, I must have sounded terribly rushed."

"No apologies, just curious. What else is happening around here?" He dropped her hand when the waiter cleared away for the next course. "How are the ceramics classes?"

"I haven't been there in quite a while."

"Getting bored with your art already?" His hand was pinioning hers; she made no effort to break free.

"I would hardly call it art," she protested, laughing. "I don't, I'm afraid, have the talent. Besides, how many ashtrays can you use around the house or give away for Christmas?"

Across the table, his face mirrored the stains she could feel spreading from earlobe to hairline, daubed Indian-fashion across the cheeks. "Who can tell," he suggested, "if you applied yourself, you might have other talents?"

"Who can tell?" she was forced to agree.

When they stepped out of the taxi, Ada took a deep breath. "Well, I can tell you this. I can't say I feel like a movie right now."

"No more do I. I'd say stop at another bar, but after all that—"

Irresolute, they stood at her corner. "Here's a good laugh for you." Ada fished inside her coat pocket. "We've been invited to a party tonight."

"Anybody I know?"

"Nobody you'd care to. I forgot—you did see them once. Remember that—cat-and-dog fight across the street?"

"The apache dancers?" He frowned. "They're giving a party? How come they invited *you*?"

Ada sighed. "It's rather annoying. They give tremendous lots of parties and try to get everyone in the neighborhood. I don't know who comes, or why. I opened the mailbox today and found this." She handed over the scrap of laundry paper. "I shoved it in my pocket and forgot entirely, I hadn't intended . . ."

Roy held the jagged edges up to the street light. "Dear Miss Wintergreen: Heap big party, Casa Jenner, Saturday 9 p.m. to 9 a.m. Come any old way, any old time, with anybody, but come."

By then they were at her street door. He was sounding a little less censorious. "Is it worth going? What kind of parties do they give, anyway?"

"I wouldn't dream of it," Ada said cheerfully. "If you want to come up I'll make some coffee. I've got a bottle of Scotch, if we feel like drinking later." She swerved out of his arms in the darkened hallway. "Wait a sec. Don't step in yet! I have to remember to fix the windows before I can turn on the lights. You have no idea how persistent—this way, I can always say I wasn't home."

"You were home all right, last night," Bob Jenner insisted. "Don't give me any of that jazz. We saw your bathroom light going off and on—until pretty damned late in the morning, too."

"Bob, please," Mrs. Jenner pleaded.

After their nearly forced entrance, with the wife in the role of flaming spearhead, she was the first to settle down. "You have a nice place here," she commented sociably, taking a look around. "Are those pieces all Early American?" In general, she was comporting herself as an invited guest—rather than someone who had pushed her way into a stranger's home at eleven on a Sunday morning. She managed even a wry, extra-communicative smile.

"Just don't let her pass any of that off on me," her husband announced. He shoved back his jacket and undid the buttons with paint-smeared, shaking fingers. Underneath he was wearing an extremely soiled pajama-top. His unblinking inventory named, priced, tested each object in the room; acknowledging the waxed pine chests and spool-back chairs dusted off from the attic back home;

passing with no comment over the shelves of irregularly shaped handmade bowls, with their mottled, pimply glazes. What do you have that we don't, his red-rimmed truculent gaze demanded. You're no better than we are.

"You know what, Hildy? I think we called the wrong number on this gal. I'd say now she's just an old-time local snob."

"I wouldn't let it get you down," the woman responded. Not having been asked, she sank into a chair and lit a cigarette. "I told you it wasn't worth the trouble. If your neighbors aren't interested—the hell with them. Let them stew in it."

"But what right does she have to treat us this way?"

From the beginning, pushing in with their vehement "Where were you last night?"—they had been acting between the two of them as though Ada wasn't there, as though her entrances and exits, her apartment, her privacy, were under their jurisdiction.

"I put it to you this way. The woman's alone, she's not, to be frank, too attractive—"

"I don't exactly agree with you." Hilda Jenner shyly stretched a hand up to Ada's head, touching the rolls and curves set into place a few nights before, now beginning to unspring. "I'm glad you're finally doing something about your hair. Hasn't she, when you get a look at her, Bob, almost classically perfect . . ."

"To me she looks hard up—in need of an outlet. We try to be friendly. We make the overtures. All right, she can't make it this week, she's busy, she can't make it that. We put ourselves out on a limb one more time—then she has the gall to tell us she wasn't home."

"Well, they're all the same. Look at Seligmann, look at DiMarco, Boland . . ."

"They're throwing it right in my teeth. What kind of freak do they take me for?"

"See here——" Once more Ada tried to cut past the barrier of their voices. She cleared her throat, wound the cord of her robe very tightly around the middle. "Just what do you mean walking in like this, what do you want of me, anyway?"

"I warned you from the start," Mrs. Jenner commented mournfully, flicking ashes on the floor. "She looked a little too reserved."

"I'd like to know what's good enough for her then," the man asked. "If not us, by God, who?" He whirled back to the original question, bearing straight down on Ada: "Why didn't you come over last night?"

"I told you people, I was out. I had a date."

"You were home while the party was going strong. By God, it lasted till five in the morning. Why didn't you bring your friend along? Who's good enough for you then? General Motors? U. S. Steel? Or are you such a sick puss you're afraid to associate with us because we're not married?"

"Bob, dear, please." The woman began pulling him gently toward the door. "Don't excite yourself, remember what Keller told you. Don't let their dirt become part of you. Let it go, drop it—breathe it out."

"Get out of here!" Ada shouted, jumping at the sound of her own voice. "Get out. This minute. What right do you have to barge in asking questions? I can come and go as I please."

As she said it, she realized with a new fear that she was speaking from a center of her experience having nothing to do with them. Her words produced no observable impact. Jenner stood hulking and inert in her doorway, looking around for means of coping with a deadly insult. He was so large, about him there was something so formless and without boundary, he made everything in her place look fussy, cramped, and spindly.

"Right now!" Ada shrieked. She was rapidly losing control. "Or I call the police."

When her hand closed over the phone, he began buttoning up his jacket. "A stinking god-damn snob," he summed it up, as the red-haired woman hurried him along. She shot one vicious parting glance at Ada, the understanding between them, whatever it had been, finally shattered. The Lorelei at the window turned into a tiny pioneer woman, spunky and tenacious, fighting with any weapon on hand to secure her mate and home. Through the closing door Ada heard his voice, low-toned and chagrined, demanding: "What right does she have to treat us this way?"

After they left, Ada sank down on the couch and gave way to tears. She could not indulge them long, however, because pretty soon there was Roy—whose hat and gloves had been in plain sight all this time on the mantel next to the used glasses and half-empty whiskey bottle, whose conservatively striped tie was openly on view slung over a chair—running upstairs with fresh rolls and the Sunday papers.

EUNICE LUCCOCK CORFMAN has written short stories for *Harper's*, *McCall's*, and *The Texas Quarterly*, and her novel entitled *THE ROARING SHOCK TEST* appeared in 1967. She lives in Washington, D.C., with her husband, a physician, and their four children.

To Be an Athlete

THE new tenant's luggage—one Sears under-the-bed flat trunk, eight crates of books trussed in bailing wire, marked on every side in red Magic Marker with threats of reprisal if damage were done —had been dumped on the front porch by the trucker while Miss Everleave was away at the Glen Rock Invitational. She saw the boxes as she turned in her drive, but no sign of the new tenant. First things first, she unloaded the MG, covered it and put away her rackets. Now she contemplated the oversized crates and single, shabby trunk. It was none of her affair, but she didn't like to see them left overnight with rain threatening.

So before she went in to take her shower she unlocked the tenant's apartment and one after another hauled his crates and trunk into the sitting room. When it began to rain, she felt vindicated. Miss Everleave locked her tenant's front door and went to take her shower.

In the bathroom she stripped, then stood still a minute. She had just moved several hundred pounds of books, played two matches today—one this morning, one this afternoon, at which she had been eliminated—and driven home in sweater and whites directly, without stopping to bathe, change, or eat. She let herself acknowledge that she ached.

Leaning against the tile, Miss Everleave crooked her leg and examined the blisters on the soles of her feet, touched the big one on her right heel. She scolded herself briefly: who plays on her

heels gets blisters there. She studied her right hand, stretching it so
the calluses stood out in yellow islands—no damage. She lifted her
right arm to the cabinet mirror and saw what a red welt her bra had
incised between her breast and armpit. She pressed it gently with
her fingertips and out loud said, "Ouch." In close-up she squinted at
her face: nobbled leather, drawn with fatigue but not gaunt,
unabsorbed Noxema lining the big nose, flakes of salt clinging in the
webbing each side of the eyes, gray-streaked hair crimped now to
kinky ringlets because she had not stopped to comb it out right
after the match while it was wet. She turned to the shower, twisting
the HOT handle.

Miss Everleave stood for some time in the beating spray, again
and again stooping—for she was tall—to pass her head through it,
offering her shoulders to it, her neck and ribs and back. She
methodically massaged her legs—white at the hip, cordovan the
length of thigh and shank, abruptly white again at the ankle, and
white, battered feet—digging in her fingers. She turned off the
water and, stepping into the hall where it was cool, rubbed herself
down.

Now. Now we face it, she ordered. That she had lost the match
this afternoon had been a failure not of legs but of concentration, far
more nettling. The defect first appeared earlier in the summer, at
the Longacre Open and again in the first match of the Burning
Tree Invitational: a disconnection between directions she gave
herself and the manner of her body's response. Miss Everleave sat
at her kitchen table wrapped in a robe and, reflecting, kneaded a
handball, an exercise that over the years had made the dimensions
of her right wrist three-quarters of an inch larger than her left.

She took a steak from the freezer; she would have to wait while it
defrosted. There was nothing much to eat—she had not expected
to be eliminated until the quarterfinals on Friday. She heard noise
from the tenant's apartment next door, someone stumbling over the
crates. It had started, she decided, in the second set, the third
game, when she had lost her serve for no good reason. She was
staying in the backcourt to save her legs for the days ahead but
playing carefully, stroking hard, placing well; that was when it had
fallen, this cut or curtain between directives and her muscles' reply.

Miss Everleave poked the steak and found it still hard at its
center. She put on slacks and went down into the basement, her
workshop where over the years she had accumulated the equip-

ment of a modest gymnasium—mats, the old-fashioned Indian clubs, a set of pulleys, and her great extravagance, parallel bars, set where the ceiling had been built high to house a coal bin.

Miss Everleave went to the parallel bars and began to swing, slowly, for she knew her body was tired. But it had not behaved well today; it had not been obedient. Upstairs the new tenant knocked at his boxes. After the isolation of the summer, she regretted having to share the house again with someone else's noises. It was unavoidable. In any case, classes would start in another week and any isolation at all would be gone for another nine months. She swung off the bars. The steak would be ready now.

Eating her steak, Miss Everleave reviewed the third set stroke by stroke. Next door the new tenant made banging and unpacking sounds. She became aware her review was turning into wishful thinking—"if only . . ."—she caught herself and clucked with contempt. She decided to spend the evening answering some letters.

Though sometimes it seemed to her the letters took an unconscionable amount of time wasted at a desk, she would not have had it any other way. These letters written to or on behalf of former students were connections she prized. Her relation to these correspondents was not "family" at all; the term made her bridle. If she had been male, her relation to them would have been obvious to anyone—they had in common that she had once been their coach. They were related to her by having once been athletes. To be an athlete among athletes was why, though overage and legs going, rarely a finalist, she continued the tennis circuit and, more indirectly, why she always answered these letters. To be an athlete was so clear a definition of herself that in twenty-seven years of teaching—she preferred to call it coaching—it had never occurred to her that for most people there is no such thing as a female athlete.

There was a knock at her door: it would be the new tenant. She tried to recall: a new man for the—history? economics? something like that—department. She hurried to the desk drawer and found the card: Ekstein. Hector Ekstein. She went to the door and opened it.

She said, "Dr. Ekstein? Come in. Get out of the rain." Another disappointment in a day of them. He was fat, how fat! And quite ugly, though she did not mind ugliness. Thick glasses and small, ripe lips. A little chin that nestled in folds of flesh, pale skin liberally moled, and a gross body below. He looked a larded forty in wet shirt and unbelted pants strained at the fly. Miss Everleave turned politely away in confusion, afraid she might have without intending betrayed her distaste.

But when he stepped into the light and spoke, the impression he made was entirely otherwise, she couldn't say exactly why, since he certainly became no thinner. His voice was pleasant, very pleasant, what she would call chuckly. He seemed to find the rain, the lack of furniture—he had understood the apartment would be furnished —the absence of bookshelves when all he had brought were his books, the crowded College Inn which could not give him a room for the night, from which he had just hiked through the storm, all a conspiracy put together for his amusement and hers. Behind the lenses his eyes shone at her, coaxed her to join the fun at his expense. She liked the shyness of his manner, though it threw her off stride that he seemed to use it in order to be outspoken. He gave out first impressions of the town and campus on an hour and a half's acquaintance with a candor and assurance that amazed her. The remarks flew from his curling lips; his shoulders shrugged to deprecate them as they came; all she had to do was listen. She did not know whether to laugh or take offense, but she was shrewd enough to recognize he was trying to be friendly.

"I'm Sam Johnson come to Scotland," he confessed and when she did not catch the allusion, interpolated quickly, "Strong suspicions of Ohio all my life and never been west of the Hudson till last night."

He went too fast. "You mean the Hudson River?" she asked. How could he never have been west of the Hudson? What was east of the Hudson? Was he foreign? He sounded American. "There's nothing east of the Hudson, is there?"

He seemed to think she had made a joke. He laughed happily. "Right, east of the Hudson is nothing. Offshore islands. I'm from one of them."

She racked her brain. Islands off the coast? She changed the subject. "You have no furniture. Where will you sleep tonight?"

"I don't know!" he said gaily. "In the bathtub?"

She gave him her sleeping bag and he thanked her effusively and had to be shown how it worked. Later, ready for bed, rubbing ointment on her welt, she heard him still moving around, cracking loose a tray of ice in his kitchen. He had left a warm feeling behind him. Miss Everleave liked and admired warm people; she knew her height and posture and untalkativeness sometimes gave an impression of coolness, which she recognized as a defect. It came to her; he must have meant Long Island. Or even Manhattan, for that matter. Of course! She grinned. That would explain why he'd never used a sleeping bag. She began to review the third set again, dozing off. But became aware Hector Ekstein was coming regularly into his kitchen, its wall adjacent to her bedroom, for water, the pipes thucking each time he turned the tap.

She told her brain to stop listening and it did. She fell asleep. The cracking of another tray of ice waked her. She sat up and checked her clock. Two A.M.! Why was he not asleep? Why drinking ice water? Had he had no dinner? Chewing ice from having had no dinner! Miss Everleave swung her long legs out of bed.

She got out of bed and padded to the closet, threw on a robe, and crossed the porch to his front door. Hector opened it and stepped back, arms spread in welcome. "My God! A *droit du seigneur* I don't know about?" He ushered her in. "I'm game if you are. Have a drink?"

She drew her bathrobe closer and wondered what he meant. He held up what was left of a quart of whiskey. Yet he seemed completely sober, moving for his weight with agility between the boxes toward the kitchen. The air in the room was hazed and stung her nose. Two full ashtrays and eight or nine open books were spread out around her sleeping bag, which he had not even unrolled. "I'm sorry to intrude, Dr. Ekstein, but I wondered if you'd had your dinner?"

Again, that shy smile. "How considerate. Yes, I ate at the Inn. Here." He handed her whiskey, which she did not tell him she rarely touched.

She watched him closely. "You're not a drinker, are you?"

"Gracious, no. Not unless you are. I'm sipping while I—" she was surprised to see him blush and falter, "—prepare my first lecture."

"It's almost two-thirty in the morning!"

"I hope you don't mind. I do appreciate the sleeping bag. It seemed simpler to stay up." He was a puppy dog, placating.

Involuntarily, she asked, "How old are you?"

He blushed more deeply. "Twenty." And snickered painfully. "Not even into my majority."

She was shocked. Twenty and all that flab! Quickly, she said, "That's very good to have your Ph.D. at twenty." And added, "Don't you worry. Lectures are easy." Again she watched him closely, for a sign of sneer. He would know, of course, her lectures were physical education.

But he seemed genuinely thankful. She said, "You must get yourself some furniture in the morning. I'll lend you my car if you like."

"That's so good of you." His whole face crinkled. She thought: what a merry type of person. He said, "But on my island many natives grow up without ever learning how to drive."

Now that she guessed he must mean Manhattan, she could see he was being amusing, so she laughed. "All right, I'll drive you." She put down her drink, untasted. "Since you're fed, that's all I came for. I'll get back to bed."

"So soon? I hope you'll come again, often."

"I won't. I rarely interfere with my tenants and vice versa. It's better that way. Unless you need something."

By November Miss Everleave had learned she need not have reassured Dr. Ekstein about his lectures; he had become a quick sensation on campus. Auditing Ekstein had become a Thing to Do. His coterie of student familiars was becoming the most select on campus. One of her Phys Ed majors told her he had scheduled private conferences with every one of his students about the reading they would do for their term paper from a reading list of hundreds of titles any of which he could talk about. He discarded the Economic History textbook and switched entirely to paperbacks; the local bookstore had to set up a special corner to house them. He ate regularly in the student dorms and seemed to think it a delight instead of a duty. One of Miss Everleave's own juniors defected to become a History major. He had become Prominent.

In what spare time she had, Miss Everleave spent the fall working on her lob topspin. Against her age, she undertook an extra conditioning program for the winter to keep her legs in shape: isometrics, ankle weights, a bicycle machine. And of course, she continued kneading the handball.

A matter that troubled her more than a little as fall turned cold was the incredible quantity of beer Dr. Ekstein consumed, leaving four or five cases of empties on the porch each Saturday to be picked up by DeFazio's delivery boy. He had been truthful in saying he was not a liquor drinker—there had been no bottle in the garbage since the first one. And town beer, she had been told, was only 3.2, scarcely more than a beverage. He must eat and drink nothing but 3.2 beer.

She appreciated the price Dr. Ekstein was paying for his phenomenal popularity: each night he came home with a green bag full of books from the college library, in addition to those he already had of his own, lined up along every wall and around each scanty piece of furniture. She watched him trudge up the drive, merry, fat, burdened as Santa Claus with his bag, heard him while he read each night until all hours, regularly every half-hour or so noisily snapping the cap off a bottle in his kitchen next to her bedroom.

But she was on good terms with him she believed, only once despite herself moved to suggest to him Diet-Pepsi instead of beer, for his weight's sake. He had replied with his shy smile, thanking her, that he certainly ought to and so much would like to, but Diet-Pepsi put him to sleep—this when he had bags under his eyes the size and color of olives. His cases of empties continued to appear on her porch each Saturday. He lost no weight and she continued to hear him in his kitchen late at night and early morning snapping his caps. During the day he was indefatigable; her History defector, aware she was his landlady, confided even Science majors were switching schedules to take Econ Hist and that his three History II sections would be reassigned to the largest hall in Wentworth at the new semester.

For the Christmas holidays Dr. Ekstein went home to his island, giving her a begonia for a present before he left, lugging it all the way from town. They said goodbyes with warmth; she called him Hector, he called her Florence.

But two days into the holiday she heard in the night sounds coming from his apartment. Investigating the next morning, she found no one there and nothing missing she could see. The next night, Christmas Eve, down in the basement on the parallel bars, she thought she heard sounds again. She went up and knocked at his door, but there was no answer. Christmas Day she drove to her old friend Coach Ben Kashimoto's home, as she had for years, bringing presents for him, his wife, the children. As always, it was a jovial day. He was Kashie, best backstroke in the Midwest, she was Everleave, toasted in tomato juice, the best forehand east of Pasadena and north of Houston. She enjoyed Kashie's heavy kindness, his wife's interminable rituals of the holiday, seeing the four children one year older.

Returning at dusk, she was surprised to see the lights on in Dr. Ekstein's apartment. This time knocking and knocking again, she was answered by an undressed young man and just behind him, in black lace, one of her sophomores. "Oh," exclaimed the surprised girl, "we thought you'd be someone else." The unperturbed young man answered her request for an explanation by saying Dr. Ekstein had given them his key for the holidays, and produced it. Miss Everleave took the key and told them they had three minutes to get out. They were not at all ashamed, seemed even angry.

When Dr. Ekstein returned the evening of January first, she asked him for an explanation. He was mild. "What kind of explanation, Florence? He's exceptionally promising, he's charming. They're two friends that wanted an apartment for the holidays."

She studied him, trying to figure his meaning. "I'm not running a brothel, Dr. Ekstein."

"I should hope not, you'd scare me into town if you were." His chuckle coaxed her. She felt mocked. "What's the problem?" he asked.

"Are they secretly married?"

He in turn seemed scandalized. "Certainly not. He's only nineteen, after all. Give him a fighting chance."

Again she wondered what in his brilliance he could be talking about. She said in growing wonder, "Why, you're not reliable, Dr. Ekstein."

He spread his hands. "But why, Florence, *please*, why?"

Her tongue was stiff. She could not tell him why when it was so unspeakably obvious. In her own house. All she said was, at last, "It must never happen again."

But the satisfaction she had taken in his success and his living beside her, as wholly given to his calling as she was to hers, satisfaction despite his empties on her porch and night noises that kept her awake, was gone. She saw that he continued overworking himself, single-minded as ever, as chaste as she and as uncaring, but always now there loomed for Miss Everleave the enormous, threatening unknown of great difference between them.

With the new semester she began a gymnastics seminar she gave in alternate years, which she anticipated especially this year because she had three good athletes, one of them outstanding. Because gym facilities were crowded—coeducational folk dance and modern dance had recently been approved for a quarter credit, neither of them legitimate sports in Miss Everleave's judgment, and the flatfooted were flocking to take advantage—she decided to hold the seminar in her own basement.

The three girls arrived on their bicycles at seven, warmed up for a half-hour with calisthenics, worked separately for an hour as she moved between them, holding a leg, straightening a back, slapping a stuck-out bottom, speaking infrequently and quietly, while the room warmed, silent except for their sighs and pants. They rested briefly and then together spent the final hour on the parallels, the best hour. She would demonstrate, they would repeat, again and again. There was hardly a word. When they had gone, Miss Everleave, drenched and extremely happy, would spend another hour writing up notes, working out regimens for each of them, blocking sequences for the next seminar while this one was still fresh in her mind.

One snowy morning she offered Dr. Ekstein a ride to Wentworth for his eight o'clock, not because she distrusted him less but because he would otherwise get his feet wet. Since the holidays they had exchanged scarcely a word. He did not look well. The hours he kept, his pace, his diet, were showing on his face, but still he was no thinner. He was always fastidious in dress, but today she noticed his fingernails, raggedly bitten to the quick. He made an effort to be genial. He told her he was taking a leaf from her book and moving one of his unofficial seminars, currently meeting at DeFazio's which closed at eleven, out to his apartment, which needn't close at all. As she let him out at Wentworth, she saw even at 7:45 A.M. of this snowing cold morning a waiting circle of students moving forward to enclose him.

Initially apprehensive, Miss Everleave was reassured when Dr. Ekstein's seminar proved to be all male and noncarousing. Though they stayed late, they were not loud. All they seemed to do was talk, steadily, for hours. At first they came once a week, then two or three times a week, talking endlessly into the night and early morning. Wholesome enough, she decided, trying to put herself to sleep.

Chapel speakers were elected by student ballot at the end of
March, five of the faculty invited to give a paper on a subject of his
(or, theoretically, her, but that had never happened) choice at a
series of Chapels the whole college attended. This March, Instructor Hector Ekstein won in a remarkable landslide. No one before had ever won by such a landslide, least of all a first-year
lecturer. Miss Everleave was both pleased and puzzled. Hector was
likable enough and certainly worked too hard; she had been told
his lectures were dazzling; she heard his quips quoted here and
there. But why it should all erupt in this overwhelming vote she did
not understand, nor the extraordinary jubilance it caused among the
students.

Over milk and graham crackers she questioned her seminar girls.
One of them burst out, "It's his charisma and his fantastic scholarship. He's out of this world. He's a showman, he's intrepid, he's got
character, he's *engagé*, he loves us, he's against *locum parentis*, it's
the concatenation." Miss Everleave sighed. She wished people
would speak simply. The girl added, "And he knows more about
parallel-bar technique than I do." Miss Everleave was startled.

In due course Hector gave his Chapel paper, which ended in a
standing ovation. The title of his talk was "Lonely Man on a Rock"
and the gist of it seemed to be a plea for understanding toward
those who chose or are condemned to spend their lives out on a
lonely rock, alone in their singular perception. Miss Everleave felt
her core touched. He seemed under the welter of words to be ad-
dressing her directly, to have singled her out for his topic. She was
bewildered by the clapping and fervent cries that followed his
speech. Everyone else seemed to feel just as she did. How many
lonely men on how many rocks could there be?

Nevertheless, that evening when he trudged up the drive, she
crossed the porch to tell him, "That was a fine speech, a great
speech. I wanted to thank you." His eyes gleamed; she knew in the
dark he was blushing; he made her feel she had crowned his day.
Feeling as warm toward him as she ever had, she teased him,
"Where did you learn parallel-bar technique? One of my girls tells
me you know more than she does."

His lips curled in their tentative way, his voice was chuckly as of
old. "You keep a text in the back seat of the MG. I read it one day
you gave me a lift, while you stopped for a head of lettuce." He

grinned. "I *don't* know more than she does. I'd break my legs if I actually *tried*."

Mollified, Miss Everleave suggested, "You've made quite an impression in your short time here. My students tell me you're leading a Reformation." She was not sorry to use the word. It hinted, since he knew parallel bars, she, also, knew history.

He laughed, this time without his twinkle. "Oh, well." Then in a rush, confessed with urgency, "Yes, like Luther. Faced with a peasants' revolution and wanting to backtrack. I want the study, Flo, and the protection of Princes; I'm ashamed of myself. But I *won't* be Luther, I can't, that constipated funk, I despise his bones. I'll stick with the peasants. Though they don't know anything. Anything at all."

Overpowered, lost, Miss Everleave wondered what to say. She hadn't an idea what he meant. She knew he was telling her something important and she wanted to help. She should never have pretended to know about the Reformation. Now he was waiting for some kind of answer. He was used to people he could talk to and who talked back. Mortification brought her to her height, her chin lifted. "I'm sorry, I don't know anything about it."

A step below, he looked up at her a moment and said, "You're very handsome, you know that?" Her words had been rebuffing, he was responding with tact.

She nodded. It was not the first time she had been told. He was changing the subject. She had wanted to help him and he had had to help her. The failure was upsetting. It spoiled her good mood.

She returned to her kitchen. Restless there, she went to the basement. She did swings and turns and leg crosses for a while, soon she was concentrating. What she desired of a sequence was that it should climb slowly to a strong finish; she despised a fake build more than incompetence. The series began to take a shape. She did a stand, two full turns, a pike, dive, save, final arm stand, brace and swung to the mat. She would have to quit. It was seminar night and the girls would be coming soon. She went upstairs.

Across the porch Hector's seminar had already begun. Through the thin wall and open windows she heard their male voices already edged, argumentative before the argument. Always the roosters, she thought, smiling, scrubbing her arms and legs with a towel. They couldn't find a bottle opener.

"Get it, can't you?"

"I'm hastening all I can. It isn't here is what."

"Find it yourself." Noise, shuffled silverware, clatter. "Hector! Where's your bottle opener!"

"So use your teeth. Don't be helpless. I'm extremely dry if you don't mind."

"Up you, pardon me. Use your own."

Miss Everleave stripped off her damp T-shirt and put on a fresh one. She sat on the edge of her bed and strapped on her ankle weights.

"Go next door and borrow one."

"Heh. After you."

"Chicken. Always."

"Go ahead. Get us a bottle opener from next door. Your idea. Get for us a bottle opener from her."

"The girls here yet?"

"Nope. She's all alone yours."

"I'll wait. Hector! Please! We can't find the opener!"

At her bureau Miss Everleave pared her nails, grinning. She could take a bottle opener over, except they'd think she'd been eavesdropping.

Hector's voice, coming into the kitchen, "I own at least three bottle openers."

The first voice, light and hoarse, "Contrary to fact. Find one."

The second voice, deep, "I told him go next door for one. He's chicken."

Light voice, "When the girls come."

"Chicken, chicken."

Miss Everleave, flexing her weighted ankle, paused: why chicken?

Light voice, "I do not provoke, see?"

Deep voice, "Go, boy, gird your loins. Storm Lesbos, come back a man."

Miss Everleave closed her eyes and sucked air in slowly, waited —waited for Hector to come down hard on the deep voice.

Light voice, "I wait for the girls. It's safer."

Miss Everleave waited, breath held.

Hector's voice, chuckly, said, "Why safer? One is safe. Four together could be an orgy."

Light and deep blended in laughter, rooster crows. Miss Everleave's lips loosened and the breath came out.

Too little, too late, Hector's voice added, "Enough time wasted?"

Miss Everleave's hand sought her pin tray, where she kept one of her handballs, found it, began to squeeze. But no footsteps came along the porch. And then because she was accustomed to disregard pain, she straightened, put the ball back in the pin tray, went to her desk to review her notes until the girls came.

After the girls had gone she remained at the parallels, instead of coming upstairs to do her written work. But there was no assuagement in it. At last she gave up, showered, and sitting at the kitchen table wrote a short note to Dr. Ekstein suggesting he seek other quarters.

She left the note in his mailbox on her way to class and when she returned that evening he was waiting for her on the porch steps with her note in his hand, anxiety on his pale, olive-bagged, and mole-flecked face. He wrung his hands. "But Florence! What did I do! What have I done!" His consternation was clear, the only clear element in the cloud of unknown he was.

She said, "Less said, the better." She dreaded that he might become vindictive. On the courts, proximity to a poor loser could make her physically ill.

He flapped his arms vaguely toward his door. "But I have to talk about it. Can't you say why? It's all so—inexplicable. I thought we got along so well, I thought . . . Won't you come in, have some . . . milk?" She was relieved to see his shoulders drop, his hand flutter; he was not going to be nasty.

"No. You can stay till the end of the school year." The concession made her feel better.

But he would not let her have it. Again that trick of opening himself, deliberately courting invasion, he said, "It's not losing the apartment, Florence; it's losing you." How easily he did it—zzip! open, walk in, I'm all yours—she drew back, an actual step backward on the porch. She had almost gone ahead and thrown it at him, so bold, ignorant, sure of himself, asking for it, sent all her anger screaming cold into that stupidly young unzipped pouch. Even as she smothered her anger, fumbling for her key, she gloated at what it could have done to him. She walked to her door.

From the steps he called after her, tentative but stubborn. "You're one of the Counter-Reformation?"

She turned around to look at him, her key in the lock and the door half-open. He stood with podgy hands half-raised toward her, upper lip lifted in inquiry, for all the world as if he thought he was talking sense. "Gibberish," she told him and went in.

But she sought out her former junior who had defected to history. Last year the girl had adored her, now she was brusque. "For God's sake, you don't *know* what's going on? I mean, Miss Everleave, I don't want to be *rude*." There were, the girl said, in fact, two camps, the Reform and the Counter-Reform. They had always been there, the contentions, the proposals, the battle lines. The girl was a talking encyclopedia of classified faculty infighting. "But now all this a*morph*ous matter has been given bones, oh, Miss Everleave. *Hector*'s bones." She flipped open her spiral notebook and fired, "*Why* have *three* Faculty Committees issued recommendations this year, *why* has the Administration promised a White Paper for June, *why* will there be an Alumni Magazine Special Issue at graduation, *why* is the Student Council revolutionizing house rules, *why* is the Reporter printing Manifestos, *why, why,* Miss Everleave?" She scarcely paused. "On the other hand is the enemy. *You* know. Anti. As-you-were. Dump-Ekstein. Be grateful. Jesus."

"What do you mean, dump-Ekstein?" she asked the girl in parting.

"Naturally. Arch Seven leaked that two weeks ago." The girl rushed off for a class.

This Arch Seven innovation Miss Everleave had heard of from Ben Kashimoto. Each evening at seven at the Memorial Arch students were gathering to hear anyone speak about anything. At the same time, Ben also told her about the decision to rewrite the course curriculum of the Physical Education Department, a suggestion she had last made thirteen years ago. Miss Everleave by virtue of seniority was offered the chairmanship of the committee, but declined because the meetings would fall during the only hours the courts were free enough of students for her own practice.

She found her legs had weathered the winter and her hours of work against the gym wall had given her lob topspin a jump it had never had before. Her net game was the next obstacle.

At home Miss Everleave tried to carry on, but Hector Ekstein's apartment had become, practically, a student lobby. Because the house was a mile and more from campus, the students rode bicycles, which continually blocked her drive and gouged her lawn.

At night knots of students retired to the porch to finish arguments too subtle for the din of Hector's sitting room; they lay together on their backs on the grass, elucidating to the moon. Some nights Hector spent shut away in his bedroom trying to keep up his reading or prepare his lectures, for she heard the voices calling out to him at midnight, to unlock his door. Other nights he took the floor and she heard, blurred by the walls, the lilt that launched the Reformation. In either case, she had much less sleep, but said nothing.

One raining morning two weeks before exams she pulled the cover off her MG and noticed Hector's door was open, banging in the wind against the doorstop. She went to close it and saw rain had wet the whole hall, stood in puddles on the oak floor. She went for mop and towels and on her knees in his hall began to sop up water. As she was doing this she looked into his sitting room and saw him lying in his last night's clothes asleep on his blue sofa. Surprised—she knew he had an eight o'clock—and shamed—celibate and forty-six, she found a sleeping male an unnatural sight—she could not decide whether she wanted to get out or finish. How terrible he looked—even, at last, losing weight. In sleep the folds under his eyes, his cheeks, his jowls were sunken, unpleasantly colored, hanging loose; it was his fastidiousness that had made him seem much healthier than he was. Asleep he had no such protection. Her consternation grew. He was sick! This whole year long it had been happening! Her hands wrung the towel and excess water dripped, splashing on the floor and waking him. He opened his eyes and saw her, sat up unsteadily, feeling his beard. "What's it—" he began, then slumped, holding his head.

"Are you all right?" she asked.

"What is the time of day?"

"About a quarter of eight."

His head jerked. "I'll be late!" He stood up, holding his pants.

"Why don't you be sick today? You are."

"No, no." He rubbed his scalp and scrubbed his cheeks. "Shower!" He headed away and stopped, turning to her, hesitated. No, she noticed, he no longer unzipped so easily. "Uh, look. I know you don't like me, but would you give me a lift to Wentworth?"

"All right. You'll have to hurry."

In the car he leaned back and closed his eyes. His bulk cramped them, made the cabin small as a fitted sock, their laps and knees conspicuous. She backed down the drive. "You should have stayed home. I could have come home at noon and fixed soup or something."

He rubbed his eyes. "If I had stayed home, soup would not have been the problem. If I had missed my class by noon I would have had twenty bowls and twenty of them swarming out to feed me." It struck her. The same tone as when he had said, one is safe; four might be an orgy. She perceived that it was his way. He could betray with a joke his students' loyalty as easily as he had her. The pleasure of helping him out melted away. She regretted having felt pleasure.

He was not aware of the change. "Anyway, this is good again." He rested. At the red light he made an overture. "The old days were nicer, weren't they, Flo?" She was glad to feel him waiting for an answer until it was clear she was not going to give him one. He looked down at his bitten nails. He rummaged in his pockets for his lecture notes.

And then just before exam week everything seemed to happen at once: two of the faculty reform reports came out, her own department's curriculum revision, the administration's white paper, the alumni magazine's extra issue, the student newspaper's *Complete Manifesto for Change*, Arch Seven's *56 Intolerables* written out on lavender toilet-paper streamers and flung over the Memorial Arch, all the activated matter Hector's bones had pulled together and set dancing.

Miss Everleave kept herself aloof as best she could, agreeing when she was spoken to, avoiding being spoken to when possible. She knew her tolerance for talk was low, but it seemed to her it had never been put to such a strain. No one would be quiet, absolutely no one. Even Ben Kashimoto was full of opinion when she retreated to his home, even his turkey-baking wife, even his two daughters roller-skating in the hall. Everything alive wherever she looked was jittering to the dance.

Miss Everleave refused to read the documents, she refused to sign anything, she refused to disagree. It made no difference at all. There was no sanctuary, not her office, not the courts, least of all her own home around which the bicycles lay drunkenly everywhere. The students lounged along the porch and in the windows and on the grass, leaning at each other exchanging paragraphs. Even into her most private precinct, her basement gym, the three seminar girls arrived for their final exam and spent time heatedly whispering, until she sent them away with a rare show of temper.

And just as she believed things could not possibly be worse, news of the nonrenewal of Hector Ekstein's contract leaked. A departmental document, to be held secret until the campus was vacated for the summer, was stolen; Xeroxed copies spread over the campus within two hours of the theft. She was handed one in the grocery store.

As she brought her grocery bag into her kitchen she saw Hector's seminar Regulars around his door, eyes bright with pain, one of them, whose deep voice she would never forget, openly crying. She heard them proposing through her kitchen window as she unpacked her sack: black armbands, a bonfire, an effigy hanging of the History Department head, a funeral procession with coffin—all rejected as puerile. Then: mass resignations and transfers, diploma burning, honors rejection. The cursing became obscene and Miss Everleave shut her window.

Shortly, someone knocked. It was her junior student who had defected to History. "Please, Miss Everleave, I have to talk to you?"

"Sure. What about?" The girl's face was blotched. Her hand held a pen, papers.

"We want faculty protest signatures. I've got one for simple protest and one for threat to resign, whichever you choose." She laid them on the table.

"I'm sorry, I don't sign things."

"Yes, I know. But this is different. We can't let this happen. We can't." Her hands made fists, her elbows hugged her body.

Miss Everleave's sense of fair play made her say, "It is sad news. He's been good for the college."

"He has! Has he ever!" The girl was radiant. "Which one do you want to sign?"

"Neither."

"But you just *said* . . . if you feel that way don't you *want*—"

"No."

"It's un*just* . . . We *can't* let . . . We *have to* . . ." Barely controlled, she paused.

"I don't ever sign, however I feel."

"But for *him*, your own *neighbor*, *shafted* in broad daylight." The girl's voice rose.

"Even so." Miss Everleave smiled slightly.

The girl studied her, but Miss Everleave made no move to pick up the pen. The girl's expression changed slowly, she uttered a long, extended guttural, "Ugggggh," she breathed. "You. You . . . non-combatant." She swept up her petitions and left.

But Hector declined to be martyred. He refused all efforts on his behalf. He dissuaded the petitioners and curbed his Regulars. He was asked to prevent a History *magna cum laude* from a public repudiation of it and he did so. He was asked to speak at Arch Seven and did, to a hushed mob of students which blocked Miss Everleave in her MG, coming home after a net-practice workout. She watched the Ekstein magic at work as his squat figure paced and wheeled, paced and wheeled along the Arch dais telling them that to make an issue of one dismissed instructor was not nearly as important as getting on with the real options the year had opened. He did not deny he thought injustice had been done him, which comforted them; they noisily approved. "But which do you want?" he challenged them, "justice or solutions? You can't have everything!"—which fell like a blasphemy, thrilling them to silence.

The sum effect, after so many days of collective tension, was a growing approval of the wise young man who behaved and spoke so well. No one wanted him a martyr—except his Regulars and even they were wavering. Reforms had become possible. On the whole, one and all were grateful to Hector that they could have his bones and eat them, too.

Miss Everleave observed that at last faculty, students, administration were turning faces in a slow pivot toward commencement. Without the threat of brutal confrontations all parties had much to gain. Much had been accomplished by the Reformation, much proposed, there was welcome room for positively oriented, temperate consolidation. A weighty consensus of hope, concluded the student *Reporter* in its final issue of the year. Miss Everleave read the editorial as she used the pages to wrap her dinner scraps for the pail.

Late in the night Hector knocked at her kitchen door. He asked to come in. Much earlier she had heard him send away his Regulars so he could finish up his blue books and for several hours Miss Everleave had enjoyed a quiet she had not known for weeks. She had been on the bars, was drinking a glass of water at the sink in her T-shirt and track shorts, enjoying the slow, earned relaxation of her muscles and mind. The knock was an intrusion.

"I'm all done!" he exclaimed. "Finished! Phut!" He spread his clumsy fingers. "You want to have a goodbye drink with me?" It was the opposite of unzipping, a guarded dare; the year had taught him something.

She would have much preferred another time. Out of courtesy, one final one, she said, "Oh, well. Sit down. I'll be back in a minute." She had to shower in a hurry and skimp the rubdown. Incompletely dry, her skin resisted, twisted her underwear. Cheated of their slow massage, her thighs felt heavy, her calves lumpy. She pulled on a shirt and slacks and combed the kinks out of her hair. Be a sport, she ordered.

He was waiting at the kitchen table with two drinks, hers pale, his dark amber. She fished the ice cubes from hers and added hot water to reduce the chill. "To the soul's ease," he toasted and they both sipped.

"It's a shame you have to leave. I can't see you did a thing wrong to them."

"I can't either." He tipped back his chair, awkwardly sporty.

"They'll do it every time," she ventured, irritated at his smartiness but wishing him well enough.

"Will they now." From his precarious balance he looked directly at her.

She saw her remark was tactless and also not very true. It made them stupid instead of wrong. It didn't do justice to the large injustice she could see he felt under the thin sportiness. "You had a raw deal here," she amended, "a very raw deal. They should be ashamed. After you've been gone awhile they will be. Don't worry." She shifted slightly because the elastic of her underwear was binding at her hip.

That was all it took, that one polite concession. "Christ!" he choked. The chair legs banged on her linoleum, he hit her table with the flat of his palm. "Oh, Christ, a raw deal!" His fingers curled over his mouth to shut it.

For a terrible moment Miss Everleave thought he was going to weep. Her superbly trained body and brain reacted instantly; gland discharge, tensed buttocks, nape pricks, sharpened vision. Warily, she watched his struggle, waited.

He won. He shrugged and drank. "That's the way the cookie bounces," he said with the merest edge of bitterness.

Relieved, Miss Everleave let her tension slack. She smiled and sipped, too. She wanted to find words to tell him she approved of him. "You're okay," she said.

Then without warning, in a fury, he said, "And a raw deal from you, too." Everything about his face was tight—shooting lips, pinched nose, eyes like forced screws splintering the skin around.

Once on the parallel in a split moment of slack attention her grip had slipped and the bar had caught her under the chin, jamming her sense. The bleakness of his voice had the impact of that blow. "Me? I?" she murmured. Even as her brain fought to recover it recognized his bleakness and how extreme it was.

The bleakness was a toad he had let jump on the kitchen table between them. A toad with whose back markings her own life had made her familiar. She knew her toad. She could and had at other times examined it without fright or repulsion, in the small cage she allowed it. It was a double jamming that slowed her brain's recovery: that someone else could have a toad like hers, that he could let it loose. Hector had flipped his on the table, not horny side up but all soft green tummy pulsing. She saw the moist, delicate membrane, unseen, unimagined until now.

Miss Everleave was appalled but she was not a coward. An Imperative faced her. She must do something: flip it back, pick it up and hold it gently and return it to Hector. She must do something for it, felt herself moving to a verge. But her head cleared a little and she perceived the toad was only an impression, not actually there on the table, and the verge receded.

It had, so to say, jumped back into Hector. She must do something for *him*. Almost, she felt her arms lift to extend across the table and take his head between her hands. But her head cleared a little more and Hector's white face and speckly moles came into focus and she perceived how inappropriate and embarrassing such an impulse would be for both of them, and the verge moved off again.

But she must do something, anything, a gesture of comfort. Must, she pleaded to her brain, tried to think of various beginnings, raked to catch a snag of one, none came to mind. Raked, raked, did not know how to go about it further. Help, help me, she cried out to herself.

All that occurred to her was to act in accordance with her manner of procedure on the bars: build a deliberate sequence leading to a strong but unhoked finish. She raised her glass and drank it all down, to make clear to Hector she entirely accepted his invitation to drink goodbye. She smiled to show that she considered all was well between them. She spoke. "I want you to know that your Chapel speech was the finest I have ever heard. I'll remember it the rest of my life." And lastly, she went to the drawer beside the sink and came back with a bottle opener. She gave it to him. "It's a present. So in an emergency you'll never be without one."

They shook hands and said goodbye. When Hector had left, Miss Everleave pulled the door to and leaned on it. She looked around her kitchen, once more hers alone. In a day or so the whole house would be once more hers alone. She bowed her head. Not by a mile had the manner of her procedure been up to what was needed. Steps taken in a sequence toward a verge gone out of sight. She went to the sink to close the drawer and picked up her handball to knead. Her fingers dented into it, her fingernails pierced its surface. Against a rising panic her fingers pressed, rolled it, pressed again. Why couldn't I? Why not up to it? When the little thing had first jumped out and been capsized, that would have been the moment, even a moment later, time enough, even . . .

Miss Everleave sat down in the chair beside the kitchen table and clasped her hands together and squeezed the handball till her arm shook. And the seat where she sat was a high hard rock and every bit as cold.

PETER TAYLOR was born in Trenton, Tennessee in 1917, and grew up in Tennessee and Missouri. He is married to the poet Eleanor Ross Taylor, and they live in Charlottesville, Virginia, where Mr. Taylor teaches in the English Department of the University of Virginia. Mr. Taylor has published four volumes of short stories, a novel, and a play, and is about to have a new collection of stories published. He is working on a novel and a new play. This is his fourth story to receive an O. Henry Award.

First Heat

HE turned up the air conditioning and lay across the bed, wearing only his jockey shorts. But it didn't stop. Two showers already since he came in from the afternoon Session! Showers had done no good. Still, he might take another presently if it continued. The flow of perspiration was quite extraordinary. Perhaps it was the extra sleeping pill he took last night. He had never been one to sweat so. It was rather alarming. It really was. And with the air conditioner going full blast he was apt to give himself pneumonia.

What he needed of course was a drink, and that was impossible. He was not going to have a single drink before she arrived. He was determined to be cold sober. She would telephone up from the desk—or from one of the house phones nearby. He always thought of her as telephoning directly from the desk. Somehow that made the warning more official. But she did always telephone, did so out of fear he might not have his regular room. So she said. He knew better, of course. Married for nearly fifteen years, and at home she still knocked on doors—on the door to his study, on the door to the bathroom, even on the door to their bedroom. She even had the children trained to knock on doors, even each other's doors. Couldn't she assume that since he knew she was on the way, knew she was by now wheeling along the interstate—doing seventy-five and more in her old station wagon—couldn't she assume that whatever kind of fool, whatever kind of philanderer she might suspect him of being, he would have the sense to have set matters right by the time she got there? But what rot! As if he didn't *have* a problem, as if he needed to make one up!

He could hear his own in the Senate Chamber that afternoon. Not his words, just his guilty voice. Suddenly he got up off the bed, pulled back the spread, the blanket, the top sheet. He threw himself down on his back, stuck his legs in the air and pulled off his shorts. They were wringing wet with his damnable perspiration! He wadded them into a ball, and still lying on his back, still holding his legs in the air, he hurled the underwear at the ceiling, where it made a faintly damp spot before falling to the carpeted floor. And she—she would already know what his voice in the Senate Chamber had said. (His legs still in the air) And knowing how the voting went, know who betrayed whom, who let whom down, who let what bill that was supposed to go through intact be amended. It would all have been reported on the local six o'clock State news, perhaps even with his taped voice uttering the words of betrayal. She would have picked it up on the radio in the station wagon just after she set out, with her evening dress in a suitbox beside her. Maybe she would even have turned back, feeling she just couldn't face certain people at the Mansion reception tonight . . . or couldn't face him.

Now—only now—he let his legs drop to the bed, his feet coming down wide apart on the firm, first-rate-hotel mattress. And he threw out his arms, one hand palm upward landing on each pillow of the double bed. He *would* relax, *would* catch a quick nap. But a new charge of sweat pressed out through every pore of his skin, on his forehead, on his neck, in the soft area just above his collar bone, from the exposed inner sides of his thighs and his ankles, from the exposed arm pits and upper arms and forearms, from the palms of his hands and the soles of his feet. He felt he was aware of every infinitesimal modicum of sweat that was passing through every pore of every area of his body. Somehow it made him feel more utterly, thoroughly naked than he had ever before felt in his entire life. Yes, and this time the sweat came before the thought—just a little before the thought this time. The thought of what he had done and left undone concerning the amendment, said and left unsaid concerning the amendment, the thought of the discrepancy between his previously announced position and the position he finally took on the floor all thought of *that* seemed something secondary and consequential to the sweat. Perhaps he was ill, really ill! Perhaps it was only a coincidence that this sickening sweat had come over his body. But no, he was not that sort—to claim illness. One thing for certain, though, the sweat was already like icewater on his skin.

Now he would have to get up and dry himself off again. There was a scratching sensation in his throat. He even coughed once. He would have to turn *down* the air conditioner. And he would have to find something else to focus his mind on. After all, he had not betrayed his country or his family. And not, God knew, his constituents. Was it only old man Nat Haley he was worrying about? He had agreed to support Nat Haley's waterways bill, had been quite outspoken in favor of it. The newspapers all over the State had quoted him. And then, yesterday, he had received promises from other sources, promises so much to the interest of his constituents that he could not resist. By God, it was the sort of things he—*and* she—had known he would have to do if he stood for the legislature and got elected, the sort of thing he would have to face up to if he went into politics, where everybody had said *he* ought not to go. He and she had looked each other in the eye one day—before he ever announced—and said as much. . . . Well, at the last minute he had agreed to support the very amendment which Nat Haley had said would be ruinous, would take all the bite out of his bill. But Nat Haley was, himself, the damnedest kind of double-dealer. Even *he* had observed that. Ah, he was beginning to know politics. And he was beginning to understand what "everybody" had meant. Old Nat Haley was well known for the deals he arranged and didn't live up to. Everyone knew about Nat Haley. Nat Haley wouldn't have hesitated to fight this bill itself if he had discovered, even at the last minute, that that was to his advantage.

Who, then, was he betraying? And it wasn't a bill of any great import, either.

He sat up and swung his feet over the side of the bed. His hand came down briefly on the moisture his body had left on the otherwise starchy hotel sheet. He glanced backward and saw the wet shadow of himself that his perspiration had left there, and he turned away from it. But as he turned away from his silhouette on the sheet, there he was, in all his nakedness, in the large rectangu-

lar mirror above the dresser. And there he was in the mirror on
the open bathroom door. He reached to the floor and took up a
bath towel he had dropped there earlier and began drying himself—and hiding himself. He stood up and went over his body
roughly with the towel; then, his eyes lighting on the mirror on the
bathroom door, he wadded up the towel, just as he had the jockey
shorts, and hurled it at the door. It came right up against his face
there! And when it had fallen, he realized that this time it wasn't
—as so often—his face in the mirror that offended him. He didn't
care about the face. He knew it too well and what its every line
and look meant. The body interested him as never before, or as it
had not in years. For a moment, it was like meeting someone from
the past, someone he had almost forgotten—an old friend, an old
enemy. It was—almost—a young man's body still; he was not forty
yet and he exercised as much as he ever had and ate and drank
with moderation. The body in the door mirror and in the large
mirror over the dresser had good tone, was only a little heavier
about the hips than it had once been, and the arm muscles were
really better developed than when he was twenty. Taking in the
different views he had of the body in the two mirrors he recalled
that as late as his college days he had sometimes shadow boxed before mirrors, usually wearing his ordinary boxer shorts and imagining they were made of silk with his name, or some title like *The
Killer*, embroidered on them in purple or orange letters. He didn't
smile over the recollection. But neither did he take any such
stance before the mirrors now. The body in the mirrors was tense,
as if prepared to receive a blow; and he looked at it objectively as
a painter or a sculptor might, as a physician might. He observed
features that particularized it; the modest island of dark hair on
the chest, which narrowed into a peninsula pointing down below
the navel and over the slightly rounded belly, almost joining the
pubic hair above the too innocent looking penis; the elongated
thighs; the muscular calves; the almost hairless arms; the shoulders, heavy and slightly stooped. Presently his interest in himself
seemed entirely anatomical. And all at once it was as though his
eyes were equipped with X-rays. He could see beneath the skin and
under the flesh to the veins and tendons and the ropelike muscles,
the heart and lungs, the liver, the intestines, the testicles, as well
as every bone and joint of the skeleton. And now it was as though
a klieg light—no, a supernatural light shone from behind him and

through him. Only when at last he moved one foot, shifting his weight from one leg to the other, did the flesh and the covering skin return. Had it been a dream? A vision? It seemed to him now that he was not naked at all, or that this was not the nakedness he had sought when he removed his clothes. At any rate, his body had ceased to sweat.

He stepped back to the bed and lay down on his side, his back to the mirrors. He experienced momentary relief. It was as though he had seen beyond mere nakedness of body and spirit, had looked beyond all that which particularized him and made his body and his life meaningful, human. Was that the ultimate nakedness? Why, it could just as well have been old Nat Haley's insides he had seen. And he did relax now. He closed his eyes. . . . But then it came on again. Only this time there was no sweat. There was just the explicit dread of that moment—soon now, soon—when he would open the door to her. And he thought of how other, older politicians would laugh at his agonizing over so small a matter. *They* would know what a mistake politics was for him. Or perhaps they would know that, like them, he was *made* for politics. Wasn't this merely his baptism—in betrayal? In politics the ends were what mattered, had to matter. In politics that was the only absolute. If you were loyal to other men, you were apt to betray your constituency. Or did he have it all backward? No, he had it right, he was quite sure. And for that very reason, wasn't the State Senate as far as he would go and farther than he should have gone? Friends had warned him against State politics especially. His father had said to him: "You are the unlikeliest looking political candidate I have ever seen." But it was a decision she and he had made together, and together they had agreed that one's political morality could not always coincide with one's private morality. They had read that somewhere, hadn't they? At any rate, one had to be prepared to face up to that morality. . . . And now, though he felt chilled to the bone, the sweat came on again. He rolled over and reached for the towel on the floor, forgetting he had thrown it at the mirror. As he got off the bed, the same hand that had reached for the towel reached out to the wall and turned down the air conditioner. He went into the bathroom and got a dry towel and came back drying himself—or those two hands were drying him. He stopped before the long mirror on the bathroom door, the hands still drying him. He remembered something else

his father had said to him once when they were on a fishing trip at
Tellico Plains. He had gone for a swim in the river and stood on
a rocky slab beside the water afterward, first rubbing his chest and
his head with a towel and then fanning his body with it before and
aft. His father, watching the way he was fanning himself with the
towel, said, "You do cherish that body of yours, don't y'?" But what
mistaken notions his father had always had about him. Or perhaps
it was only wishful thinking on his father's part. Perhaps he had
only *wished* that kind of concern for him. Ah, if only his body
had been his great care and concern in life—his problem! And no
doubt that's what his sweating meant! He *wished* it were only a
bodily ill!

He wasn't, as a matter of fact, a man who was given to lolling
about this way with no clothes on—either at home or in a hotel
room. And it occurred to him now that it wasn't sweat alone that
had made him do so today. As soon as he had walked into the
room and closed the door after him he had begun pulling off his
clothes. It seemed to him almost that the sweat began *after* he had
stripped off his clothes. But he couldn't definitely recall now
whether it had begun before or after he got to the room. At any
rate, he wasn't *sure* it had begun before. Had it? Else, why had
he undressed at once? . . . He lay down on the bed again and his
eye lit on the black telephone beside the bed. The first thing some
men did when alone in a hotel room, he knew, was to take up the
telephone and try to arrange for a woman to come up. Or that was
what he always understood they did. The point was, he should
have *known*. But he—he would hardly know nowadays how to
behave with such a woman. He would hardly know what to say
or do if one of those hotel creatures came into the room. Or would
he know very well, indeed! Yes, how simple it all would be. What
a great satisfaction, and how shameful it would seem afterward.
How sinful—how clearly sinful—he would know himself to be.
There the two of them are, in bed. But suddenly there comes a
knock on the door! He will have to hide her. His wife is out there
in the passage. The baby sitter came a little early. And the traffic
was not as bad as she had anticipated. With the new interstate, a
forty-mile drive is nothing. He has no choice. There isn't anything
else he can do: He will have to hide the creature. She will have to
stand naked, her clothes clutched in her arms, behind the drapery
or in the closet, while he and his wife dress for the reception at the

Governor's Mansion. If only—. But the telephone, the real, black telephone was ringing now, there on the real bedside table.

He let it ring for thirty seconds or so. Finally he took up the instrument. He said nothing, only lay on his side breathing into the mouthpiece.

"Hello," she said on the house phone. He could hear other voices laughing and talking in the lobby.

"Hello," he managed.

"I'm downstairs," she said, as she always said, waiting for him to invite her to come up. He invited her now, and she replied "Is everything all right? You sound funny."

"Everything's fine. Come on up," he said. "You've heard the news?"

"I listened in the car, on the way over."

"I changed my mind about the Bill," he said.

"Is Mr. Haley pretty angry?"

"He cut me cold on the Capitol steps afterward."

"I thought so," she said. "He was icy to me when I passed him in the lobby just now. Or I imagined he was."

"Do you still want to go to the reception?"

She laughed. "Of course I do. I'm sure you had good reasons."

"Oh, yes, I had good reasons."

"Then, shall I come on up?"

"Do," he said. But then he caught her before she hung up. "Wait," he said. He sat on the bed, pulling the sheet up about his hips. "Why don't you wait down there? Why don't we go some-where and have a drink and something to eat before we dress for the reception? I'm starved."

"I'm starved, too," she said. "I had only a very small snack with the children at four-thirty."

"I'll be right down," he said.

"Well—" She hesitated and then said, "No, I have my dress with me in a box—my dress for tonight. I want to put it on a hanger. I'll be right up—that is, if you don't mind."

"Good," he said.

"And why don't we have our drink up there. It might be easier."

"Good," he said.

As soon as he had put down the telephone, he sprang from the bed, ran to pick up his sweaty shorts and the sweaty hotel towels. He began straightening the room and pulling on his clothes at the

same time, with desperate speed. She must not find him undressed, this way. It would seem too odd. And if he should begin
the sweating again, he was lost, he told himself. He would have to
to try ignore it, but she would notice, and she would know. . . .
She would be on the elevator now, riding up with the other members of the legislature and their wives, wives who had also come
to town for the reception at the Mansion. He felt utterly empty, as
though not even those veins and tendons and bones and organs
were inside him. Wearing only his shirt and fresh shorts and his
black socks and supporters, he stopped dressing long enough to
give the bed a haphazard making up. He yanked the sheet and
blanket and spread about. Fluffed the pillows. But if only there
were something besides his body, something else tangible to hide.
Catching a glimpse of himself in the mirror, he blushed bashfully
and began pulling on his trousers to cover his naked legs. While
slipping his tie under his collar, he was also pushing his feet into
his shoes. As he tied the necktie and then tied the shoe strings,
he was listening for her footsteps in the passage. Oh, if only, if
only—if only there were a woman, herself covered with sweat, and
still—still panting, for him to hide. What an innocent, simple thing
it would be. But there was only himself. . . . When the knock
came at the door, he was pulling on his jacket. "Just a second," he
called. And for no reason at all, before opening the door he went
to the glass topped desk on which lay his open briefcase and
closed the lid to the case, giving a quick snap to the lock. Then
he threw open the door.

It was as though only a pair of blue eyes—bodiless, even lidless
—hung there in the open doorway, suspended by invisible wires
from the lintel. He read the eyes as he had not been able to read
the voice on the telephone. They were not accusing. They had
done their accusing in the car, no doubt, while listening to the
radio. Now they were understanding and forgiving. . . . He bent
forward and kissed the inevitable mouth beneath the eyes. It too
was understanding and forgiving. But if only the mouth and eyes
would not forgive, not yet. He wanted their censure, first. She
entered the room, with the suitbox under her arm, and went
straight over to the closet. He held his breath, his eyes fixed on the
closet door. She paused with her hand on the doorknob and looked
back at him. Suddenly he understood the kind of sympathy she
felt for him. Is it the lady or the tiger? her hesitation seemed to

say. If only, she seemed to say with him, if only it *were* the lady, naked and clutching her bundle of clothing to her bosom. But he knew of course, as did she, it would be the tiger, the tiger whose teeth they had drawn beforehand, whose claws they had filed with their talk about the difference between things private and things political. The tiger was that very difference, that very discrepancy, and the worst of it was that they could never admit to each other again that the discrepancy existed. They stood facing each other well and fully clothed. When, finally, she would open the closet door they would see only his formal evening clothes hanging there, waiting to be worn to the Governor's Mansion tonight. And while he looked over her shoulder she would open the cardboard box and hang her full-length white evening gown beside his tuxedo. And after a while the tuxedo and the evening gown would leave the hotel room together and go down the elevator to the lobby and ride in a cab across town to the Governor's Mansion. And there was no denying that when the tuxedo and the evening gown got out of the taxi and went up the steps to the Mansion and then moved slowly along in the receiving line, he and she, for better or worse, would be inside them. But when the reception was over and the gown and the tuxedo came down the steps from the Mansion, got into another taxi, and rode back across town to their empty hotel room, who was it that would be in them then? Who?

THOMAS STERLING has lived in Rome for the past nine years, and traveled extensively in Africa. He is the author of five novels, including *SILENT SIREN, THE EVIL OF THE DAY,* and *STRANGERS AND AFRAID.*

Bedlam's Rent

The trouble with me, if you want to know, Mr. Winter—doll, do find a match for me. *Must* I beg, for God's sake? Thank you. I don't really look like this. Christ, there I go. Stop it, Maggie. The trouble with me is that I'm not worldly. Find me another drink. I won't go into that terrible room again. You do it. I know you can. No ice. And don't tell anyone it's for me. They won't give it to you. I like your hands. And please, please give me a light. Hurry!"

It was never an ordinary companionship. And John Winter sometimes felt it wasn't a companionship so much as an exercise in patience; but at this point he was merely being what he looked: an upright, pink-faced young man who frequently used patience as a weapon against what he did not understand. He was a "member of life," as she later informed him.

The party had ebbed and surged through the flimsy suburban house, threatening at moments to break out to the lawn where expectant garden chairs waited in the dying light. During one of the surges John found himself watching the greening light that came through a prim wood of poplar. A voice behind him said: "Of course you *did* run away from me. I'm not chasing you. God, I can't stand Siamese couples. One woman . . . Don't gossip, Maggie. Look at the yellow coming through *now. Please* sit down. Oh, the fools. Why don't they come out? No, I don't want them. I don't want anything but peace—go away. I didn't mean that. You are sweet. At least *you* had the sense to come out. *Look* at the sky. Look!"

She had been married many times, although she appeared to be

"Bedlam's Rent" – Thomas Sterling, *The Paris Review*, First published in *The Review*, Issue No. 42.

a few years under thirty. She had come here alone tonight. She had a smattering of knowledge of a great many things, not for the knowledge, it appeared to John, but for the things. She rushed into intimacy and rushed away again, with the scorn of the rejected; but it didn't seem to him that she cared much, one way or the other.

"You *really* have good hands, that's why I asked you to get me a drink. I wanted to see them. All right, *don't* say anything about my hands. To hell with you. I'm going." But she didn't go. Not then. John felt it was the evening light that held her, however, not him. He noticed that her hands were extremely beautiful. Her face, at certain angles, was attractive and her body was appropriate. That relieved him. He preferred to share his tastes with others.

She gripped his forearm. "What's the date! No, don't tell me. I don't want to know. I'd hate you if you knew. Imagine *paying* to live in a house like this. Such a nice view—don't you think? No, you don't. You want to be in there with the rest of them. Go then. I don't care. Is it near the end of the month?" She buried her face for a split-second in expressive hands. Then she said, "Oh God!" and looked up, smiling. She patted John's arm. "There, there. It'll be all right."

"I don't suppose you have a car. None of my beaux ever do. Excuse me, you're not my beau, are you? That's a nice word, isn't it? It makes you think of blazer jackets. I wouldn't have you if they stuffed you with gold. Oh God, I'm being silly. Please don't let me go on like this. Say something. Oh, I know—go away. You'd say something rude like that. I'm tired. *Haven't* you any matches? Or any of those machines which shoot up flames and substitute for your . . . Oh, you see, you are a dear. I always think the worst. Curable pessimist. Oh, stars! 'I see the starres at bloodie warres in the wounded welkin weeping.' You know that. Say you do. I don't really care if you do, damn it. Just say it. Let's go in."

At the close of the evening he was listening to a young television actor telling of his part in a half-hour version of *The Respectful Prostitute*. He had always thought the word was Respectable. Maggie joined them. After a while she said, with no venom, "But I think it's wonderful that you can be an actor and raise a family and live so sensibly. And you don't even have to be *good*, do you?" After that, John agreed to take her home, although he guessed that she had run through everyone else before she considered him.

They got a ride back to New York in the station wagon of an unsuspecting couple. Maggie opened a brown paper bag and took out two beer cans and an opener. She had raided the host's refrigerator. "How could I know it was his best friend? He brought Bellevue up himself. Open this, doll. One big hole and a *little* hole on the other side for air. Don't slop for God's sake. Of course you won't do it right. No one ever does. After all, I've been to Bellevue—and Pilgrim State. Oh, now you *have* slopped. Haven't you? And I said, there's a little sadist there who force-feeds you Philip Wylie. Why not Addison and Steele, for God's sake? And it was his very best friend—the sadist. I couldn't know, could I? Be careful! I hate station wagons. I can't think why anyone would be stupid enough to buy one."

The couple who owned the car fell silent. Maggie sipped her beer. John spent the rest of the trip trying to understand his feeling for her. He was never comfortable when he couldn't understand feelings.

He went to her appartment. She hadn't asked him to come, but neither had she asked him not to. "Sit down—I have some beer. No —not there. Someone I love sits there. Any place, just *light* somewhere. You make me nervous. This was my first husband's furniture. I married him the last time, too, but I'm free now. Except for Billy. Here. Too much foam, I know. Go fix it yourself. I can't wait on everyone. Take off your jacket. It suffocates me to look at you. No, *not* there. I told you about that chair!"

He didn't feel that she was abusing him, but of course she must have been.

". . . I was furious with him. I sent him the second notice, said if he was *going* to pay my rent why didn't he do it. I wouldn't take it from anyone else, but he was my first and last husband and he has *all* the money in the world. And I'll be evicted, probably. Oh, I don't care. Stop tapping. You don't tap well, anyway. You haven't any sense of rhythm."

Her apartment was a large single room with a kitchenette. The paint was beginning to crack and the Venetian blinds were broken.

". . . of course I never was a good actress. I didn't like it. Actors are better when they're stupid. And I would cut—cut my own lines and pick up the cue at the end. I never missed a cue. I only

did it for the poor male lead who would have to stand around
fidgeting until I finished. Such a good-looking boy. I almost married him. He didn't know Laertes was Polonius' son. He never
bothered to read any part but his own. Well, Laertes was like that,
too. Darling, please sit on the bed. You look uncomfortable there.
That *silly* tie. Take it off. Will you do me *one* favor? No, I'll do it
myself. Turn off the kitchenette light. Oh God. I only want you
around because I can't sleep."

John went to turn off the light and when he came back to the
bed he took off his shoes.

"And when I was divorced, the last time, my husband tried to
stop me. Stay married to me, he said, and go off and do what you
please. You won't know what to do alone. But I wouldn't listen
and in two months I lost about fourteen jobs. I was a riveter once.
That was the only job I liked but I menstruated three times a
month."

She had miserably failed a filing-girl's test and a Fifth Avenue
department store had kept her one day. She had not been able to
master the skills of a receptionist, and she was a hazard as a
waitress. She hadn't made out as a telephone operator because she
couldn't keep from breaking in on conversations. She had several
times been taken off to state hospitals for trying to kill herself—
usually with sleeping pills. "I never could take *enough*. And you
know I can't sleep. No, you don't know yet, do you?" She spoke
matter-of-factly of the wrackful siege of battering days as though
it were a platitude and not, as John was vaguely aware, a quotation.

"So I thought, why should I look around for a way to earn
money when God knows I *have* one talent. I decided to be kept,
so I wrote letters. Very business-like. 'Dear Sir'—not even dearest
sir, you see—'I should like to make application to enter your
employ as a full-time mistress. I am 28 years old' . . . body
measurements, past experience, skills. I chose all the names from
a mailing list of the New York Chamber of Commerce. Pour me
another beer, doll . . . I'm afraid there's nothing else here. Billy
gives me some house money—not much, God knows—but when I
buy Scotch with it he makes it even less. Scratch every man and
you find a boy scout. Do I judge his rotten home life? Well, yes,
I do. *Do* get the beer. I'm not fair to Billy. He's very sweet. Thank

you. Beautiful hands. His aren't. Do I look terrible? I know I do. Sit down, honey. I won't *bite* you."

John reminded her that she had been writing letters.

"Yes. I got dozens of answers. I knew I was going to be a success. And I chose one. He wasn't so bad, really—oh horrible, but you know what I mean. For him it was lust—for me it was just business. Except *he* was the one who knew about business. I was faithful because I wanted to do a good job. But after a year I slipped. Well, you *really* aren't interested. I think you'd better go."

John took a last sip of his beer and slid toward the edge of the bed.

"You're not leaving, darling? Why do people take everything literally? Well, go if you want—or stay. I don't care. After that I was interviewed—*interviewed.* I practically had to fill out a questionnaire for a job as a call-girl. Does that shock you? You're sweet. Oh, a well-paid one. He said we'll start you off at seventy-five and I said you'll give me one hundred and fifty or nothing. I thought I could just work one night a week, you know. There would be two kinds of men, he said. He had it all worked out. One was the family type who would want to show you to his friends and would probably let you off easily. They really want a decent night's sleep. The other kind would make trouble. But I knew *that* kind already.

"Are you tired, sweet? I know you are. And I just go on and on. Tell me to shut up. Can I play you one piece of music? It's Villa-Lobos. I always play it when the light's coming up. You see, it's morning already. You are a doll to listen. Why don't you get into bed? *Please* put on slippers. You know I . . . But you don't know at all. We've just met, haven't we? There're slippers in the closet. And I have a guest toothbrush, brand new. Go to sleep or go wash your teeth. Do something. I can't stand to see you looking like that. Or go home, if you like. Be quiet."

She had put on the record and John shuffled to the bathroom in oversized slippers. She handed him a new toothbrush. From the other room he heard a moaning soprano.

But several minutes or several hours after he had gone to sleep he felt her beside him. He turned toward her as though that had been the plan from the beginning.

He woke in the afternoon and found a note on his clothes telling him to make some coffee. It described the cup the coffee was to be served in and told him how to place it on the table beside the bed. He was to put *two* pillows behind her and give her an old shirt to cover nakedness. He was then to say, "Here's your coffee, darling," and go to the *other* side of the room. The note was deadly serious and he obeyed. For ten minutes she sat in bed, scowling, sipping coffee.

Then she said, "Thank you." She looked into the empty cup. "Would you do me *one* favor?"

He brought her a second cup.

She wound up slowly. "I have to be careful. Really I do. I lost so much sleep last week that I had to get my doctor to come and drug me. I just couldn't stop. I was so tired the sheets hurt my toes. You don't know how nice you were to do what I said. I was so afraid you wouldn't. I think I could love a man just for that. Don't be afraid. Don't you have to work or something?"

He explained that he did not.

"Doll, do you have a *lot* of money or none? It's not important, but I wish you did. Well, of course I can see you don't. People I like never do, or they have to spend it on someone else. Oh God! I'm so sick of worrying about rent. I don't know how to worry about rent. Don't get upset. It hasn't anything to do with you. I was thinking about Billy. After all, I am his mistress. When I think of that fish in Mamaroneck. Do you know she came all the way back from Reno in a private ambulance? It was her way to keep from getting the divorce. Clever. That was after she heard about me. Women like that get divorces when they're punishing a man, not when they're doing him a favor. I think he was glad to have her back, only because he'd begun to realize he was left with me. Full time I frighten *every*body."

She told him about Billy, then. He seemed an ordinary, confused, hopeful man, with enough money to pay for an ambulance from Reno, and a bit left over.

"I don't take anything from him but house money. He lives here part of the week. He's away on a trip now. Don't get nervous. Well, you know there *would* be a scene. Still, I'm on my own. If there were only something I could do. Some other thing. Hand me that book there, sweet."

There seemed to be no definite line to mark the new day from the old, except that they were more intimate now. The book she had asked for was a copybook. It contained scribbled quotations which she read aloud, he felt, for medicinal reasons. There were Emerson's gliding snakes, bits of Matthew Arnold and Gerard Manley Hopkins and lines from speeches of Abraham Lincoln. She wasn't very learned. She had picked these things up like beads or pretty stones. Electic, John thought, using the first reasonable word that came to him.

"John, I must have a drink."

He had only four dollars, which he thought might buy a pint. "Oh don't. It costs so much to be poor! I have a few dollars. I didn't want to touch them but we ought to have a fifth."

He bought it and they spent the rest of the day and night in idleness and friendly passion. But before he went to sleep he heard her mutter, "Oh God! *Must* he be so careless?" John wondered if he should do something about her rent.

He left the next morning before she got up. He had an appointment at noon and he had promised to call Maggie at two o'clock. When he did call she was cool. She couldn't see him, she said. Perhaps she could never see him, but if he would call again at seven she would know about that for sure.

He wasn't angry.

"I have to do something important," she said. "It's a business thing and I certainly can't think of seeing anyone—least of all you."

After he hung up he began to wonder what business she had.

At seven he called, and continued to call until eight, when she breathlessly answered, saying that he *might* wait until she paid the little boy.

"What little boy?" he asked, when she came back to the phone.

"The little boy who carried my packages. His mother always says don't give him anything but that's only because she's jealous. Oh, I mean it. She thinks he likes me too much. I did come all the way down in a taxi, you know—just to get your damned call. Can't you wait till I get my breath? Oh, I can't speak. I can't do *anything* till I take a bath. I want to scrub and scrub and . . ."

He heard her crying. It was intimate crying, quickly over, like one of her thoughts.

"You know, of course. You *do* know, don't say you don't. Oh, this smell! I earned seventy and I need sixty but I think I've spent more—I don't know how . . ."

She began to cry again and he asked searching, nervous questions.

"Gilbert. Mr. Gilbert. *Do* I have sixty? I can't even look. Well, I don't suppose you want to see me. I don't want to see you. I just want some peace. God! Won't you say something! No. All I want is a bath. I *can't* see you. If you want to come later . . ."

John said he would come right away. He searched his apartment for money and collected twelve dollars. There was no more cash, even in coins. He bought some dwarf roses and a fifth of Scotch.

Her room smelled of steam from the bath and her hair fell limply down her back. She had washed it, she told him, washed, washed, washed. But she liked the roses. Always bring prostitutes flowers, she said. And they would drink his whiskey, not Mr. Gilbert's. But she had already had a quarter of Mr. Gilbert's.

"Of course that wasn't his name. He keeps an apartment in the Beresford just for this. I'll *swear*, when I walked in, in my whore-suit—you know, simple with white gloves, no jewelry and a little hat—and asked for Mr. Gilbert at the desk, the clerk looked disappointed. Too subtle. *Don't* sit in that chair. No. I don't mind. Sit anywhere you like, but don't tap. You have no sense of rhythm. I didn't *want* ice. I told you—no, I'm being horrid. You didn't know. And he had a pleasant voice on the phone. He wasn't so bad. Except they all do the same thing. They all ask you how you got into this. It's inevitable. They want to know, as if it were any of their goddamn business. Certainly you tell a story—that's part of what you're paid for, maybe even most of it. The old Scheherazade. And another thing. You know how you always try to get free advice from a doctor? Well, it's the same. They have love problems. His wife is crazy about golf tournaments. What should he do? She goes off every afternoon and plays golf and he goes to play man. Jesus, Joseph and Mary! I thought I was going to get out after all. I talked. And you know what that can do. Doll, pour this out. Make me one with soda and *no* ice. You can do one thing for me, can't you?

"But he came around. He wasn't so bad. I mean he may even have been a decent man. Oh, I don't know what I'm saying. He's a cheat, like all the rest. They really want romance. They'd be sure to call it that. He wasn't bad-looking. He could have gone out looking for it. It's not so difficult. Oh, but I was *late*. Can you imagine being scolded for being late, like a secretary? And then, certain kinds of men always take everything out of their pockets and lay them neatly on a table—keys, wallet, loose change . . .

"And now, I'll tell you. Because I had almost talked him helpless he was afraid, you see, and he had to prove it again and that was a little sweet—or do you see that? So I began to like him a little. Well, that did it. It's enterprise, you see. If I had objected I would have a double fee—one hundred—but because I felt . . . Oh God, did I spend too much?"

John was shaken, in a familiar, unemotional way.

"Here, let's count." She pulled five dirty ten-dollar bills from a wallet. "I *must* have more. I walked past the subway but I couldn't take it. Then the whiskey and—oh yes. The perfume. I couldn't wear *my* perfume. I borrowed money from my hairdresser. Do you know? I can't scrub it off. I tried. Really, I tried.

"Doll, please sit here on the bed. Don't touch me. I'm sorry. I'm a fool. Everyone I know I could borrow from is out of town. *Will* you take off those shoes! Oh, I know. I look terrible. Stop it, Maggie. Can't you make me shut up? *Such* pretty roses."

John kept thinking about the money. It was not enough. And that was as bad as not having it at all. He explained to Maggie that he couldn't find cash for at least two days, when his quarterly check was supposed to come in, and that he would have to live on credit.

She was amused. "How sweet you are!"

She began to talk without a stop. She told of a bus trip in the middle of which she had asked a young Mexican soldier to step off with her to pick flowers. They hadn't got back on and didn't see a town for two days. And somehow, in Mexico also, she met a millionaire who kept her locked in the house. She enjoyed that, she said, until he refused to let her take sunbaths on the roof. The next moment she was in a powder-blue Cadillac racing for New York. (Somehow he could believe this more than all the rest.) But she forgot to give the machine oil and it stalled in the middle of Thirty-fourth Street at the intersection of Seventh Avenue, where she abandoned it. She spoke of Bellevue, "And this fool. You know, I told you, the friend of that psychiatrist the other night. He said he didn't believe I had enough intellectual companionship. So every *day* he read me the *complete* works of Philip Wylie. I'd rather have given him personal illustrations of the *entire* Kama Sutra and ordinarily he was the last man on earth I'd let put a finger on me—well, especially a finger. You know those scrubbed fingers with hair on the backs, like caterpillars? And I didn't dare say . . . If you've ever been in a hospital like that you keep your mouth shut. You put up with any kind of insanity just to keep from being called insane. The worst thing is being told you aren't unhappy, just crazy. Sweet, do you mind this? Sometimes I thought they were right—that I was. And sometimes I even knew it. But most always I wasn't. You *do* believe that, don't you? Oh, what do I care. Believe anything you like."

The night went on, and somewhere in the middle of it John realized that the next day was the thirty-first, the last day for her to pay her rent. "They *want* to get me out. I made so much trouble. And they want to charge more for it. They can do that if they get me out. My lawyer said that I would have to send the rent in a registered letter on the last day or . . ."

Then she told him a long story about her lawyer, who, she said, had been in love with her.

She would not go to sleep. At four o'clock they went for a walk. He had to drag her away from a hamburger stand where she tried to pick up a customer. They went home at six in the morning and she talked until nine. He made love to her, desperately, and fell into a deep sleep from which he woke at twelve, thinking about the rent. He found another note: "Darling, I called the bank. I have $8.50. Somebody didn't cash a check or something. So if you have about 95 cents and I have change that will make it. We've *got* to get to the bank."

He woke her at one, with coffee, knowing her well enough now to see that two hours was a very short time in which to get her to the bank. His head ached.

She was wild at being wakened. And when the telephone rang a few minutes later she grew maniacal. "Jesus!" she screamed at the mouthpiece. "How dare you call me so early. How *dare* you. I don't care if you've made a million. When did you get back? Go polish your badges. Don't *ever* call me again." She banged the phone down and rolled over in a naked ball of rage.

But he got her to sit up. "Here's your coffee," he said, stiffly. She brooded, like a banked fire sprinkled with new coal. Then she broke into flame.

"God. If you only knew how I hate you all! Two thousand dollars, he says. Now we can do this, do that. If his wife doesn't take another ambulance trip. Someone who claims to love you and he calls now! Get up on time, he says, don't drink, don't make a fool of yourself, don't, don't. Oh, I despise them. Golden-rule boys, righteous boys. Not you, darling, you . . . I hate this. You're like all the rest. The only people I could ever stand were in three state hospitals—the private one was just like everything else. You all stood in line together, you all did *everything* together. And I said it! These people are too crazy to be cold and stupid. And you know they put me in that thing you're not supposed to call a strait jacket. I didn't *dare* call it that. I will *not* go on like this."

But he got her to go on. She dressed, finally, and they took a taxi to the bank. They arrived just in time.

Filling out the check she said, "Do you know, I was sent down from the Irving Trust? I mean it. Just like Cambridge or Oxford or someplace. I didn't know how to handle a checking account. The National City is fairly nice."

She had a special teller. He seemed fond of her and certified her check with a minimum of suspicion. They mailed the money at the post office and registered it.

Maggie fell silent after that. She asked him back for a drink, half-heartedly. They were both exhausted. He said good-by at the subway station. "You *will* call again, doll?"

He said that he would and at that moment in his crisp life he believed that he surely would, if only for the pity one classically owes superior whores. Later—years later—he realized that her future had been as promising as his and, even at that age, that they were both heading down to a casual, inconsequent end. And maybe she had more fun getting there.

MICHAEL RUBIN is the author of two novels, *A TRIP INTO TOWN*, which was published in 1961, and *WHISTLE ME HOME*, published in 1967. His stories have appeared in the *Quarterly Review of Literature, Antioch Review, Cosmopolitan*, and *Redbook*. Mr. Rubin now lives in New York City where he divides his time between teaching and writing.

Service

A DOZEN times that week Sheila had warned herself to *listen* for a change when the alarm rang at 9:00, at least on Tuesdays and Fridays when the cleaning girl came. Now there was the Service bus down the street already, and here she was just pulling herself out of bed again. Not that she really blamed herself. Harry was up and out by 7:00 to find his breakfast in the city, and the kids preferred messing around in the kitchen on their own before school. It was her Puritan upbringing, she supposed, that made her feel at all guilty about it. The TV commercials, too, those gay breakfast scenes with super-charged cereals and morning mouthwash.

Pulling on her woolen wrapper, she began to brush her fine, blond hair for her beauty parlor appointment this afternoon. Mr. Tony had absolute fits if she came in looking shabby—a personal insult to his integrity and his art, he always said. He was funny and faggoty that way, but she couldn't help admiring him for sounding as though he really *cared* about it, that it was a genuine affront to him, as he said, if his "do's were unduly undone."

She yawned at her face in the mirror. She knew she hadn't felt concerned about *anything* for a long time now. Sometimes she wondered why she ever got out of bed at all.

Well, for one thing, she had to let in the girl. "My mission in life is to let in the colored girl!" she announced as she groped her way down the staircase, and laughed to hear herself sounding like some kind of civil rights worker. Not that she was unsympathetic to their cause. As a matter of fact, once she'd even planned to go into the city to watch a demonstration. One of the neighbors—a girl who had since moved out of the development—had managed to convince her of her responsibility. But at the last minute something had come up, she couldn't remember just what, now. And then, when she'd read in the papers what had happened—two white workers being attacked by the Negroes *themselves* right on the street—she'd told Harry (who hadn't liked the idea to begin with) that if that's the way they felt about it, she'd just as soon spend her time collecting for the Cancer Fund. She hadn't done that yet, either, because she didn't know exactly where it was you applied.

The back door bell rang just as she reached the playroom of their split-level, still brushing out her hair and yawning. "Hello!" she said at the opened door with a brave effort to sound cheerful, her flip hanging down to her chin. "Don't look at me. I'm an absolute mess!"

She climbed back upstairs. What a relief it was to have a steady girl at last, or at least what *passed* for steady these days. This one had been with them for over three months now, which was probably some kind of *record* around here. She knew where everything was and didn't have to be told what to do, but usually just started right in where she left off the last time.

She suddenly had the wildest idea. Suddenly she thought it wouldn't be the worst thing in the world to hire *herself* out. Why not? She had the time for it, God knew. Lots of women around here went back to work as soon as their kids were old enough. But most of them had office skills or some kind of profession. With no education to speak of, what was she fit for but housework? Still, the pay was pretty good—she should know. And the Service even gave their girls transportation all the way from St. Albans. Except for the dirt, who could complain?

As a matter of fact, a few weeks ago her friend Harriet had been thinking about giving up *her* girl altogether because the Service had raised its prices again. Not only that, but the one they'd assigned to her had also been getting very snippy. But then, when Harriet called the Service to complain, they'd immediately changed women for her. That seemed a little odd and unfair; Sheila thought for sure the Service would have defended an employee. Instead, they'd actually *thanked* Harriet, and told her they hoped in time to weed out all their potential troublemakers. Funny, when it was an absolute fact that the Service was owned and operated by Negroes *themselves*, and no one else. Anyway, she supposed Harriet's new girl had worked out better, because Harriet had stopped threatening to do her own housework.

Sheila had to laugh to herself. Here she was thinking of becoming a cleaning woman when she knew she would probably die if she didn't have help in her *own* house. And it had nothing to do with what the commentators said about white or black power, or about status-seeking or the lack of values in the U.S.A. and/or the twentieth century. She was spoiled, simple as that. Housework was a pain in the behind. She could afford help. It was no crime having it. And at this late date it would almost be hypocritical of her to give it up. Who knew, maybe it *was* some kind of cultural or psychological dependency problem, the way one liberal writer— the one who was always having trouble with his wives—had said. Some dependency problem. The colored girls these days were hardly old Southern mammies cottoning up to Vivien Leigh.

Not that she'd ever found any of them abusive or unco-operative. Just the reverse, in fact. The ones the Service sent *her* had always worked away quietly and steadily, humming to themselves like a floor waxer. Oh, once or twice she'd found one of them sitting down at the dining room table in a funny, wornout way, just sitting there for a while, not so much catching her breath, it seemed, as wondering why she was there at all. Well, Sheila had those feelings too. Didn't everybody? Anyway, that didn't happen very often, and she supposed the Service was probably very canny to keep hiring the dopey kind, the near feebleminded, or the done-in, because in this day and age who *else* could be relied on to do a decent job?

When she came downstairs again, she noticed that the girl had finished the living room and was working in the dining area now, even taking down the knickknacks from the dutch hutch for a good dust and polish. She was pleased by such initiative, though a little uneasy about it, too. More so when she glanced around to realize that her living room had really never looked lovelier. She had many pretty things, of course, but today the satin pillows had been set on their points as never before, the drapes really straightened out for a change, the ashtrays absolutely glistening. This girl of hers seemed to improve with age. Who knew, maybe she'd fallen in love with the things she was paid to care for. If that were so, then, in a way, she envied her.

"There's coffee when you want it," Sheila called as she headed for the kitchen. The kids always plugged in the automatic percolator for her before leaving the house in the morning.

So that the girl wouldn't think her a total loss, she washed the children's dishes before sitting down at the table with a second cup of coffee. She hoped she could finish it before the girl came in for her own. Then she could go upstairs and make her morning phone calls while waiting to leave for her appointment. Frankly, she just never liked being around when the girl was here. And since the Service guaranteed against theft, she usually scheduled her card games and beauty parlor dates on those days.

No such luck today. The girl appeared at the door and languidly said, "'Scuse me, ma'am. I don't rightly think this is the house."

Sheila, who had averted her face when she saw her coming, looked up. "What?"

"This here house. It ain't the one."

"The one *what?*"

"The one where I suppose to *be.*"

Sheila's hand trembled, her cup clattering. It couldn't be true. It was. The wrong girl was standing there. She wasn't *hers.*

"You—you mean you just came in—and started cleaning and—didn't even *know?*"

"Do now. This ain't the one. It sure enough ain't."

For all their vacancy of expression, the girl's eyes kept Sheila pinned to her chair. "Well—where *should* you be?"

The girl shrugged. "Lord know."

This was impossible. "But—you've been *cleaning—*"

"Yes, ma'am," the girl assured her. "I been cleanin'—"

"I mean—you couldn't tell? My *things?*"

The girl shrugged her narrow shoulders again, neither embarrassed nor pained, as though the mistake was a natural one, nothing to fuss so much about.

"But how did you find the vacuum cleaner—and the dust mitt you're using?"

"In the closet. They's always in there."

"What?"

"Same's every house hereabout. Same closets, same things

mostly. Can't hardly tell no difference. How you like that bus driver, though, didn't even say a blessed word."

"Well, but, I mean—why should *he* have to tell you?"

"Ask you a question, ma'am?"

Sheila hesitated. "Yes?"

"How come *you* didn't?"

The cigarette flew from Sheila's mouth, hit her coffee dead center, sent up smoke to sting her eyes.

"You let me go on workin' all this here time without you tell me I weren't the one. That ain't nice. I prob'ly lose my whole day pay now."

"No. No—I'll pay you," Sheila muttered.

"Yeah—*you*, maybe—but the Service, they maybe not. They very strick down there, you know."

"I'll fix it with the Service. I promise."

The girl seemed satisfied, but only stood there now as though, oh God, waiting to be plugged in again!

"Look, why don't you—just go on with what you were doing while I figure out what's—what."

Without so much as a nod, the girl turned around and seemed to glide from the room. In spite of herself, Sheila crept to the doorway to watch her mindlessly moving around the dining area again, a cleaning machine with arms like broom handles, sponges for feet, the mouth and nose a vacuum to pull up the dirt with dumb efficiency. She was ready to weep. No, not for the girl—which made it all the worse—but for herself! Oh, if necessary she could swallow the galling truth that all her pretty things were like everyone else's pretty things. In a way that was why they'd been bought, wasn't it? But, oh, "How come *you* didn't?" had been the girl's simple question, and in it Sheila had suddenly seen too much.

The phone rang. She jumped for it, almost desperate to hear a human voice, to ascertain her own again.

"Hello, Sheila? It's Martha. Sheila—the most peculiar thing's happened—"

"I know, I know."

"What do you know?" asked Martha.

"Nothing. Tell me."

"Well, there's a girl here that I think belongs to you."

"*What?*"

"Did *yours* come today, Sheila?"

"Well—"

"This one's sitting on my easy chair crying her eyes out."

"Cr—crying?"

"For a while I thought she was going into *shock*. I almost called the doctor. She was cleaning the living room quietly enough, but then suddenly she let out this loud—well, *whoop*, of all things, and actually threw her apron over her head, and started laughing like a hyena. Then she sank down into my best chair and began *bawling*. I finally got her to calm down a little, but she started babbling on and on about how her life had probably given her the brain fever or something. Of course, by this time I'd realized she wasn't *my* girl. I don't know where *my* girl is at all."

"How—how do you know that one's mine?"

"Well, first she said she thought she worked for a woman with two kids or maybe three."

"I have two children. Two girls. Ages ten and twelve. Toby and Geraldine. Toby is learning to play the piano and is doing very nicely."

"Sheila, what's *wrong* with you today? *Listen* to me. Anyway, *that* didn't help, so I asked her to try describing the house. But, do you know, for all I could tell it might have been the Van Hornes' or the Brodies'? Then, finally, she mentioned a woman with blond hair. She went on and on about how much she loved and admired this blond hair. She wouldn't stop. She kept calling it 'angel hair,' Sheila, so I suppose you're supposed to be flattered, if you're the one. Honestly, I think she's ready for a straight jacket. Is she yours? Should I call the Service?"

"No! My God, no! They're very strict down there! She's mine. Look, Martha. I think—I think I have *yours*. The same thing's happened here, more or less."

"What? Well, why didn't you *say* so?"

"Well, I don't really *know* if she's yours. I mean—she didn't say you had angel hair. She couldn't even remember your house at *all*."

"Of all the goddamned nerve. I've fed that girl royally. I've *talked* to her!"

"She was working here almost an hour before—she—*we* found out."

"Oh, this is ridiculous. Sheila, you don't think they're putting us *on?* I mean, you know how they are these days."

"I don't think so. In a way, I wish they were. I don't even think this one knows about the revolution."

"Well, what do we *do?*"

"I guess we've got to start thinking, Martha. We've got to start thinking very hard."

"Thinking about what?"

"Oh, I don't know. About what to *do* about it, I suppose. And whose *fault* it is. Why is it that we've let ourselves get so—"

"Sheila, I have company coming tonight. That's all I'm worried about at the moment. Paul has the car today or I'd drive yours over and pick mine up. Is your car available?"

"I think I have a slow leak."

"That's just fine. Well, you *know* we can't just send them out into the street. They'd get lost in no time flat around here. Look, why don't I just keep yours for today, and you mine?"

"Martha, they're not interchangeable parts!"

"Did I say *that?* It's just that—well, if you want to know the truth, *yours* has been absolutely terrific. She's much better than mine. My kitchen's never been cleaner."

"But—you said my girl was *crying.* You said she missed me, she misses my house."

"For God's sake, Sheila, she didn't even know she wasn't *there.*"

"Martha, listen to me. That's what I'm trying to tell you. *I* didn't know she wasn't here, *either.* Neither did you. Or your girl *here.* Can't you understand? That's *terrible!*"

"Sheila, I have company coming tonight—"

"Well, I want mine back. I'll walk over and get her."

"And bring mine with you, okay?"

"Martha—please—let me—let me keep them *both.*"

"Are you crazy? What am *I* supposed to do?"

"Clean your own house, I guess."

"Sheila, you bring my girl back or you don't get yours, do you understand?" shouted Martha as the phone clicked down.

Now what? Now what? Suddenly, Sheila felt like rushing inside and screaming at the girl to stop working, to beat her until she lay down her dust mitt. But she was so afraid the girl would only stand there staring at her, or she would stare back as in a mirror, doing nothing, nothing. Oh, God, what *could* be done to set things right in herself or in the world? Maybe, she could organize a kind of group therapy session with all the ladies and their

maids getting together once a week to talk out the whole frightening mess. Or should she just give the girl her old clothes, the
money in her purse, and tell her to get the hell out of her house
and never come back again? No, no, no. Harry's tape recorder!
Maybe she could get the girl to talk into it, tell her life story,
and publish it for all the world to know. Better yet, she could
record her own, two sides of the same sad story, both of them
winding it up by singing folk songs together, love songs, songs
by those who'd sinned against themselves. No. Instead, she should
just get down on her knees and help the girl wax the floors. Or
do them herself while the girl whipped her every time she
wanted to stop. Or send her to night school. Or back to Africa.
Or trade houses with her. Swop husbands. Take up a sign. Stretch
herself across Southern trolley tracks. What action was opened to
her? What drinking fountain? Oh, God, revelations were so easy to
come by. What to *do* with them was the killer!

She braced herself to enter the living room, hoping just the
sight of the girl itself would suggest something to her, something
worth something to both of them. But, as she moved from the
kitchen, she saw down the hallway the day's mail being slipped
under the door. Without looking in at the girl, she rushed for
it and shuffled through several bills and advertisements. The
last one caught her eye, an announcement sent out by a new
beauty salon along Sunrise Highway:

INTRODUCING OUR LATEST SERVICE

COME IN AND

MEET MR. MACHINE

OUR FABULOUS NEW COLORIST

WHY WASTE HOURS WHEN YOU CAN BE COLORED IN MINUTES?

She screamed. The girl, on her haunches to pick up stray
nap from the carpet as though she were gathering cotton, looked
up without surprise. Rushing toward her, Sheila dropped heavily
to her knees and grabbed the girl's narrow shoulders, shaking her
and pleading pitifully, "Don't you—don't you even want to know
my name?"

GRACE PALEY was born and educated in New York City, where she is now living. She has taught at Columbia University and at Sarah Lawrence. A collection of her short stories, *THE LITTLE DISTURBANCES OF MAN,* was first published in 1959, and re-issued in 1968. Her stories have also appeared in *New American Review, Esquire,* and *The Atlantic.* Miss Paley is currently working on a novel.

Distance

You would certainly be glad to meet me. I was the lady who appreciated youth. Yes, all that happy time, I was not like some. It did not go by me like a flitting dream. Tuesdays and Wednesdays was as gay as Saturday nights.

Have I suffered since? No, sir, we've had as good times as this country gives; cars, renting in Jersey summers, TV the minute it first came out, everything grand for the kitchen. I have no complaints worth troubling the manager about.

Still it is like a long hopeless homesickness my missing those young days. To me, they're like my own place that I have gone away from forever, and I have lived all the time since among great pleasures but in a foreign town. Well, OK. Farewell, certain years.

But that's why I have an understanding of that girl Ginny downstairs and her kids. They're runty, underdeveloped. No sun, no beef. Noodles, beans, cabbage. Well, my mother off the boat knew better than that.

Once upon a time, as they say, her house was the spit of mine. You could hear it up and down the air shaft, the singing from her kitchen, banjo playing in the parlor, she would admit it first, there was a tambourine in the bedroom. Her husband wasn't American. He had black hair—like Gypsies do.

And everything then was spotless, the kitchen was all inlay like broken-up bathroom tiles, pale lavender. Formica on all surfaces, everything bright. The shine of the pots and pans was turned to stun the eyes of company . . . you could see it, the mischievousness of that family home.

Of course, on account of misery now, she's always dirty. Crying crying crying. She would not let tap water touch her.

Five ladies on the block, old friends, nosy, me not included, got up a meeting and wrote a petition to Child Welfare. I already knew it was useless as the requirement is more than dirt, drunkenness, and a little once in a while whoring. That is probably something why the children in our city are in such a state. I've noticed it for years, though it's not my business. Mothers and fathers get up when they wish, half being snuggled in relief, go to bed in the afternoon with their rumpy bumpy sweethearts pumping away before three P.M. (So help me.) Child Welfare does not show its concern. No matter who writes them. People of influence, known in the district, even the district leader, my cousin Leonie, who put her all into electing the mayor, she doesn't get a reply if she sends in a note. So why should I as I'm nothing but a Primary Day poll watcher?

Anyhow there are different kinds coming into this neighborhood, and I do not mean the colored people alone. I mean people like you and me, religious, clean, many of these have gone rotten. I go along with live and let live, but what of the children?

Ginny's husband ran off with a Puerto Rican girl who shaved between the legs. This is common knowledge and well known or I'd never say it. When Ginny heard that he was going around with this girl, she did it too, hoping to entice him back, but he got nauseated by her and that tipped the scales.

Men fall for terrible weirdos in a dumb way more and more as they get older; my old man, fond of me as he constantly was, often did. I never give it the courtesy of my attention. My advice to mothers and wives: Do not imitate the dimwit's girlfriends. You will be damnfool-looking, what with your age and all. Have you heard the saying, "Old dough won't rise in a new oven?"

Well, you know it, I know it, even the punks and the queers that have wiggled their way into this building are in on the inside dope. John, my son, is a constant attendant now at that Ginny's poor grubby flat. Tired, who can blame him, of his

Margaret's shiny face all pitted and potted by Jersey smog. My grandchildren, of which I have close to six, are pale, as the sun can't have a chance through the oil in Jersey. Even the leaves of the trees there won't turn a greenish green.

John! Look me in the eye once in a while! What a good little twig you were always, we did try to get you out with the boys and you did go when we asked you. After school when he was eight or so, we got him into a bunch of Cub Scouts, a very raw bunch with a jawful of curse words. All of them tough and wild, but at attention when the master came among them. Right turn! You would've thought the United States Marines was in charge they was that accurate in marching, and my husband on Tuesday nights taught them what he recalled from being a sergeant. Hup! two, three, four! I guess is what he knew. But John, good as his posture was, when he come home I give him a hug and a kiss and "what'd you do today at Scouts, son? Have a parade, darling?"

"Oh, no, Mother," says he. "Mrs. McClennon was collecting money the whole time for the district-wide picnic, so I just got the crayons and I drew this here picture of Our Blessed Mother," he says.

That's my John. And if you come with a Polaroid Land Camera you couldn't snap much clearer.

People have asked and it's none of their business. Why didn't the two of you (meaning Jack and me—both working) send the one boy you had left to college?

Well now to be honest, he would have had only grief in college. Truth: He was not bright. His father was not bright, and he inherited his father's brains. Our Michael was clever. But Michael is dead. We had it all talked over, his father and me, the conclusion we come to: A trade. My husband Jack was well established in the union from its early struggle, he was strong and loyal. John just floated in on the ease of recommendation and being related. We were wise. It's proved.

For now (this very minute) he's a successful man with a wonderful name in the building trade, and he has a small side business in cement plaques, his own beautiful home, and every kid of his dressed like the priest's nephew.

But don't think I'm the only one that seen Ginny and John when they were the pearls of this pitchy pigsty block. Oh, there

were many, and they are still around holding the picture in the
muck under their skulls, like crabs. And I am never surprised when
they speak of it, when they try to make something of it, that
nice-looking time, as though *I* was in charge of its passing.

"Ha," Jack said about twenty times that year, "she's a wild little
bird. Our Johnny's dying . . . Watch her."

OK. Wild enough. I guess. But no wilder than me when *I* was
seventeen, as I never told him, that whole year, long ago, mashing
the grass of Central Park with Anthony Aldo. Why I'd put my
wildness up against any wildness of present day, though I didn't
want Jack to know. For he was a simple man . . . Put in the
hours of a wop, thank God pulled the overtime of a decent
American. I didn't like to worry worry worry him. He was kindness
itself, as they say.

He come home 6:00 P.M. I come home 6:15 P.M. from where
I was afternoon cashier. Put supper up. Seven o'clock, we ate
it up and washed the dishes; 7:45 P.M. sharp, if there was no
company present and the boy out visiting, he liked his pussy.
Quick and very neat. By 8:15 he had showered every bit of
it away. I give him his little whiskey. He tried that blabbermouth
Journal American for news of the world. It was too much. Good
night, Mr. Raftery, my pal.

Leaving me, thank goodness, the cream of the TV and a cup
of sweet wine till midnight. Though I liked the attentions as
a man he daily give me as a woman, it hardly seemed to tire me
as it exhausted him. I could stay with the late show not fluttering
an eyelid till the very end of the last commercial. My wildness as
a girl is my own life's business, no one else's.

Now: As a token for friendship under God, John'd given Ginny
his high school G O pin, though he was already a working man.
He couldn't of given her his union card (that never got customary),
though he did take her to a famous dinner in honor of Klaus
Schnauer: thirty-five years at Camillo, the only heinie they ever
let into that American local; he was a disgusting fat-bottomed
Nazi so help me, he could've turned you into a pink Commie,
his ass, excuse me, was that fat. Well, as usual for that young-
hearted gang, Saturday night went on and on, it give a terrible
jolt to Sunday morning, and John staggered in to breakfast, not
shaved or anything. (A man, husband, son, or lodger should be

shaved at breakfast.) "Mother," he said, "I am going to ask Virginia to marry me."

"I told you so," said my husband and dropped the funnies on his bacon.

"You are?" I said.

"I am, and if God is good, she'll have me."

"No blasphemy intended," I said, "but He'll have to be off in the old country fishing if she says yes."

"Mother!" said John. He is a nice boy, loyal to friends and good.

"She'll go out with anyone at all," I said.

"Oh, Mother!" said John, meaning they weren't engaged, and she could do what she wanted.

"Go out is nothing," I said. "I seen her only last Friday night with Pete, his arm around her, going into Phelan's."

"Pete's like that, Mother," meaning it was no fault of hers.

"Then what of last Saturday night, you had to go to the show yourself as if there wasn't no one else in the Borough of Manhattan to take to a movie, and when you was gone I seen her buy two Cokes at Carlo's and head straight to the third floor to John Kameron's . . ."

"So? So?"

". . . and come out at 11 P.M. and *his* arm was around her."

"So?"

". . . and his hand was well under her sweater . . ."

"That's not so, Mother."

"It *is* so, and tell me, young man, how you'll feel married to a girl that every wild boy on the block has been leanin' his thumbs on her titties like she was a Carvel dairy counter, tell me that?"

"Dolly!" says Jack. "You went too far . . ."

John just looked at me as red and dumb as a baby's knees.

"I haven't gone far enough into the facts, and I'm not ready to come out yet, and you listen to me, Johnny Raftery, you're somebody's jackass, I'll tell you, you look out that front window and I bet you if you got yourself your dad's spyglass you would see some track of your little lady. I think there are evenings she don't get out of the back of that trailer truck parked over there and it's no trouble at all for Pete or Kameron's half-witted kid to get his way of her. Listen Johnny, there isn't a grown-up woman who was sitting on the stoop last Sunday when it was

so damn windy that doesn't know that Ginny don't wear underpants."

"Oh, Dolly," says my husband, and plops his head into his
hands.

"I'm going, Mother, that's libel, I'll have her sue you for libel,"
dopey John starts to holler out of his tomato-red face. "I'm going
and I'll ask her and I love her and I don't care what you say.
Truth or lies, I don't care."

"And if you go, Johnny," I said, calm as a dead fish, my eyes
rolling up to pray and be heeded, "this is what I must do,"
and I took a kitchen knife, a bit blunt, and plunged it at least
an eighth of an inch in the fat of my heart. I guess that the
heart of a middle-aged lady is jammed in deeper than an eighth
of an inch, for I am here to tell the tale. But some blood did
come soon, to my son's staring, it touched my nightie and spread
out on my bathrobe, and it was as red on my apron as a picture
in an Italian church. John fell down on his knees, and hid his
head in my lap. He cried, "Mother, Mother, you've hurt yourself."
My husband didn't say a word to me. He kept his madness in
his teeth but he told me later, Face it: the feelings in his heart
was cracked.

I met Ginny the next morning in Carlo's store. She didn't look
at me. Then she did. Then she said, "It's a nice day, Mrs. Raftery."

"Mm," I said. (It was.) "How can you tell the kind of day it is?"
(I don't know what I meant by that.)

"What's wrong, Mrs. Raftery?" she said.

"Hah! wrong?" I asked.

"Well, you know, I mean, you act mad at me, you don't seem
to like me this morning." She made a little laugh.

"I do. I like you a great deal," I said, outwitting her. "It's
you, you know, you don't like Johnny. You don't."

"What?" she said, her head popping up to catch sight of that
reply.

"Don't, don't don't," I said. "Don't, don't!" I hollered, giving
Ginny's arm a tug. "Let's get out of here. Ginny, you don't like
John. You'd let him court you, squeeze you, and he's very good,
he wouldn't press you further."

"You ought to mind your business," says Ginny very soft, me
being the elder (but with tears).

"My son is my business."

"No," she says, "he's his own."

"My son is my business. I have one son left, and he's my business."

"No," she says. "He's his own."

MY SON IS MY BUSINESS. BY LOVE AND DUTY.

"Oh, no," she says. Soft because I am the older one, but very strong. (I've noticed it. All of a sudden they look at you, and then, it comes to them, young people, they are bound to outlast you, so they temper up their icy steel and stare into about an inch away from you a lot. Have you noticed it?)

At home, I said, "Jack now, the boy needs guidance. Do you want him to spend the rest of his life in bed with an orphan on welfare?"

"Oh," said Jack. "She's an orphan, is she? It's just her mother that's dead. What has one thing to do with another? You're a pushy damn woman, Dolly. I don't know what use you are . . ."

What came next often happens in a family causing sorrow at the time. Looking back, it's a speck compared to life.

For: Following this conversation, Jack didn't deal with me at all, and he broke his many years after-supper habits and took long walks. That's what killed him, I think, for he was a habitual person.

And: Alongside him on one of these walks was seen a skinny crosstown lady, known to many people over by Tompkins Square —wears a giant Ukrainian cross in and out of the tub, to keep from going down the drain, I guess.

"In that case, the hell with you," is what I said. "I don't care. Get yourself a cold-water flat on Avenue D."

"Why not? I'll go. OK," said Jack. I think he figured a couple of weeks vacation with his little cuntski and her color television would cool his requirements.

"Stay off the block," I said, "you slippery relic. I'll send your shirts by the diaper-service man."

"Mother," said poor John, when he noticed his dad's absence, "what's happening to you? The way you talk. To Dad. It's the wine, mother. I know it."

"You're a bloated beer guzzler!" I said quietly. (People that drink beer are envious against the ones in favor of wine. Though my dad was a mick in cotton socks, in his house, we had a choice.)

"No, Mother, I mean you're not clear sometimes."

"Crazy, you mean, son. Huh? Split personality?"

"Something's wrong!" he said. "Don't you want Dad back?" He was nervous to his fingernails.

"Mind your business, he'll be back, it's happened before, Mr. Two-Weeks Old."

"What?" he said, horrified.

"You're blind as a bat, Mr. Just Born. Where was you three Christmases ago?"

"What! But Mother! Didn't you feel terrible? Terrible! How'd you stand for him acting that way? Dad!"

"Now quit it, John, you're a damnfool kid. Sure I don't want to look at his dumb face being pleased. That'd kill."

"Mother, it's not right."

"Phoo, go to work and mind your business, sonny boy."

"It is my business," he said, "and don't call me sonny."

About two months later, John came home with Margaret, both of them blistered from Lake Hopatcong at ninety-four degrees. I will be fair. She was not yet ruined by Jersey air, and she was not too terrible-looking, at least to the eye of a clean-minded boy.

"This is Margaret," he says. "She's from Monmouth, Jersey."

"Just come over on the *Queen Mary*, dear?" I asked for the joke in it.

"I have to get her home for supper. Her father's strict."

"Sure," I said, "have a Coke first."

"Oh, thank you so much," says Margaret. "Thank you, thank you, thank you, Mrs. Raftery."

"Has she blood in her?" hollered Jack after his shower. He had come home by then, skinny and dissatisfied. Is there satisfaction anywhere in getting old?

John didn't inquire an OK of his dad or me, nor answer to nobody Yes or No. He was that age that couldn't live without a wife. He had to use this Margaret.

It was his time to go forward like we all did once. And he has. Number 1: She is kept plugged up with babies. Number 2: As people nowadays need a house, he has bought one and tangled it around in Latin bushes. Nobody but the principal at Holy Redeemer High knows what the little tags on the twigs say. Every evening after hard work you can find him with a hose scrubbing down his lawn. His oldest kid is now fourteen and useless. The littlest one is four, and she reminds me of me with the flashiest eyes and a little tongue sharpened to a scrappy point.

"How come you never named one for *me*, Margaret?" I asked her straight in her face.

"Oh," she said, "There's only the two girls, Teresa, for my mother, and Cathleen, for my best sister. The very next'll be for you."

"What, next! Are you trying to kill my son?" I asked her. "Why he has to be working nights as it is. You don't look well, you know. You ought to see a smart Jewish doctor and get your tubes tied up."

"Oh," she said, "Never!"

I have to tease a little to grapple any sort of a reply out of her. But mostly it doesn't work. It is something like I am a crazy construction worker in conversation with fresh cement. Can there be more in the world like her? Don't answer. Time will pass in spite of her slow wits.

In fact it has, for here we are in the present, which is happening now, and I am a famous widow baby-sitter for whoever thinks I am unbalanced but within reason. I am a grand storybook reader to the little ones. I read like an actress, Joan Crawford or Maureen O'Sullivan, my voice is deeper than it was. So I do make a little extra for needs, though my Johnny sees to the luxuries I must have. I won't move away to strangers. This is my family street, and I don't need to.

And of course as friendship never ends, Johnny comes twice a week for his entertainment to Ginny. Ginny and I do not talk a word though we often pass. She knows I am right as well as victorious. She's had it unusually lovely (most people don't)— a chance to be some years with a young fellow like Blackie that gave her great rattling shivers, top to bottom, though it was all cut off before youth ended. And as for my Johnny, he now absolutely has her as originally planned and desired, and she depends on him in all things. She requires him. Her children lean on him. They climb up his knees to his shoulder. They cry out the window for him, *John, John,* if his dumb Margaret keeps him home.

It's a pity to have become so right and Jack's off stalking the innocent angels.

I wait on the stoop steps to see John on summer nights as he hasn't enough time to visit me and Ginny both, and I need the sight of him, though I don't know why. I like the street anyway, and the hot night when the ice-cream truck brings all the dirty kids and the big nifty boys with their hunting-around eyes. I put a touch of burgundy on my strawberry ice-cream cone as my father said we could on Sunday, which drives these sozzle-headed ladies up the brown brick wall, so help me Mary.

Now, some serious questions, so far unasked:

What the devil is it all about, the noisiness and the speediness, when it's no distance at all? How come John had to put all them courtesy calls into Margaret on his lifelong trip to Ginny? Also, Jack, what was his real nature? Was he for or against? And that Anthony, what *did* he have in mind as I knuckled under again and again (and I know I was the starter)? He did not get me pregnant as in books it happens at once. How come the French priest said to me, crying tears and against his order, "Oh, no, Dolly, if you are enceinte (meaning pregnant), he will certainly marry you, poor child, now smile, poor child, for that is the church's promise to infants born." To which, how come, tough and cheery as I used to be, all I could say before going off to live and die was: "No, Father, he doesn't love me."

BEN MADDOW is the author of a novel, *FORTY-FOUR GRA-VEL STREET*, and of many short stories. This is his second O. Henry Award—"In A Cold Hotel" appeared in the 1963 volume. Mr. Maddow lives in Los Angeles.

You, Johann Sebastian Bach

THE drapes had gone to the cleaners the Tuesday she had come back from Italy; furious, cold, and already ill.

When she awoke, she saw, as if it were not hers but a lover's, a fine plump foot, with a cinquefoil of gleaming creamy nails thrust out below the stitched deep blue silken rolls of her familiar quilt. And with the same fine detachment, the joyful clarity that one feels only on that first long day of convalescence, Irene let herself be overwhelmed by sheets and waves of rising sunlight which splashed westward toward her through the curtainless windows, and reached and wrapped the great black Bluthner concert grand, open as she had left it weeks ago. She half arose, bulky and naked, bending herself at buttock and knee, hoping to make breakfast and review the inferior world again.

The cablegram was still open, where she had left it three weeks before, on the heavy, horizontal strings of piano. Irene knew it by heart: "MAMA DARLING COULD YOU POSSIBLY POST-PONE TOUR I THINK I AM DYING."

But as she twisted, still in bed, reluctant, scratching the coils of her belly as she turned, that mad cat of hers leaped out of hiding and dug her unpadded claws into Irene's left thigh. Perversely then, avoiding with practiced skill the clutch of those monstrous pianistic hands, she sprang away and under the great bed, whence her blue eyes, fiercely and ridiculously crossed, like a Japanese demon, stared toward the blank, blinding window; and a pink mouth yowled for sympathy.

Irene got up and switched on the recorder; the tape slid left to right, silent as a lizard. Irene walked back and forth in the apartment, at first aimlessly. Her own familiar playing rang out, tumbling upwards in the arpeggios of the opening movement. Then, as she felt better, she began to make fresh coffee; while it was brewing, she still paced round and round, heavy, naked, and nimble, from kitchenette to bathroom to the black knob of the tone control, and then stooped down to the door where a fan of yesterday's late mail lay still unopened. There was the expected letter from Padua, and though her heart immediately banged between her two breasts, she put it aside, unable to read it so soon. Instead, she phoned Sysmanski at home; he was her agent at the Hurok office, but he would scarcely be sensible for another two hours.

"Did I wake you, Arthur darling?"

"Hell, no. It'd take a lot more than that."

"This is Irene Packer."

"Funny, I thought it was somebody important."

"Baby," she said, "do you have a pencil?"

"No. Why? You want to borrow a pencil at this time in the morning?"

"I want you to wire the coast I'll do their concert, after all."

"But Irene, please, no, I wouldn't, take my advice."

"I would."

"You were deathly sick only two days ago."

"I'm well enough to eat breakfast, so I'm well enough to do the program."

"You want to get out of New York."

"I want to get out of New York."

"Have you heard anything from the girl?"

"I got a letter from Elinor only this morning."

"And—?"

"And—I haven't read it yet."

"You're made of iron, aren't you?"

"I have to be."

Sysmanski said, "Irene, if I were the right sex—"

"You mean, if I were—"

"I'd marry you in a little minute. In the meantime, come and have lunch with me tomorrow."

"No, Arthur. I'll be practicing like mad. Thanks."

She smiled, and hung up. Then she had her coffee and found

two pecan rolls, stiff and stale but all the more sugary, and gave herself a chocolate mint as a present, and then switched off the tape. She stretched her arms and did some setting-up exercises, at a slow pace; and then sat down on the leather bench, still nude, before the great black piano. She listened to its heavy silence.

"Oh, you monster, you're waiting for me, aren't you?" she said to the instrument. That cat, forgotten, jealous at the sound of her voice, made an irritable sound under the shelf of the bed. Irene turned to glare back; she massaged her cold wrists, and then thought, acutely, painfully, of her daughter Elinor, and pushed the image far to one side in her mind. That cat was called Rusty, though it was not her color. She had muscles made of barbed wire. She responded only to violent noises, or to a newspaper hurled and opening like a dangerous bird. Her reply, bristling and hissing, may have been all pretense, but for some minutes, at least, the beast was tame.

Irene's next concert was two days off. She was aware of a double danger. When she had not practiced, even for a day, she could feel a tiny stiffness in the joints of her fingers, the signs of her future arthritis. On the other hand, there was the danger of practicing too much, so that the performance itself was easy, smooth, perfect—and without that strange, almost painful energy that derived from some uncertainty, that doubt as to the ultimate meaning of what she was playing, that effort which her friend Artur Rubinstein called, "one extra drop of blood." She let her hands strike down at the cool, flesh-like ivory, and then began to unwind the opening arpeggios. Bach had published this last Partita when he was past forty-five; there were no dynamics, one could play the piece boldly (she did), or softly, amoroso—however one chose; yet his strong and melancholy wisdom never changed. She played the whole composition, right through to the intense and syncopated Gigue; and only then, her mind going backward in perception, did she lean forward and take the rustling cablegram off the open and still faintly vibrating strings.

The cablegram had arrived at about four in the afternoon. On that evening she'd had a concert with the Boston Symphony. She had therefore to put the whole thing resolutely out of her mind. She took several aspirins, went to the Lincoln Center, played, even by her own standards, with magnificent force, and then took the earliest possible plane (it was a Sunday morning) straight on to Rome. She had spent that awful night drinking cups of chocolate, to which she was vaguely addicted, especially when depressed or anxious. All that thick, sweet liquid seeped through her stomach and irritated her nerves. She slept uneasily on the plane, waking only once. They were flying through a turbulence of towering clouds, as gigantic above as below; she began to imagine that her pulse beat more and more feebly; she was convinced, quite calmly, that she was about to die. But the panic slowly passed. She phoned from the airport in Rome. The connection to Padua was alive, that early evening, with an irritable, cosmic crackling of some sort; she could scarcely hear her daughter, who was in the University Hospital, but apparently not in bed.

"An accident, Mama darling!" said Elinor; she had to shout, but that very fact reassured her mother.

"Now tell me, baby! Exactly what kind of accident? Have you been driving on these awful Italian roads? You haven't bought a car or a scooter, have you?"

"Oh, you hate Italy worse than you hate me, don't you Mama!"

"No, Elinor," she said, quite calmly, "I happen to love Italy. I'm not sure about you, that's true. Now what kind of an accident, and how are you hurt? Your silly skull is all right, I hope?"

"Perfect, Mama. But please don't cross-examine me."

"How do you feel?" asked her mother.

"I don't know. They've given me sleepy pills. . . ."

("Why does she say *sleepy*, why not *sleeping*? That girl is so corny!" her mother cried out inside herself. It was a criticism far more profound than it seemed.)

"—Aren't you coming to see me? If you can't just say so. And I'll try to adjust. Oh, Mama, are you really calling from Rome?"

"Of course I'm in Rome!" They discussed the time she was coming, and set it for noon tomorrow, for Irene was exhausted. "I'll fly, of course, though I hate planes, as you damn well know."

Irene took a taxi into Rome; she felt marvelously light, somehow; excitement was good for her; the ruins of Roman tombs, overgrown with purple wisteria, gleamed as the sky grew slowly dark, with a dull, historical glow. When she arrived, she pulled off her stifling clothes and immediately went to bed.

Once, she remembered, when Elinor was barely fourteen, and
Irene had begun to despair of her musical education, Elinor persuaded her to switch from piano to organ. After several months
of remarkable progress, Irene got permission for Elinor to practice
very early in the morning at St. Catherine's Cathedral. She could
imagine Elinor sitting high up in the church, on the organist's
bench, in the cold of an early morning in March, and rubbing
her hands to keep them warm, and with her feet, monstrously
long, and wearing high sneakers with a black rubber patch at
the ankle bone. What must have happened, was that high up
on the organist's bench, Elinor could look down obliquely through
the enormous, frigid space of the church; and sometimes, not
always, see small groups of nuns come in through the distant
door, and kneel, genuflect, and look up toward the altar, above
which hung a commonplace and not even particularly lurid cruci-
fixion; they were mostly young and ugly, with standard metal-
rimmed glasses, but sometimes on the faces of one or two was
such purity of feeling, such exaltation, such tender stretching
toward ecstasy, that Elinor, young as she was, one early morning
became a fanatic convert. At night, and secretly, she read the
pamphlets of the Society for the Propagation of the Faith; and
in her room, with the latch hooked into its rusty loop, did penance
for masturbation, and other mortal sins, by sleeping all night long
on the naked floor; and once or twice, in cases of stubborn
pleasure, she would lie down on rude stones which she had
stolen from the Botanical Park nearby. When Irene, the outraged
daughter of an anarchist family, found these Catholic stones and
pamphlets under the folded blouses in the third drawer from the
bottom, she went into such a rage that she seized Elinor and
beat and slapped her with the coarse, utilitarian paper of which
all religious literature seemed to be made.

It was the middle of June, and school had just ended. She
arranged for Elinor to go to a strictly atheist camp in the Pocono
Mountains; but Elinor and Elinor's newest friend, a thin blonde
girl whom Elinor called Toothpick, with a silly smile and long
thin feet and little buds of breasts, pooled their pocket money
and jumped the train just as it began to move. Burning with
excitement, they got a bus to as far north as possible, and when
most of their money was gone, hitchhiked all the rest of the way to
Montreal; their goal was the Shrine of St. Ursula the Compas-

214   BEN MADDOW

sionate, where you could earn remission of sins by climbing one
hundred forty-one concrete steps, especially if you did them on
your knees. The two girls spent their last cash on a taxi from
the outskirts of Montreal; they arrived just behind a chartered
bus of pilgrims from Bloomington, Indiana. The taxi driver, a
French Canadian whom Elinor described as an incarnation of
Santa Claus, warned the girls that a female could not enter the
Shrine without a hat. All the ladies going up the steps had fancy
hats of one kind or another; straw and flowers were the fashion
that year. The taxi driver loaned Toothpick his taxi driver's cap,
absurdly too big for her, for the sweat band came down until
it was stopped by the ridge of her protruding ears, and he knotted
his handkerchief in four corners for Elinor to wear over her hair.
Thus capped, the two teenagers began to kneel up the steps,
counting as they went. They had gone about twenty steps, when,
looking at each other, they began to giggle, and each giggle fed
the other until they were both bent double with violent attacks of
laughter. Thus the martyrdom of St. Elinor ended.

Irene, her great, restless body tranquilized with the memory
of silly laughter, fell asleep at last. She was in her favorite Roman
hotel, a rather formal and ornate building whose name, Il Massimo d'Azeglio, matched its prandial designs: the great cakes and
cheeses on the dessert table, the glazed fowl and the pinkly
phosphorescent beef, and the enormous scalloped pies of truffle
and minced veal. The bathtubs in the hotel were invariably huge;
the soap was specially wrapped and smelled of some bitter masculine perfume. It was only a few streets from the "New" railway
station, a post-war shell of thick glass and airy steel. A moment
after she fell asleep, she had several nightmares in succession;
they were all familiar, a replay from her prolonged and uneasy
pregnancy. She was giving birth to a child. Was it Elinor? Impossible; the baby was covered with sharp scales like a fish.

Accustomed to the exercise of her will, even in sleep, she tried
to force these stupidly symbolic dreams to end. She assured herself
(there were several selves in the dream) that Elinor was perfectly all right; anyway, she was no longer a baby, even a painful
one. After that, she had a second dream of an elaborate glass
funeral coach in which there was a wedding cake as large as a
mountain; she knew quite well that the mountain was herself.

She awoke, thinking she heard a locomotive close by. But it

was only some distant nocturnal thunder. Rain began to splash the tall windows of the room; she got up and went to the one on the north side, and unfolded the shutters; they were waxy to the touch, she wouldn't sleep any more, or so she decided. She sat in an easy chair, naked as usual; would she have time to practice tomorrow morning, before flying to Padua?

Insensibly the rain stopped, but the lightning continued: ultramarine flashes accompanied by a metallic scraping and crackling; no, they were only sparks from the short-circuits of the electric trolleys that turned the corner at five-minute intervals. Irene swung open one shutter and cranked the left upper pane into the weather above the street. She thought, absurdly but sadly, that she heard Elinor's voice speaking Italian. Was she still dreaming?

She leaned out; rain fell on her thick, dyed, black hair, wound in a single braid that now fell forward over the arch of her powerful neck; pure drops blown out of the sky brushed at both her nipples. Down below, a woman was screaming curses at a couple of policemen on the opposite corner. Thin, she was bulked out by a black raincoat; and this, and her cropped gold hair, gleamed as if enameled. Diagonally across the street, in one of Rome's beautiful doorways, another woman, older, square, and disconsolate, held a handkerchief to her cheek and looked at it, occasionally weeping and exlaiming at what apparently were stains of blood. This got nothing but scorn from the blonde.

"*Ehi! Ragazza—!*" called Irene. The gold head looked up; and shouted, as if to the galleries of a theatre, her dramatic complaint that here, here entirely, here by the grace of St. Jude of Lost Causes, here was her corner, she had worked this corner since the beginning of the year, but now this diseased, ignorant and Neopolitan whore. . . .

And suddenly she ceased her complaint, and asked, would Irene want her to come up? She would make it a nice adventure, and because it was late, it would be ridiculously cheap. "What room?" she inquired. Irene stared down at the woman's face; she was pretty, with eyes markedly oval, and a beaked mediterranean nose. Irene drew back and shut the window and laughed and went back to bed. Oh, things were going to be fine, and the world, which consisted of those who went to her concerts and those who did not, was quite unchanged by Elinor's cablegram.

Next morning, she cancelled the piano she had ordered, and

flew very early into Padua, and took a room in the large commercial hotel on the main corner. At about nine o'clock, as she was having mixed coffee and chocolate, with the consolation of globs of ricotta spooned onto flat, fresh bread, a small but splendid brass band began to march around the corner. In her quilted robe, still munching and drinking, she looked down to read the banner that followed. They were the names of various groups and groupings and grouplets; one sign said, DOVE LA PACE DI DEO?— but that was about as blood-thirsty as they got. Irene's mother had been a Polish anarchist; in the old yellow snapshots, taken for subversive picnics, she wore a workman's cap with a visor, and parted her straight hair in the center of a wide pure forehead; her eyes burned like feverish stars. In those days, the oligarchic world was about to crumble, and May First was always a great harsh holiday, and legless veterans were wheeled forward in slow ranks, singing *Bandiera Rosa*, in translations that were equally hideous in every country in the world.

Irene dressed and went down into the streets. She found herself tremendously excited. "Strike, strike, strike!" she chanted to herself, as she had once done as a child on her father's sickly, bony shoulders. A float representing *Labor in Chains* was just going by. It was towed by an enormous brand-new truck, property of the *Fraterni Gatti Furniture Factory*, and there were samples of the furniture in the truck, too, with prices prominently displayed; evidently Padua had a tame bourgeoisie. A sour dark man in a frayed suit was passing out leaflets. Irene pursued him and got one; he seemed rather reluctant. WARNING! it said, in great red letters. She got a taxi (the price was doubled because of the holiday) and bent her head to imbibe the fiery message. The taxi driver smoked an abominable local brand of cigar, jutting it up toward his nose, and inhaling it thus, from both ends. She asked for his help in the translation, but the leaflet was disappointing: it advertised a cure, not for capitalism, but for venereal disorders.

Aha! Was this the trouble with Elinor? It would account only too nicely for her gaiety, her evasions, for the ambiguous word "accident," and was only too consistent with her daughter's character. It was rash, restless, and obsessive, and in that respect, exactly like her own; but, in her absolute lack of any talent whatever, she was like Rabinowitz. Because Elinor was the child of rape; not by her father, but by her mother.

Well, naturally: all the men she'd known were cowards; they were as frightened of sex as a rabbit seduced by a fox. Rabinowitz was the worst; but before that there was Jay Louis Vicker, a handsome and ridiculous man, a writer who slept all day and revised his one published and unperformed play all night long and every night, smoking cigars and drinking *ouzo,* for which he had developed a passion when Irene took him on tour with her to Greece; and there were other men, even feebler and funnier. At her friend Sylvia's she'd been to a birthday dinner; all the guests were professional women, most of them with good income, heavy eaters like herself, with decisive and quarrelsome voices. Irene was past forty, and Sylvia's birthday disturbed her; she began to get drunk on the authentic raspberry brandy she herself had brought as a dinner present.

She found herself standing in a corner, making a passionate defense of one of Bach's sons, Carl Emanuel, though no one present knew enough music to attack him. The women, all a bit tight by now, and slouched or squatting on Sylvia's marvelous new light Danish furniture, simply roared at everything she said. Suddenly, horribly, she had two concurrent feelings: she wanted to get out, and she wanted a child. She rushed down a flight of linoleum stairs and onto Second Avenue near 68th Street, where she roamed silently back and forth before the dark antique shops, till at the corner she collided at last with a small man, close-shaven, and wearing what she later described as "a black, flat, immaculate hat." He had difficulty, at first, understanding her question. Would he like to come and sleep with her? She asked him the same thing in several languages. "Ach, no!" he said. He explained that he had no money to spare; he was a refugee from Vienna, via Vichy France.

Irene kept him in her apartment almost three weeks; as soon as he would show signs of restlessness or irritation, she would serve food that she regarded as especially aphrodisiac, such as rich cheeses, tins of pâté, smoked shrimp, and champagne; and then, opening her thick velvet robe, without bothering to take it off, she would press herself heavily upon him. She weighed thirty pounds less, in those days, and she was solid, voluptuous, and skillful. He told her all about himself, but she rarely listened.

One day, when she was practicing a particularly loud passage in the first Brahms Sonata, he took advantage of all that *martellato* to dress, shave, and escape. However, he abandoned his ridiculous felt hat, which had a famous Portuguese label, and which she kept for years, in case he returned. Poor Rabinowitz, she had a curious affection for the man; for the body is stubborn and sentimental; and Elinor was the product of their dark collaboration.

"I may go on and study medicine," Elinor was saying to her mother. They had come to the open sundeck on the second floor of the University Hospital, in a fine, open part of Padua. A young man with a spinal injury, suffered at soccer, hung upright in a padded frame, grinning lewdly at Elinor. Her daughter was beautiful; thinner than she need be, of course; her broad, wide, doubly curving mouth was accentuated by the darkness under her cheekbones and beyond the outer folds of her enormous pale green eyes. A tiny shadow, faint and luxurious, arched under each twisted nostril. Elinor had both forearms suspended in a black silk sling.

"How's my friend Rusty?" Elinor said.

"She's fallen in love with a fish."

"What, Mama? You're joking. Did somebody give Rusty a fish?"

Irene said yes. She didn't say from whom she had received the gift; actually, it was from Sylvia, who was Head of Publicity at Saks-Fifth. "It's beautiful," she continued. "It's black, with black fins. Not fins—underwater wings, really."

"How lovely!" said Elinor. It was impossible to tell, from the very day that she learned to talk, whether she was being sarcastic or not.

Elinor had been baptized under her mother's maiden name; she was a prodigy, but only up to the age of five; she could read music and played a quarter-size violin; but then slowly, stubbornly, she resisted all further education. At six, she ran away from home, and was found next day, quite unharmed, in the apartment of a moronic but polite New York City apprentice fireman who moonlighted as a plumber, and who had come to their place with a box of tools, on the inside cover of which he had scotch-taped the photo of a girl wearing only a fishnet, cork floats and all, which both Elinor and her mother, in possibly different ways, had found so astounding. At nine, Elinor failed arithmetic and became passionate about horses; she kept a saddle over the arm of a chair in her room, and wore riding boots to private school. Four years later, in fact, she won three blue ribbons at the Horse Show in Madison Square Garden. A year later, she turned Catholic. At sixteen, she was an alcoholic, and Irene, secretly proud of this disaster, took her along on an international tour that lasted well over a year; but her daughter wept for hours out of boredom. She convinced her, at last, that she hated music, and she took to spending hours in her mother's room, particularly during concerts, trying, on the inner skin of each forearm—the memory gave Irene an instant feeling of dread— various perfumes from her mother's collection of tiny crystal decanters. At times, Irene was convinced that her daughter was simply illiterate; but then, after some horrible, screeching quarrel between them had cleared the air of all emotion whatsoever, Elinor would go to bed and write pages and pages of a kind of crude, raw, and original poetry, in which she mingled slang, musical terms, and obscenities in several languages, which she had learned from hotel employees all over the world.

And once—was it in Brussels? Elinor had swallowed all of Irene's cough medicine. Some day she must ask her if it was an accident or revenge. It was curious that she had forgotten all about this horrible episode, as if it were a paragraph on the inside page of a Flemish newspaper; as indeed it nearly was. Elinor was then almost eleven, and Irene had just refused to buy her a horse they had seen galloping past in the public park. Elinor could not be wakened for almost seventy-two hours. Did the accident imply another act of this sort? But Irene pointed out to herself, with some scorn, that one doesn't commit suicide by spraining both wrists.

Elinor had continued gaily chattering, while Irene, safe in the awful past, chose not to listen; but her particularly childish tone, imitation Joe-jah, Atlanta actually, where they had spent all of one Sunday together, penetrated Irene's defense at last, and slowly enraged her. "Mama," Elinor repeated, "would you please, pretty please, get me a po'table American TV?"

"No! Of course not!" Irene told her. They shifted their chairs on the hospital sundeck; it was getting very warm again.

"Well, then ah won't tay you," said Elinor.

"Tell me what?"

"Haow it happened."

"Well, how did it happen?"

"No, I'm going to let my Mama purely die of curiosity."

"I'll bet it was one of those scooters, wasn't it? A Vespa, or a Yamaha, or one of those horrible items."

"No, ah reckon ah just won't tell you, Mama, evah, evah."

"I suppose that's because you took my Christmas money and bought one, and you're afraid to admit it."

"It wasn't on a scoota," sing-song sang Elinor.

"I suppose you would have enjoyed the whole thing immensely if I had been present, screaming my head off, while you skidded out of control and tore your arms open on a clump of trees somewhere?"

"Oh, you're right! Right, right, right. Except there wah no clump of trees, Mama."

"Well, whatever. I'm told you may recover. I sincerely hope not."

"Oh, Mama mia, you are truly so funny?"

Irene rose and looked for her raincoat. That they loved each other, they denied; but it was true and it was often frightening. Once, in her lonely rage (Irene had dressed elaborately and gone to dinner with an oboe player, mad, naturally, as all oboe players must be), Elinor had smashed Irene's whole collection of perfumes and hurled their travelling case after them, down into the crowded street outside the Rasoumovsky Hotel. Two men were hurt by broken glass, and Elinor's jealous rage cost Irene several thousand guilders. Yet it wasn't this particular act that broke them apart, but Elinor's renewed and tearful insistence on creeping into Irene's bed. She knew that Irene had always slept alone; it was a form of secret self-protection. The presence of another person in her bed made her feel at once restless and exhausted; this was true even during her marriage to Rabinowitz, especially with his pale, icy, nervous feet. And the touch of her daughter, coming to her full of grief and kisses, in the rainy morning of a Dutch November, curving herself against Irene like a spoonful restoring itself to the inside of a spoon, made Irene sick with a sensual terror.

Next day, she had phoned Hurok himself, and made him pull strings to get Elinor into the University of Padua, in spite of her curious and uneven education; they took her on as a probationary

student. So mother and daughter parted, as they had innumerable
times, on sullen terms with one another. Six months passed and
Irene heard little, and was hurt by her silence; but she put the
slow accumulated pain far back in her mind, as something she
must face and kill eventually; and then the cablegram came, and
all the old sutures were torn violently open.

Elinor said, in her normal husky voice again, "Will you give a
concert while you're here?"

"No. Why should I?"

"Suppose I asked you?"

"Look here," Irene said. Her voice was darkening and trembling.
"I want to know why you're being so kind?"

"Oh, just to make you mad, ah raykon."

"Elinor, when I look at you objectively, all I can see is a truly
horrible person. Of course you're attractive, I don't mean that.
But your soul, if you'll give me permission to use that word, is
just perfectly sick."

"I know, Mama."

"And sometimes I think it's all my fault. And other times, I
don't. People have to be responsible for themselves, certainly at
your age."

"Well, but will you?" said Elinor again.

"Would you really like me to play? Do they have a decent
hall?"

"Should be. It's got a wooden ceiling a thousand years old."

"Today is Monday. Maybe Wednesday, the night before I go."

Elinor said, "Goodness, we're in a hurry, aren't we."

Irene said, "Look, dearest. We'll spend all of Tuesday together.
Maybe go to a play or something. I saw a notice in the hotel."

"Better yet, maybe I could go home with you?"

"We'll see. I have two concerts in L.A. I could meet you in
New York in about a month."

"Play some Bach, will you, Mama, at the University?"

"You really want me to, darling? But I haven't practiced in
two days. It makes a difference, you know. Not to others, but to
me."

Elinor smiled. "You know you'd love to, Mama. The fact is,
you love Johann Sebastian Bach far more than you love me,
don't you?"

"That's so true," said Irene.

"It's quite hopeless, Mama," Elinor continued. "He's married. Twice, in fact."

Irene felt the familiar awful softening of love toward her daughter. She said, "Isn't it time for your pills?"

"Will you give them to me?"

"Why, are your arms that badly hurt? Can't you bend at the elbow?"

"Yes," said Elinor. "But I just like you to do it." Irene bent down and kissed her several times, then called a nurse for a glass of water, and gave her daughter the medicine.

Yet Irene left the hospital with tremendous relief. Instead of taking a taxi she walked through Padua, past the open air markets and toward her hotel, where she'd gotten, through the hotel porter, a pair of seats for the theatre tomorrow night. It was Zefirelli's new production of *Romeo and Juliet*, to be staged in English at the Teatro La Fenice in Venice, thirty miles away.

She went downstairs and ordered an enormous lunch in the dining room. As she ate, she felt an irritable apprehension at the very edges of her mind; did that accident really happen on the road? And wasn't there a man involved? The idea of a lover for Elinor—and one as selfish, young, and clumsy as he was bound to be—was so repulsive to Irene that she gave up the idea of resting after lunch. Instead, she took a benzedrine, and had the chief porter downstairs get her a rented car. She drove the Fiat down the river road, past the Palladian villas with their classic columns and their stucco walls the color of scorched clay. There were people everywhere walking in their holiday clothes, and a pair of lovers hugging behind a tree; they had a beautiful green glass bottle, floating, empty now, in a tub of melted ice. There were some odd traffic signs along the way; one of them announcing, with a great yellow numeral, how many people had been killed in traffic accidents at this precise curve of the road.

At one crossroad, about halfway to Venice, a hideously crushed car had been lifted and balanced on to a concrete pillar; it was the very epitome of popular art—morbid and moral at the same time. Yes, that's how it happened; Elinor, she was sure, had been riding pillion, with her arms clasped around the belt of some dark-lashed boy, and a truck, no doubt, came past in the opposite direction (one roared by her now, hooting its illegal electric horn), and Elinor must have been flung through the air when they skidded; hurled the fence and into one of these ancient vegetable fields.

Oh, it was perfectly clear now; Elinor was evasive, naturally, because of the boy; probably he was not even a student, but some baker's apprentice or even common laborer; for her daughter was at once intrigued by any sort of tool working in a man's hand. Irene parked the car in the multi-layered garage at Venice and got on a *vaporetto*. Many of the passengers carried tiny red flags.

The sun burned over the water, bursting into fragments as a wind arose from the Adriatic. The skipper of the *vaporetto* leaned out of the open window of the pilot house, cursing; a passenger next to Irene, with an unrolled black umbrella, was cursing him back; they were engaged in a dispute about the fact that the *vaporetto* had forgotten to stop at one of the islands. "Revolutionary Holiday!" cried the captain of the *vaporetto*, and made a hairy fist; he knew the complainant by sight, as a Bureau Chief of Traffic Planning and a clerico-crypto-fascist from baptism onward. The other passengers waved their arms and with a nice impartiality, encouraged them both. "Stop the boat! Stop! Stop!" shouted the man with the umbrella. The skipper pulled the visor of his cap down over his eyes and disappeared into the pilot-house. Ten seconds later, the boat came to a shuddering halt in the midst of open water.

The sea was ink black; like the bottle that Elinor had discovered in her mother's desk at the age of eighteen months, and while Irene napped, had opened and emptied every closet, and smeared clothes, music, and mementoes from every one from Mahatma Ghandi to Huey Long, with splotches of Jet Black Indelible. It was Ink Day. Irene wanted to kill her, and the feeling had never quite vanished.

Meanwhile, the skipper emerged from the window of the pilot-house and politely invited the passenger with the rolled umbrella to get the hell off the boat; Christ could walk on the waters, possibly a Bureau Chief could, as well. All three hundred passengers on the boat commented on this sacrilegious insult. The man with the umbrella put on a marvelous performance, full of groans, tears, and bitter imprecations. But the skipper smiled; he sat in the window of his pilot-house and fanned himself with his cap, as if he were utterly and serenely alone. The rich salt tide, on which Venice appears to float, nudged the boat first in one direction, then another, but only very slowly and capriciously. Irene felt marvelous again; she was free of any responsibility. Perhaps death was like this: a numb drifting, a *vaporetto* on the soiled waterways of a romantic and banal Italian eternity; surely it was not the vengeful and chiaroscuro cave invented by Dante.

As the shouts, the lapel-seizures, the self-administered slaps of the forehead, all grew more and more violent, Irene became more and more calm. She bitterly acknowledged to herself that she didn't want Elinor to see *Romeo and Juliet*, after all. Actually, it was a rather incredible play about an incredible teenage love, pandered to a farethewell by an incredible priest who made incredibly stupid blunders, and which ended with an incredible orgy of double suicide in a marble family vault already crowded to the rafters by recent corpses. No, *Romeo and Juliet* was definitely not the right entertainment for herself and Elinor. For the girl was quite wild and melancholy enough, without the sanction of Shakespeare. Literature, she thought, was by its nature corruptive; but never music. She began her favorite daydream: herself as Bach; in the last month of life, writing bar by bar, absolutely complete as it went along, two voices, three, six, canon and inverse canon, and all in the service of one's own proper voice, wiry, strong, somewhat sad, and yet, quite amoral; creating, with antiphony and counter-force, these galaxies, these cloudy harmonies, resolving one into another; as great as God, while one held the proud note-scribing pen. She wiped the point, in her imagination, on a piece of old linen, part, very possibly, of an old and worn altar-cloth. For Bach, she told herself, was a great hypocrite, serving only himself; he had worked so hard, not for the glory of God, but to satisfy the terrible metabolism of his own soul.

Was this piece for herself? Sadly, no. She was too entangled in human connections; a man could have a child—Bach had seventeen—yet never feel more than love. But a woman's child is the branch of one's self-made, tree-like self; not to be severed except with the teeth of the saw. Yet how much of herself was truly Elinor? Nothing, really; yet at the very moment she knew this to be quite true, she saw Elinor on the *vaporetto*, laughing near the upper rail, and with her head turned away. Now she turned toward Irene, and looked down; it was someone older, though with the same turn of the jaw and temple. She began to shout and push, along with the other passengers. By now, they had floated till they were only twenty yards from the cement shore. Lines were tossed aboard, and Irene herself, along with many others standing near the rail, stretched out her hands and seized the wet hemp ropes, pulling in the wrong direction. Thus, by contradictory garrulous human force, the boat was hauled into dock.

Irene was mad with the pleasure of this incident. She loved to be surprised, or even cheated, by the world; it served to make things real for a moment. Sweating and smiling, she disembarked, feeling the bodily pleasure of the crowd as if it were an enormous single person, and no longer a stranger. On the dock were two lovers, holding hands, waiting to get on. She greeted them in Italian, asking if they wanted two seats to *Romeo and Juliet* Tuesday night.

"*Davvero?*" they said, both at once; were they frightened of her? They began to talk to each other in English. So she had them all wrong: they were English tourists, very young and fair, and brother and sister.

"Wouldn't we have to ask Mum?" said the girl.

"I imagine, yes," said the boy.

Irene assured them the offer would cost them nothing, absolutely nothing. "I was going to take my daughter, but she's been in a traffic accident, nothing serious, but she should rest, you see." They agreed to meet later, at 4 p.m., in the piazza in front of the theatre, when their parents would both be there.

"Thank you so much, it's really very decent of you," said the girl.

"But we'll have to persuade Mum, you know," said the boy.

"Why," asked Irene, "is she such a monster?"

"Yes," said the girl.

And she laughed, touched the girl's sleeve, and strode off. She had her Belgian walking shoes on her feet; they cost an enormous sum, because she'd had them hand made in Bruges almost ten years ago; like a painting or a sculpture, they would last far beyond her own life; they were made of some sort of pliable tawny, soft iron. Irene felt extremely, ridiculously, unreasonably happy; as if not taking Elinor and herself to see a pair of adolescent lovers solved all their nagging problems. For what was the dilemma, exactly? Wasn't it that Elinor, in spite of the laws of nature, was not her daughter, but the pale and morbid progeny of poor Rabinowitz.

The crowds were dense, and when the sky became overcast and it rained, although fitfully, she would find herself penned into a covered alley, or into a rectangle under a cafe awning, or into a stifling doorway. Even when the rain stopped, it was impossible to hurry, for the holiday crowds were slow and even stubborn, and her idea of the right direction was continually confused by the irregular, branching, angulating streets of this part of Venice. How to kill the hours agreeably? All the cinemas were closed, but from the posters moldering on the walls she learned there was a Regatta today, in honor of May First. The Union of Venetian Gondoliers was to stage a race down the Grand Canal. She made her way toward the water and rented a seat in a gondola that was tied to one of the jetties. The young gondolier loaned her a moth-eaten parasol. The balconies up and down the Canal were hung with scarlet banners decrepit from a couple of centuries of aristocratic use; behind them, in the shadows, people sat with plates of food and glasses of wine. Almost two hours passed in the parked gondola. Irene dozed several times, her thick round body rising and falling blissfully to the rhythm of the brilliant, black water. In a dream, she heard someone say, in a high-pitched voice—"Astonishing . . . The greatest woman pianist of the age . . . Formidable. . . ."

Slowly, reluctantly, she awoke. She complained of the heat, and the young gondolier gave her mixed wine and water to drink from the neck of the green bottle which he had brought for himself. Irene cleaned the rim, more or less symbolically, with her dark silk sleeve. As she drank, she thought she heard her name called out; she stood up, but it was only a girl crying, "Anna, Anna!" Hundreds of people took up the cry. It was their amusement till the race should begin. Just above Irene, in one of the windows of the palazzo behind her, there was a middle-aged film star, waving her love to the customers down below; visible behind her was a morose young man in pink, horizontally striped pajamas, thrusting his rather prominent chin out of the window and eating a sandwich. He became, for her, the image of Elinor's boyfriend, Roman, agreeable, useless, and dangerous. She saw him lift both hands and cry, "Bravo! Bravo!" The race had begun; in the middle distance, twenty-three gilded gondolas came rushing on, each poled forward by a single gondolier who prodded the water like Neptune with his spear.

Irene's own gondolier rose with his green bottle and began to scream, *"Papa! Papa! Papa!,"* which Irene took to mean that the Pope had arrived; but it appeared that the gondolier's father was one of the racers. He was a stocky man with a slow, powerful stroke and looked, as he came straining by, to be almost fifty. That's the sort of man she should have married, thought Irene; by him, she'd have a clutch of thick, dark, belligerent sons —though this particular son was little more than a pale and pleasantly lazy young man. He left the race to his father. *"Non sono vano*—I'm not vain," he told her.

Meanwhile, the race of the gondoliers passed the finish line and was over. His father got second place, which, said his son, meant a silver-plated medal worth a few hundred lire, at most. Irene got off the parked boat. It was almost four by now, and the first thing she did was lose the way toward her appointment at La Fenice. This was absurd: now she would have to keep the tickets and go to the theatre with Elinor; mother and daughter tied together forever by a bloody birth; for Elinor, characteristically, was a Caesarean child; both of them dressed uncomfortably in the early heat and seated, like two pretty bon bons, in that candy box of a theatre; pure sugary sentiment; quite unbearable. No, she had to find the English couple.

She had a glimpse of herself, stubbornly advancing, with her fine proud face thrust forward, in a shop window full of elaborate pastry. She went in to inquire the direction. Then, as long as she was there anyway, she bought a half-kilo of little cakes decorated with spangles of chocolate and halves of walnuts. She began to eat before she left the shop; as she came out, a bitten fragment of a cake fell out of her thick hand and was seized by some sort of black animal, with wings as dusty as a bat's, which darted out of a narrow doorway: it was an old woman in faded mourning clothes, tall, with a startling pink ball in each eye socket. At a distance, now, of ten feet, the two women stared at each other, the famous, aging concert pianist and the hungry, dotty grandmother, and each chewed voraciously at their bit of cake.

"Buon appetito!" Irene said to the woman, and grinned at her; but got no response. She left the rest of the oil-stained paper bag on the edge of a dry fountain in the little square, and looking back

saw the old woman swoop forward and take it and hide it under
her flaps and rags. So, with this hasty sacrifice, Irene felt she had
pacified the Fates, those old, hungry, triple monomaniacs, with
their clothes the color of ancient umbrellas. It was true, but she
turned the corner of a church, and, suddenly, there was the
theatre on the other side of the piazza, but it was a quarter of five;
the young English couple had obviously come and gone. Only
a group of twenty German tourists, thick-legged and handsome,
were standing on the broad steps of La Fenice. A hoarse feminine
guide was explaining to them the trade routes and sordid commercial origins of all that splendid Venetian art. Beyond them
were two men, one in shorts, and the other with large glasses, a
pale moustache, and a kind of tweed kilt; a little to the left of
this pair, and listening at the edge of the German group, were
a couple of young tourists holding hands. The girl turned, and
seeing Irene far off, smiled; Irene recognized her, rather slowly,
as the English girl; now her brother raised his hand as if to wave,
but touched and twisted his cropped hair instead. Irene, laughing,
strode down the long flight of outside steps, and, as she came toward
them, cried, "Oh, I am so sorry! I'm late, but then I'm always late!
Well here you are, so it doesn't matter. Wait, now. Have you
asked—" she said with unavoidable irony, "—your parents?"

The English girl led Irene toward the man in kilts. "This is the
person who offered the tickets," she told him.

"We're very grateful," he said; his voice was not particularly
high, but it was certainly not a man's either; and his kilt was really
a skirt of some English or Irish tweed. But the other, the shorter
man, nodded and smiled; he took out an empty pipe and put it
back again; he was rather pleased, on the whole, but nervous.
The young girl looked off into the sky; the boy, though, felt he
should explain. "This is my Mum," he told Irene. He meant the
one with the moustache, and now that Irene looked at her closely,
it was not trimmed and neat like a man's, but luxuriant and somewhat unkempt, of that indeterminant British color between pale
and gray. Irene gave this hairy Mum the tickets, excused herself,
and went off. She immediately felt sick and yet excited.

"Fate has struck at me twice," she said, almost aloud; she always
addressed herself in these corny and melodramatic phrases—"and
fate will strike again."

Irene had returned to the *vaporetto* now; she was going back in the late heat of the day, utterly dulled and exhausted. The boat now stopped at every island; friends and relatives shouted from windows above, to whom Irene was forever a fat old stranger. Suddenly, that cat, Rusty, sprang uninvited into her mind; who, in her periodic desperation, would whine and mutter and back up to Irene, wriggling and flaunting her inflamed and furry behind, until Irene, disgusted, would seize her by the skin back of the head, as if she were a kitten, and shut her up in the bathroom. Every season there were new scarifications on the enamel of the bathroom door, marks of feline obscenity.

Irene had named that cat in memory of a redheaded cousin, nicknamed Rusty, with whom she had sat in a car that had been abandoned in an empty lot full of immense, prickly weeds, to eat sticky candy and press noses fiercely together; both of them were about eight years old, athletic and filthy brats, forever at war with their great square bosomy female relatives. And then there was the second Rusty, a swimming counselor at a girl's camp—God! More than forty years ago!—the shimmering, slim, muscular, thick-handed, sun-golden idol of all the girls' cabins. Irene was not quite twenty, in charge of chorus and campfire musicales; at the time she was pink and shy, with great tangles of tar-colored hair. They all went walking in groups every night, on the path through young pines bordering the lake. When the moon sank, it grew absolutely dark. Irene and a group of older girls were walking on an invisible road, pressing their faces into all that yielding, gently swimming darkness. She heard Rusty, moving nearby, exclaim as she struck the edge of her right bare foot on a boulder that protruded from the road; and Rusty's expletive, that simple word spoken aloud for the first time in Irene's life, and not merely thought or seen or imagined, was not brutal, but simply mysterious. Someone took her hand, a moment later, and holding Irene still as the others in the group advanced, bent her backward as she was kissed; lifting her face till her eyes were full of the vast meander of the Milky Way, a soft and glowing sisterhood of stars.

Irene dressed all in white for her concert at Padua University. She had gained weight even in the brief period since the cablegram from her daughter; the silk that she loved was tight and twisted at her armpits. The Massimo d'Azeglio served vast meals, cooked with the delicate Roman cuisine that she so loved. She had seen Elinor about once every day. They had taken to cross-examining one another; once Irene asked Elinor, "Are you in love?"

"I've been in love every three weeks since I've been a baby," said Elinor. Then she added, "They're all such little kids around here, even when they're 21 or 22, or even 25. Why don't you introduce me to some nice old man? Somebody you've discarded, I don't care."

On the morning of the concert, Elinor no longer wore the sling for her arms, but had a large new bandage on each, from the forearm to the base of the fingers; it was already soiled, with traces of lipstick and some sort of anonymous gravy, and also various of her fellow students had signed their names; *Con Amore Eterna*, said one of the inscriptions, in blue ink.

Irene said, "Where were you going with this man when you were hurt?"

"When did I say I was going anywhere?"

"I don't know if you did or you didn't. It doesn't matter. Is he an Italian?"

"Italians!" said Elinor. "I hate Italians, they talk a great game. But they're like rabbits. Two minutes, then they scootch back on the pillow, heave a sigh of relief, and borrow a cigarette."

Irene laughed and told her about the English woman on the steps before La Fenice; her anecdotal style was in the family tradition, detailed and witty; but she censored all mention of the tickets she'd given away. Elinor only stared, and said, finally, "Did you ever consider growing a moustache, Mama?" So they parted, as usual, on bad terms.

Yet Elinor was there in the audience, in the very front row of uncomfortable wooden folding seats; she was restless, and glanced frequently and coquettishly to each side. She wore long sleeves and appeared rather pale. She didn't applaud as her mother came to the piano; no doubt her injuries would hurt if she banged her palms together. Irene adjusted the knob on the leather stool, rubbed her wet hands on her handkerchief, and began.

Her program was deliberately unconventional. She turned the history of music backward, and began the concert with Schoenberg's piano pieces, the earliest group, morose, languid, romantic, and yet full of acid qualifications; they were frequently marked with quadruple piano and quadruple forte; after these, and the polite applause—for most Italians hated everything from Wagner onward—she plunged into the supernatural passions of Op. 111, Beethoven's last sonata. There were only two movements; the first was a condensation, a summary, of the whole furious and seductive world; but the second movement, with its extended, hovering, wing-like trills, was a preview of Hell disguised as Paradise; *Sensana—Nirvana*. She hurled this monstrous masterpiece at her young audience with superb defiance. The first movement bristled with passion; the second had the perfection of icy and crystalline technique. At the end, the audience sat still; Irene rose and bowed, rather ironically; then, as she left the piano, indeed after almost half a minute, the students came out of their hypnotic trance and began to applaud rather timidly. Little by little, as she returned and bowed again, they began to shout and stamp their feet. Irene looked toward her daughter. Elinor sat quite still, her head somewhat to one side, clasping her tapered, long-phalanged fingers. For the first time, Irene noticed there was a boy with a face like an adolescent Cupid, sitting at her daughter's left. He leaned over and whispered to Elinor. Irene tried to read her daughter's lips; she was saying something like "No, no, man, no,"—it was certainly something negative, for the boy sat back, hurt and sulky. Elinor yawned; she became all tongue and teeth; she gaped like a fledgling.

Irene watched her as she took a seventh bow. She had heard much applause in her long concertizing life; unlike love, it was never tiring; maybe because it was a gift without responsibility. She sat down again for an encore, and said, in Italian, "My daughter, who's here at the University—." There were cries of *brava, bravissima,* and she looked again toward Elinor, noting, in the oblique light, the marvelous hollows at the base of her long neck,—"has especially requested that I play some—" she smiled maternally at the audience—"Johann Sebastian Bach." Now she let her hands sink down, with sudden instant pleasure, into the beginning of Partita VI, letting its curious seven-headed rhythm ring out, one after another, like amethysts on a chain. She played the fugue with marked sadness, and then brought back the septimate chords to enclose it. Irene moved on toward the final harmony, which shifted, at the last possible moment, from minor into major, with that one new bright G sharp; and then Irene lifted her hands into silence, but only for a couple of seconds. Her daughter Elinor, in the front row, was looking upward, her eyes tracing the ancient wooden squares on the ceiling. Irene let her fingers strike down toward the keyboard again, sloping her heavy wrists, feeling the thick elliptical muscles still tense in each palm, and began the opening delicacies of the Allemanda—and as she played this dance, she looked again toward her daughter.

Poor Elinor, her head to one side, was asleep.

The final Gigue, ending the Partita, Irene played as a fury of conflicting voices; never before this had she understood the violence of their measured, syncopated cacophony. She played this movement as if with one long-held, cramped, but prevailing and conquering breath. It helped her to endure the future which she still had to face, quite alone, in a foreign city, with a foreign girl, whom in every way except financially, formally, and physically, she must now begin to recognize as in no way her own child.

She was finished. She got up from the piano.

She saw Elinor wake, rather slowly, at the applause, and saw her smile, but still she didn't clap her hands. Irene went out into the lecture room which had been provided for her rest between numbers. It was horribly vacant. Already sobbing, she found a door on the other side, beyond the blackboards, and emerged into a small, closed, and little-used courtyard, in which grew several orange trees. Burst and rotten fruit had fallen unattended on to the pale brick walk: they were the characteristic sweet, small blood-oranges of the Mediterranean.

She was crying and shaking. She wanted desperately to shed her body like a crustacean. She had the repeated empty nausea of crisis; and felt some painful effort to conceive a third and happier life (her second had begun with the birth of Elinor), though of what sort, at sixty, she had no idea. Her heavy, somewhat hairy thighs were like two weights that drew and bent her down, and bent her great, white, plump back under the silk, down, down toward the brick-plated ground, pressing both knees against the spatter where red oranges had fallen and burst.

Elinor said, "Mama, what in hell is the matter with you?" Irene rose at once in the darkness, and sat down, still sick and crying, on a curved marble bench that had sunk into a patch of flowers, lopsided, and so low that now her two flanks were raised as if she were giving birth. Elinor, moving away, began to pluck and examine oranges from the nearest bough of one of the trees.

"You're always angry and I never know why," said Elinor; and bit a hole in one of the fruits, and began to suck through the skin, rather noisily. There was still applause from inside the hall, two walls and a room away.

"I'm so stupid!" said Irene.

"Oh, mother, don't upset yourself so much about me. It's not that important."

"You asked me to play Bach, why?" Irene said. She gasped and sobbed, alternately; like a child out of breath, having run a long way and fallen at the very steps of her house. "You deliberately asked me for Bach, and I did what you asked me, I played Bach. And you fell asleep." Then she added, "Why are you so sleepy? Are you taking drugs? Is that what happened? Is that the accident, you were so awful, you won't tell me about?"

"Oh, Mama, for heaven's sakes," said Elinor. "If I'm going to go ape, I'll let you know in advance," and began to spit out seeds. Her mother began to control herself: it was a matter of breathing; she remembered this from the year and a half she had spent in learning Yoga.

Elinor was saying, "It's so silly. You're upset because Bach makes me sleepy. Well, he does! I'm never going to be like you. Why can't you get that through your great big famous head? You're rich, talented, intellectual. So it's not your fault, is it? That you have a stupid daughter. Or mine, either."

"I'm not rich. Where in hell did you get that idea?" So, with great fat tears running down into her mouth, Irene vented her grief in an easier form; she truly and deeply hated her daughter; there was no escape from that fact; her present mockery was a knife that divided them, like the one sentence of sarcasm that sums up and breaks a marriage.

"You don't particularly like me, so what's the difference?" said Elinor. Irene laughed, that statement was so true and so small a part of the truth. Elinor went on, "Well, do you? I don't think you ever did. So why worry about it—want an orange?" With her left fist, in a curve, that went from her own belly to her daughter's hand, Irene struck the offering away. Elinor fell backward slightly, recovered, looked steadily at Irene, though with a curious, downward smile. She began to push up her long sleeves straightening her arms as she did so, and lifting both, alternately toward her mother to see and judge—

No, it was quite impossible! Children are secret maniacs,

thought Irene. Elinor was saying, "—Quite a week! We had finals in practically everything, my Italian of course is great, why not, the best dictionary in the world is to be found in bed, you said so yourself. Well, anyway, I may possibly pass, but just. International Relations is not only boring, but terribly bloody. When you come to think of the people who die just to change some line on a map! And by the way, I changed my room. I don't know if I can get along with this new girl. Her name is Amy Poinceau, her father's a painter, do you know him? She's from Alsace-Lorraine, and is she ever a freckled mess—"

—Elinor was coming forward, still, an action that took only half a second, but was augmented, stretched, into an agony of boundless time, lifting her arms and turning her palms upward toward Irene—

"And that boy Filoso, really cute!" She said to her mother, "Believe me, you're not feeling any worse about the situation than yours truly, though right now I'm fully recovered, believe me. There's just a couple of interesting scars, just for memory. No one will notice them, particularly Italian boys, who tend to attack you in quite a softer part of your geography. Which reminds me, I am not seeing Signor Filoso any more, he's just too sickening. And anyway, and this is really big news, last night at last *ho le mie cose*, so therefore *tutto va bene*."

—Elinor was thrusting her exposed wrists toward her mother's face; on each of them was an identical two inches of surgical tape.

Elinor was saying, and very flatly, too, "—anyway, Filoso, he would never condescend to marry me. I'm too silly. He said so. I wasn't under any particular illusion as to that. Or I hope not, anyway. So anyway, anyway,"—she mocked her mother's customary postponement of sadness or disaster—"I stole the razor blade he uses for paper collages—" Irene began to faint; which was silly, because how could Elinor be capable of suicide when she was capable of nothing else? No, it was a trick, like her excursion into Catholicism, to astonish and appall one's parent.

Elinor continued, "—anyway, Mama, you're always preaching freedom. Well, don't you see that no freedom is possible or means anything, does it? Unless you have the freedom to kill yourself?" And when this had no affect on her mother's face, with thumb and forefinger she tore off the bandage, the one on her left wrist, and turned the palm upward so Irene could see the new drops of blood rising in a jagged line between the stitches.

"My God, ridiculous," cried Irene. She was lying on the floor in the adjacent classroom with the view of the underside of twenty old fashion desks, all slowly revolving. Some of them had the customary black splotches of gum, due to the influx of the last few years of American students. Irene got up at once, but the room continued to swim past; and also Padua, and Rome and the lounges of various airplanes, with steaming cups of soluble coffee, and loud voices in that universal and incomprehensible language spoken only by loud-speakers and at last, the artificial silence of New York City; for her apartment was on the eighteenth floor, far above the filthy River.

She went to the window and touched it with her hands to judge the outside weather. The angel-fish had died long ago, and some time in the past week she had buried it in a pot of geraniums, as a sort of symbolic fertilizer. However, she had forgotten to empty the tank, and a small jungle of underwater greenery still thrived, slowly bubbling.

Rusty, back from her ill-tempered stay at the vets, was convinced the fish was still alive, but in hiding. She was sure that one day its huge protuberant eye would emerge from its vegetable refuge at the bottom of the tank. She therefore acquired a new habit; she would leap to the narrow sill, and keeping one cross-eyed glance alert for possible flying objects would dip her small sleek head and begin to lap up the empty water in the tank. Hopeless, of course; but Irene wondered whether it was feline strategem —or a sort of twisted love. She got up and opened the letter from Padua; returning, still naked, to sit on the leather bench; she rarely used the glasses which had been prescribed for her five years ago, but now she was obliged to find them in order to read her daughter's writing: there were two sheets of paper, of different colors.

The first was a review torn out of *Il Progresso Padovano*, praising her concert as "worthy of the best tendencies of modern pianistic culture," etc., etc. At the end of the article was a short paragraph regretting her recent illness, and expressing hope for her quick recovery, in the interest of Italian-American relations. The other sheet was a page of ugly typewriter paper, smudged with, possibly, thick Italian coffee. It was another one of Elinor's detestable poems. She read it as fast as possible:

> *Blood oranges*
> *Nobody eats a big breakfast around here*
> *Nothing*
> *Nipples and salt*
> *I wish I could remember one little thing*
> *Nothingness twice in succession*
> *Oh, you're ever so sweet, aren't you*
> *Edge of a used*
> *Raw mineral*
> *Rude sucking*
> *Blue razor blade*
> *Child.*

Irene tore it up and let it fly out the window toward the River. The wind took it over the morning tide and toward that Island where they kept drunks, whores, arteriosclerotics, and suicides, all under sedation. She shut the window firmly, and then, by way of consolation, bent forward and kissed the envelope and pressed it against her cheek. For the girl was still her daughter: her one procreation, her baby, her wild, cold manic bird. She folded the letter, with the cablegram, and locked them both away in the case where she kept her smaller mementoes; the worn gold ring she had gotten from Rabinowitz, and one of one pair of garnet earrings which the original Rusty had once hurled in frustrated passion, into a small lake filled with moonlight and then with ambiguous darkness.

Oh, there was no doubt about one thing, anyway. The black fish was dead; yet Irene took to refilling the tank every day; and eventually Rusty would drink nowhere else.

MAX STEELE is the director of the Creative Writing Program at the University of North Carolina in Chapel Hill, where he lives with his wife and two-year-old son. He was born in Greenville, South Carolina, and was educated at Furman University, Vanderbilt, Chapel Hill, and the Sorbonne. He has published recently a collection of short stories, *WHERE SHE BRUSHED HER HAIR*, and stories in *The New Yorker, Esquire, Harper's, The Atlantic, Southwest Review, Mademoiselle,* and many quarterlies including *The Paris Review,* of which he is an advisory editor. In addition to his short stories, Max Steele is the author of a Harper Prize novel, *DEBBY*.

Color the Daydream Yellow

DURING the two years when Roger Blair was married, living in Santa Monica, a graduate student at UCLA, he daydreamed (mainly after visits from Katherine's dyke-like mother) about being single again and living in some great city: Paris once more, or Cairo, Athens, or Rome. In the daydream he had money to live, say in Paris, on the Left Bank and to drink on the Right. And the women in the daydreams were incredibly soft. In the large apartments he shared with them there was no rigid place for shoes, ties, raincoats, no exact times for breakfast, lunch, and so on, literally and so on.

Late that afternoon, the same as any afternoon, he glanced quickly up from his 3×5 note cards (Thomas Paine; Paris; In Pay of the French?) just as Katherine said: "We eat in two minutes. O.K.?" Without even looking toward the red alarm clock on the terrible pink, formica headboard (the bed catty-cornered because there was no other way to reach the closet door and the clothes hanging in neat rows on hooks) he knew it was precisely two minutes till six. He lifted the cardtable-desk, the cards sliding, back into the corner in order to get out the door and into the other

room, the "social" room which included pullman kitchen, dining
area, and "living" area.

Their calibrated life was resuming again. He tried to raise the
venetian blind enough to watch the sunset over the Pacific as they
ate. As usual the blind went up fast on one side and almost not at
all on the other. The landlord who owned a dozen such student
apartments would neither have the blinds retaped nor allow him to
remove them. Today as they began (the hamburger was, as usual
near the end of the month, smaller) the lower edge of the sun was
already dissolving in the Pacific. Tomorrow at this same time it
would be deeper under water and by midwinter, completely gone
at six o'clock, with no red streak of wave and cloud to remind one it
had ever existed. "Color the experience red," he thought. They were
still a little annoyed with each other and would not talk during this
meal.

When she spoke she said, "It's 6:25." She meant: "Don't dawdle."
She would insist on washing the dishes before leaving the house at
6:40 to be at the corner for the 6:45 bus. At 7:30 she would walk
through the back door of the Wilshire Bank where she would sit
until midnight playing the computing machines as if they were
pipe organs. He had heard enough from her violent mother (who
always imagined the worst possible things happening to her
daughter) how dangerous it was for Katherine to be out catching
busses after dark; and so now he walked with her to the corner and
stood with her.

Tonight they were a minute or two early and waited without
talking. It was a false sort of intimacy because she really was tired
of the job and resented another year of graduate work ahead for
him before she could quit. And all the time her mother, with the
instant values of a waterfront whore, was putting ideas of divorce
into her head, just as the old gal herself had got rid of Katherine's
father. But she wanted Katherine pregnant first. The original Black
Widow.

Katherine was nothing like her mother and seemed sometimes
almost soft; such times as now when she gazed up the long street,
her mouth not smiling, but pleased, with some inner secret. Often,
in silence, their thoughts arrived at exactly the same point by
wildly circuitous paths. He asked the familiar question, the utmost
invasion of privacy which for some reason they allowed each other:
"Where were you?"

"In Paris," she said.

"With me?" he asked. It would be nice if they could be back on, maybe not warm, but at least civil terms with each other.

"No," she said, a little annoyed, a little shy. "Before I met you."

"That Italian?" His face was flushing already with fury.

"What difference does it make?" She sounded edgy.

"This difference": Not he, himself, not any rational part of himself, but a fury took over his speech. "This difference: you mentioned it because you want a fight. Just as you get on the bus. So I'll be too angry to study. Well, I'll tell you one thing, you'd better come back on the bus and not let that fat idiot drive you. . . ."

Already the bus was pulling to the curb. "I hate you," she said.

"Not as much . . ." he started but then turned away and walked furiously toward the apartment. Hell is all he can think.

Sitting in the dark kitchen, a second cup of coffee before him on the table, he realized how foolish maybe he had been. Maybe at nine, during her coffee break he would phone her. Apologize. Mention, if she sounded all right, how easy it will be to get a teaching job once he has the degree. Not that bluntly. Maybe just that his research is coming along great now. No, a simple apology: at least that, so they would not have to sleep another night without touching.

The ocean is black and only one star shines over it. He sees himself watching the black sky and sees himself two years ago, as lonesome then as now, regarding the sky over Paris. (Is it a daydream, the essence before an experience; or a memory, the essence after? And who can separate daydream, experience, memory and say which is which?) He watches the first sun rays find steeples, rooftops, the broad boulevards and sinuous river.

Below him on the lawn, an airline pilot with twenty hands, all rounded palms, is measuring a plump dark girl for a dress, stockings, brassiere, all of which he promises to bring on his next flight. The pilot is drunk, pretending to be sober; and she is sober, pretending to be drunk. And Roger Blair watching from his parapet, is alive, pretending to be a stone gargoyle, staring down with stone eyes at the embrace.

When he turns away, he finds exactly what during the night he had imagined: a dark-haired American girl with a guidebook using the inlaid brass diagram to find, in a systematic sweep the Trocadero, the Tower, the Military School, the Invalides, and the spire of St. Germaine. For awhile he helps her, but is defeated by her academic determination to see in two days all the French have built in twenty centuries. Besides which she must meet her mother at the American Express at nine. Maybe when she comes back from Italy, alone, in September, they can see some things together. She prints his name and Paris address in a neat leather notebook.

Such had been the day: the studious outsider looking in on the warm and warm-flushed couples (the Beaux Arts students, younger and wiser than he had ever been or would ever be), playing touching games with their lips and fingertips on the sun-warmed cobblestones sloping to the river); or wandering aimlessly or not courageous enough to admit an aim (from Montmartre to Montparnasse); making tentative approaches, his shyness frightening the young girls into a shyness which seems aloof.

"Ah now!" Roger Blair says, sitting down at last on a terrace near the Odéon. He stretches his legs until his desert boots are in the last remaining sun slanting down from the Luxembourg. Now at last, his feet are beginning to be warm; and into the pool of sunlight, two lizards, cleverly disguised as slippers, slide. He is absently studying the feet, the fine-boned tops and ankles, the tight black ski pants, when a voice says: "Can I have some of your sunshine?"

The accent is Swedish, husky, mournful, a winterful of nights, moons warmer than polar suns, a touch of bleak wind off a frozen lake.

He looks up quickly at her and quickly away. Thinks quickly of Garbo. No, that's ridiculous. Forgets her. Thinks of Grace Kelly. Forgets her. Sees the best skier he knows as she stoops to take the crest of a hill, then lets her fly out of sight. None of these. Seeks reality. Thinks of the boniest girl he ever saw swinging a racket in an awkward backhand. Sees all the tall girls he danced with out of pity at every high school dance. Shuts his eyes again and reconciles the images. Then dares to look again.

Is that high forehead with the heavy-lidded blue eyes and high cheekbones too strange, too oriental to be beautiful, framed by the incongruous silver-blond hair? Is the mouth too large, the lips too pale and too full? The teeth too small? The neck, even in the black turtle-neck sweater certainly is too long, as is the body with the small breasts. Later Roger Blair will ask for reassurance and will be told: "She's all right if the only thing you want is a handsome woman with flawless skin, perfect teeth, and elegant bones, along with a beautiful, sensual body."

What is confusing is this: she does not know she is exotic, delicious, elegant, all those things. She thinks of herself as shy, a little dull, boring, and has no pride in her looks. She is so convinced of her unattractiveness she convinces others of it. Or almost.

Roger Blair is confused only a moment and then moves his feet slightly to make room for her feet and says she can share his sunshine with him.

She is holding a leash and on the leash, asleep under an empty chair is a miniature schnauzer. It is not much of a dog but it is better than shyness and silence and so he asks if it is her dog.

"I keep him for my friend," she says the words cautiously in her heavy voice as if she is not at all sure the words mean anything at all. "And now they have runned off and lefted me."

Roger asks her in French if it has been a long time since they have abandoned her. She counts on the tips of a fan of fingers. "Un, deux, trois, quatre, cinq. Cinq. Cinq hours." She looks distressed but then smiles wistfully before looking distressed again. "I do not mind. It has been sun. But now the sun sits."

He orders a Dubonnet and when offered, she accepts a Coca-Cola. Wine, she has had so much wine all afternoon that now she is thirsty. Talk about Coca-Cola establishes him as an American and her as a Swede from Stockholm where Coca-Cola is also drunk.

"Isn't dot funny?" she asks with a smile too narrow and long. From a photograph one would suspect that the smile concealed bad teeth. But not at all. Evidently someone told her at eight that her mouth was too big; at twelve that she was too tall (hence the slightly stooped shoulders); her breasts too small (the loose sweater which flows about them when she moves); her feet too large—and there they were right. Yet it is her feet now that she has made no effort to hide, touching his with them lightly.

And during her second coke ("Oh my God, but how I am thirsty!") Tilde's ridiculous plight is revealed in her great funereal voice: Lilibet, the girl she has come to Paris with from Sweden this very day, has left her here in this cafe while Lilibet and her French boy friend, a medical student (named Jean-Pierre of course) whom they met the summer before in Copenhagen, have gone off to find a room for the two girls. Lilibet's parents are very strict (the blue eyes roll at thought of the puritanical parents) and

Lilibet has promised them she will have a room. And now five hours have gone and the dog has not eaten and won't eat the roll she has tried to feed him. And Lilibet has all the money and their baggage is still at the station and she doesn't know how to get there and now she is afraid to leave. And the dog that belongs to Jean-Pierre! It is all so tragic as told.

"And," she announces after a long silence. "Do you know what Jean-Pierre calls the dog? Its name?"

He assures her he doesn't.

"Martini!" she is aghast. "Imagine, calling a dog, 'Martini'." At the sound of his name the schnauzer thumps his stubby tail and rolls over in the sun. "Look at him," she says. "Joost look." The dog, warmed by the sun and his name, pretends to sleep again; he is grinning; he is dreaming; he is playing dead and does not know he is asleep. Roger Blair explains the dog to her and she is delighted.

She whispers: "Because he drinks martini and likes to be drunk." At the sound of his name the dog's ear twitches and as if to prove his lack of character, his sinful ways, he groans comfortably, opens one eye and shuts it again. The sober world is too much for him.

"My first day in Paris!" Tilde pouts.

Before they leave the cafe to buy meat for the dog, they write a note for Lilibet and Jean-Pierre; but when they come back at nine, after feeding the dog in the park and themselves in a bistro, there is a note from Lilibet saying Tilde should find a hotel room, just for the night. Tomorrow at noon they will all meet at the cafe.

To everything he has suggested, walking, shopping, eating, drinking, she has said "Yah!" easily and with no hesitation. So at ten, when she has yawned several great, wet-eyed yawns, he says: "Would you like to see my place?"

"Yah!" she says.

In silence they walk along to the Place St. Sulpice. There on the fifth floor, he points, is his apartment. On the sixth floor, his landlady lives in the maid's room when she is in Paris. Her light is on now and he does not want to see her tonight. Therefore it will be better if they do not talk on the stairs. "Yah," she whispers. "Yah!"

The next day as he slips out of the building he runs into his landlady talking to the concierge. Apparently she has been waiting for him all morning, though at the moment she seems absorbed in her mail. He gets almost to the street before she says: "Mr. Roger." Will she ask him to move? Will she want more rent for an extra person? "Mr. Roger, you do remember our agreement when you took the apartment?"

In his embarrassment he remembers nothing.

"No pets," she says, rather amused by her ambiguity.

His face grows warm.

"No dogs," she says.

He is not sure.

"One cannot risk fleas in summer," she says blandly and then there is a smile only in her voice. "A sympathetic young man like yourself can find better company than dogs I'm sure. So shall we agree again: no dogs?"

Thus begins the honeymoon. At the cafe Lilibet and Jean-Pierre are happy that the morose Swede will not be alone and will that very day deliver her baggage and pick up Martini. When he arrives back at the apartment with red wine and cheese, bread and ham, Tilde is happy. "Yah," she says, sitting in the sun on the balcony. Even with her mouth full of bread and ham she can say it. "Yah. Is good."

Everything is good. "Yah" she says at night. "Yah. Yah." Until it almost becomes a playground taunt. "Yah yah yah." But the nights are the nights that a young man should experience if he is to be a complacent old man. "I have done my best and my best was good." But the mind seeks proof of its own sanity. Thus all honeymoons end; all plots thicken; every lover must have his rival (if Tilde is so marvelous as she seems, then other men must, by a lover's logic, see her as marvelous too); bliss without jealousy does not remain bliss. By its shadow we measure the height of a steeple. A steeple without a shadow may be no steeple at all. So now he needs to put in shade to make sunlight. He reaches for the black crayon:

And touches the fingers of Garcia Limon. *Don* Garcia Limon, one would guess from the slight bow the Spaniard gives as he shakes hands. The Spaniard's hand is thin and strong. His clothes are genteel, shabby: suit jacket, tie, odd pants, pointed shoes, worn heels, polished. Son of a refugee. Medical student. Roommate, until the appearance of Lilibet, of Jean-Pierre. Now living in bleak poverty alone. Damn the sad eyes, the handsome brow and mustache, the dancer's body.

Torture time.

But if it is not Garcia Limon, the mind conjures another who sits at an unknown cafe, waiting for an unguarded moment to lure

Tilde away. For now he knows "easy come, easy go" applies more
to women than to money.

"Limon," Tilde says in the apartment. "He is nice. I like him.
He is so poor. Lilibet and Jean-Pierre like him. He is nice." It is all
she says.

But it is too much. He hears: "Limon is nice. You are not. He is
poor. Therefore I like him, I feel sorry for him, I want to mother
him, to feed him, to warm him with the warmth of my own body.
Lilibet and Jean-Pierre like him better than they like you. Because
he is nice."

He is silent.

"I am so tired." She stretches her arms into a wide bronze V
above her body.

But why should she be so tired? It is only ten p.m. and what
has she done today? It is he who has made the bed, swept up,
emptied the trash, marketed, cooked supper, stacked the dishes.
What has she done besides bathe and wash her hair and dry it in
the sunlight, lying naked on the plum-colored velvet spread, her
hair hanging down into the droprug of sunlight.

But while he was marketing, where had she gone? Today.
Yesterday? Everyday? For two weeks now. Isn't her explanation too
strange? She cannot stay in an apartment alone because once in
Gottenburg as a student she returned from a weekend and found
her landlord, an old man, a distant relative, dead, with the morning
mail, the envelopes still unopened, about him like playing cards
where he threw them in his fall toward the hearth. Who is to
believe she leaves the house because the ghost of Cousin Augustus
comes and rattles the skillets in every apartment where she is
alone?

Now it is late July and the five of them have been swimming on
the barge pool in the Seine. Garcia, Lilibet, Jean-Pierre, Tilde and
himself. How soft, American, he seems amongst them with their
thin, European, student bodies. The slightly immoral look of an
athlete out of season, he sees himself, his own body. And as heavy
in mind as body, trying to follow as they race across the verbal
steppingstones from English to French and Spanish, resting on a
German boulder before disappearing into a Scandinavian thicket,
all laughing and understanding and waving kindly to him on his
English shore. They come back for him as for a child and explain
that he has missed nothing. It is unbearable. And what difference

does it make if Tilde's shoulder is smooth and cool against his own if at the same time her warm toes are touching Limon's hairy thighs?

"But they weren't," she protests over hot chocolate in the middle of the night in the exact middle of the bed. "I don't know. I don't understand you. What if they were? Toes don't mean anything. *Toes!*" She exclaims something amusing (she claims untranslatable) to herself in Swedish. "Toes, my God!" She sits in the center of the bed hugging her knees. On her back the lamplight makes gold dust of the fine blond hairs. "You are no fun anymore. At first you were fun."

Jean-Pierre when Roger finds him alone is no help. He says: "You are so serious. You're probably worse than those Swedish men they come here to get away from." Jean-Pierre tries to explain: all winter it is dark, cold, unfriendly. Paris by contrast is a party. They dream of Paris, sunshine. Fun. They have not come down to get married. "Are you wanting to marry Tilde? Is that why you are so serious?" Roger Blair says he has not thought of it.

"Then how can you demand so much? Tilde thinks what you really want is a housewife. To make beds, sweep, wash dishes. Cook."

"Someone has to do it."

Jean-Pierre shrugs. Someday Roger feels he may hit a shrugging Frenchman.

"I know," Roger says. The truth is: at first, before the appearance of Limon, he did not mind that sort of housework. But now it adds to the silly picture he has of himself. He, out haggling for fresh eggs while Tilde sits somewhere listening to the motor-purr of Limon's Spanish-French.

The mind seeks before all things equilibrium. The bliss must not become too heavy or the scale will tumble, taking reason with it. Now Roger Blair adds, to the other side of the scale, his grievances: Garcia Limon and housekeeping. The two are really one, for if she kept house she would not have time to sit on a terrace with Limon.

"I sit in the sun," she states.

"It is strange no other sun is as warm as the sun where that Spaniard sits."

"Garcia likes the sun too." Tilde clips her toenails straight across and regards her biscuit-brown toes. "Yah, we are just alike, Garcia and I . . . me . . . we love the sun."

She loves fish for lunch and so he cooks fish for lunch and hates every bite she takes from her upside-down left-hand fork. He hates the way she raises her eyebrows and opens her eyes wide as she rakes the flakes of fish off the prongs with her small, even, bottom teeth. "Ah, it is so good!" she says now in her throaty voice. Only his cooking now receives such throaty compliments.

Then it happens, as he has imagined it would, and perhaps because he imagined it would. He comes by the cafe with a heavy net of groceries and she is not there waiting. Nor does she come home to supper. Nor is she there when he returns from a movie which he does not see, though he knows the shape of every blond head in the audience.

At two o'clock, has he been asleep since midnight?, the light clicks on in the kitchen and he hears her voice: "Roger! Roger!" Tilde is afraid. A voice in a well. A whisper echoed in tile. Cousin Augustus may answer first. Certainly Roger Blair has no intention of answering. She enters still calling, as always, "Roger, Roger." The child-woman, infinitely appealing. Infinitely forgivable.

But not at two a.m. and where in hell will she say she's been? Oh, that she would only name the theatre where he has waited in ambush.

He pretends sleep, more silent and regular than sleep itself. Better than Martini had played dead. Apparently she sees his clothes, scattered over the living room, and stops calling. She pushes back the velvet draperies from the bedroom arch and crosses on barefeet. In the windowlight she glides and disappears behind the draperies that hide the bathroom door.

She emerges after a curiously long time, drying her hands in that peculiar night time way: pressed together as if for prayer but rubbed against each other, first in glee, and then for warmth.

"Get out," he says before she has a chance to sit down on the foot of the bed.

The argument begins, first in the dark, then in the light of the overhead fixture; they say absolutely nothing new in this argument, but the words are louder, more bitter and bitten, and finally she adds a new line: "I hate you."

He says it back to her: "And I hate you."

But though she does leave the apartment immediately, whoever parts for good on such fierce words?

Of course he tries to find her before she reaches the cafe. And of course she watches him running, then turns back and takes another street: toward Lilibet's and Jean-Pierre's; toward Limon's. He lets her go.

Now it is late August. The Paris shopkeepers have not yet returned from the South of France. The streets are hot and almost deserted. Flocks of American tourists, bright-colored and clear-voiced, descend suddenly on a street and light on terraces, tables and chairs. Off the main boulevards the little cafes continue with their habituals. Tilde now sits often where Roger Blair first saw her and often alone.

Sometimes Roger Blair sits at a table nearby or even at the same table if Lilibet and Jean-Pierre are present. Limon is in Spain and even if he comes back it is all right. Summer is at an end. Soon Limon and Jean-Pierre will be thinking only of their work; soon the Swedes will go back to Stockholm; soon Roger Blair himself will be leaving for New York or California. The world at the table is more tired than sad; more flat than round.

Lilibet to make conversation says to Roger: "The girl I saw you with yesterday, is she American?"

"The black-headed girl?" he asks, knowing it is Katherine she has seen.

"The most beautiful black hair, Tilde," Lilibet says. "Like we've always wanted. Long." She strokes imaginary tresses. "Black as ivory."

"Ebony!" Tilde says. "Yah?"

"Ebony, the black keys. As black as that."

"Yah!" Tilde says. "How beautiful!"

Are they teasing him?

"Oh," Tilde says, "how I have always wanted hair like that. What clothes you could wear! What hats! You can't wear hats with straw like this." She holds out her ponytail of sun-bleached hair. "Yah, beautiful." She turns directly to Roger. "Is she American?"

He nods, not trusting yet his voice to say she has been all summer in Rome.

"The one you used to mention sometime."

He shakes his head. "No. She didn't come over. She got married instead."

"I didn't like her," Tilde says. "She was so proper." They both are embarrassed a little by talk of the early summer. "Lilibet," Tilde says, "remember the time we rubbed carbon paper on our hair to make it black."

"And it came out marine blue. . . ."

"Purple!"

During their delight, Roger Blair leaves to arrange to meet Katherine the next morning. "In front of Sacré Coeur, then," he says over the telephone. "We can have breakfast in the nunnery behind the cathedral." He listens to her plans for the morning. Yes, he will take her to buy kitchen gadgets if that's really what she wants most to do. But tonight, dinner, she cannot change her evening. She must see an Italian friend who has been very nice and who wants to take her to a special restaurant.

He walks back to St. Sulpice satisfied. At least he will have someone to daydream about between pages of his book, sips of his brandy, puffs on his pipe. She is, he admits, even now he admits, pedantic, a real graduate student, not prim, but virginal, aggressively intellectual though soft spoken. Nevertheless, her bottom lip is full and her eyes show mischief when they move too swiftly. It will not be easy.

He climbs the five flights to his apartment. Who would ever think of being homesick for an elevator? He sits with the windows open until the sky is darker than the mansard roofs, then turns on the tiny desk lamp which seems not bright enough to attract a moth.

Yet, within a few minutes, there is a fluttering at the door. Tilde, warm-bodied and furry, enters, bumping the hallway, the doorway, the desk, before settling in the chair near the lamp. "Everything is so neat," she says. "Yah, like you like it."

It is the first time she has been back and she has dressed for the occasion: a soft white stole over a black cotton dress that looks like a petticoat. White cotton gloves that float near then far from her face and body.

How can he say to her: "I have another daydream going now?" Back to America on the same boat, reading the same books, holding hands, nothing more, just holding hands with her till she gets used, first to his hands, then his cheeks, and gradually, maybe not even on the boat. Tilde does not belong in this dream. How to finish the first without having it overlap with the new one? Perhaps another argument?

"I am so hungry," she says.

So that is it. For a second the daydreams mingle and it is New York or California and Katherine is serving roast beef to him and Tilde. He looks out the window and the montage fades.

"I've been eating out," he says. Meaning: there is nothing in the house. "Since I planned to leave."

"Those good omelettes you used to make," she says wistfully.

"While you sat and did nothing," he wants to say; but that is the conversation that has become so hateful and slippery with repetition. "And the dishes I washed afterward," he wants to say, "while you slipped off to Limon." He is too angry to say anything.

"You always have something to eat in the house, here."

"Tea," he says. "That's all."

"Tea! Yah! Tea." She is delighted.

"Do you mind making it?" he asks. "While I change clothes?"

"You are going out." Her voice pleads and the melancholy note holds so that "out" goes on and on.

Until that moment he had not known he was. "Over to the Opera," he says.

Before he can take off his shirt, she calls to him from the kitchen. She cannot remember where the tea is kept. He goes in. She is trying to heat water in a pyrex bowl. It will be easier to make the tea for her than to mop up afterward; but she does not move from the tiny kitchen. "Go sit down, I'll bring it to you."

She is entranced by something on the top shelf.

"Is that good to eat?" She points with white-gloved finger to a can on a top shelf.

"It's beets," he says.

"They're delicious," she says. "I love them." She watches as he unbuttons his shirt. "I wish you did not go out tonight."

He reaches for the can of beets. "Do you want some?"

"If you open it for me. Those open-canners never work for me."

He opens the can and places a dish beside it and goes back

to the bedroom to take off his shirt and to the bathroom to
shave.

He comes out wiping the last of the lather from his chin and
neck and chest. She is sitting at the desk. In the circle of light
under the small lamp sits the open can of beets. As if she is
daydreaming (does she see herself in a satin chaise lounge, in
white feathers and furs, lifting a bonbon from a box and while
the maid massages her insteps, biting through the hard chocolate
shell to the liquid cherry?) she reaches out and with delicate,
gloved fingers dips into the can and lifts out, by its edge, a slice
of pickled beet. She holds her other gloved hand under it as
she brings it up, dripping, above her head and lowers it into her
mouth. The red drops on the left glove spread out on the palm.
She turns her hand admiring the polka dot effect. She swallows
almost without chewing; then almost licks the stained glove finger.
She looks up to see him watching and laughs, red fleshy bits
of beets glistening as they slide across her teeth before being
captured by the tip of her artful tongue. "Did you see me?" she
asks. "I almost licked my glove."

Again, while he stands hypnotized, she fishes for another beet
slice and dangles it above her mouth and cupped hand. "Yah,
they are so good," she says and says something else that is munched
up with the beet.

With her mouth full, studying her ruined gloves, she munches
and laughs and tries to say something. "What a mess I am!" she
finally says.

Such words have a final, definitive ring and it is on such
casual phrases that lovers can finally part. He feels the daydream
slipping. She glances at him as she reaches for another beet
and sees herself dissolving, becoming thin, transparent, and nowhere.

"Don't you want one?" she offers him the can.

For a little while he wants to hold on to the dream, the memory,
and so he takes a beet and eats it, wiping his mouth with the
towel. Now she feels more real and moves toward him to test
again her reality against his. The night is still dark when he wakes
but she is gone.

So he lets Paris sink in the ocean wake, and lets himself walk
now to the bow of the boat and think serious thoughts ("What
I Did on My Summer Vacation.") In the deck chair behind him,

he knows he has only to turn to see her, Katherine is stretched out, her neck bent, a book in hand, her black hair still brushed to a high sheen by the Swedish admiration, as pedantic and dull and essentially domestic as himself. No, he must not begin another daydream. Instead he must think serious thoughts and organize them well (What Do I Want Out Of Life?)

Beyond the kitchen window the ocean pitches black and white. There are no red waves and no red clouds to remind one the sun ever existed. Gradually, over the white ruffles of the waves he sees one star, and then another, until the sky and his brain itself seem to be dancing with them. The touch of the cold coffee cup to his lip startles him and he is frightened. For a little while he has been outside himself, for a little while he has cleared his head of all thought, his heart of all anger; and he feels both weak and drunk. Where was he? Where is he? What was he thinking? Paris? Is he in Paris imagining a girl named Katherine, or in California imagining a girl named Tilde?

And Katherine, was she part of a daydream once or is she a memory too? Was it really two weeks ago she got on the bus? And the supper tonight was it merely a sweet memory of all their suppers? Or was it tonight she got on the bus and is he merely daydreaming that she has left him?

He tells himself not to panic. In the blue glow from the pilot light on the stove he can see the dish drainer. The dishes: two plates, two salad bowls, two glasses, two knives, forks, spoons, two saucers, one cup, all neatly slanted, still spotted with water. Through the doorway to the bedroom he can read the luminous dial of the traveling clock. Thank God, he still has time to get to the drugstore and call her at her coffee break. He will meet her at the bank and buy her a beer. Yes, and over the phone he will tell her he loves her so she will be through with her crying when he tells her again in the bar.

For a moment longer he sits at the table and fills in the outlines of familiar objects with familiar colors. "Color the dish drainer white. Color experience red and color the dream blue; color the daydream yellow and memory green, and shade one into the other like lights on water. And if one fades into the other or even if the colors run together, it will last only a little while. For like the ocean, soon it will be all dark. Then color my soul red and color me quick!"

H. L. MOUNTZOURES was born on Fishers Island in New York, and graduated from Wesleyan University in Connecticut with a degree in English. *THE EMPIRE OF THINGS AND OTHER STORIES*, a collection of his stories was published in 1968, and many of his stories have also appeared in *The Atlantic, The New Yorker,* and *Redbook.* Mr. Mountzoures is now living in New London, Connecticut, and working on a novel and stories.

The Empire of Things

WE walked through the vast Tudor building. There were many of us registering. I was surprised and happy to see college friends from ten years ago whom I had not seen since graduation. Don Fielding came in. His face was red and shiny, and he had all of his hair; he looked exactly as he had in first-year French; only a class beanie was lacking. "What are you doing here?" I asked him. Shyly, he pulled at his crew-neck sweater and said, "The same thing you are."

We shuffled through a long line. Trembling little old women gave us our clothes and gear. At the end of the first line, a fat woman handed me a folded green entrenching tool. "You must be careful of color and concealment," she said. I looked at her closely. She was my elementary-school physical-education teacher —Miss Holstein. Her face was very tan. There was no lipstick on her mouth. She had short, fuzzy brown hair and bowling-pin legs, and she wore a plain mauve suit and pale calfskin flat shoes with thick soles. She held a big brown rubber dodge ball in her left hand.

I started to acknowledge her. She raised a finger and frowned. I moved on to another line. One of my best friends from college, Tim O'Connell, came in through a dark-stained door full of tiny

"The Empire of Things" – H. L. Mountzoures, *The New Yorker,* Copyright © 1967 by Harry L. Mountzoures. Originally appeared in *The New Yorker.* From *The Empire of Things and Other Stories* by H. L. Mountzoures. Reprinted by permission of Charles Scribner's Sons.

glittering windowpanes. We embraced and shook hands. He, too, had not changed. He was huge and burly as always, and his laughter was exactly as I remembered it—deep, throaty, almost mournful. He had a large mouth.

I said, "You look the same after all this time."

"So do you," he said. "You haven't changed a bit."

"But I'd have thought everyone would look older."

He shrugged. "How's your family?"

"Great. I miss them. Especially my son. He's seven. The last time I saw him, he was boarding a big yellow school bus on the hill in front of our house. I'd just turned to get into my car when I saw the red signals of the bus flashing. It was raining, and Charlie—that's my son—was the last one on, because he was having trouble closing his umbrella. It was a red umbrella. He's so little I wondered if he was ever going to get it down, but he finally did. I waved with my briefcase, he waved back, and the bus shut off its signals and chugged up the hill. That's the last I saw of him. The rascal."

The huge room, nostalgically like my college dining hall, bustled with men getting their packs together. Someone blew a whistle. Milling and chatting, we settled on the floor. How odd. Now it was kindergarten, with narrow planks beneath us, shiny oak, and we were very close to earth, to the bottom. Would there be a piano and singing? Or cutout time, and furtive eating of paste that tasted of wintergreen?

Miss Holstein came to the front. We stood. She pulled down a silvery granulated screen. There was a flag behind her. We pledged allegiance, sang "God Bless America," and sat down again. With pointer in hand, she said softly, "I am going to give a very brief orientation. Then we will go into the warehouse."

As she talked slowly on and on, the sun shone on her tan, fuzzy face. How much it was like the sun of childhood autumns, early Septembers, when school started. ". . . here to help the troops," she was saying. "We are brave little soldiers in our own way." There was a squirming around me. "Soldiers of mercy. Soldiers of peace, dealing with *things*. We are going to help our fighting men not with prayer, not with entertainment, not even with coffee and doughnuts, but with concrete things that will remind them of home, and civilization, and history, and meaning. Things that will boost our men's morale and help them see it through. Do you understand?"

We all droned peacefully.

"Pull the shades. First slide, please." The windows became deep, warm yellow, the room pleasantly dark. Several maps flashed onto the screen. They showed crude road lines, supply lines, chow areas, latrine areas, the combat zone. Company headquarters—our location—lay on the west. From it three fat black arrows flared north, east, and south. Miss Holstein swept the pointer over the arrows. She said, "This part of the jungle is your working radius. You will use compasses. Next slide, please. Ah. Here are some of the things." Slides flashed in rapid succession. They showed small articles of furniture, glassware, china, toys, linen. The slides ended.

We were taken to an adjoining room, the warehouse. It turned out to be an immaculate museum, with much the same kind of things we had seen on the screen. Each was encased in glass and labelled. "Chippendale chair." "Porringer, 1784." "Hand mirror of Mme. Pompadour." "Earrings from Knossos, 1600 B.C." Stuff like that. We were all impressed.

Miss Holstein gathered us around like a large group of tourists. Pointing, she said, "When you go through that door, you'll be on your own. Remember to gather your things compactly in a container you'll find, such as a chest or a bureau. And don't take more than you can carry alone. By the time you fill your containers, you should be near enough the combat zone to deliver them personally to our fighting men. Then your mission is done. You will return here. It'll be cookies and milk and a long rest. You'll have earned it. Good luck."

We applauded respectfully. She marched to the door and opened it. Everyone filed through.

The jungle was like home—the woods in New Hampshire. I did not understand. Maple trees, birch, oak, beech, pines. Some swamp. Rocks. But no open fields.

We spread out to find containers for our things. It was fun—like a large Easter-egg hunt. We discovered dust-covered chests; spider-webbed bathtubs with claw feet; old, discarded refrigerators with no doors; abandoned automobiles, upholstery coming out of the seats; huge Victorian trunks. Everything was hidden among bushes, under trees, behind boulders. My collegues cheered as they found suitable containers. Tim O'Connell was using a baby-blue Volkswagen with no wheels and no engine.

I am not a big man. I chose a strange combination of small
bureau and chest. I had never seen such a piece of furniture, so I
did not know the name of it. I called it a trunk. It had six big brass
handles—three on each long side. Drawers with cut-glass knobs
pulled magically out of the narrow ends. Yet the top opened like a
lid, and inside there was no sign of the drawers. It was roomy, and
you could store a lot in it if you were eclectic and not greedy for
large, ostentatious things.

All the men had chosen containers. One picked a 1940-vintage
washing machine. It had a small black rubber knob that you
turned to let out the water. A stick to stop the agitator. No hose.
As I walked by, I peeked in; the large, propeller-like agitator was
still in place. I wondered how he expected to fit much in it at all.

Everyone moved out smartly with his empty container. I dragged
mine for a while, then shouldered it. It got heavier and heavier.
How rapidly we tire, I thought. How frail we are.

When we reached the first large cache, we shouted, "Hurrah!"
Men put down their containers and began to scoop up things. We
gathered glittering identification necklaces from the green-leaved
trees. Sunlight made the quick-moving men shimmer. I stopped.
Was it innocence I saw on their faces? The jungle was filled with a
shadowy, dappled glow and the sneaky, lithe movements of small
boys. Who were the Indians, I wondered. The cowboys. Who were
the bad guys and who were the good? I plucked two splendid ruby
earrings from a bush where they were hanging and laid them carefully in the flowered fabric bottom of my trunk. No. They would
be lost there. They were too small. I put them in one of the small
end drawers instead. The drawer was lined with maroon-and-
écru striped silk. It smelled of old perfume, talcum powder.
Ephemera. Death. I shook my head.

I found a tortoiseshell comb, a satinwood natural-bristle brush. I
wondered whose they had been as I laid them gently in the
drawer. A bag of marbles, with "Joe—1876" embroidered on it. A
First World War lead soldier. He had a pink painted face and a
brilliant red dot of a mouth.

I spotted a large, beautiful white porcelain Cheshire cat. I must
have dragged the trunk a mile farther before I found some burlap,
wrapped the cat up, and put him in the bottom of the sweet-sour
trunk. Next to a tree stump, I found a long leather change purse
divided into two compartments, with two snap prongs to open and

close it. It smelled wonderfully of leather, slightly moldy. Someone
could use it. I put it in one of the drawers. This drawer was lined
with an old yellowed newspaper. The visible headlines were about
a Senate debate, a stock-market decline, and an accidental drowning. I came on two hurricane lamps tangled in brambles. They
would do to light a soldier's reading and correspondence. I
wrapped the lamps in many green leaves and placed them gently
in the trunk.

I heard a bullet zing. Must be getting near the front line. Act
fast, I told myself, but choose. Here was a hobbyhorse with one of
its madly staring agate eyes missing. Painted spots on its rippling
body were fading, gone. I wanted to take that, but I had to be
selective. Beside it stood a squat black iron play stove. Charming
but useless. A pair of opera glasses. Perfect for reconnaissance. Into
the trunk with them. Seven home-knitted brown woollen mufflers.
Four sealed pints of brown, coagulated Red Cross blood dated
January, 1944. Good.

The mosquitoes were intolerable. It was getting hotter. Creatures
were screaming and moving in the brush. I found a toy drum. That
would do. For signals, maybe. But it dissolved when I picked it up
—rust. Suddenly Tim O'Connell was in front of me. He had taken
off all his clothes. He was hairy and laughable, his beer belly
hanging out. With palette in one hand and brush in the other, he
was painting his baby-blue Volkswagen khaki and brown, green
and black, beige and gray, in patches like pieces of a jigsaw puzzle.

"Miss Holstein," he said. "Concealment."

I went on, dragging my trunk. As I passed, I looked at what he
had in his Volkswagen. An enormous clear-plastic bag of popcorn.
An elaborate Telefunken radio. Several red-and-black plaid blankets. An embalming kit. An old, mineral-stained porcelain toilet
bowl. About ten pairs of ladies' highheel pumps, an ostrich boa, and
a large goldfish bowl full of packs of prophylactics. A sawhorse,
and two stuffed baby alligators. Not very selective, I thought. Yet I
must not judge. "I'll see you later," I said. "That's quite a fine
collection of things."

"Thanks."

I heaved my trunk onto my back. The terrain was changing.
There were vines. Huge tropical flowers. Sweet-smelling, rotting
fruit underfoot, and elephant droppings. Monkeys swinging,
screeching. Screaming parrots, birds of paradise. Sweat. Flies. The

roar of a tiger? You could not be certain. I was groaning under the
load of my trunk. God help us, I thought. I heard someone thrash-
ing nearby (cutting with machetes?), and voices. "A thirteenth-
century triptych!" "Gramophones!" "Spanish armor!" Squeals of
delight.

I wandered frantically. For a while, I could find no things. I was
lost. The needle of my compass spun and spun. I just missed a
quicksand pit. A nearly endless python slithered past. I walked for
a long time.

All at once I was in a dark, misty paradise of things. I could hear
no one. The others had gone. I began to gather the things as
swiftly as I could, shoving them into drawers, into the trunk. It
became a hungry mouth. Rain was threatening. I worked fast. I put
in a dozen candlewick cutters and snuffers—silver. Sixteen morning
suits, complete with striped cravats. Two beautiful heavy green-
and-white croquet mallets, six croquet balls. From a tree, a large,
delicate, empty gilded birdcage. Three small crystal chandeliers. A
satin wedding gown. The Regent diamond. A music box, a pillbox,
and a snuffbox, all carved and jewelled. A complete moroccan-
leather-bound and gold-edged set of Shakespeare. An enormous
string of black pearls. A silver carving set, with jade handles.
Four sets of diamond-studded andirons and pokers. An Indian
inlaid-ivory jewel box.

Not bad duty, I thought. Not a bad way to serve your country.
Some poor soldier will be very happy with these. I kept stuffing
things into the trunk. I wanted to make someone happy. To do my
part.

The heat; my khaki shirt was dripping wet. Thunder. Hurry. I
found a large cut-glass fruit bowl and placed it carefully in the
trunk. A great pile of stage costumes with "Traviata, Act I" labels
attached to them with rusty common pins. Four cylinder Edison
records, a dozen thick 78s. One was "Annie Laurie," sung by John
McCormack. I didn't read the others. What treasures. A thick
velvet-covered footstool. A Louis XV commode. The throne with
the Stone of Scone. Two American Colonial corner cupboards. All
of Bach's original music scores in seventy-three huge bundles. A
forty-room English castle, furnished. The trunk took everything. An
old, ornate wood-and-glass hearse. Napoleon's and Josephine's bed.
Three stuffed owls, a Victorian coach. The Venus de Milo. She was
sticking out of the dirt, and I spent a long time carefully digging

her up with my entrenching tool. She excited me as I uncovered her, but I had no time. "La Gioconda." I discarded it. Must choose with care. Michelangelo's "Pietà." The original puppet Pinocchio. All the drapes and mirrors from Versailles. And sixty-seven issues of the *Saturday Evening Post* from 1928 and 1929. Riches. I was a conquistador. Ah, a jewelled dagger. I put it in my belt. A sword. I hung that beside the dagger, swashbuckling at my side. A pirate's pistol, loaded. Three rifles, a flamethrower, four hand grenades, two bazookas, a tank, seven napalm bombs.

Let them come, the bastards. I was ready. My things were heaped high, spilling out of the trunk. I could get anyone—pick them off one by one—anyone who tried to take my things. Mosquitoes buzzed and bit me. Men's shouts in my ears: anguish. *My* stuff. I found it. Natural rights—stake a claim. Noise. Scuffles. Machine-gun fire. Snipers? I took out my weapons. I flung hand grenades. Fired the bazookas. Used the flamethrower. Scores of the enemy screamed and fell at my feet. I looked. Tim O'Connell lay there, dead, his face grinning.

It began to rain, making the flamethrower useless. A red thing was coming at me. Fast. The rain was thick and hot, steaming. The red thing ran. I could not see. I took out the pirate's pistol, aimed as best I could, and fired. It went off with a tremendous boom. There were blood flecks on my hand from the powder. The red thing quivered and fell. I looked to my side. My treasure was safe. I eased forward a few steps. The rain was pouring down like hot silver coins, and I slogged ahead in the mud and vines. The form was still. I turned it over quickly with my foot.

It was my son, Charlie, the red thing his umbrella. It stood bottom side up, filling fast with water. Charlie's tiny red mouth was open slightly. I snatched him to me. I was crying, and the rain kept coming. I kissed his limp and weightless body again and again. I carried him to the trunk. I flung out all the stuff. It took me hours. I put Charlie in gently among the cloth flowers, got the umbrella, put that in beside him. I closed the trunk. Slowly, dragging my treasure, in the stupendous jungle rain, I began to try to find my way back.

SUSAN ENGBERG was born in 1940, raised in Iowa, and educated at Lawrence College in Wisconsin. She is now living in Chicago with her husband, who is an architect, and their daughter.

Lambs of God

EVERYTHING was coming to life, Helene said. Did the girls see how green the willows were? She pointed to a watery fissure between mounded fields. If Leonard wouldn't drive so fast—she looked sidelong past little George to her husband—they would all enjoy the scenery more. She lowered her sewing to her knees and winced as the car plunged down a hill and dipped up to the next rise. It wasn't even pleasant driving that way, she said. Why was he in such a hurry? Why couldn't he just relax and enjoy the trip? They were only going down to the farm, after all.

Sixty was a good speed, he said. Didn't she want to get there before dark?

Not if it meant making everyone sick and missing all the spring sights besides. The new lambs were out, and the baby pigs, she said. It was important for the children to see all that. There, look. Had they missed it? They had passed a pungent-smelling barnyard turned to choppy brown sea by the footprints of animals. In the muck had been sows weighted down in their own eating by suckling farrows. She sighed. The burdens were great; sometimes it seemed to her that she was fighting all alone, that to her only it now seemed unbearable, altogether wrong that they should be going sixty miles an hour through Iowa farm land which at no other time of day, at no other time of year would look exactly this way—opened by the plow, misted by the evening, gauzed in hollows and on distant ridges by palest green. Had they seen it? Baba? Sarah?

Sarah pressed into her corner of the back seat, her head against the jolting window, and tried to protect her trance-like abstraction

of wires and flying telephone poles from the intolerable bombard-
ment of her mother's words. She put up a finger, the better to upset rows of birds along the swooping wires, and left the encum-
brance of answering on Baba, whose duty it was anyway, being
the eldest. Yes, said Baba, she had seen it. But she was so miserable, she added: her eyes watered, her nose itched; couldn't anything be done for her?

Sarah only pressed harder to the window when her sister's body,
slumping fretfully against the seat, gave in to its restless discomfort, and mother said, poor Baba.

Sarah must close up her window—right away, said mother. Poor
Baba. Where on earth had she gotten these allergies? All from his
father, no doubt, she said to daddy; and Sarah envisioned the red
face of grandpa and the way he would look that night, standing
with grandma on the yellow-lighted back porch of the farm house
to welcome their arrival.

"All that hurry was for nothing then," said mother; for it was
already so dark as they lurched up the lane past the garden that
the car lights threw beams on swarms of insects while daddy
stopped to open the wide white gate, and as the car curved
around the pump house, the startled eyes of cats glowed and
vanished in the unfathomable dark spaces beneath the slatted
corncrib. They were waiting on the porch as Sarah had imagined
them; grandpa came forward; the engine was shut off. It was
necessary now to rouse herself and carry in the picnic basket, the
empty egg crate, to accept a kiss from grandpa's stubbled cheek,
an embrace against grandma's pillowed bosom. She shivered from
a sense of open space and unlit night beyond their small illumined
circle, out there space vast enough, or so it seemed to her, shivering, her arm crooked inside the old wooden egg crate, to surround
the farm with the entire dome of moon and stars.

"No, you're going right upstairs to bed," said mother to little
George. "You'll have time for all that tomorrow."

"Here, my fine friend," said daddy, lugging his son beneath one
arm to the hand pump beside the stoop, "we'll give you one
squirt," and Sarah, hearing the wheeze and clank of the straining
pump, remembered her old joy in the gushing water, so that she
shouted, urgently, for the water had not yet rounded the crook,
"I will—let me," while she dropped the basket and the loose-jointed

crate and ran to put her full weight on the clammy handle that
brought out the first rush of brown water into George's hands.
Again and again she threw herself on the handle until mother's
voice was saying, "All right, all right! Leonard, you've let them get
all wet."

Beneath the nursery window as she fell asleep she heard the soft
bells of sheep, and her hand beside her face was perfumed with
the earthbound scent of iron rust.

Sarah woke in the night to the wind, throwing itself against the
loose nursery windows. In its troughs of quiet she heard the chime
of a clock from some lower hollow of the drafty house and the
sonorous push and pull of heavy people sleeping: she was at the
farm. The room had its own smell. She lay high up on the hard,
humped bed, exposed to the air, to the dark spaces around the
radiator, to the light that seemed to come from inside the vanity
mirror itself. On the ceiling the circle of stars and moons and
animals still faintly glowed. Grandpa had put them up for George.
They were magic, he said. She stared until she wasn't even sure she
saw them any more.

The windows rattled, and a glide of white passed through the
doorway and took the shape of mother over George's bed. Then the
form came to her; she saw a limp bit of ribbon at a nightgown's
neck.

"Mom?"

"Sarah, are you awake?"

"Where are the sheep?"

"The sheep? Somewhere safe, I'm sure. Did the wind wake you
up?"

"Where is Baba sleeping?"

"In with grandma. Are you warm enough?" Mother tucked the
covers around her face, and Sarah felt eased into a cave of
muffled sound.

"Then where is grandpa?"

"He's in his own room, of course. Now you must go back to sleep.
Are you warm enough?"

"When does the clock go?"

"Did you hear it just now? In another fifteen minutes it will
strike three times for 3.00 o'clock. But you'll be asleep by then,"
said mother.

"Why are you up?"

"Well, you know I don't sleep too well when daddy snores. But someone has to get up to cover you children. Why, if I didn't, our George-boy would sleep all night without a single cover on." Mother stood up.

"Do I need covering?"

"There now, you're sleepy. Do you hear how sleepy you sound?" Sarah listened, and she heard the wind. An extra blanket, smelling like the closets, was pulled up.

"Mom, put the lights on once more so the stars shine. Please."

"It will wake George."

"Please."

"All right. Close your eyes." Sarah felt the body coming closer and the lips touching her forehead. Then she was alone; beyond her eyes the light flared a moment and was gone, and the voice whispered from the doorway, "Now. Open."

She opened her eyes and saw shining animals swimming in space; especially she stared at a round moon within a ring that grandpa said was a planet. "Good night," said the voice. The new blanket was tucked all around her ears. And though she waited for another chime, trying to keep her eyes on the glowing circle above, she didn't hear again the clock that would still go off every fifteen minutes, even in the middle of the night.

Finally it was morning. All night, it seemed to Helene, she had been fitfully riding the tops of waves, barely sleeping, until a moment ago when the first bird calls washed her up to solid wakefulness. It was a relief to see light at the lace curtains, to smell the optimistic freshness that separated morning from night air. Early morning: this was her time; it had been ever since the end of those drugged, slow-motion days of early marriage when the very atmosphere in which she moved seemed to have been formed of thick fluids. The difference had come gradually, a slow recovery from the shock of discovering herself a woman. A little common sense applied here and there, and she had managed to emerge from those persistent waters. She stretched in the old double bed beside heavily breathing Leonard and began exercising her feet, pointing her toes in a rhythmic, rolling motion. Well, for one thing, she knew a great deal more about the simple facts of health than she ever had as a young woman—decent breakfasts, enough milk and protein and exercise, sensible shoes and coats. She knew that when she was tired, she must either sleep or eat something nourishing and that when her eyes began to smart with the difficulty, the sadness of what could happen to people, even beyond the cause of their follies, she must set her mind on doing something practical and generous and near at hand. Rolling and stretching her feet one last time, she felt the muscles tighten all the way up her legs.

It hadn't been easy, teaching herself all these lessons. She had never had a mother to do what she was doing for her daughters, and she had had to come around to most things by herself. There had been people, of course; all along the way there had been dear people. She sighed. Some of them were even dead now: Mrs. Knack who had boarded her as a young teacher and who had embroidered and edged with handmade lace three sets of pillowcases for her small dowry; Professor White who had said for her to put away his busy work and run along to the lecture, a fine girl like her; Vera Bell, taken so soon, a real painter, who had said she would give anything for a fresh complexion and strength of mind like hers. She sighed again. And then there was her father.

She sat up abruptly and let her bare feet down to the stiff wool guest room carpet. At least she had learned enough to get out of bed when she woke and not waste these peaceful hours. She moved quietly around the room with her dressing, at which she had trained herself to be quick, knowing from experience what a waste of time it was, what a giving in to emotional backwaters, to ponder oneself in front of a mirror. The maddening thing was how difficult it had become lately to put herself together properly. So often now her stomach felt heavy and bloated, her feet ached, and her hair seemed stiff and unmanageable. She hooked her stockings and straightened up in front of the old vanity mirror. Behind her in the dim light was the heavy walnut bed, draped at the foot with the white bedspread and filled in the center with the mound of Leonard's body, which could sleep in such exhausted weight and dampness, could be so insistent, so masculine, and was so quietly aging. As was hers.

She lowered her eyes and pressed her lips together. There were some magazines with articles on education in her basket downstairs; she could begin those while she had her coffee. George had spilled food all over his sweater in the car last night; she must wash that out. And the bathrooms, she had noticed, smelled of urine; she must find some disinfectant and see if she could, without grandma's knowing it, get those toilets cleaned: they simply weren't safe for the children this way. She hung up her night clothes and took a last look around the room. Sunrise was close.

Downstairs she pulled up the dining room window shades. The sun would come in directly there, in the window by the drooping fern plant overlooking the barnyard with its walnut tree, grassy cistern mound, and red and white buildings. The rising sun would fall upon the far sides of the buildings, it would warm her face and touch the oak wall paneling behind her. She turned. Halfway up the wall, where the paneling stopped, a shelf supported a row of decorated plates and mugs. In the center of the room was the heavy table, covered with a green cloth. By the big window was the magazine table and the rocking chair with the handwoven rag mat that she admired, in the corner the tall clock that she seemed to have heard each time it struck the night before, and beside her the divan of rough wool where her father-in-law slept after each meal, turned on his side toward the wall, his wide overall straps crossing over his back, his fringe of white hair damp and curly over his red ears, and his deplorably enormous stomach hugged like a watermelon in the curve of his body.

She saw the body as it would lie there; it turned, it rattled in its throat, it slept face up. How little did grandma and grandpa know of her, yet over the years had she not proved herself, shown that she, too, was thrifty and hard working, in touch with the plain and the sorrowful? How could one help but learn these pains? How could one help but be overcome, subdued, saddened when glimpsing the burdened sow, hearing of a couple who had lost both their children in some freakish way, watching the mask of illness take over the face of a friend? Hard forces waited for everyone; hard forces made one humble.

Yet it was her great talent, her great mission, she told herself as she crossed decisively to the kitchen to make herself coffee and oatmeal, that she could imagine the largest effects from the smallest acts. It was a sense of history, that's what it was; the sense of her place in the historic line of Christ's servants was a disquieting nimbus around her that would not let her say, "It makes no difference." And so she had opinions—how could she help it, when she saw some child stumbling in the dark of dumbness, all because no one had ever taken the trouble to talk to him. Or when some stupid ox of a man was let into some position of authority, all because—well, sometimes she wasn't quite sure why such things happened.

By the time she had settled herself at the kitchen table with the steaming bowl and cup, the sun had risen, reflecting red in some windows, gold in others. It was very nice to be eating good oatmeal with the sun in the room like that; if the rest of them could only see her, they would know how indestructible she was, how alert, how far above the ordinary run of women. Grandpa would be coming down soon for the chores, but for the moment she was quite alone, as solitary as she had been as a girl at the lake or as a young teacher living in an upstairs room of someone else's house. But of course she had hardly known what to do with herself then, so ignorant she had been, ignorant and foolish; sometimes late at night when she would sit in the big chair under the light with her head tipped back, her eyes closed, her book fallen, she had to press her lips together and shake her head at how much she had had to learn. She wished all those people from her past could see her, then they would know that she wasn't so foolish as to go through life un-touched, that she continually gathered her energies together and did what she could. The great duty was to take a stand, to accept the terrible burdens, to survive the imperfections. Her mission, her talent was to make everything count, to put meaning into every-thing she did.

In a jagged flash she remembered her eldest daughter. The morning light faltered when she saw again the slender body, the heavy, falling hair, the stained underclothes as she had seen them last night in the hollow, drafty bathroom. Too fast, things some-times seemed to be going too fast now, so that she didn't know what to do with them; parts of herself were left behind, part of herself still stood at the basin while the water turned red and Baba shivered behind her.

It wouldn't be so difficult if only she could slow down their life; she must set her mind now on keeping it in hand. Leonard, for example, had been working entirely too hard. Why, it shocked her how battered he seemed sometimes, and yet he didn't seem to know what was happening. Did he even realize that he hardly ever read a single word that didn't have to do with his blessed business? Turning on the lamp in the alcove by the table, she crossed her legs and opened the magazine. If she thought about these things too much, she'd never get anything done.

One by one she turned the pages. The children were too young now, but some day they would understand what her world had been, what she had fought against, what she had been given to work with. Some day they would marvel at her energy and her wisdom, and because never, never had she been indifferent to them, they would also excuse her for mistakes she had never known. And didn't everyone need excusing? She excused grandpa, she excused Leonard, she forgave the spring for coming so inevitably, so sadly around again.

At a photograph of a lined, pensive face she stopped. It was the face of a famous French sculptor and beside the picture was an interview. She read quickly down the page. He ate his breakfasts of coffee and hard rolls in a resturant not far from his studio: an egg or two would do him better, she thought, and he was smoking, too. No, he answered the interviewer, he had never changed his lodgings; he had, in fact, found himself working in a smaller and smaller space in his modest studio, never feeling the need to surround himself with possessions: she raised an eyebrow; it was curious that he could work with his hands and still not have a healthy respect for the objects of life; she herself knew what it meant to have a satisfactory teapot and the right silver tray for squares of soft, fruity cake. She turned the page to see photographs of his statues. A never-ending, lifelong search, the editorial caption said, for the essence of man. Of course, what was wonderful about these magazines was that they brought you up close to things you'd never see otherwise. The same with television. Why, she heard lectures and interviews there that put her in touch with the whole world. She took a sip of coffee, and it was deliciously fragrant and warm. In a moment she would get up and start being useful. She finished the last of her oatmeal. Here she was eating her breakfast and looking at the studio of a famous sculptor.

In the corner of the page was a picture of the artist's wife in a loose, untailored dress, and beside her a row of figures for which she had been the model. The sculpted breasts seemed to hang directly from the sinews of the neck. Well, it certainly would be strange having a husband like that and sitting naked in front of him all day. She wondered if this were his first wife, but the caption didn't say. A never-ending, lifelong search: she looked up from the magazine to the gleaming stove, the glass cracker jar, the cross-stitched sampler on the wall. It would be something, all right, to be

married to someone so wrapped up in a single purpose: with a man
like that she might have been a much different person. She would
have lived in Paris; she would have met such a different lot of
people. And it was the people one met, she was firmly convinced,
that made all the difference. Think how far she had come since she
had left home. And yet sometimes she felt that she had never met
quite the right people; somehow no one understood quite what she
might have done. Again she looked at the picture of the sculptor's
wife. It was very possible, of course, that this poor woman did
nothing but pose for her husband all day, cook his food, make his
bed and lie in it with him, all necessary and worthy duties, but
perhaps she slouched about unkempt; perhaps neither of them
cared a bit about the education of their children. Now, what
Leonard had was a love of solid, basic things; that was what had
appealed to her, the idea of being a good wife to a solid man, of
making herself a positive force against discomfort and disorder and
sorrow. For of what good was her mind, she had asked herself in
those early days, until she had first tied herself to the solid, basic
things? One shouldn't stay untouched; one shouldn't be too proud.
And what she had already learned about life was more real than
anything these artists, or those questionable psychologists, for instance, could discover. One didn't know anything about life until
the children came, and the sorrows, and the sacrifices, and the
terribly difficult times.

From upstairs she heard the creaking of a metal bed and the
long wheezing coughs that meant grandpa was getting up for the
chores. She patted back her hair and took another sip of coffee.
Maybe it would be better if he found her at work. She rinsed her
dishes at the sink by the wide kitchen window overlooking the
orchard, made up some nice rich suds in a basin, and began washing out George's little sweater. Apple trees, in full bloom, spread
like layers of lace down the sloping orchard. The wind was still up,
she saw; in the pasture valley the cottonwoods sustained one
slanted, shivering pose after another. He would be down soon. She
worked at the spotted sweater. One step at a time he was coming,
in a labored, arthritic tread, his low groans mingling with those of
the wooden banister that bore his tremendous weight with each of
his downward lunges. She sighed, she pressed her lips together.
The morning was coming on too quickly. Grandpa lumbered so
painfully down.

"Good morning, grandad," she said in her brightest, most practical voice as he came wheezing into the kitchen.

He unlocked the back door, opened the screen, and spat into the yard.

"I've made some oatmeal," she said. "You'll have some, won't you?" She saw with horror that he was wearing no underpants beneath his loose-fitting overalls, for at their side openings his white flesh showed smooth and round and promised to plunge to an abyss beneath the stomach that he was forced to heave along with each rocking, stiff-legged step.

"Oatmeal? Nah, no oatmeal." He was putting on a denim jacket and an engineer's cap. His taciturnity, familiar as it was to her by now, still set off eddies of uneasiness around her, especially in the early morning with only the two of them in the kitchen that was usually staged with the squat figure of grandma at the spotless sink. Sometimes it seemed to her that he would die, and he would never know any more about her than he did now. But he loved the grandchildren; that she knew. She had given him the only grandchildren he would ever have, and thinking this, she said brightly, "But of course you're going to have something to eat. Can I fix you an egg?"

"I'll wait," he said and went down the steps and the walk and through the gate into the barnyard. She watched as he went first to the windmill to turn on the pump; then he disappeared, and she knew he was urinating on the far side of the tool house. At the corncrib he disappeared again and a few moments later emerged with two buckets of corn. "Shee-eep, shee-eep, shee-eep," she heard him call. "Shee-eep, shee-eep, shee-eep." Leaning on the pasture gate, he threw the cobs one at a time. The sheep came in a wave over the crest of the hill, nodding, running as if they were one amorphous animal. She watched until he had thrown all the corn, and then she turned back to the kitchen.

When Sarah woke, she heard bells, one alone, two never quite together, perhaps more, and kneeling at the low, dark wood window sill, she saw that there were indeed three black-faced sheep almost directly beneath her at the drinking trough by the orchard fence. Now and then a head was raised, a pink mouth opened, for a jerking bleat. She put out a hand to touch the light curtains that puffed out and sank back with the wind. The air that surrounded her had been over the numberless fields, through the blooming orchard, and like the trees, she shivered in the vast breezes. Below her the sheep moved slowly and absently; absently, softly she stroked the filmy curtain.

At breakfast grandpa said he had a surprise for the girls, but mother said Sarah couldn't leave the table until she had eaten some protein. "You simply can't go out in that wind with nothing but sweets in your stomach. I won't have you girls eating only cookies and waffles."

"Won't hurt 'em," said grandpa, who poured thick sorghum from a white crockery pitcher into the hollows of his waffle. The light from the big window gleamed on his bald head.

"Grandpa, tell us the surprise," said Baba. Her heavy blond hair was clipped neatly back on one side, and Sarah saw that she was sitting up very straight and eating her boiled egg. The night before Baba had had some secret with mother in the bathroom, and this morning, too, she had locked the door and told Sarah through the fuzzy, patterned glass to wait a few minutes. "Tell us what it is," she was saying, but in a grown up voice.

Taking George up on his lap, daddy tried to get the boy to finish his egg and oatmeal, but Sarah saw that he cleaned up the bowls himself.

"Leonard, won't he eat?" asked mother.

"Slick as a whistle," said daddy, holding up an empty bowl and winking at Sarah beside him.

"It won't be no surprise if he tells you," grandma was saying to Baba. Her voice sounded high and tight, what mother called strained. "Those waffles are made with eggs," she said to mother.

Sarah took a mouthful of egg and then another. Breakfast seemed to have been going on for a long time. Beyond grandpa's molded head a green dust sifted from the trees; across the fields she could see deep brown and yellow-green and brown and green in endless rolls and strips; a black and white and yellow spotted cat stopped before the low window and lay down at the edge of the walk under the green, sifting dust. Somewhere upstairs a door slammed, and the glass fringe on the lamp by the rocking chair tinkled with sounds that weren't even notes. Mother was saying something to grandma about being anemic and white in the face and tired, and Sarah saw that the small, pouched face of grandma at the end of the table was very white. She probably needed iron, was mother's opinion.

"How are the thistles, dad?" asked daddy, still playing games with George, who leaned far back against his arm and looked at Sarah upside down.

"You want to salt 'em down?"

"And the orchard needs clearing, too. Come on, my fine friend," he said to George. "Up you go. We've got work to do."

Helene put up a hand to protest: Leonard toted the boy so rakishly under his arm. "Leonard, he has just eaten." George's laughter rippled, was sucked in, and gushed forth in uncontrollable delight. But the next moment the boy was on his own two feet in the kitchen, and so she relaxed her arm, took a sip of coffee, and said instead, "He's had a cold, you know. You'll have to watch him every minute to see that he keeps his ears covered."

The girls, too, would have to wear scarves, she said, as she stacked up dishes. These spring winds could be so dangerous. And then she looked at Baba, her eldest girl, because she had felt again the jagged memory, and she said, "And you should keep absolutely warm all over today, do you hear? Try not to get a bit chilled."

"Why? Why shouldn't she?" Sarah heard her own voice almost shouting out.

"Because. That's why," said mother, and her voice sounded tired; it lingered wearily after her as she carried the dishes to the kitchen.

Kittens were the surprise. "Oh-h," Sarah stooped down in the dusty summer kitchen to the rag-filled box, "how old are they? I want the yellow one."

"They ain't very old." Grandpa stood in the doorway. "A week maybe. We've been keepin' 'em for you."

Daddy lifted George down from his shoulders. The kittens lay in a silky heap beside their long black mother. They were all different colors, like the discarded bits of cloth in the box.

"Why don't they move?" asked Sarah. They lay so still she was afraid they were dead.

"Go ahead. Pick one up," said grandpa.

But of course she had played with kittens before; she knew how to pick them up. You pinched a little fold of fur at the back of their necks and dangled them up through the air to your arms. They liked it because that was the way their own mother carried them. She reached into the box and pinched up a fold of fur. The kitten dangled in the air, it curved itself up like someone poked in the middle, it opened its mouth. Then she had swung it up to cradle it under her chin and all was safe. Her fingers twitched with how easy it had been to pluck up the scrawny living bit and swing it up through the air. She reached down and took up another one and held them close to her cheek. They squirmed and curled delightfully, and she could manage them both very well in her hands.

"I want," fussed George until he was told to sit on the cracked cement floor and a kitten was put in his lap. Baba took hers to the rocking chair. There were six kittens in all. The black cat sat up stiffly, and Sarah saw that her stomach was white.

"Does she mind?" she asked. The black cat seemed to blink directly at her through slits of eyes.

"You go ahead," said grandpa. "I saved 'em for you."

"I'm taking mine for a walk," she said and slipped around grandpa's stomach into the sun, ducked under the dish towels snapping on the line, and came out at the front of the farm house, never used as an entry, where a half-finished sidewalk from the white porch ended in spongy lawn beneath the mulberry trees. With each step she sank down upon the burrows of moles that crossed beneath the trees like humped veins; with each step she saw ceilings of tunnels crashing to floors. Well, it couldn't be helped: she had to walk, but sometimes she did follow deliberately the crest of a tunnel, making sure that she had leveled it neatly down. The moles were a nuisance. Grandma had said so.

"Hey, stop it," she cried as a kitten wriggled from her grasp and clawed its way across her shoulders. She ripped him from her neck. "Naughty cat. Bad cat." She shook him in her hand. It was so easy; he weighed almost nothing. She shook him again, and he panted soundlessly through his pink mouth. "Naughty cat," she said, but less fiercely, while she zipped down her jacket and made a warm pocket for the kittens in the crook of her arm. It would have been easy to clamp her arms over them and press hard until they could no longer breathe; they were about the size of two furry tennis balls, only soft—bellies as soft as pulpy fruits.

"We'll go to the barn now," she said, "and then I'll take you back to your mother." She peered into the jacket and saw that they were lying one on top of the other, very still. Sometimes tremors passed from the kittens into her own arm and side.

She turned down the driveway through the wide gate into the barnyard, past the corncrib where she breathed the half-musty, half-fresh odor of the million tumbled cobs. Beneath the crib, between its high, piled stone foundations, was the home of all the cats, an uneven bed of dirt and rock whose innermost shadows were never touched by light. Kneeling, she saw not a single cat, yet imagined she heard them. "This is where you'll live," she said into her jacket, but the kittens seemed asleep. She jostled them, but they only nosed more deeply against each other. Funny little things, they might have been sleeping safe against their mother, the way they looked. She wondered if they were hungry.

She took them to the barn, through the lower half of the heavy side door, over the high, worn stone sill, up into the dim room where stiff and dusty harnesses hung along the wall and the small panes of the windows were crusted with dirt and cobwebs. The barn was formed of so many stalls and separate rooms and rafters and hayracks sticking up like slanted fences that there were places where she had never been—rooms behind rough doors whose wooden latches she could not turn, stalls separated from her by insurmountable partitions beyond which she could only hear muffled thuds of animals enclosed. Even now, as she stood, holding the kittens tightly, her shoes already deep in the smelly straw, she saw the cap of grandpa appear on the far side of a room through dust and stripes of sun and disappear as a door opened and closed. "Grandpa!" she called, but he must not have heard. She waded past a row of stalls to a door that she could open by lifting a peg. Surely he would be there. She sat on the sill and slid down into the hay of the two-story, center section of the barn that ran like a cavernous avenue between the two enormous doors she had seen opened only once, to let a hay wagon in. "Grandpa?" A pigeon flew high among the rafters with a brushing sound, settling far back over a loft. The kittens were making noises now, urgent peeps. "Okay," she said, "wait a few minutes and then I'll take you back."

"Grandpa?" she said, but all the high, cupboard-like doors along the wooden avenue were closed. Surely a door would open, and he would come out. From the spaces above her a shaft of sun fell through swirling straw dust to her feet. "Grandpa?" she called out again, but she heard only the bleat of a sheep. The wagon doors strained against their heavy bars and a sudden shower of straw fell loosely from the loft for no reason. Whirling around, she saw nothing behind her, and then she could not be quick enough in climbing back up through the door and straining toward the sunny opening that framed a warm brown field and far away the rises and dips of the yellow road.

The light in the barnyard dizzied her with its brightness. She needed to go to the bathroom and to wash away the taint of breakfast syrup from her mouth. "Shut up," she said to the kittens in her jacket. "Quit it," she almost shouted, for they were curling their claws into her side. What was going wrong? She shuddered to remember the obscurity of those interior spaces, the way she had glimpsed in secret the back of grandpa's cap as he worked, the mysterious whirr of birds in the far reaches of the lofts. Running as if the shadow of the great building were at her heels, she came at last to the familiar cistern mound, her place, to whose grassy top she could climb in the same way the sheep did, by a long gang-plank of heavy boards. Here she was high enough to command the whole yard; from here the barn looked as it always did, and she might never have been inside, hearing her own voice as it died in the dusty silence. She sank down and let the kittens into the grass. Yes, here, certainly, she was safe. There was the back door of the house, where she had come from breakfast, where she would go for lunch. Continually, absently, she turned the groping kittens like mechanical toys from the perilous edge of the cistern. She would forget about the barn.

Anyway, she had done nothing wrong, for she was allowed in there. Seeing grandpa that way, though, made her feel alone and strange with herself. It was like the time she had glimpsed him tinkling on the tool shed, or when she had come upon mother crying in the bathroom, or when they had gone over to the other farm, which was rented out to the family with all the children, and she had seen in the barn the terrible metal milking machines, making noises like grandma's old washing machine, hitched up to the soft, round cows. She hadn't been able to tell anyone how she had stared at those pumping cups; still in her mind the sex of the animals wavered between the warm female of milk and the hard male of the enslaved teats.

Stupid little silly kittens. They had no idea where they were. Grabbing them up abruptly, she lolled back and dandled them above her chest. She dropped one to the forest of grass and before it could recover its balance, snatched it up again. A slow, hot shiver convulsed her as she let them both fall and watched as they righted themselves and sniffed toward each other. Above her, in a new tack of the wind, the half-dead branches of the walnut tree scraped and clacked upon each other. She saw daddy squatting far down in the pasture with George, and for a moment grandpa in his overalls appeared at a barn door to throw water from a bucket, an explosion of drops in the wind, after which he looked up at the sky and lurched back into the black interior. Inside the hollows of her body she felt vaguely sick.

She stood with the kittens and began to walk around and around the top of the cistern; the orchard and summer kitchen and walnut tree and house and garden and tool shed and barn circled around her in the opposite direction. The ground under her was strewn with dead branches and stones and sheep droppings and a rusty metal wheel with a wide rim. She shook the kittens in front of her face. "Where are you going, sillies, where are you going?" Very badly now she needed to go to the bathroom. It was the barnyard that whirled around them. And before she knew it, she had dropped a kitten to the base of the cistern; she had held it out like that by the scruff of the neck and just let go. She let go of the second kitten, and then her hands were empty. Farther down than she could jump the kittens crawled toward each other. She stood watching them, chewing hard on the end of one of her braids, until a door slammed at the house and she looked up and saw mother in someone else's old jacket and a bunched-up scarf over her head, her hand shading her eyes, walk toward the pasture where daddy stooped, killing thistle roots with spoons of salt. Sarah knew, for she had once followed behind, throwing the coarse grains into holes left by the spade.

What had happened? It was still morning, only closer to noon; mother pushed through the gate; the towels still flapped by the summer kitchen. And before it should be too late, she clambered half-crouching down the same rough planks and followed the damp bands of metal that encircled the cistern wall to the place where the kittens still stumbled near each other. She bent over them. They were all right then. Cats had nine lives, grandma had said.

Hunkering down, her chin on her knees, she pondered on the
eight remaining lives of the kittens who seemed too soft to be
crawling in the coarse rubble of the barnyard, and she pinched
them up to her arm gently and with remorse, for she had not
meant to be the one to take away their first lives.

Gently, her head bent protectively over them, she carried them
to the summer kitchen, out of the wind, and with a shudder of
relief let them down beside the black cat, who stretched up from
the mass of rags and nursing kittens and bobbed her head again
and again over the returned babies, licking their eyes, their heads,
the hollows between their forelegs and stomachs. A fly droned
against a window, and near her feet Sarah saw a black spider, its
legs groping over a crack in the cement. Never once did the black
cat cease her rhythmic caresses.

The noon dinner seemed quite satisfactory to Helene, and
everyone ate well, except that grandpa put far too much grape
jelly on his cottage cheese. There was beef that had cooked with
onions over a low heat all morning, potatoes peeled and mashed
with cream and butter by grandpa himself, applesauce and sweet
watermelon pickles put up by grandma, a good mess of last year's
asparagus from the freezer, cottage cheese and milk and bread and
butter and jelly, and for dessert strawberries unthawed to cool
sweetness and cookies stuffed with dates. She kept George beside
her, settled nicely on a chair with a farm catalogue under him, and
saw to it that he got down all his meat and potatoes before he was
allowed more applesauce. Everyone seemed sleepy, and Leonard
and the girls had new, high color in their cheeks from the wind. In
fact, Leonard looked exceedingly well; his gray hair was blown up
from his forehead, so different from the flat style he wore to the
office, and though he ate noisily and with bent concentration, she
didn't mind for once. He was relaxed; he helped Sarah to more
applesauce; he told his father that he'd build a bonfire in the
orchard, that the thistles would be done in an hour or so, that the
sheep looked good, very good—would he want to do the shearing
while they were there? She watched him sweep a piece of bread
around his plate for the last of the gravy. Projects—those were what
Leonard loved: getting a bit of garden in shape, stripping the paint
from some old chair, clearing an orchard of dead wood. Sometimes

it seemed to her that he should never have left the farm, that the way they lived now left him no freedom.

"Mo' ap'sauce," begged George, but she said, wiping his cheeks, that he had had enough, he'd get the gollywobbles if he had any more, that he must finish his milk.

"You like grandma's applesauce, don't you?" said grandma in the special tone of voice she always adopted for the children.

"We all do," said Helene. "Did you use the Wealthies for it?"

"There's all different kinds in there," said grandma. "The apples was all good last year."

After lunch grandpa slept even before the dishes were done so that Helene had to tiptoe through the dining room past the couch where he was stretched and whisper to the girls reading magazines in the darkened front sitting room that they should go up to their beds for half an hour. Daddy and George were already upstairs; grandma had just gone up. They must be very quiet. And she? Well, she was going to rest downstairs, for daddy was sure to be snoring. Now off they must go. She was too tired to argue.

But they protested. They hadn't had a nap for years. What was she thinking of? All they were doing was reading magazines, which was restful anyhow, and there they would stay.

"You at least should sleep," she said to Baba, for they were sprawled on the couch where she herself had wanted to nap. "Your body needs extra rest right now. How do you feel?"

"Achy," said Baba, looking up, "in my back and my legs. My nose itches."

There now, she might win her daughter over. "It's sleep you need," she said quickly. "Some day you girls will have to learn how to take care of yourselves." But it was no use; Baba plumped herself more deeply into the couch, and Sarah rested a flushed cheek against a crocheted tidy. "I'm too tired to stand here and argue," she said. "Only don't come to me at suppertime and say you're too sleepy to set the table or help clean up. You both left all the work to grandma and me this noon, and that's fine because you were out of doors enjoying yourselves, but it can't be that way all the time; it's too much of a strain on grandma. But I won't argue with you." She left them with a sigh she couldn't control: it was so difficult for her to get enough rest these days; her family was spreading out around her, scarcely leaving her enough peace of mind for her own needs.

Wrapping herself in a heavy tweed coat, she sighed again. All
through her dishwashing her tiredness had grown until she had
become impatient listening to grandma and had told Leonard
that if he didn't take charge of George for a while, she wouldn't
be able to get through the day. She gathered up her sewing
and basket of magazines and took herself through the dining room
—quietly, for grandpa groaned and turned in his sleep—out to the
porch swing where she sat down on the stiff wood, her hand on
the chains that supported it, and gazed out at the long veranda,
at the trees constantly in motion and full of the sound of the wind
and the soundless drifting of blossom dust, at the cut in the land
where the road ran, and at the distant farms distinguishable by
barn roofs and clumps of trees. She closed her eyes and let herself
be carried with the swing. Already she had been up over eight
hours, and there were eight more to go before she could rest again.
It was so terribly difficult to get enough sleep: if it wasn't someone's sickness, or Leonard's snoring, or her own racing mind and
aching muscles, then it would be one of the girls, off on some
adventure with her friends, or Leonard, up in that tiny company
airplane, doing more business than any man should be asked to
do; with all that going on she simply couldn't get her own rest.
She kept her eyes closed and rested her head on the back of the
swing. There had been a swing on the house her father built; for
long hours as a child she had rocked there, watching the fruit trees
and grape vines and vegetable garden dip and rise before her,
probably because, she was able to reason now, she had once been
told that her mother had often sat there with her father in the
evenings. They had been great talkers, an aunt had told her; they
talked so much the neighbors wondered how they found so much
to say to each other.

She saw them, suspended together from the porch roof, her
mother pregnant, her father dressed in his jerkin, his measuring
stick still folded in his pocket perhaps; she saw them through a
neighbor's window—it was before she had been born—through the
fruit trees and the pillars of the porch. But she couldn't hear what
they were saying. She stopped the swaying of the swing with her
foot.

And if she herself were to be seen right now? Straightening
up, she turned her coat collar against the wind, tucked her skirt
tightly around her knees and picked up her sewing. Some of the

people in the distant farms knew who she was, would recognize
her if they drove by just now, for she had spoken to them at
birthday parties or funeral dinners; they must think of her as the
clever wife Leonard had found at the university. Would they
think it strange that she should sit here spending so much time on
a little handiwork? That was what amazed people, even her own
friends: her contradictions, how she could give a lecture, or talk
with ease to the most important sort of people and still put out
a roast beef and apple pie dinner that satisfied even nameless
hungers, or know exactly how to appreciate the most common
people, or raise three children such as hers, who so far had
brought her nothing but credit, being healthy and quick at school
and already singled out by her friends and the teachers for special
talents. It was hard for people to put all this together. Why, one
time after she had spoken to a group of parents at the grade
school, a man had come up to her and said right out that he
thought her the most remarkable woman in town. After that she
had gone home in such a flush that she had put up eight quarts
of applesauce before going to bed.

The only trouble was that sometimes things seemed to be getting
out of control. She found herself objecting quite irrationally to
Leonard or the children, not being able to stop herself. But of
course she herself worked just as hard as Leonard, and it was true
that if anything went wrong, if they got sick, for instance, all the
trouble would fall back on her; she'd be the one to sit up at night
and clean up the bathroom messes and cook the special food. Yet
it frightened her sometimes the way her voice would suddenly
come out, objecting, as if the reasons for her speech were far
down, out of reach. Sometimes it seemed as if she had lost hold on
her life, as if at some imperceptible point she had been dispersed
irretrievably into the people around her.

She rocked in the swing, barely moving, and made stitches
so neat and small they were almost invisible. In the midst of this
wind, these wild dartings of cats across the lawn, these uncontrollable movements of animals—a sheep had gone into labor,
grandpa said at noon—and of the family within the house—George
would have kicked off his blankets by now, and Leonard, snoring,
would never know—she glided tightly in place, one foot on the
wooden porch floor, her fingers looping stitch after stitch through
the yellow binding and the printed cotton. Her face felt drawn

with weariness. It was so terribly difficult to make a day turn out right. She pressed her lips together and looped a series of perfect stitches.

"Sarah, do you know what's going on in this picture?" Sarah looked. Her mouth felt raw from sucking hard candies, and her whole body burned with exhaustion and excitement, for she had been reading of what people called Nazis had done to naked prisoners in cold rooms with showers and cement floors. She looked at the picture and saw two heads, a man's and a woman's, and a hand with painted fingernails pressing into flesh. "Well, do you know what's going on?" demanded Baba.

"What is?"

"If you don't know, I'm not going to tell you. Give me back the book," said Baba. "Now. Look at this one."

She looked and saw huge rocks around which stood naked, decorated Negro women with big bellies and children at their legs. "It must be in Africa," she said. "Whose is that?"

"It's a book of photographs daddy sent for. Those women are going to have babies—see? And they've all been sent up there to the rocks together."

"Why?"

"To have them, of course."

"Don't they have hospitals?"

"This is in Africa. Come on, let me finish it first," said Baba urgently and took back the book. Her hair hung down one side of her face, and she was chewing on her barette and snuffling. There was a pile of candy wrappers on the coffee table that they would have to hide later from mother. Sarah went back to her magazine.

"After insertion, the glass tubing was broken," she read, "making urination an excruciating process." The row of cows, the gleaming milking machines took places in the cold room with the cement floors. Her teeth felt as if they were rotting in her mouth; daddy had said cavities could start in five minutes. "Baba, what did you do with your kitten?" she asked.

"Put him back, naturally. Mother said mine had fleas all over it. Did yours?"

"I don't know," she almost whispered.

"The day we leave they'll all get killed, you know."

"Killed?"

"Drowned. In a bucket. Grandpa always does it that way."

"That isn't so."

"Ask and see."

"How do you know?"

"I found out."

Sarah unwrapped another candy and pressed it hard against the roof of her mouth until it was crushed and the soft center oozed out. She heard grandpa get up from the couch in the next room. "Ah!" he cried out sharply, "ah!" as he rose to his feet. She held the shattered candy firmly with her tongue so that it almost hurt and stared at a patch of sun on the dark flowered carpet until the sweetness had dissolved. Candies went quickly; the best moment was just before the centers broke out. Again her mouth felt raw and empty. She imagined shattered bits of glass within flesh in a cold room, within the cows' drooping teats which the big boy with the red face had enclosed so deftly with the metal cups. Cats had waited in the straw and muck. "They always comes around at milkin' time," the boy had said. "They sure is smart."

Throwing down the magazine, she stretched herself taut and then crumpled into the couch. How long would it take to eat every candy in the bowl? Idly she counted as many of them in their metallic wrappers as she could see. The wool sofa pricked right through her shirt.

"I think I'll go outside and look at the kittens," she said aloud, but continued to lie immobile in the stuffy room with the sun shining around the lowered shades. In her mind she was unwrapping another candy and holding it, round, uncrushed, on her tongue. It would have been better if she hadn't done that to those kittens. Every time she remembered with vague disbelief what her hands had done, how they had just let go, she wished it could be undone. She hadn't meant it at all; she had just been going round and round the cistern mound.

"I guess I'll go outside," she said again.

Baba blew her nose and lay back sighing. "Sarah, don't tell mother that I showed you that picture."

"Which one?"

"The first one."

Sarah saw painted fingernails digging into someone's skin. She thought of them all the time that she was washing her own hands and brushing her teeth hard in the bathroom by the kitchen. She

saw them again as she stood over the box in the summer kitchen
watching the kittens pressing their paws into the black cat as they
nursed. Her two kittens were there with the rest. She stooped, but
she didn't touch them. "I'm sorry," she whispered. The big black
cat stared straight ahead with half-closed eyes. A heavy flying bug
snarled against the window. "I'm sorry, kittens," she said again,
but not a single kitten turned away from his eating. What she had
done was secret, then; even the mother cat didn't know that her
kittens had fallen. Easing up so quietly she thought as she stood at
the door she could still hear their faint slurps of nursing, she
slipped outside.

So bright was the sun that she could barely open her eyes to the
blooming orchard and the white dish towels twisting from the line.
All the swift, fresh morning shadows had given way to droning
air and fierce sun, which she felt sink into her hair and neck and
back as she settled herself cross-legged on the hitching stone,
facing the broad, afternoon façade of the barn, and began twisting
her fingers, painfully, repeatedly, into the metal hitching ring. She
smelled manure and blossoms and the metal fence behind her and
the rotting walnuts on the ground. The long grass on top of the
cistern was like someone's hair, ruffled up; she thought she could
see the flattened down place where she had sat with the kittens.
That had been before lunch, when the sun had still come from the
other side of the barn, and grandpa had stepped out of the
shadowed doorway to throw water from a bucket. She twisted her
fingers again and again through the metal ring.

When she next looked up, grandpa was coming toward her
from the barn, rocking from side to side, holding something in his
arms, passing the corncrib and then crossing the gravel drive,
coming straight toward her and, she saw now, carrying in his arms
a lamb, all four of its legs thrust down.

"Here," he said. "Sit still and hold him." He put the lamb into
her lap. "Put your arm over him. Hold him tight. Hold his front
legs tight." Then he went on through the gate to the house and left
her with the wriggling, curly-haired baby lamb, who looked right
up into her face and bleated, "Mehh, mehh," with a catch in the
sound. His tongue was as pink as her own. She felt his fluttering
heart in the round, firm chest she cupped in her hand and saw
that his hair was rough and kinky even over the bones of his head
and down between his eyes. "Meh-h," he bleated and pushed his

nose hard up against her cheek and into her ear and along her neck. "Ah!" she cried and bent down to hold him close as he nosed back to the warm place on her neck where the sun sank into her braids.

"Here," said grandpa. "Give him this." He put a bottle with a long brown nipple in her hand, and she could feel that the milk inside was warm. "You'll have to push it in. Hold it up. He ain't used to this."

Grandpa held the lamb's head while she pushed the nipple through the black lips. Milk dribbled down his woolly throat. "Give him a minute. There he goes," said grandpa, as the lamb suddenly pushed against the bottle so that she had to hold it firmly as he sucked and the wool along his throat rippled with the milk going down inside.

"Is he sick?" she asked.

"Nah, he's just got a ornery mother. Won't feed him. They do that sometimes. Won't have nothing to do with their own babies— maybe a wrong smell." Grandpa took his hands from the sheep. "You like that?" he asked. He was wheezing heavily, in through his mouth, out through his nose with his lips pursed. When he opened his mouth, she could see all the gold caps along his teeth.

"Yes," she said, looking back at the lamb standing tensely on her lap, his whole body straining up to the bottle, only his short tail and his lips and throat moving.

"You can have him then," said grandpa.

"You mean I can take him around with me?"

"You got to feed him."

The lamb drank two bottles of milk right there, and she had to jump up suddenly while he tinkled all over the stone block.

"Haw, haw," said grandpa. "Did he get you wet?" He was feeling the lamb all over with his big hands. He looked into his mouth and ears and eyes and felt along his throat and legs and belly with hands that seemed to know what they were feeling for. "There ain't nothing the matter with him. Do you want to take him with you?"

"Anywhere I want? Grandpa, anywhere I want?" she had to repeat, for he had already turned away and was frowning in the direction of the barn. Still not answering, he heaved himself to his feet, steadied himself, and started off across the yard. It was as if he had forgotten her and the lamb and everything that had happened. Grandpa was funny, like the way he turned his back on the dining room when he slept on the couch, the way he could go right to sleep, even with people still at the table. "It's all right," she said softly to the lamb, and the sound of her voice talking to him was strange. She would have to go some place very quiet where she could talk to him.

"Meh-h," bleated the lamb sleepily as she carried him through the orchard, past the first rows of trees and down a slope until the house behind them was almost hidden. After they were settled in the grass, she loosened one of her hands and then the other, but he didn't run away; he stood stiff-legged beside her, his black nose twitching in the wind, and she noticed with awe that his eyes were fringed with the finest pale lashes. Talking to a lamb was not as easy as talking to a kitten. It made her feel as she sometimes did sitting on the edge of her bed in front of the mirror and pretending that she was two people, that she was herself and that she was also someone else who didn't know herself. It was as if he might be able to understand what she was saying, the way he looked at her and the way he stood so separately beside her.

She touched the high, flat hump of his head, then slipped her arm around his body, wondering if he were seeing what she did: the two rows of dark pine trees at the bottom of the orchard, the cottonwoods in the valley of the sheep pasture, the sunny fields beyond that looked as if the cupped palm of a hand had firmed them up the way one made hills in moist sand. She looked as far as she could see, and it seemed as if she had never tried to see so far; it seemed as if she had never seen how trees looked ten farms away, how the clouds piled close to the ground in the distance and burned moving shadows across the fields. "Hello, sheep," she said, stroking his back; he ducked his head up again and again under her caressing hand. She wasn't hurting him; she was being good to him. "Lamb, I dropped some kittens," she whispered suddenly, but he only ducked his head up again to receive her touch. If she were to stroke him long enough, in the right way, it wouldn't make any difference about the kittens. "Anyway, I think they're all right," she said close to his ear. He pushed his nose along her neck and she could feel his breath and the curls of wool under his chin.

Never had an afternoon been more beautiful. "Isn't it beautiful?"

she said to him, and it seemed as if she had never used the word before.

When she heard voices higher up in the orchard, she crept down the hill with the lamb to the pines where the light descended sharply into dusk. She had never been here alone before. Damp brown needles covered her shoes with each sliding step. All sound was subdued by the dense branches. She crouched at the base of a tree and from beneath the lowest shaggy branches saw again the sunlit fields; almost near enough for her to touch ran a fence and a field with plowed up chunks of earth sliced sharply down their sides as if with a knife. She looked at the slim, paired pine needles at her feet and then at the sliced sides of earth and then out to the horizon again, this time almost level with her eyes. The kittens were all right; they had forgotten everything. She would eat no more candy. Every day she would feed the lamb and bring him down here. "Don't worry," she said to the lamb, who sprawled across her lap. Leaning back, she felt how her braids got caught in the flaky bark of the odorous tree.

Helene paused, her hand still on the banister. For what had she come up the stairs? Sunlight wavered through the rough bathroom glass as if through water; late sunlight flooded from the open nursery door across the old hall carpet. Something from the nursery? She smoothed a patchwork quilt at a bed's corner. Something for George to wear? Brilliantly dappled sunlight slanted through the mulberry trees, and she heard shouts from the orchard where they all were working now, where she was going in a moment, but first having come upstairs for something, something. No, not for George: she had seen him off, bundled him up herself, made him promise not to loosen his scarf. Something for someone. "You go ahead. I'll be out in a minute," she had said at the back door, straightening up from helping George, knowing from the feel of the skin on her cheeks how tired she was. She had forced her legs to climb up the dark stairwell. She had come up into the airy hall, the bedroom doors open around it, the broad, loose windows shaking from thudding gusts of wind, sunlight streaming from the west. Now she was wandering—into the bathroom reeking of asparagus urine; into grandpa's undecorated room where the metal clock ticked loudly on the marble dresser; into grandma's room with half-drawn shades, the Bible by the bed, the glass case of Leonard's early books. She tapped the case before the books—all stories of success, rags to riches, and guides to self-improvement. Was it something for grandma? It was disgraceful to have forgotten so easily, to have come all the way up those stairs for nothing. Leonard had taken George piggyback to the orchard.

Yes, it was for Leonard. She stood in the doorway of the guest room. It was the camera, and it had been her idea, too. "We must have a picture of this," she had said as she saw even grandma dressing for the wind in a faded purple scarf and a lumpy jacket. And George had been so fresh from his nap. She tucked the leather case under her arm and touched on fresh lipstick at the mirror. "At the farm. May. From left to right Grandpa, Grandma, Helene, George at four years, Baba, Sarah." Already as she descended the stairs she was labeling the photograph, filing it; already as she put on her own coat and walked down to the orchard she was seeing her great-great-grandchildren finger the picture in some future living room. Helene, the mother of those children, the wife of that man; Helene, the intelligent one in the tweed coat; Helene, holding that little boy by the hand. She pushed open the gate. The sun was just right for a photograph.

But they had already started the bonfire; it crackled and snapped in dangerously high flames, and—she stopped dead—there was George all alone fiercely throwing sticks at the fire's edge. As she began running she could see piles of branches already gathered here and there among the trees, and as she finally reached her son Leonard was coming along the fence dragging half a tree behind him. "Leonard!" She heard her own voice, high-pitched, frantic. Indignation collected as she watched him come laboriously into earshot, but she couldn't help herself: there was no excuse for what he had done; it made her so weary to think of it. He stopped before her and let his branches crash to the ground. He was exhilarated, she could tell. "Leonard, what, what were you thinking of when you left George up here alone by the fire?"

"Why, he's all right. What are you fussing about?"

"All right! A child that age is never all right near a fire without supervision. What were you thinking of?"

"I thought he'd be all right."

Her husband's hands looked awkwardly empty at his sides, but she couldn't stop herself. "What am I to think when you do something like this?" She felt only the weariness of her life. A

flame burst near her, and a falling branch sent up a spray of
sparks. George was tearing twigs from the wood Leonard had
dragged up.

"Look at me," he said to them, and he threw the twigs hard
down into the fire.

Still she couldn't stop. "When anything happens to one of them,
I'm the one who does the worrying. You're not home enough. You
have no idea how difficult it is for me when they're sick or hurt."
She felt her eyes smarting from the difficulty of her position,
from the outrageous thing Leonard had done in leaving a little boy
alone by a fire. And in a wind, too. There was no way out but
to keep on talking and talking. A flock of birds crossed above
them in a dense, whirring fan.

Leonard interrupted her. "He's all right, Helene. He's just been
running back and forth. I've had my eye on him."

The sun was coming straight at them now, through the trees.
She pressed her lips together. "Well, I won't say any more, but you
should have known. Are you still going to take this picture? The
sun is going." He reached out for the leather case. She saw his
hand, stubby and hard, reaching out from the leather sleeve of his
jacket. It didn't seem to belong in the same place with the sound
of her voice; it shamed her. She watched the hand tilt a light
meter this way and that in front of her face. Beyond was the sun
and against it she saw grandma and Baba, coming up the slope
with their arms full of sticks and then grandpa, rocking slowly
behind them, dragging branches.

The hand folded to the precision of the camera. She closed her
eyes and stood with the sun on her face. She would have liked to
stand so still that the parts of her life came home to her in a
single luminosity; she would have liked the sun to burn into
her until she was loosened to the bone, made ready, as once she
had been, to the feel of the touch of hands.

"Leonard, you have taken so many nice pictures," she murmured, opening her eyes, but her husband was no longer near
her; he was crouched on the far side of the fire with George. Her
throat tightened with the loss of her life.

And yet there was nothing, really, that she didn't have. No, of
course there wasn't. Here they all were—her children, her husband,
the irreplaceable older generation that gave such ballast to their
lives. Everything was fine. This was just what happened. And who

after all would judge them in the end? One never knew what history would make of them. She straightened her collar. She was an extraordinary woman; that she must remember and then go about setting her mind on doing what she could. This photograph, for instance: wasn't it so typical of her, so admirable, to understand how important such a document would be for the future? Of course it was. And this trip: wouldn't it make a difference, one way or another, that the children had been driven at dusk through the spring country, in the wake of the plows and the dark nights of animal births?

"All set," said Leonard, leading George around the edge of the fire.

"Are we all here?" she asked. "Where's Sarah? Baba, come here and let me straighten your hair. Daddy wants to take a picture. Grandma. Grandpa. George, don't run away. Where shall we stand, Leonard?"

She clipped back Baba's hair. Already her daughter was taller than she. "You should have a scarf on," she said. "Does anyone know where Sarah is? Leonard, can you whistle?"

"Why, don't this look nice?" said grandma. "Leonard, I want you to make me a copy if it turns out."

Sarah was still crouched under the pine tree when she heard the whistle. For a long time she had been waiting for the lamb to finish sleeping. A chill, like a layer of colder water beneath the sunstruck surface, had settled among the trees so that she turned up her collar and burrowed her hands into her sleeves. Then for a brief time a golden slant of light had transformed the floor of drab needles into radiant copper until a rise in the field finally blocked the last of the sun. Her cheeks felt as if she had been running in water. It was important to stay absolutely still, to let the lamb sleep, to watch the light slant in and disappear as it would. Every time she remembered the kittens, the sick, rich aftertaste of the candy, the naked prisoners in rooms colder than milking stalls, she held herself even more deliberately so that nothing should now be spoiled. Yes, never had an afternoon been more beautiful. This was what could happen.

"Wee-oo." The whistle came in two tones, higher, lower.

"Wee-oo. Sar-rah."

"Now we can go," she said to the lamb. When she stood, there

was nothing around her but the black-green grove. With the
lamb under her arm, his heart thudding in her palm, she stooped beneath the branches one last time to see the place where she had
been—the fence, the plowed earth heaved up so close to her that
she might have been a creature living in its ridges, the fields of
color beyond running up the world until they merged into the
sky that arced overhead and landed someplace, always behind
her.

"Sar-rah."

"Coming," she said softly, as the lamb nuzzled in the crook of
her arm, and now there was nothing strange in the sound of her
own voice as it was let loose among the branches.

As she carried the lamb up the hill through the blooming trees,
she could see uncurling licks of flame and smoke and then the
whole fire, consuming into pure molten color the disorderly heap
of dead branches. The fire was beautiful. Everyone was standing
in a row beside it. Mother held George by the hand. "Wee-oo,"
whistled her father, waving his arm, while behind him the fire
crashed down into its center and sparks gushed up as high as the
house. She began to run. "Wee-oo."

Magazines Consulted

Analecta – Box 133, Demarest, N.J. 07627
Ante – P.O. Box 29915, Los Angeles, Calif. 90029
Antioch Review – 212 Xenia Avenue, Yellow Springs, Ohio 45387
Approach – 114 Petrie Avenue, Rosemont, Pa. 19010
Ararat – Armenian General Benevolent Union of America, 109 East 40th Street, New York, N.Y. 10016
Arizona Quarterly – University of Arizona, Tucson, Ariz. 85721
The Atlantic – 8 Arlington Street, Boston, Mass. 02116
Ave Maria – National Catholic Weekly, Congregation of Holy Cross, Notre Dame, Ind. 46556
Carleton Miscellany – Carleton College, Northfield, Minn. 55057
Carolina Quarterly – Box 1117, Chapel Hill, N.C. 27515
Chelsea Review – Box 242, Old Chelsea Station, New York, N.Y. 10011
Chicago Review – University of Chicago, Chicago, Ill. 60637
The Colorado State Review – 360 Liberal Arts, Colorado State University, Fort Collins, Colo. 80521
Colorado Quarterly – Hellums 118, University of Colorado, Boulder, Colo. 80304
Commentary – 165 East 56th Street, New York, N.Y. 10022
Confluence – Lindewood College, St. Charles, Mo. 63301
Cosmopolitan – 1775 Broadway, New York, N.Y. 10019
The Critic – 180 N. Wabash Avenue, Chicago, Ill. 60601
December – P.O. Box 274, Western Springs, Ill. 60558
The Denver Quarterly – Denver, Colo. 80210
Descant – Dept. of English, TCU Station, Fort Worth, Tex. 76129
Encounter – 25 Haymarket, London, S.W.1, England
Epoch – 159 Goldwin Smith Hall, Cornell University, Ithaca, N.Y. 14850
Escapade – 529 Fifth Avenue, New York, N.Y. 10017
Esprit – University of Scranton, Scranton, Pa. 18510
Esquire – 488 Madison Avenue, New York, N.Y. 10022
Evergreen Review – 64 University Place, New York, N.Y. 10003
Fantasy and Science Fiction – 347 East 53rd Street, New York, N.Y. 10022
For Now – Box 375, Cathedral Station, New York, N.Y. 10025
Forum – University of Houston, Tex. 77004
Four Quarters – La Salle College, Philadelphia, Pa. 19141
The Free Lance – 6005 Grand Avenue, Cleveland, Ohio 44101
Generation, the Inter-arts Magazine – University of Michigan, 420 Maynard, Ann Arbor, Mich. 48103
Georgia Review – University of Georgia, Athens, Ga. 30601
Good Housekeeping – 959 Eighth Avenue, New York, N.Y. 10019

The Greensboro Review – The University of North Carolina, Greensboro, N.C. 27412

Harper's Bazaar – 572 Madison Avenue, New York, N.Y. 10022

Harper's Magazine – 2 Park Avenue, New York, N.Y. 10016

Hudson Review – 65 East 55th Street, New York, N.Y. 10022

Impulse – Rockland Community College, Suffern, N.Y. 10901

Kenyon Review – Kenyon College, Gambier, Ohio 43022

Ladies' Home Journal – 641 Lexington Avenue, New York, N.Y. 10022

The Laurel Review – West Virginia Wesleyan College, Buckhannon, W. Va. 26201

Lillabulero – P.O. Box 1027, Chapel Hill, N.C. 27514

The Literary Review – Fairleigh Dickinson University, Teaneck, N.J. 07666

Mademoiselle – 420 Lexington Avenue, New York, N.Y. 10022

The Malahat Review – University of Victoria, Victoria, British Columbia, Canada

The Massachusetts Review – University of Massachusetts, Amherst, Mass. 01003

McCall's – 230 Park Avenue, New York, N.Y. 10017

Midstream – 515 Park Avenue, New York, N.Y. 10022

The Minnesota Review – Box 4068, University Station, Minneapolis, Minn. 55455

The Moonlight Review – P.O. Box 1686, Brooklyn, N.Y. 11202

New American Review – 1301 Avenue of the Americas, New York, N.Y. 10019

The New Mexico Quarterly – University of New Mexico Press, Marron Hall, Albuquerque, N. Mex. 87106

The New Yorker – 25 West 43rd Street, New York, N.Y. 10036

North American Review – Cornell College, Mount Vernon, Iowa 52314

The Paris Review – 45–39, 171 Place, Flushing, N.Y. 11358

Partisan Review – Rutgers University, New Brunswick, N.J. 08903

Perspective – Washington University Post Office, St. Louis, No. 63105

Phylon – 223 Chestnut Street S.W., Atlanta, Ga. 30314

Playboy – 232 East Ohio Street, Chicago, Ill. 60611

Prairie Schooner – Andrews Hall, University of Nebraska, Lincoln, Nebr. 68508

Quarterly Review of Literature – 26 Haslet Avenue, Princeton, N.J. 08540

Quartet – 346 Sylvia Street W., Lafayette, Ind. 47906

The Quest – P.O. Box 207, Cathedral Station, New York, N.Y. 10025

Ramparts – 1182 Chestnut Street, Menlo Park, Calif. 94027

Readers & Writers – 130–21 224th Street, Jamaica, N.Y. 11413

Redbook – 230 Park Avenue, New York, N.Y. 10017

Red Clay Reader – 2221 Westminster Place, Charlotte, N.C. 28207

Saturday Evening Post – 641 Lexington Avenue, New York, N.Y. 10022

Sewanee Review – University of the South, Sewanee, Tenn. 37375

Shenandoah – Box 722, Lexington, Va. 24450

Southern Review – Drawer D, University Station, Baton Rouge, La. 70803

Southwest Review – Southern Methodist University Press, Dallas, Tex. 75222

The Tamarack Review – Box 159, Postal Station K, Toronto, Ontario, Canada

The Texas Quarterly – Box 7527, University of Texas, Austin, Tex. 78712

Trace – P.O. Box 1068, Hollywood, Calif. 90028

Transatlantic Review – Box 3348, Grand Central P.O., New York, N.Y. 10017

Tri-Quarterly – University Hall 101, Northwestern University, Evanston, Ill. 60201

The University of Windsor Review – Windsor, Ontario, Canada

The University Review – University of Kansas City, 51 Street & Rockhill Road, Kansas City, Mo. 64110

Venture (for Junior High) – 910 Witherspoon Bldg., Philadelphia, Pa. 19107

Ventures – Yale Graduate School, New Haven, Conn. 06520

The Virginia Quarterly Review – University of Virginia, 1 West Range, Charlottesville, Va. 22903

Vogue – 420 Lexington Avenue, New York, N.Y. 10017

Washington Square Review – New York University, 737 East Bldg., New York, N.Y. 10003

Western Humanities Review – Bldg. 41, University of Utah, Salt Lake City, Utah 84112

Woman's Day – 67 West 44th Street, New York, N.Y. 10036

Yale Review – 26 Hillhouse Avenue, New Haven, Conn. 06520